CHILDREN OF THE GHETTO

CHILDREN
OF THE
GHETTO

A Study of a Peculiar People

by

ISRAEL ZANGWILL

BLACK
APOLLO
PRESS

Published by Black Apollo Press, 2004
ISBN 1 900 355 30 2

Originally published by Macmillan and Co. in 1895

CONTENTS

INTRODUCTION

Israel Zangwill was born in the East End of London on the 21st of January 1864, well within sound of the church bells of St Mary Le Bow, which, in later life, he proudly claimed made him an official Cockney. It was an odd connection but a significant one; growing up as the son of poor, immigrant Jews – his father from a small Baltic village, his mother from Warsaw – he knew first hand the tenuous relationship between the native Eastenders and the teaming mass of immigrants, mainly impoverished, Yiddish-speaking artisans and small traders, deposited like human flotsam by the great emigrant wave emanating from the Russian Pale and flowing, relentlessly, through an unwelcoming Germany, westward. It was only the poorest of the poor who spilled onto the shores of that island state which sat haughtily at the upper tip of Europe, separated only by a mote-like channel and a certain aloofness – a consequence of Empire which, by the time Zangwill was born, was at its height and thus acting as a magnet to those unfortunate castaways who believed the capital city of that Imperial realm must certainly have streets paved with gold (rather than the pot-holed pyrite they actually found there).

Zangwill was truly a child of the ghetto, though his parents, through fortuitous family connections, soon moved to a more salubrious locale. His father was an itinerant merchant who spoke only market English – enabling him to shift just enough from his never empty bags of sponges and lemons to keep up his patriarchal duties. An orthodox observer, he was eventually to leave his family, ending his years as a spiritual mendicant in the small, seedy town of Jerusalem, impoverished and dreary in the wake of the receding Ottomans.

His mother was a more worldly sort who saw in her children (at least in her sons) an opportunity to leave the mental ghetto she found as restricting as the physical one and so was determined that they become 'English' through hard work and a solid education, which to her (and to many like her) was the most reliable path toward the cherished dream of true emancipation and a thankful end to centuries of persecution.

Zangwill was thus a product of the push toward modern secularism exemplified by the Jews' Free School, that hot-house of assimilation which, through the largess of an earlier and very successful vanguard, sought to mould the sons and daughters of the teaming Jewish ghetto who gathered in those few acres of land known as Whitechapel – the most densely populated bit of real estate in Europe – into proper Englishmen and Englishwomen. The problem was that the swarthy ghetto urchins who flocked to the Free School shoeless, with bellies tender from lack of nourishment, had a common language that wasn't English but a raw, poetic, infinitely expressive amalgam of religious, cultural, and visceral communication known as 'Yiddish' – the mama-loshen of the scattered tribes of the Diaspora that had moved northwards many generations before from the Sephardic sunbelt into the dark and perilous Germanic kingdoms.

This 'Bastard German,' referred to contemptuously as 'The Dialect,' was anathema to the assimilated Jews, mainly Sephardic, who had come to Britain in small numbers some generations before and had managed to find an important niche in the emerging economic infrastructure which would allow them to become, a few decades after Disraeli, fully integrated into the English political and social system. These established Anglo-Jews, who counted in their number some super rich families like the Rothschilds and Montefiores, watched in horror as boatload after boatload of impoverished, unwashed and uneducated brethren flooded into London. What to do? There were only two choices, really. One was to get rid of as many of them as possible by subsidising their further voyage to the Americas (something that most of the immigrants would have done anyway had they the capital); the other was to try to make them (or their children) into proper Englishmen.

Thus the Jews' Free School was set up in the ghetto as a factory of assimilation. The first step of the process was linguistic. English was to be their *lingua franca* and dialects were not to be spoken. Yiddish was to be extirpated from their lives as quickly as possible. If the young aspirants were forced to speak it at home because their parents needed to communicate with them, then they must not degrade themselves elsewhere. For Yiddish was the language of the ghetto, of physical (if not spiritual) impoverishment, and so was a language of shame – which translated into shame for their shtetl culture.

Zangwill was a brilliant student. He excelled at his studies and was eventually rewarded at Prize Day with a commendation from the great Rothschild himself – an event which impressed itself on the young artist's memory as thoroughly humiliating since it was clear from his manner that this revered statesman of the Anglo-Jewish cause looked upon Zangwill and the rest of the ghetto children as a caste of Untouchables that Brahmins like Rothschild were duty bound to patronise, though at a healthy distance.

But Anglicised education was indeed the road out of the ghetto and the time had never been more propitious. The 1880s were a period of extraordinary transition. Enormous wealth and dire poverty existed side by side and, more than ever, people were crossing back and forth over the demarcation lines with heretofore unknown fluidity.

New technologies were emerging: the country was being electrified. New suburbs were being built with rapid transportation systems connecting people on the outskirts with their inner city workplaces. And new markets were opening especially for books, magazines and newspapers – a combination of the increased literacy rate (itself a product of the recent education act) and clever distributors like W.H. Smiths who saw a connection between the invention of the commuter and the opportunity of filling empty time with frothy reading matter for their journey.

Everything was new and newness reigned supreme – so why not new ideas and new ways of thought? Generations of Empire had given rise not only to a vast army of bureaucrats but also to a liberalised intelligentsia who used the excess wealth at their disposal to codify what was blindingly obvious to all but the very cosseted: that in the most powerful and wealthy country on earth there was a vast underworld of grinding poverty and deprivation. The science of statistical sociology was coming of age and keen practitioners like Charles Booth exposed, in intricate colour-coded charts, the true extent of this blight on their cherished fantasy – that God had ordained the English to be the 'civilising authority' for an otherwise savage world.

Booth, like others before him, concentrated his study of poverty on the East End of London. And by the midpoint of the decade Whitechapel was awash with social reformers, eager young researchers and half-penny journalists, who fell over themselves trying to expose (and often exploit) what they saw as a pit of unrelenting misery and, in the eyes of the most effective campaigners, the missionaries and salvationists, damnation. The East End, thus vilified, became synonymous with crime, pestilence and moral turpitude of the worst sort in the mind of the more protected middle class readers who found these titillating horrors often depicted in their 'penny dreadfuls' and salaciously staged in their illustrated weeklies.

This essential demonisation of the East End and its poorest inhabitants, the Russian and Polish immigrants, set off alarm bells in the Anglo-Jewish establishment. It wasn't so much that a slur on one was a slur on all, but rather what it would mean to their tenuous sinecures. For as ensconced as they may have been, they had only to look over the creek into the heartland of Europe to see the terrors unleashed in the name of *Judenhass*.

Assimilation was seen as the needed antidote to this nightmare scenario of an English pogrom. But the blunt approach of Anglicisation, extirpating centuries of historical memory from these Children of the Ghetto, could only partially work. It created a new beast – the secular Jew, cut off from his native community and forced to absorb an alien culture, complete with intricate social obligations and codes to pretend were their own.

Zangwill had left the ghetto. With febrile energy and imagination he had taken up with a group of writers – mainly other escapees from their class and social backgrounds – who, using London as their canvass, were reinterpreting the world. They met in small cafés in Soho and Bloomsbury, around the site of their Mecca, the British Museum. It was a bright and colourful assortment – people like Jerome K. Jerome, a youthful and yet unknown George Bernard Shaw, the Scotsman, J.M. Barrie and a young doctor named Conan Doyle. They wrote for the flourishing commuter magazines like the *Strand* and later, Jerome's *Idler*, which became home for a group collectively known as 'the New Humorists' (not because they were particularly funny, rather for their attempts to reshape the severe mid-Victorian melodrama with a lighter touch and a more optimistic vision of the world).

This cluster of Young Turks, of whom Zangwill was a leading figure, came to re-define the British literary scene. Writing in the vernacular, they pushed the boundaries of language, theme, story and plot, severing the class ties to tired middle-class formulas and developing in the process, original works of fiction that were unique and inventive.

But Zangwill, though very much of this movement, had an aspect of himself that harked back to the side of the ghetto experience that had nurtured him and had provided him with the pallet for his art. It was the side of the ghetto that was warm and human; brimming with life and pulsating with the primal spirit that was so much a part of the romance of the shtetl.

He was, therefore, the perfect choice to 'humanise' the immigrant Jewish community of Whitechapel. This was a project dear to the hearts of those Jewish leaders who feared that the image of the East End as a den of crime and iniquity was tarnishing the good name and gentle image of the immigrant Jews (and rather spoiling it for the rest of them). What was needed, according to their way of thinking, was a thorough P.R. makeover. Something that humanised the poor and downtrodden rather than villainise them. Something akin to Walter Besant's *All Sorts and Conditions of Men*. Or, even better, Mrs. Humphrey Ward's *Robert Elsmere*, which had become an international best-seller.

Zangwill wasn't opposed to the project when approached by the Jewish Publication Society with such a proposal – especially as there was an offer of money up front. He simply wanted the promise of total artistic freedom. And, really, it was money for old rope as he had been writing vignettes about the people of Whitechapel for some years by then. The characters had already been corralled and the locations selected.

What was left to work out had to do with Zangwill's own dilemma – his ambivalence about the process of assimilation, where it was leading and what it entailed. He could only mock Jewish orthodoxy, rabbinical sophism, and the landsman's refusal to accept that what might have been good for a shtetl community of three or four hundred in the heart of the Russian Pale might not be appropriate for a life in 1880s England. But the flip side of the coin was the cultural vacuousness of 19th century free-market capitalism and the lonesome and dispiriting consequences of submitting to its glittering but ultimately hollow allure. What was lost and what was gained? And, most important of all, where did it leave them?

Zangwill's *Children of the Ghetto* is his resultant masterpiece. Tender, loving, humorous, wise, it is essentially the story of a people from far off lands swept up onto alien shores and struggling to survive. It is the story of courage, foolishness, ingeniousness and pain, of human dignity that refuses to die. And, as such, it is a story for our time.

R. A. Biderman
Victorian Series Editor
Cambridge 2004

PROEM

Not here in our London Ghetto the gates and gabardines of the olden Ghetto of the Eternal City; yet no lack of signs external by which one may know it, and those who dwell therein. Its narrow streets have no speciality of architecture; its dirt is not picturesque. It is no longer the stage for the high-buskined tragedy of massacre and martyrdom; only for the obscurer, deeper tragedy that evolves from the pressure of its own inward forces, and the long-drawn-out tragi-comedy of sordid and shifty poverty. Natheless, this London Ghetto of ours is a region where, amid uncleanness and squalor, the rose of romance blows yet a little longer in the raw air of English reality; a world which hides beneath its stony and unlovable surface an inner world of dreams, fantastic and poetic as the mirage of the Orient where they were woven, of superstitions grotesque as the cathedral gargoyles of the Dark Ages in which they had birth. And over all lie tenderly some streaks of celestial light shining from the face of the great Lawgiver.

The folk who compose our pictures are children of the Ghetto; their faults are bred of its hovering miasma of persecution, their virtues straitened and intensified by the narrowness of its horizon. And they who have won their way beyond its boundaries still play their parts in tragedies and comedies – tragedies of spiritual struggle, comedies of material ambition – which are the aftermath of its centuries of dominance, the sequel of that long cruel night in Jewry which coincides with the Christian Era. If they are not the Children, they are at least the Grandchildren of the Ghetto.

The particular Ghetto that is the dark background upon which our pictures will be cast, is of voluntary formation.

People who have been living in a Ghetto for a couple of centuries, are not able to step outside merely because the gates are thrown down, nor to efface the brands on their souls by putting off the yellow badges. The isolation imposed from without will have come to seem the law of their being. But a minority will pass, by units, into the larger, freer, stranger life amid the execrations of an ever-dwindling majority. For better or for worse, or for both, the Ghetto will be gradually abandoned, till at last it becomes only a swarming place for the poor and the ignorant, huddling together for social warmth. Such people are their own Ghetto gates; when they migrate they carry them across the sea to lands where they are not. Into the heart of East London there poured from Russia, from Poland, from Germany, from Holland, streams of Jewish exiles, refugees, settlers, few as well-to-do as the Jew of the proverb, but all rich in their cheerfulness, their industry, and their cleverness. The majority bore with them nothing but their phylacteries and praying shawls, and a good-natured contempt for Christians and Christianity. For the Jew has rarely been embittered by persecution. He knows that he is in *Goluth*, in exile, and that the days of the Messiah are not yet, and he looks upon the persecutor merely as the stupid instrument of an all-wise Providence. So that these poor Jews were rich in all the virtues, devout yet tolerant, and strong in their reliance on Faith, Hope, and more especially Charity.

In the early days of the nineteenth century, all Israel were brethren. Even the pioneer colony of wealthy Sephardim – descendants of the Spanish crypto-Jews who had reached England via Holland – had modified its boycott of the poor Ashkenazic immigrants, now they were become an overwhelming majority. There was a superior stratum of Anglo-German Jews who had had time to get on, but all the Ashkenazic tribes lived very much like a happy family, the poor not stand-offish towards the rich, but anxious to afford them opportunities for well-doing. The *Schnorrer* felt no false shame in his begging. He knew it was the rich man's duty to give him unleavened bread at Passover, and coals in the winter, and odd half-crowns at all seasons; and he regarded himself as the Jacob's ladder by which the rich man mounted to

Paradise. But, like all genuine philanthropists, he did not look for gratitude. He felt that virtue was its own reward, especially when he sat in
Sabbath vesture at the head of his table on Friday nights, and thanked
God in an operatic aria for the white cotton table-cloth and the fried
sprats. He sought personal interviews with the most majestic magnates,
and had humorous repartees for their lumbering censure.

As for the rich, they gave charity unscrupulously – in the same
Oriental, unscientific, informal spirit in which the *Dayanim*, those cadis
of the East End, administered justice. The *Takif*, or man of substance,
was as accustomed to the palm of the mendicant outside the Great
Synagogue as to the rattling pyx within. They lived in Bury Street, and
Prescott Street, and Finsbury – these aristocrats of the Ghetto – in
mansions that are now but congeries of "apartments." Few relations had
they with Belgravia, but many with Petticoat Lane and the Great *Shool*,
the stately old synagogue which has always been illuminated by candles
and still refuses all modern light. The Spanish Jews had a more ancient
snoga, but it was within a stone's throw of the "Duke's Place" edifice.
Decorum was not a feature of synagogue worship in those days, nor was
the Almighty yet conceived as the holder of formal receptions once a
week. Worshippers did not pray with bated breath, as if afraid that the
deity would overhear them. They were at ease in Zion. They passed the
snuff-boxes and remarks about the weather. The opportunities of
skipping afforded by a too exuberant liturgy promoted conversation,
and even stocks were discussed in the terrible *longueurs* induced by the
meaningless ministerial repetition of prayers already said by the congregation, or by the official recitations of catalogues of purchased
benedictions. Sometimes, of course, this announcement of the offertory
was interesting, especially when there was sensational competition. The
great people bade in guineas for the privilege of rolling up the Scroll of
the Law or drawing the Curtain of the Ark, or saying a particular *Kaddish*
if they were mourners, and then thrills of reverence went round the
congregation. The social hierarchy was to some extent graduated by
synagogal contributions, and whoever could afford only a little offering

had it announced as a "gift" – a vague term which might equally be the covering of a reticent munificence.

Very few persons, "called up" to the reading of the Law, escaped at the cost they had intended, for one is easily led on by an insinuative official incapable of taking low views of the donor's generosity and a little deaf. The moment prior to the declaration of the amount was quite exciting for the audience. On Sabbaths and festivals the authorities could not write down these sums, for writing is work and work is forbidden; even to write them in the book and volume of their brain would have been to charge their memories with an illegitimate if not an impossible burden. Parchment books on a peculiar system with holes in the pages and laces to go through the holes solved the problem of bookkeeping without pen and ink. It is possible that many of the worshippers were tempted to give beyond their means for fear of losing the esteem of the *Shammos* or Beadle, a potent personage only next in influence to the President whose overcoat he obsequiously removed on the greater man's annual visit to the synagogue. The Beadle's eye was all over the *Shool* at once, and he could settle an altercation about seats without missing a single response. His automatic amens resounded magnificently through the synagogue, at once a stimulus and a rebuke. It was probably as a concession to him that poor men, who were neither seat-holders nor wearers of chimney-pot hats, were penned within an iron enclosure near the door of the building and ranged on backless benches, and it says much for the authority of the *Shammos* that not even the *Schnorrer* contested it. Prayers were shouted rapidly by the congregation, and elaborately sung by the *Chazan*. The minister was *Vox et proeterea nihil*. He was the only musical instrument permitted and on him devolved the whole onus of making the service attractive. He succeeded. He was helped by the sociability of the gathering – for the Synagogue was virtually a Jewish Club, the focus of the sectarian life.

Hard times and bitter had some of the fathers of the Ghetto, but they ate their dry bread with the salt of humour, loved their wives, and praised God for His mercies. Unwitting of the genealogies that would be found for them by their prosperous grandchildren, old clo' men plied their trade in ambitious content. They were meek and timorous outside the Ghetto, walking warily for fear of the Christian. Sufferance was still the badge of all their tribe. Yet that there were Jews who held their heads high, let the following legend tell: Few men could shuffle along more inoffensively or cry "Old Clo'" with a meeker twitter than Sleepy Sol. The old man crawled one day, bowed with humility and clo'-bag, into a military mews and uttered his tremulous chirp. To him came one of the hostlers with insolent beetling brow.

"Any gold lace?" faltered Sleepy Sol.

"Get out!" roared the hostler.

"I'll give you de best prices," pleaded Sleepy Sol.

"Get out!" repeated the hostler and hustled the old man into the street. "If I catch you 'ere again, I'll break your neck." Sleepy Sol loved his neck, but the profit on gold, lace torn from old uniforms was high. Next week he crept into the mews again, trusting to meet another hostler.

"Clo'! Clo'!" he chirped faintly.

Alas! the brawny bully was to the fore again and recognized him.

"You dirty old Jew," he cried. "Take that, and that! The next time I sees you, you'll go 'ome on a shutter."

The old man took that, and that, and went on his way. The next day he came again.

"Clo'! Clo'!" he whimpered.

"What!" said the ruffian, his coarse cheeks flooded with angry blood. "Ev yer forgotten what I promised yer?" He seized Sleepy Sol by the scruff of the neck.

"I say, why can't you leave the old man alone?"

The hostler stared at the protester, whose presence he had not noticed in the pleasurable excitement of the moment. It was a Jewish young man, indifferently attired in a pepper-and-salt suit. The muscular hostler measured him scornfully with his eye.

"What's to do with you?" he said, with studied contempt.

"Nothing," admitted the intruder. "And what harm is he doing you?"

"That's my bizness," answered the hostler, and tightened his clutch of Sleepy Sol's nape.

"Well, you'd better not mind it," answered the young man calmly. "Let go."

The hostler's thick lips emitted a disdainful laugh.

"Let go, d'you hear?" repeated the young man.

"I'll let go at your nose," said the hostler, clenching his knobby fist.

"Very well," said the young man. "Then I'll pull yours."

"Oho!" said the hostler, his scowl growing fiercer. "Yer means bizness, does yer?" With that he sent Sleepy Sol staggering along the road and rolled up his shirt-sleeves. His coat was already off.

The young man did not remove his; he quietly assumed the defensive. The hostler sparred up to him with grim earnestness, and launched a terrible blow at his most characteristic feature. The young man blandly put it on one side, and planted a return blow on the hostler's ear. Enraged, his opponent sprang upon him. The young Jew paralyzed him by putting his left hand negligently into his pocket. With his remaining hand he closed the hostler's right eye, and sent the flesh about it into mourning. Then he carelessly tapped a little blood from the hostler's nose, gave him a few thumps on the chest as if to test the strength of his lungs, and laid him sprawling in the courtyard. A brother hostler ran out from the stables and gave a cry of astonishment.

"You'd better wipe his face," said the young man curtly.

The newcomer hurried back towards the stables.

"Vait a moment," said Sleepy Sol. "I can sell you a sponge sheap; I've got a beauty in my bag."

There were plenty of sponges about, but the newcomer bought the second-hand sponge.

"Do you want any more?" the young man affably inquired of his prostrate adversary.

The hostler gave a groan. He was shamed before a friend whom he had early convinced of his fistic superiority.

"No, I reckon he don't," said his friend, with a knowing grin at the conqueror.

"Then I will wish you a good day," said the young man. "Come along, father."

"Yes, ma son-in-law," said Sleepy Sol.

"Do you know who that was, Joe?" said his friend, as he sponged away the blood.

Joe shook his head.

"That was Dutch Sam," said his friend in an awe-struck whisper.

All Joe's body vibrated with surprise and respect. Dutch Sam was the champion bruiser of his time; in private life an eminent dandy and a prime favourite of His Majesty George IV, and Sleepy Sol had a beautiful daughter and was perhaps prepossessing himself when washed for the Sabbath.

"Dutch Sam!" Joe repeated.

"Dutch Sam! Why, we've got his picter hanging up inside, only he's naked to the waist."

"Well, strike me lucky! What a fool I was not to rekkernize 'im!" His battered face brightened up. "No wonder he licked me!"

Except for the comparative infrequency of the more bestial types of men and women, Judea has always been a cosmos in little, and its prize-fighters and scientists, its philosophers and "fences," its gymnasts and money-lenders, its scholars and stockbrokers, its musicians, chess-players, poets, comic singers, lunatics, saints, publicans, politicians, warriors, poltroons, mathematicians, actors, foreign correspondents, have always been in the first rank. *Nihil alienum a se Judaeus putat.*

Joe and his friend fell to recalling Dutch Sam's great feats. Each out-vied the other in admiration for the supreme pugilist.

Next day Sleepy Sol came rampaging down the courtyard. He walked at the rate of five miles to the hour, and despite the weight of his bag his head pointed to the zenith.

"Clo'!" he shrieked. "Clo'!"

Joe the hostler came out. His head was bandaged, and in his hand was gold lace. It was something even to do business with a hero's father-in-law.

But it is given to few men to marry their daughters to champion boxers: and as Dutch Sam was not a Don Quixote, the average peddler or huckster never enjoyed the luxury of prancing gait and cock-a-hoop business cry. The primitive fathers of the Ghetto might have borne themselves more jauntily had they foreseen that they were to be the ancestors of mayors and aldermen descended from Castilian hidalgos and Polish kings, and that an unborn historian would conclude that the Ghetto of their day was peopled by princes in disguise. They would have been as surprised to learn who they were as to be informed that they were orthodox. The great Reform split did not occur till well on towards the middle of the century, and the Jews of those days were unable to conceive that a man could be a Jew without eating *kosher* meat, and they would have looked upon the modern distinctions between racial and religious Jews as the sophistries of the convert or the missionary. If their religious life converged to the Great *Shool*, their social life focused on Petticoat Lane, a long, narrow thoroughfare which, as late as Strype's day, was lined with beautiful trees; vastly more pleasant they must have been than the faded barrows and beggars of after days. The Lane – such was its affectionate sobriquet – was the stronghold of hard-shell Judaism, the Alsatia of "infidelity" into which no missionary dared set foot, especially no apostate-apostle. Even in modern days the new-fangled Jewish minister of the fashionable suburb, rigged out like the Christian clergyman, has been mistaken for such a *Meshumad*, and pelted with gratuitous vegetables and eleemosynary eggs. The Lane was always the great market-place, and every insalubrious street and alley abutting on it was covered with the overflowings of its commerce and its mud. Wentworth Street and Goulston Street were the chief branches, and in festival times the latter was a pandemonium of caged poultry, clucking and quacking and cackling and screaming. Fowls and geese and ducks were bought alive, and taken to have their throats cut for a fee by the official slaughterer. At Purim a gaiety, as of the Roman carnival, enlivened the swampy Wentworth Street, and brought a smile into the unwashed face of the pavement. The confectioners' shops, crammed with "stuffed monkeys" and "bolas," were besieged by hilarious crowds of handsome girls and their young men, fat women and their children, all washing down the luscious spicy compounds with cups of chocolate; temporarily erected swinging cradles bore a vociferous many-coloured burden to the skies; cardboard noses, grotesque in their departure from truth, abounded. The Purim *Spiel* – or Purim play – never took root in England, nor was Haman ever burnt in the streets, but *Shalachmonos*, or gifts of the season, passed between friend and friend, and masquerading parties burst into neighbours' houses. But the Lane was lively enough on the ordinary Friday and Sunday. The famous Sunday Fair was an event of metropolitan importance, and thither came buyers of every sect. The Friday Fair was more local, and confined mainly to edibles. The Ante-Festival Fairs combined something of the other two, for Jews desired to sport new hats and clothes for the holidays as well as to eat extra luxuries, and took the opportunity of a well-marked epoch to invest in new everythings from oil-cloth to cups and saucers. Especially was this so at Passover, when for a week the poorest Jew must use a supplementary set of crockery and kitchen utensils. A babel of sound, audible for several streets around, denoted Market Day in Petticoat Lane, and the pavements were blocked by serried crowds going both ways at once.

It was only gradually that the community was Anglicised. Under the sway of centrifugal impulses, the wealthier members began to form new colonies, moulting their old feathers and replacing them by finer, and flying ever further from the centre. Men of organizing ability founded unrivalled philanthropic and educational institutions on British lines; millionaires fought for political emancipation; brokers brazenly foisted themselves on 'Change; ministers gave sermons in bad English; an English journal was started; very slowly, the conventional Anglican tradition was established; and on that human palimpsest which has borne the inscriptions of all languages and all epochs, was writ large the sign-manual of England. Judæa prostrated itself before the Dagan of its hereditary foe, the Philistine, and respectability crept on to freeze the blood of the Orient with its frigid finger, and to blur the vivid tints of the East into the uniform grey of English middle-class life. In the period within which our story moves, only vestiges of the old gaiety and brotherhood remained; the full *alfresco* flavour was evaporated.

And today they are all dead – the *Takeefim* with big hearts and bigger purses, and the humorous *Schnorrers*, who accepted their gold, and the cheerful pious peddlers who rose from one extreme to the other, building up fabulous fortunes in marvellous ways. The young mothers, who suckled their babes in the sun, have passed out of the sunshine; yea, and the babes, too, have gone down with grey heads to the dust. Dead are the fair fat women with tender hearts, who waddled benignantly through life, ever ready to shed the sympathetic tear, best of wives and cooks, and mothers; dead are the bald, ruddy old men, who ambled about in faded carpet slippers, and passed the snuff-box of peace; dead are the stout-hearted youths who sailed away to Tom Tiddler's ground, and dead are the buxom maidens they led under the wedding canopy when they returned. Even the great Dr. Sequira, pompous in white stockings, physician extraordinary to the Prince Regent of Portugal, lies vanquished by his life-long adversary and the Baal Shem himself, King of Cabalists, could command no countervailing miracle.

Where are the little girls in white pinafores with pink sashes who brightened the Ghetto on high days and holidays? Where is the beauteous Betsy of the Victoria Ballet? and where the jocund synagogue dignitary who led off the cotillion with her at the annual Rejoicing of the Law? Worms have long since picked the great financier's brain, the embroidered waistcoats of the bucks have passed even beyond the stage of adorning sweeps on May Day, and Dutch Sam's fist is bonier than ever. The same mould covers them all – those who donated guineas and those who donated "gifts," the rogues and the hypocrites, and the wedding-drolls, the observant and the lax, the purse-proud and the lowly, the coarse, and the genteel, the wonderful chap-men and the luckless *Schlemihls*, Rabbi and *Dayan* and *Shochet*, the scribes who wrote the sacred scroll and the cantors who trolled it off mellifluous tongues, and the betting-men who never listened to it; the grimy Russians of the capotes and the earlocks, and the blue-blooded Dons, "the gentlemen of the Mahamad" who ruffled it with swords and knee-breeches in the best Christian society. Those who kneaded the toothsome "bolas" lie with those who ate them; and the marriage-brokers repose with those they mated. The olives and the cucumbers grow green and fat as of yore, but their lovers are mixed with a soil that is barren of them. The restless, bustling crowds that jostled laughingly in Rag Fair are at rest in the "House of Life;" the pageant of their strenuous generation is vanished as a dream. They died with the declaration of God's unity on their stiffening lips, and the certainty of resurrection in their pulseless hearts, and a faded Hebrew inscription on a tomb, or an unread entry on a synagogue brass is their only record. And yet, perhaps, their generation is not all dust. Perchance, here and there, some decrepit centenarian rubs his purblind eyes with the ointment of memory, and sees these pictures of the past, hallowed by the consecration of time, and finds his shrivelled cheek wet with the pathos sanctifying the joys that have been.

CHAPTER I

The Bread of Affliction

A dead and gone wag called the street "Fashion Street," and most of the people who live in it do not even see the joke. If it could exchange names with "Rotten Row," both places would be more appropriately designated. It is a dull, squalid, narrow thoroughfare in the East End of London, connecting Spitalfields with Whitechapel, and branching off in blind alleys. In the days when little Esther Ansell trudged its unclean pavements, its extremities were within earshot of the blasphemies from some of the vilest quarters and filthiest rookeries in the capital of the civilized world. Some of these clotted spiders' webs have since been swept away by the besom of the social reformer, and the spiders have scurried off into darker crannies.

There were the conventional touches about the London street-picture, as Esther Ansell sped through the freezing mist of the December evening, with a pitcher in her hand, looking in her oriental colouring like a miniature Rebecca going to the well. A female street-singer, with a trail of infants of dubious maternity, troubled the air with a piercing melody; a pair of slatterns with arms akimbo reviled each other's relatives; a drunkard lurched along, babbling amiably; an organ-grinder, blue-nosed as his monkey, set some ragged children jigging under the watery rays of a street-lamp. Esther drew her little plaid shawl tightly around her, and ran on without heeding these familiar details, her chilled feet absorbing the damp of the murky pavement through the worn soles of her cumbrous boots. They were masculine boots, kicked off by some intoxicated tramp and picked up by Esther's father. Moses Ansell had a habit of lighting on windfalls, due, perhaps, to his meek manner of walking with bent head, as though literally bowed beneath the yoke of the Captivity. Providence rewarded him for his humility by occasional treasure-trove. Esther had received a pair of new boots from her school a week before, and the substitution of the tramp's foot-gear for her own resulted in a net profit of half-a-crown, and kept Esther's little brothers and sisters in bread for a week. At school, under her teacher's eye, Esther was very unobtrusive about the feet for the next fortnight, as the fear of being found out died away, even her rather morbid conscience condoned the deception in view of the stomachic gain.

They gave away bread and milk at the school, too, but Esther and her brothers and sisters never took either, for fear of being thought in want of them. The superiority of a class-mate is hard to bear, and a high-spirited child will not easily acknowledge starvation in the presence of a roomful of purse-proud urchins, some of them able to spend a farthing a day on pure luxuries. Moses Ansell would have been grieved had he known his children were refusing the bread he could not give them. Trade was slack in the sweating dens, and Moses, who had always lived from hand to mouth, had latterly held less than ever between the one and the other. He had applied for help to the Jewish Board of Guardians, but red-tape rarely unwinds as quickly as hunger coils itself; moreover, Moses was an old offender in poverty at the Court of Charity. But there was one species of alms which Moses could not be denied, and the existence of which Esther could not conceal from him as she concealed that of the eleemosynary breakfasts at the school. For it was known to all men that soup and bread were to be had for the asking thrice a week at the Institution in Fashion Street, and in the Ansell household the opening of the soup-kitchen was looked forward to as the dawn of a golden age, when it would be impossible to pass more than one day without bread. The vaguely-remembered smell of the soup threw a poetic flagrance over the coming winter. Every year since

Esther's mother had died, the child had been sent to fetch home the provender, for Moses, who was the only other available member of the family, was always busy praying when he had nothing better to do. And so tonight Esther fared to the kitchen, with her red pitcher, passing in her childish eagerness numerous women shuffling along on the same errand, and bearing uncouth tin cans supplied by the institution. An individualistic instinct of cleanliness, made Esther prefer the family pitcher. Today this liberty of choice has been taken away, and the regulation can, numbered and stamped, serves as a soup-ticket. There was quite a crowd of applicants outside the stable-like doors of the kitchen when Esther arrived, a few with well-lined stomachs, perhaps, but the majority famished and shivering. The feminine element swamped the rest, but there were about a dozen men and a few children among the group, most of the men scarce taller than the children – strange, stunted, swarthy, hairy creatures, with muddy complexions illumined by black, twinkling eyes. A few were of imposing stature, wearing coarse, dusty felt hats or peaked caps, with shaggy beards or faded scarfs around their throats. Here and there, too, was a woman of comely face and figure, but for the most part it was a collection of crones, prematurely aged, with weird, wan, old-world features, slip-shod and draggle-tailed, their heads bare, or covered with dingy shawls in lieu of bonnets – red shawls, grey shawls, brick-dust shawls, mud-coloured shawls. Yet there was an indefinable touch of romance and pathos about the tawdriness and witch-like ugliness, and an underlying identity about the crowd of Polish, Russian, German, Dutch Jewesses mutually apathetic, and pressing forwards. Some of them had infants at their bare breasts, who drowsed quietly with intervals of ululation. The women devoid of shawls had nothing around their necks to protect them from the cold, the dusky throats were exposed, and sometimes even the first hooks and eyes of the bodice were unnecessarily undone. The majority wore cheap earrings and black wigs with preternaturally polished hair; where there was no wig, the hair was tousled.

At half-past five the stable-doors were thrown open, and the crowd pressed through a long, narrow white-washed stone corridor into a barn-like compartment, with a white-washed ceiling traversed by wooden beams. Within this compartment, and leaving but a narrow, circum-scribing border, was a sort of cattle-pen, into which the paupers crushed, awaiting amid discomfort and universal jabber the divine moment. The single jet of gas-light depending from the ceiling flared upon the strange simian faces, and touched them into a grotesque picturesqueness that would have delighted Doré.

They felt hungry, these picturesque people; their near and dear ones were hungering at home. Voluptuously savouring in imagination the operation of the soup, they forgot its operation as a dole in aid of wages; were unconscious of the grave economical possibilities of pauperization and the rest, and quite willing to swallow their independence with the soup. Even Esther, who had read much, and was sensitive, accepted unquestioningly the theory of the universe that was held by most people about her, that human beings were distinguished from animals in having to toil terribly for a meagre crust, but that their lot was lightened by the existence of a small and semi-divine class called *Takeefim*, or rich people, who gave away what they didn't want. How these rich people came to be, Esther did not inquire; they were as much a part of the constitution of things as clouds and horses. The semi-celestial variety was rarely to be met with. It lived, far away from the Ghetto, and a small family of it was said to occupy a whole house. Representatives of it, clad in rustling silks or impressive broad-cloth, and radiating an indefinable aroma of super-humanity, sometimes came to the school, preceded by the beaming Head Mistress; and then all the little girls rose and curtseyed, and the best of them, passing as average members of the class, astonished the semi-divine persons by their intimate acquaintance with the topography of the Pyrenees and the disagreements of Saul and David, the inter-course of the two species ending in effusive smiles and general satisfaction. But the dullest of the girls was alive to the comedy, and had a good-humoured contempt for the unworldliness of the semi-divine persons who spoke to them as if they were not going to recommence squabbling, and pulling one another's hair, and copying one another's sums, and stealing one another's needles, the moment the semi-celestial backs were turned.

Tonight, semi-divine persons were to be seen in a galaxy of splendour, for in the reserved standing-places, behind the white deal counter, was gathered a group of philanthropists. The room was an odd-shaped polygon, partially lined with eight boilers, whose great wooden lids were raised by pulleys and balanced by red-painted iron balls. In the corner stood the cooking-engine. Cooks in white caps and blouses stirred the steaming soup with long wooden paddles. A tradesman besought the attention of the Jewish reporters to the improved boiler he had manufactured, and the superintendent adjured the newspaper men not to omit his name; while amid the soberly-clad clergymen flitted, like gorgeous humming-birds through a flock of crows, the marriageable daughters of an East-End minister.

When a sufficient number of semi-divinities was gathered together, the President addressed the meeting at considerable length, striving to impress upon the clergymen and other philanthropists present that charity was a virtue, and appealing to the Bible, the Koran, and even the Vedas, for confirmation of his proposition. Early in his speech the sliding door that separated the cattle-pen from the kitchen proper had to be closed, because the jostling crowd jabbered so much and inconsiderate infants squalled and there did not seem to he any general desire to the President's ethical views. They were a low material lot, who thought only of their bellies, and did but chatter the louder when the speech was shut out. They had overflowed their barriers by this time, and were surging cruelly to and fro, and Esther had to keep her elbows close to her sides lest her arms should be dislocated. Outside the stable doors a shifting array of boys and girls hovered hungrily and curiously. When the President had finished, the Rabbinate was invited to address the philanthropists, which it did at not less length, eloquently seconding the proposition that charity was a virtue. Then the door was slid back, and the first two paupers were admitted, the rest of the crowd being courageously kept at bay by the superintendent. The head cook filled a couple of plates with soup, dipping a great pewter pot into the cauldron. The Rabbinate then uplifted Its eyes heavenwards, and said the grace: "Blessed art Thou, O Lord, King of the Universe, according to whose word all things exist."

It then tasted a spoonful of the soup, as did also the President and several of the visitors, the passage of the fluid along the palate invariably evoking approving ecstatic smiles; and indeed, there was more body in it this opening night than there would be later, when, in due course, the bulk of the meat would take its legitimate place among the pickings of office. The sight of the delighted deglutition of the semi-divine persons made Esther's mouth water as she struggled for breathing space on the outskirts of Paradise. The impatience which fretted her was almost allayed by visions of stout-hearted Solomon and gentle Rachel and whimpering little Sarah and Ikey, all gulping down the delicious draught. Even the more stoical father and grandmother were a little in her thoughts. The Ansells had eaten nothing but a slice of dry bread each in the morning. Here before her, in the land of Goshen, flowing with soup, was piled up a heap of halves of loaves, while endless other loaves ranged along the shelves as for a giant's table. Esther looked ravenously at the four-square tower built of edible bricks, shivering as the biting air sought out her back through a sudden interstice in the heaving mass. The draught reminded her more keenly of her little ones huddled together in the fireless garret at home. Ah! what a happy night was in store. She must not let them devour the two loaves tonight; that would he criminal extravagance. No, one would suffice for the banquet; the other must be carefully put by. "Tomorrow is also a day," as the old grandmother used to say in her quaint jargon. But the banquet was not to be spread as fast as Esther's fancy could fly; the doors must be shut again, other semi-divine and wholly divine persons (in white ties) must move and second (with eloquence and length) votes of thanks to the President, the Rabbinate, and all other available recipients; a French visitor must express his admiration of English charity. But at last the turn of the gnawing stomachs came. The motley crowd, still babbling, made a slow, forward movement, squeezing painfully through the narrow aperture, and shivering a glass window pane at the side of the cattle-pen in the crush; the semi-divine persons rubbed their hands and smiled genially; ingenious paupers tried to dodge round to the cauldrons by the semi-divine entrance; the tropical humming-birds fluttered among the crows; there was a splashing of ladles and a gurgling of cascades of soup into the cans, and a hubbub of voices; a toothless, white-haired, bleary-eyed hag lamented in excellent English that soup was refused her, owing to her case not having yet been investigated, and her tears moistened the one loaf she received. In like hard case a Russian threw himself on the stones and howled. But at last Esther was running through the mist, warmed by the pitcher which she hugged to her bosom, and suppressing the blind impulse to pinch the pair of loaves tied up in her pinafore. She almost flew up the dark flight of stairs to the attic in Royal Street. Little Sarah was sobbing querulously. Esther, conscious of being an angel of deliverance, tried to take the last two steps at once, tripped and tumbled ignominiously against the garret-door, which flew back and let her fall into the room with a crash. The pitcher shivered into fragments under her aching little bosom, the odorous soup spread itself in an irregular pool over the boards, and flowed under the two beds and dripped down the crevices into the room beneath. Esther burst into tears; her frock was wet and greased, her hands were cut and bleeding. Little Sarah checked her sobs at the disaster. Moses Ansell was not yet returned from evening service, but the withered old grandmother, whose wizened face loomed through the gloom of the cold, unlit garret, sat up on the bed and cursed her angrily for a Schlemihl. A sense of injustice made Esther cry more bitterly. She had never broken anything for years past. Ikey, an eerie-looking dot of four and a half years, tottered towards her (all the Ansells had learnt to see in the dark), and nestling his curly head against her wet bodice, murmured:

"Neva mind, Estie, I lat oo teep in my new bed."

The consolation of sleeping in that imaginary new bed to the possession of which Ikey was always looking forward was apparently adequate; for Esther got up from the floor and untied the loaves from her pinafore. A reckless spirit of defiance possessed her, as of a gambler who throws good money after bad. They should have a mad revelry tonight – the two loaves should be eaten at once. One (minus a hunk for father's supper) would hardly satisfy six voracious appetites. Solomon and Rachel, irrepressibly excited by the sight of the bread, rushed at it greedily, snatched a loaf from Esther's hand, and tore off a crust each with their fingers.

"Heathen," cried the old grandmother. "Washing and benediction."

Solomon was used to being called a 'heathen' by the *Bube*. He put on his cap and went grudgingly to the bucket of water that stood in a corner of the room, and tipped a drop over his fingers. It is to be feared that neither the quantity of water nor the area of hand covered reached even the minimum enjoined by Rabbinical law. He murmured something intended for Hebrew during the operation, and was beginning to mutter the devout little sentence which precedes the eating of bread when Rachel, who as a female was less driven to the lavatory ceremony, and had thus got ahead of him, paused in her ravenous mastication and made a wry face. Solomon took a huge bite at his crust, then he uttered an inarticulate "pooh," and spat out his mouthful.

There was no salt in the bread.

CHAPTER II

The Sweater

The catastrophe was not complete. There were some long thin fibres of pale boiled meat, whose juices had gone to enrich the soup, lying about the floor or adhering to the fragments of the pitcher. Solomon, who was a curly-headed chap of infinite resource, discovered them, and it had just been decided to. neutralize the insipidity of the bread by the far-away flavour of the meat, when a peremptory knocking was heard at the door, and a dazzling vision of beauty bounded into the room.

"'Ere! What are you doin', leavin' things leak through our ceiling?"

Becky Belcovitch was a buxom, bouncing girl, with cherry cheeks that looked exotic in a land of pale faces. She wore a mass of black crisp ringlets aggressively suggestive of singeing and curl-papers. She was the belle of Royal Street in her spare time, and womanly triumphs dogged even her working hours. She was sixteen years old, and devoted her youth and beauty to buttonholes. In the East End, where a spade is a spade, a buttonhole is a buttonhole, and not a primrose or a pansy. There are two kinds of buttonhole – the coarse for slop goods and the fine for gentlemanly wear. Becky concentrated herself on superior buttonholes, which are worked with fine twist. She stitched them in her father's workshop which was more comfortable than a stranger's, and better fitted for evading the Factory Acts. Tonight she was radiant in silk and jewellery, and her pert snub nose had the insolence of felicity which Agamemnon deprecated. Seeing her, you would have as soon connected her with Esoteric Buddhism as with buttonholes.

The Sweater

The *Bube* explained the situation in voluble Yiddish, and made Esther wince again under the impassioned invective on her clumsiness. The old beldame expended enough oriental metaphor on the accident to fit up a minor poet. If the family died of starvation, their blood would be upon their granddaughter's head.

"Well, why don't you wipe it up, stupid?" said Becky. "'Ow would you like to pay for Pesach's new coat? It just dripped past his shoulder."

"I'm so sorry, Becky," said Esther, striving hard to master the tremor in her voice. And drawing a house-cloth from a mysterious recess, she went on her knees in a practical prayer for pardon.

Becky snorted and went back to her sister's engagement-party. For this was the secret of her gorgeous vesture, of her glittering earrings, and her massive brooch, as it was the secret of the transformation of the Belcovitch workshop (and living room) into a hall of dazzling light. Four separate gaunt bare arms of iron gas-pipe lifted hymeneal torches. The labels from reels of cotton, pasted above the mantelpiece as indexes of work done, alone betrayed the past and future of the room. At a long narrow table, covered with a white table-cloth spread with rum, gin, biscuits and fruit, and decorated with two wax candles in tall, brass candlesticks, stood or sat a group of swarthy, neatly-dressed Poles, most of them in high hats. A few women wearing wigs, silk dresses, and gold chains wound round half-washed necks, stood about outside the inner circle. A stooping, black-bearded, bleary-eyed man in a long, threadbare coat and a black skull cap, on either side of which hung a corkscrew curl, sat abstractedly eating the almonds and raisins, in the central place of honour which befits a *Maggid*. Before him were pens and ink and a roll of parchment. This was the engagement contract.

The damages of breach of promise were assessed in advance and without respect of sex. Whichever side repented of the bargain undertook to pay ten pounds by way of compensation for the broken pledge. As a nation, Israel is practical and free from cant. Romance and moonshine are beautiful things, but behind the glittering veil are always the stern realities of things and the weaknesses of human nature. The high contracting parties were signing the document as Becky returned. The bridegroom, who halted a little on one leg, was a tall sallow man named Pesach Weingott. He was a boot-maker, who could expound the Talmud and play the fiddle, but was unable to earn a living. He was marrying Fanny Belcovitch because his parents-in-law would give him free board and lodging for a year, and because he liked her. Fanny was a plump, pulpy girl, not in the prime of youth. Her complexion was fair and her manner lymphatic, and if she was not so well-favoured as her sister, she was more amiable and pleasant. She could sing sweetly in Yiddish and in English, and had once been a pantomime fairy at ten shillings a week, and had even flourished a cutlass as a midshipman. But she had long since given up the stage, to become her father's right hand woman in the workshop. She made coats from morning till midnight at a big machine with a massive treadle, and had pains in her chest even before she fell in love with Pesach Weingott.

There was a hubbub of congratulation (*Mazzoltov, Mazzoltov,* good luck), and a palsy of handshaking, when the contract was signed. Remarks, grave and facetious, flew about in Yiddish, with phrases of Polish and Russian thrown in for auld lang syne, and cups and jugs were broken in reminder of the transiency of things mortal. The Belcovitches had been saving up their already broken crockery for the occasion. The hope was expressed that Mr. and Mrs. Belcovitch would live to see "rejoicings" on their other daughter, and to see their daughters' daughters under the *Chuppah,* or wedding-canopy.

Becky's hardened cheek blushed under the oppressive jocularity. Everybody spoke Yiddish habitually at No. 1 Royal Street, except the younger generation, and that spoke it to the elder.

"I always said, no girl of mine should marry a Dutchman." It was a dominant thought of Mr. Belcovitch's, and it rose spontaneously to his lips at this joyful moment. Next to a Christian, a Dutch Jew stood lowest in the gradation of potential sons-in-law. Spanish Jews, earliest arrivals by way of Holland, after the Restoration, are a class apart, and look down on the later imported *Ashkenazim,* embracing both Poles and Dutchmen in their impartial contempt. But this does not prevent the Pole and the Dutchman from despising each other. To a Dutch or Russian Jew, the "Pullack," or Polish Jew, is a poor creature; and scarce anything can exceed the complacency with which the "Pullack" looks down upon the "Litvok" or Lithuanian, the degraded being whose Shibboleth is literally Sibboleth, and who says "ee" where-rightly constituted persons say "oo." To mimic the mincing pronunciation of the "Litvok" affords the "Pullack" a sense of superiority almost equalling that possessed by the English Jew, whose mispronunciation of the Holy Tongue is his title to rank far above all foreign varieties. Yet a vein of brotherhood runs beneath all these feelings of mutual superiority; like the cliqueism which draws together old clo' dealers, though each gives fifty per cent more than any other dealer in the trade. The Dutch foregather in a district called "The Dutch Tenters;" they eat voraciously, and almost monopolize the ice-cream, hot pea, diamond-cutting, cucumber, herring, and cigar trades. They are not so cute as the Russians. Their women are distinguished from other women by the flaccidity of their bodices; some wear small woollen caps and sabots. When Esther read in her school-books that the note of the Dutch character was cleanliness, she wondered. She looked in vain for the scrupulously scoured floors and the shining caps and faces. Only in the matter of tobacco-smoke did the Dutch people she knew live up to the geographical "Readers."

German Jews gravitate to Polish and Russian; and French Jews mostly stay in France. *Ici on ne parle pas Français,* is the only lingual certainty in the London Ghetto, which is a cosmopolitan quarter.

"I always said no girl of mine should marry a Dutchman." Mr. Belcovitch spoke as if at the close of a long career devoted to avoiding Dutch alliances, forgetting that not even one of his daughters was yet secure.

"Nor any girl of mine," said Mrs. Belcovitch, as if starting a separate proposition. "I would not trust a Dutchman with my medicine-bottle, much less with my Alte or my Becky. Dutchmen were not behind the door when the Almighty gave out noses, and their deceitfulness is in proportion to their noses."

The company murmured assent, and one gentleman, with a rather large organ, concealed it in a red cotton handkerchief, trumpeting uneasily.

"The Holy One, blessed be He, has given them larger noses than us;" said the *Maggid*, "because they have to talk through them so much."

A guffaw greeted this sally. The *Maggid's* wit was relished even when not coming from the pulpit. To the outsider this disparagement of the Dutch nose might have seemed a case of pot calling kettle black. The *Maggid* poured himself out a glass of rum, under cover of the laughter, and murmuring "Life to you," in Hebrew, gulped it down, and added, "They oughtn't to call it the Dutch tongue, but the Dutch nose."

"Yes, I always wonder how they can understand one another," said Mrs. Belcovitch, "with their *chaluchayacatigewesepoopa*." She laughed heartily over her onomatopoetic addition to the Yiddish vocabulary, screwing up her nose to give it due effect. She was a small sickly-looking woman, with black eyes, and shrivelled skin, and the wig without which no virtuous wife is complete. For a married woman must sacrifice her tresses on the altar of home, lest she snare other men with such sensuous baits. As a rule, she enters into the spirit of the self-denying ordinance so enthusiastically as to become hideous hastily in every other respect. It is forgotten that a husband is also a man. Mrs. Belcovitch's head was not completely shaven and shorn, for a lower stratum of an unmatched shade of brown peeped out in front of the *shaitel*, not even coinciding as to the route of the central parting.

Meantime Pesach Weingott and Alte (Fanny) Belcovitch held each other's hand, guiltily conscious of Batavian corpuscles in the young man's blood. Pesach had a Dutch uncle, but as he had never talked like him Alte alone knew. Alte wasn't her real name, by the way, and Alte was the last person in the world to know what it was. She was the Belcovitches' first successful child; the others all died before she was born. Driven frantic by a fate crueller than barrenness, the Belcovitches consulted an old Polish Rabbi, who told them they displayed too much fond solicitude for their children, provoking Heaven thereby; in future, they were to let no one but themselves know their next child's name, and never to whisper it till the child was safely married. In such wise, Heaven would not be incessantly reminded of the existence of their dear one, and would not go out of its way to castigate them. The ruse succeeded, and Alte was anxiously waiting to change both her names under the *Chuppah*, and to gratify her life-long curiosity on the subject. Meantime, her mother had been calling her "Alte," or "old 'un," which sounded endearing to the child, but grated on the woman arriving ever nearer to the years of discretion. Occasionally, Mrs. Belcovitch succumbed to the prevailing tendency, and called her "Fanny," just as she sometimes thought of herself as Mrs. Belcovitch, though her name was Kosminski. When Alte first went to school in London, the Head Mistress said, "What's your name?" The little "old 'un" had not sufficient English to understand the question, but she remembered that the Head Mistress had made the same sounds to the preceding applicant, and, where some little girls would have put their pinafores to their eyes and cried, Fanny showed herself full of resource. As the last little girl, though patently awe-struck, had come off with flying colours, merely by whimpering "Fanny Belcovitch," Alte imitated these sounds as well as she was able.

"Fanny Belcovitch, did you say?" said the Head Mistress, pausing with arrested pen.

Alte nodded her flaxen poll vigorously.

"Fanny Belcovitch," she repeated, getting the syllables better on a second hearing.

The Head Mistress turned to an assistant.

"Isn't it astonishing how names repeat themselves? Two girls, one after the other, both with exactly the same name."

They were used to coincidences in the school, where, by reason of the tribal relationship of the pupils, there was a great run on some half-a-dozen names. Mr. Kosminski took several years to understand that Alte had disowned him. When it dawned upon him he was not angry, and acquiesced in his fate. It was the only domestic detail in which he had allowed himself to be led by his children. Like his wife, Chayah, he was gradually persuaded into the belief that he was a born Belcovitch, or at least that Belcovitch was Kosminski translated into English.

Blissfully unconscious of the Dutch taint in Pesach Weingott, Bear Belcovitch bustled about in reckless hospitality. He felt that engagements were not everyday events, and that even if his whole half-sovereign's worth of festive provision was swallowed up, he would not mind much. He wore a high hat, a well-preserved black coat, with a cutaway waistcoat, showing a quantity of glazed shirtfront and a massive watch chain. They were his Sabbath clothes, and, like the Sabbath they honoured, were of immemorial antiquity. The shirt served him for seven Sabbaths, or a week of Sabbaths, being carefully folded after each. His boots had the Sabbath polish. The hat was the one he bought when he first set up as a *Baal Habaas* or respectable pillar of the synagogue; for even in the smallest *Chevra* the high hat comes next in sanctity to the Scroll of the Law, and he who does not wear it may never hope to attain to congregational dignities. The gloss on that hat was wonderful, considering it had been out unprotected in all winds and weathers. Not that Mr. Belcovitch did not possess an umbrella. He had two – one of fine new silk, the other a medley of broken ribs and cotton rags. Becky had given him the first to prevent the family disgrace of the spectacle of his promenades with the second. But he would not carry the new one on week-days because it was too good. And on Sabbaths it is a sin to carry any umbrella. So Becky's self-sacrifice was vain, and her umbrella stood in the corner, a standing gratification to the proud possessor. Kosminski had had a hard fight for his substance, and was not given to waste. He was a tall, harsh-looking man of fifty, with grizzled hair, to whom life meant work, and work meant money, and money meant savings. In Parliamentary Blue-Books, English newspapers, and the Berner Street Socialistic Club, he was called a "sweater," and the comic papers pictured him with a protuberant paunch and a greasy smile, but he had not the remotest idea that he was other than a God-fearing, industrious, and even philanthropic citizen. The measure that had been dealt to him he did but deal to others. He saw no reason why immigrant paupers should not live on a crown a week while he taught them how to handle a press-iron or work a sewing machine. They were much better off than in Poland. He would have been glad of such an income himself in those terrible first days of English life when he saw his wife and his two babes starving before his eyes, and was only precluded from investing a casual twopence in poison by ignorance of the English name for anything deadly. And what did he live on now? The fowl, the pint of haricot beans, and the haddocks which Chayah purchased for the Sabbath overlapped into the middle of next week, a quarter of a pound of coffee lasted the whole week, the grounds being decocted till every grain of virtue was extracted. Black bread and potatoes and pickled herrings made up the bulk of the everyday diet. No, no one could accuse Bear Belcovitch of fattening on the entrails of his employees. The furniture was of the simplest and shabbiest – no æsthetic instinct urged the Kosminskis to overpass the bare necessities of existence, except in dress. The only concessions to art were a crudely-coloured *Mizrach* on the east wall, to indicate the direction towards which the Jew should pray, and the mantelpiece mirror which was bordered with yellow scalloped paper (to save the gilt) and ornamented at each corner with paper roses that bloomed afresh every Passover. And yet Bear Belcovitch had lived in much better style in Poland, possessing a brass wash-hand basin, a copper saucepan, silver spoons, a silver consecration beaker, and a cupboard with glass doors, and he frequently adverted to their fond memories. But he brought nothing away except his bedding, and that was pawned in Germany on the route. When he arrived in London he had with him three groschen and a family.

"What do you think, Pesach," said Becky, as soon as she could get at her prospective brother-in-law through the barriers of congratulatory countrymen. "The stuff that came through there" – she pointed to the discoloured fragment of ceiling – "was soup. That silly little Esther spilt all she got from the kitchen."

"*Achi nebbich*, poor little thing," cried Mrs. Kosminski, who was in a tender mood, "very likely it hungers them sore upstairs. The father is out of work."

"Knowest thou what, mother," put in Fanny. " Suppose we give them our soup. Aunt Leah has just fetched it for us. Have we not a special supper tonight?"

"But father?" murmured the little woman dubiously.

"Oh, he won't notice it. I don't think he knows the soup kitchen opens tonight. Let me, mother."

And Fanny, letting Pesach's hand go, slipped out to the room that served as a kitchen, and bore the still-steaming pot upstairs. Pesach, who had pursued her, followed with some hunks of bread and a piece of lighted candle, which, while intended only to illumine the journey, came in handy at the terminus. And the festive company grinned and winked when the pair disappeared, and made jocular quotations from the Old Testament and the Rabbis. But the lovers did not kiss when they came out of the garret of the Ansells; their eyes were wet, and they went softly downstairs hand in hand, feeling linked by a deeper love than before.

Thus did Providence hand over the soup the Belcovitches took from old habit to a more necessitous quarter, and demonstrate in double sense that Charity never faileth. Nor was this the only mulct which Providence exacted from the happy father, for later on a townsman of his appeared on the scene in a long capote, and with a grimy woe-begone expression. He was a "greener" of the greenest order, having landed at the docks only a few hours ago, bringing over with him a great deal of luggage in the shape of faith in God, and in the auriferous character of London pavements. On arriving in England, he gave a casual glance at the metropolis and demanded to be directed to a synagogue wherein to shake himself after the journey. His devotions over, he tracked out Mr. Kosminski, whose address on a much-creased bit of paper had been his talisman of hope during the voyage. In his native town, where the Jews groaned beneath divers and sore oppressions, the fame of Kosminski, the pioneer, the Croesus was a legend. Mr. Kosminski was prepared for these contingencies. He went to his bedroom, dragged out a heavy wooden chest from under the bed, unlocked it and plunged his hand into a large dirty linen bag, full of coins. The instinct of generosity which was upon him made him count out forty-eight of them. He bore them to the "greener" in over-brimming palms and the foreigner, unconscious how much he owed to the felicitous coincidence of his visit with Fanny's betrothal, saw fortune visibly within his grasp. He went out, his heart bursting with gratitude, his pocket with four dozen farthings. They took him in and gave him hot soup at a Poor Jews' Shelter, whither his townsman had directed him. Kosminski returned to the banqueting room, thrilling from head to foot with the approval of his conscience. He patted Becky's curly head and said:

"Well, Becky, when shall we be dancing at your wedding?"

Becky shook her curls. Her young men could not have a poorer opinion of one another than Becky had of them all. Their homage pleased her, though it did not raise them in her esteem. Lovers grew like blackberries – only more so; for they were an evergreen stock. Or, as her mother put it in her coarse, peasant manner, *Chasanim* were as plentiful as the street dogs. Becky's beaux sat on the stairs before she was up and became early risers in their love for her, each anxious to be the first to bid their Penelope of the buttonholes good morrow. It was said that Kosminski's success as a "sweater" was due to his beauteous Becky, the flower of sartorial youth gravitating to the work-room of this East London Laban. What they admired in Becky was that there was so much of her. Still it was not enough to go round, and though Becky might keep nine lovers in hand without fear of being set down as a flirt, a larger number of tailors would have been less consistent with prospective monogamy.

"I'm not going to throw myself away like Fanny," said she confidentially to Pesach Weingott in the course of the evening. He smiled apologetically. "Fanny always had low views," continued Becky. "But I always said I would marry a gentleman."

"And I dare say," answered Pesach, stung into the retort, "Fanny could marry a gentlemen, too, if she wanted."

Becky's idea of a gentleman was a clerk or a school-master, who had no manual labour except scribbling or flogging. In her matrimonial views Becky was typical. She despised the status of her parents and looked to marry out of it. They for their part could not understand the desire to be other than themselves.

"I don't say Fanny couldn't," she admitted. "All I say is, nobody could call this a luck-match."

"Ah, thou hast me too many flies in thy nose," reprovingly interposed Mrs. Belcovitch, who had just crawled up. "Thou art too high-class."

Becky tossed her head. "I've got a new dolman," she turning to one of her young men who was present by special grace. "You should see me in it. I look noble."

"Yes," said Mrs. Belcovitch proudly. "It shines in the sun."

"Is it like the one Bessie Sugarman's got?" inquired the young man.

"Bessie Sugarman!" echoed Becky scornfully. "She gets all her things from the tallyman. She pretends to be so grand, but all her jewellery is paid for at so much a week."

"So long as it is paid for," said Fanny, catching the words and turning a happy face on her sister.

"Not so jealous, Alte," said her mother. "When I shall win on the lottery, I will buy thee also a dolman."

Almost all the company speculated on the Hamburg lottery, which, whether they were speaking Yiddish or English, they invariably accentuated on the last syllable. When an inhabitant of the Ghetto won even his money back, the news circulated like wild-fire, and there was a rush to the agents for tickets. The chances of sudden wealth floated like dazzling Will o' the Wisps on the horizon, illumining the grey perspectives of the future. The lottery took the poor ticket-holders out of themselves, and gave them an interest in life apart from machine cotton, lasts or tobacco leaf. The English labourer, who has been forbidden State Lotteries, relieves the monotony of existence by an extremely indirect interest in the achievements of a special breed of horses.

"*Nu*, Pesack another glass of rum?" said Mr. Belcovitch genially to his future son-in-law and boarder.

"Yes, I will," said Pesach. "After all, this is the first time I've got engaged."

The rum was of Mr. Belcovitch's own manufacture; its ingredients were unknown, but the fame of it travelled on currents of air to the remotest parts of the house. Even the inhabitants of the garrets sniffed and thought of turpentine. Pesach swallowed the concoction, murmuring "To life" afresh. His throat felt like the funnel of a steamer, and there were tears in his eyes when he put down the glass.

"Ah, that was good," he murmured.

"Not like thy English drinks, eh?" said Mr. Belcovitch.

"England!" snorted Pesach in royal disdain. "What a country! Daddle-doo is a language and ginger-beer a liquor."

"Daddle-doo" was Pesach's way of saying "That'll do." It was one of the first English idioms he picked up, and its puerility made him facetious. It seemed to smack of the nursery; when a nation expressed its soul thus, the existence of a beverage like ginger-beer could occasion no further surprise.

"You shan't have anything stronger than ginger-beer when we're married," said Fanny laughingly. "I am not going to have any drinking."

"But I'll get drunk on ginger-beer," Pesach laughed back.

"You can't," Fanny said, shaking her large fond smile to and fro. "By my health, not."

"Ha! Ha! Ha! Can't even get *shikkur* on it. What a liquor!"

In the first Anglo-Jewish circles with which Pesach had scraped acquaintance, ginger-beer was the prevalent drink; and, generalizing almost as hastily as if he were going to write a book on the country, he concluded that it was the national beverage. He had long since discovered his mistake, but the drift of the discussion reminded Becky of a chance for an arrow.

"On the day when you sit for joy, Pesach," she said slyly, "I shall send you a valentine."

Pesach coloured up and those in the secret laughed; the reference was to another of Pesach's early ideas. Some mischievous gossip had heard him arguing with another Greener outside a stationer's shop blazing with comic valentines. The two foreigners were extremely puzzled to understand what these monstrosities portended; Pesach, however, laid it down that the microcephalous gentlemen with tremendous legs, and the ladies five-sixths head and one-sixth skirt, were representations of the English peasants who lived in the little villages up country.

"When I sit for joy," retorted Pesach, "it will not be the season for valentines."

"Won't it though!" cried Becky, shaking her frizzly black curls. "You'll be a pair of comic 'uns."

"All righty Becky," said Alte good-humouredly. "Your turn'll come, and then we shall have the laugh of you."

"Never," said Becky. "What do I want with a man?"

The arm of the specially invited young man was round her as she spoke.

"Don't make *schnecks*," said Fanny.

"It's not affectation. I mean it. What's the good of the men who visit father? There isn't a gentleman among them."

"Ah, wait till I win on the lottery," said the special young man.

"Then, vy not take another eighth of a ticket?" inquired Sugarman the *Shadchan*, who seemed to spring from the other end of the room. He was one of the greatest Talmudists in London – a lean, hungry-looking man, sharp of feature and acute of intellect. "Look at Mrs. Robinson – I've just won her over twenty pounds, and she only gave me two pounds for myself. I call it a *cherpah* – a shame."

"Yes, but you stole another two pounds," said Becky.

"How do you know?" said Sugarman startled.

Becky winked and shook her head sapiently. "Never you mind."

The published list of the winning numbers was so complex in construction that Sugarman had ample opportunities of bewildering his clients.

"I von't sell you no more tickets," said Sugarman with righteous indignation.

"A fat lot I care," said Becky, tossing her curls.

"Thou carest for nothing," said Mrs. Belcovitch, seizing the opportunity for maternal admonition. "Thou hast not even brought me my medicine tonight. Thou wilt find it on the chest of drawers in the bedroom."

Becky shook herself impatiently.

"I will go," said the special young man.

"No, it is not beautiful that a young man shall go into my bedroom in my absence," said Mrs. Belcovitch blushing.

Becky left the room.

"Thou knowest," said Mrs. Belcovitch, addressing herself to the special young man, "I suffer greatly from my legs. One is a thick one, and one a thin one."

The young man sighed sympathetically.

"Whence comes it?" he asked.

"Do I know? I was born so. My poor lambkin (this was the way Mrs. Belcovitch always referred to her dead mother) had well-matched legs. If I had Aristotle's head I might be able to find out why my legs are inferior. And so one goes about."

The reverence for Aristotle enshrined in Yiddish idiom is probably due to his being taken by the vulgar for a Jew. At any rate the theory that Aristotle's philosophy was Jewish was advanced by the medieval poet, Jehuda Halevi, and sustained by Maimonides. The legend runs that when Alexander went to Palestine, Aristotle was in his train. At Jerusalem the philosopher had sight of King Solomon's manuscripts, and he forthwith edited them and put his name to them. But it is noteworthy that the story was only accepted by those Jewish scholars who adopted the Aristotelian philosophy, those who rejected it declaring that Aristotle in his last testament had admitted the inferiority of his writings to the Mosaic, and had asked that his works should be destroyed.

When Becky returned with the medicine, Mrs. Belcovitch mentioned that it was extremely nasty, and offered the young man a taste, whereat he rejoiced inwardly, knowing he had found favour in the sight of the parent. Mrs. Belcovitch paid a penny a week to her doctor, in sickness or health, so that there was a loss on being well. Becky used to fill up the bottles with water to save herself the trouble of going to fetch the medicine, but as Mrs. Belcovitch did not know this it made no difference.

"Thou livest too much indoors," said Mr. Sugarman, in Yiddish.

"Shall I march about in this weather? Black and slippery, and the Angel going a-hunting?"

"Ah!" said Mr. Sugarman, relapsing proudly into the vernacular, "Ve English valk about in all vedders."

Meanwhile Moses Ansell had returned from evening service and sat down, unquestioningly, by the light of an unexpected candle to his expected supper of bread and soup, blessing God for both gifts. The rest of the family had supped. Esther had put the two youngest children to bed (Rachel had arrived at years of independent undressing), and she and Solomon were doing home-lessons in copy-books, the candle saving them from a caning on the morrow. She held her pen clumsily, for several of her fingers were swathed in bloody rags tied with cobweb. The grandmother dozed in her chair. Everything was quiet and peaceful, though the atmosphere was chilly. Moses ate his supper with a great smacking of the lips and an equivalent enjoyment. When it was over he sighed deeply, and thanked God in a prayer lasting ten minutes, and delivered in a rapid, sing-song manner. He then inquired of Solomon whether he had said his evening prayer. Solomon looked out of the comer of his eyes at his *Bube*, and, seeing she was asleep on the bed, said he had, and kicked Esther significantly but hurtfully under the table.

"Then you had better say your night-prayer."

There was no getting out of that; so Solomon finished his sum, writing the figures of the answer rather faint, in case he should discover from another boy next morning that they were wrong; then producing a Hebrew prayer-book from his inky cotton satchel, he made a mumbling sound, with occasional enthusiastic bursts of audible coherence, for a length of time proportioned to the number of pages. Then he went to bed. After that, Esther put her grandmother to bed and curled herself up at her side. She lay awake a long time, listening to the quaint sounds emitted by her father in his study, of Rashi's commentary on the Book of Job, the measured drone blending not disagreeably with the far-away sounds of Pesach Weingott's fiddle.

Pesach's fiddle played the accompaniment to many other people's thoughts. The respectable master-tailor sat behind his glazed shirt-front beating time with his foot. His little sickly-looking wife stood by his side, nodding her bewigged head joyously. To both the music brought the same recollection – a Polish market-place.

Belcovitch, or rather Kosminski, was the only surviving son of a widow. It was curious, and suggestive of some grim law of heredity, that his parents' elder children had died off as rapidly as his own, and that his life had been preserved by some such expedient as Alte's. Only, in his case, the Rabbi consulted had advised his father to go into the woods and call his new-born son by the name of the first animal that he saw. This was why the future sweater was named Bear. To the death of his brothers and sisters, Bear owed his exemption from military service. He grew up to be a stalwart, well-set-up young baker, a loss to the Russian army.

Bear went out in the market-place one fine day and saw Chayah in maiden ringlets. She was a slim, graceful little thing, with nothing obviously odd about the legs, and was buying onions. Her back was towards him, but in another moment she turned her head and Bear's. As he caught the sparkle of her eye, he felt that without her life were worse than the conscription. Without delay, he made inquiries about the fair young vision, and finding its respectability unimpeachable, he sent a *Shadchan* to propose to her, and they were affianced; Chayah's father undertaking to give a dowry of two hundred gulden. Unfortunately, he died suddenly in the attempt to amass them, and Chayah was left an orphan. The two hundred gulden were nowhere to be found. Tears rained down both Chayah's cheeks, on the one side for the loss of her father, on the other for the prospective loss of a husband. The Rabbi was full of tender sympathy. He bade Bear come to the dead man's chamber. The venerable white-bearded corpse lay on the bed, swathed in shroud, and *Talith* or praying-shawl.

"Bear," he said, "thou knowest that I saved thy life."

"Nay," said Bear, "indeed, I know not that."

"Yea, of a surety," said the Rabbi. "Thy mother hath not told thee, but all thy brothers and sisters perished and, lo! thou alone art preserved! It was I that called thee a beast."

Bear bowed his head in grateful silence.

"Bear," said the Rabbi, "thou didst contract to wed this dead man's daughter, and he did contract to pay over to thee two hundred gulden."

"Truth," replied Bear.

"Bear," said the Rabbi, "there are no two hundred gulden."

A shadow flitted across Bear's face, but he said nothing.

"Bear," said the Rabbi again, "there are not two gulden."

Bear did not move.

"Bear," said the Rabbi, "leave thou my side, and go over to the other side of the bed, facing me."

So Bear left his side and went over to the other side of the bed facing him.

"Bear," said the Rabbi, "give me thy right hand."

The Rabbi stretched his own right hand across the bed, but Bear kept his obstinately behind his back.

"Bear," repeated the Rabbi, in tones of more penetrating solemnity, "give me thy right hand."

"Nay," replied Bear, sullenly. "Wherefore should I give thee my right hand?"

"Because," said the Rabbi, and his tones trembled, and it seemed to him that the dead man's face grew sterner. "Because I wish thee to swear across the body of Chayah's father that thou wilt marry her."

"Nay, that I will not," said Bear.

"Will not?" repeated the Rabbi, his lips growing white with pity.

"Nay, I will not take any oaths," said Bear, hotly. "I love the maiden, and I will keep what I have promised. But, by my father's soul, I will take no oaths!"

"Bear," said the Rabbi in a choking voice, "give me thy hand. Nay, not to swear by, but to grip. Long shalt thou live, and the Most High shall prepare thy seat in Gan Iden."

So the old man and the young clasped hands across the corpse, and the simple old Rabbi perceived a smile flickering over the face of Chayah's father. Perhaps it was only a sudden glint of sunshine.

The wedding-day drew nigh, but lo! Chayah was again dissolved in tears.

"What ails thee?" said her brother Naphtali.

"I cannot follow the custom of the maidens," wept Chayah. "Thou knowest we are blood-poor, and I have not the wherewithal to buy my Bear a *Talith* for his wedding-day; nay, not even to make him a *Talith*-bag. And when our father (the memory of the righteous for a blessing) was alive, I had dreamed of making my chosen a beautiful velvet satchel lined with silk, and I would have embroidered his initials thereon in gold, and sewn him beautiful white corpse-clothes. Perchance he will rely upon me for his wedding *Talith*, and we shall be shamed in the sight of the congregation."

"Nay, dry thine eyes, my sister," said Naphtali. "Thou knowest that my Leah presented me with a costly *Talith* when I led her under the canopy. Wherefore, do thou take my praying-shawl and lend it to Bear for the wedding-day, so that decency may be preserved in the sight of the congregation. The young man has a great heart, and he will understand."

So Chayah, blushing prettily, lent Bear Naphtali's delicate *Talith*, and Beauty and the Beast made a rare couple under the wedding canopy. Chayah wore the gold medallion and the three rows of pearls which her lover had sent her the day before. And when the Rabbi had finished blessing husband and wife, Naphtali spake the bridegroom privily, and said:

"Pass me my *Talith* back."

But Bear answered: "Nay, nay; the *Talith* is in my keeping, and there it shall remain."

"But it is my *Talith*," protested Naphtali in an angry whisper. "I only lent it to Chayah to lend it thee."

"It concerns me not," Bear returned in a decisive whisper.

"The *Talith* is my due and I shall keep it. What! Have I not lost enough by marrying thy sister? Did not thy father, peace be upon him, promise me two hundred gulden with her?"

Naphtali retired discomfited. But he made up his mind not to go without some compensation. He resolved that during the progress of the wedding procession conducting the bridegroom to the chamber of the bride, he would be the man to snatch off Bear's new hat. Let the rest of the riotous escort essay to snatch whatever other article of the bridegroom's attire they would, the hat was the easiest to dislodge, and he, Naphtali, would straightway reimburse himself partially with that. But the instant the procession formed itself, behold the shifty bridegroom forthwith removed his hat and held it tightly under his arm.

A storm of protestations burst forth at his daring departure from hymeneal tradition.

"Nay, nay, put it on," arose from every mouth.

But Bear closed his and marched mutely on.

"Heathen," cried the Rabbi. "Put on your hat."

The attempt to enforce the religious sanction failed too. Bear had spent several gulden upon his head-gear, and could not see the joke. He plodded towards his blushing Chayah through a tempest of disapprobation.

Throughout life Bear Belcovitch retained the contrariety of character that marked his matrimonial beginnings. He hated to part with money; he put off paying bills to the last moment, and he would even beseech his "hands" to wait a day or two longer for their wages. He liked to feel that he had all that money in his possession. Yet "at home," in Poland, he had always lent money to the officers and gentry, when they ran temporarily short at cards. They would knock him up in the middle of the night to obtain the means of going on with the game. And in England he never refused to become surety for a loan when any of his poor friends begged the favour of him. These loans ran from three to five pounds, but whatever the amount, they were very rarely paid. The loan offices came down upon him for the money. He paid it without a murmur, shaking his head compassionately over the poor ne'er do wells, and perhaps not without a compensating consciousness of superior practicality.

Only, if the borrower had neglected to treat him to a glass of rum to clench his signing as surety, the shake of Bear's head would become more reproachful than sympathetic, and he would mutter bitterly: "Five pounds and not even a drink for the money." The jewellery he generously lavished on his woman-kind was in essence a mere channel of investment for his savings, avoiding the risks of a banking account and aggregating his wealth in a portable shape, in obedience to an instinct generated by centuries of insecurity. The interest on the sums thus invested was the gratification of the other oriental instinct for gaudiness.

CHAPTER III

Malka

The Sunday Fair, so long associated with Petticoat Lane, is dying hard, and is still vigorous; its glories were in full swing on the dull, grey morning when Moses Ansell took his way through the Ghetto. It was near eleven o'clock, and the throng was thickening momently. The vendors cried their wares in stentorian tones and the babble of the buyers was like the confused roar of a stormy sea. The dead walls and hoardings were placarded with bills from which the life of the inhabitants could be constructed. Many were in Yiddish, the most hopelessly corrupt and hybrid jargon ever evolved. Even when the language was English the letters were Hebrew. Whitechapel Public Meeting, Board School, Sermon, Police, and other modern banalities, glared at the passer-by in the sacred guise of the Tongue associated with miracles and prophecies, palm-trees and cedars and seraphs, lions and shepherds and harpists.

Moses stopped to read these hybrid posters – he had nothing better to do – as he slouched along. He did not care to remember that dinner was due in two hours. He turned aimlessly into Wentworth Street, and studied a placard that hung in a bootmaker's window. This was the announcement it made in jargon:

Riveters, Clickers, Lasters, Finishers,
Wanted.
BARUCH EMANUEL,
Cobbler.

MALKA

Makes and Repairs Boots.
Every Bit as Cheaply
as
MORDECAI SCHWARTZ,
of 12 Goulston Street.

Mordecai Schwartz was written in the biggest and blackest of Hebrew letters, and quite dominated the little shop-window. Baruch Emanuel was visibly conscious of his inferiority to his powerful rival, though Moses had never heard of Mordecai Schwartz before. He entered the shop and said in Hebrew "Peace be to you." Baruch Emanuel, hammering a sole, answered in Hebrew:

"Peace be to you."

Moses dropped into Yiddish.

"I am looking for work. Peradventure have you something for me?"

"What can you do?"

"I have been a riveter."

"I cannot engage any more riveters."

Moses looked disappointed.

"I have also been a clicker," he said.

"I have all the clickers I can afford," Baruch answered.

Moses's gloom deepened. "Two years ago I worked as a finisher."

Baruch shook his head silently. He was annoyed at the man's persistence. There was only the laster resource left.

"And before that I was a laster for a week," Moses answered.

"I don't want any!" cried Baruch, losing his temper.

"But in your window it stands that you do," protested Moses feebly.

"I don't care what stands in my window," said Baruch hotly. "Have you not head enough to see that that is all bunkum? Unfortunately I work single-handed, but it looks good and it isn't lies. Naturally I want Riveters and Clickers and Lasters and Finishers. Then I could set up a big establishment and gouge out Mordecai Schwartz's eyes. But the Most High denies me assistants, and I am content to want."

Moses understood that attitude towards the nature of things. He went out and wandered down another narrow dirty street in search of Mordecai Schwartz, whose address Baruch Emanuel had so obligingly given him. He thought of the *Maggid's* sermon on the day before. The *Maggid* had explained a verse of Habakkuk in quite an original way which gave an entirely new colour to a passage in Deuteronomy. Moses experienced acute pleasure in musing upon it, and went past Mordecai's shop without going in, and was only awakened from his day-dream by the brazen clanging of a bell. It was the bell of the great Ghetto school, summoning its pupils from the reeking courts and alleys, from the garrets and the cellars, calling them to come and be Anglicised. And they came in a great straggling procession recruited from every lane and by-way, big children and little children, boys in blackening corduroy, and girls in washed-out cotton; tidy children and ragged children; children in great shapeless boots gaping at the toes; sickly children, and sturdy children, and diseased children; bright-eyed children and hollow-eyed children; quaint sallow foreign-looking children, and fresh-coloured English-looking children; with great pumpkin heads, with oval heads, with pear-shaped heads; with old men's faces, with cherubs' faces, with monkeys' faces; cold and famished children, and warm and well-fed children; children conning their lessons and children romping carelessly; the demure and the anæmic; the boisterous and the black-guardly, the insolent, the idiotic, the vicious, the intelligent, the exemplary, the dull – spawn of all countries – all hastening at the inexorable clang of the big school-bell to be ground in the same great, blind, inexorable Governmental machine. Here, too, was a miniature fair, the path being lined by itinerant temptations. There was brisk traffic in toffee, and grey peas and monkey-nuts, and the crowd was swollen by anxious parents seeing tiny or truant offspring safe within the school-gates. The women were bare-headed or be-shawled, with infants at their breasts and little ones toddling at their sides, the men were greasy, and musty, and squalid. Here a bright earnest little girl held her vagrant big brother by the hand, not to let go till she had seen him in the bosom of his class-mates. There a sullen wild-eyed mite in petticoats was being dragged along, screaming, towards distasteful durance. It was a drab picture – the bleak, leaden sky above, the sloppy, miry stones below, the frowsy mothers and fathers, the motley children. "Monkey-nuts! Monkey-nuts!" croaked a wizened old woman.

"Oppea! Oppea!" droned a doddering old Dutchman. He bore a great can of hot peas in one hand and a lighthouse-looking pepper-pot in the other. Some of the children swallowed the dainties hastily out of miniature basins, others carried them within in paper packets for surreptitious munching.

"Call that a ay-puth?" a small boy would say.

"Not enough!" the old man would exclaim in surprise. "Here you are, then!" And he would give the peas another sprinkling from the pepper-pot.

Moses Ansell's progeny were not in the picture. The younger children were at home, the elder had gone to school an hour before to run about and get warm in the spacious playgrounds. A slice of bread each and the wish-wash of a thrice-brewed pennyworth of tea had been their morning meal, and there was no prospect of dinner. The thought of them made Moses's heart heavy again; he forgot the *Maggid's* explanation of the verse in Habakkuk, and he retraced his steps towards Mordecai Schwartz's shop. But like his humbler rival, Mordecai had no use for the many-sided Moses; he was "full up" with swarthy "hands," though, as there were rumours of strikes in the air, he prudently took note of Moses's address. After this rebuff, Moses shuffled hopelessly about for more than an hour; the dinner-hour was getting desperately near; already children passed him, carrying the Sunday dinners from the bakeries, and there were wafts of vague poetry in the atmosphere. Moses felt he could not face his own children.

At last he nerved himself to an audacious resolution, and elbowed his way blusterously towards the Ruins, lest he might break down if his courage had time to cool.

"The Ruins" was a great stony square, partly bordered by houses, and only picturesque on Sundays when it became a branch of the all-ramifying Fair. Moses could have bought anything there from elastic braces to green parrots in gilt cages. That is to say if he had had money. At present he had nothing in his pocket except holes.

What he might be able to do on his way back was another matter; for it was Malka that Moses Ansell was going to see. She was the cousin of his deceased wife, and lived in Zachariah Square. Moses had not been there for a month, for Malka was a wealthy twig of the family tree, to be approached with awe and trembling. She kept a second-hand clothes store in Houndsditch, a supplementary stall in the Halfpenny Exchange, and a barrow on the "Ruins" of a Sunday; and she had set up Ephraim, her newly-acquired son-in-law, in the same line of business in the same district. Like most things she dealt in, her son-in-law was second-hand, having lost his first wife four years ago in Poland. But he was only twenty-two, and a second-hand son-in-law of twenty-two is superior to many brand new ones. The two domestic establishments were a few minutes away from the shops, facing each other diagonally across the square. They were small, three-roomed houses, without basements, the ground floor window in each being filled up with a black gauze blind (an invariable index of gentility) which allowed the occupants to see all that was passing outside, but confronted gazers with their own reflections. Passers-by postured at these mirrors, twisting moustaches perkily, or giving coquettish pats to bonnets, unwitting of the grinning inhabitants. Most of the doors were ajar, wintry as the air was; for the Zachariah Squareites lived a good deal on the door-step. In the summer, the housewives sat outside on chairs and gossiped and knitted, as if the sea foamed at their feet, and wrinkled good-humoured old men played nap on teatrays. Some of the doors were blocked below with sliding barriers of wood, a sure token of infants inside given to straying. More obvious tokens of child-life were the swings nailed to the lintels of a few doors, in which, despite the cold, toothless babes swayed like monkeys on a branch. But the Square, with its broad area of quadrangular pavement, was an ideal playing ground for children, since other animals came not within its precincts, except an inquisitive dog or a local cat. Solomon

MALKA

Ansell knew no greater privilege than to accompany his father to these fashionable quarters and whip his humming-top across the ample spaces, the while Moses transacted his business with Malka. Last time the business was psalm-saying. Milly had been brought to bed of a son, but it was doubtful if she would survive, despite the charms hung upon the bedpost to counteract the nefarious designs of Lilith, the wicked first wife of Adam, and of the Not-Good Ones who hover about women in childbirth. So Moses was sent for, post-haste, to intercede with the Almighty. His piety, it was felt, would command attention. For an average of three hundred and sixty-two days a year Moses was a miserable worm, a nonentity, but on the other three, when death threatened to visit Malka or her little clan, Moses became a personage of prime importance, and was summoned at all hours of the day and night to wrestle with the angel Azrael. When the angel had retired, worsted, after a match sometimes protracted into days, Moses relapsed into his primitive insignificance, and was dismissed with a mouthful of rum and a shilling. It never seemed to him an unfair equivalent, for nobody could make less demand on the universe than Moses. Give him two solid meals and three solid services a day, and he was satisfied, and he craved more for spiritual snacks between meals than for physical.

The last crisis had been brief, and there was so little danger that, when Milly's child was circumcised, Moses had not even been bidden to the feast, though his piety would have made him the ideal *sandek* or Godfather. He did not resent this, knowing himself dust – and that anything but gold-dust.

Moses had hardly emerged from the little arched passage which led to the Square, when sounds of strife fell upon his ears. Two stout women chatting amicably at their doors, had suddenly developed a dispute. In Zachariah Square, when you wanted to get to the bottom of a quarrel, the cue was not "find the woman," but find the child. The high-spirited bantlings had a way of pummelling one another in fistic duels, and of calling in their respective mothers when they got the worse of it – which is cowardly, but human. The mother of the beaten belligerent would then threaten to wring the "year," or to twist the nose of the victorious party – sometimes she did it. In either case, the other mother would intervene, and then the two bantlings would retire into the background and leave their mothers to take up the duel while they resumed their interrupted game.

Of such sort was the squabble betwixt Mrs. Isaacs and Mrs. Jacobs. Mrs. Isaacs pointed out with superfluous vehemence that her poor lamb had been mangled beyond recognition. Mrs. Jacobs, *per contra*, asseverated with superfluous gesture that it was her poor lamb who had received irreparable injury. These statements were not in mutual contradiction, but Mrs. Isaacs and Mrs. Jacobs were, and so the point at issue was gradually absorbed in more personal recriminations.

"By my life and by my Fanny's life, I'll leave my seal on the first child of yours that comes across my way! There!" Thus Mrs. Issacs.

"Lay a finger on a hair of a child of mine, and, by my husband's life I'll summons you; I'll have the law on you." Thus Mrs. Jacobs; to the gratification of the resident populace.

Mrs. Isaacs and Mrs. Jacobs rarely quarrelled with each other, uniting rather in opposition to the rest of the Square. They were English, quite English, their grandfather having been born in Dresden; and they gave themselves airs in consequence, and called their *kinder* "children," which annoyed those neighbours who found a larger admixture of Yiddish necessary for conversation. These very *kinder*, again, attained considerable importance among their school-fellows by refusing to pronounce the guttural "ch" of the Hebrew otherwise than as an English "k."

"Summons me, indeed," laughed back Mrs. Isaacs. "A fat lot I'd care for that. You'd jolly soon expose your character to the magistrate. Everybody knows what *you* are."

"Your mother!" retorted Mrs. Jacobs mechanically; the elliptical method of expression being greatly in vogue for conversation of a loud character. Quick as lightning came the parrying stroke.

"Yah! And what was your father, I should like to know?"

Mrs. Isaacs had no sooner made this inquiry than she became

conscious of an environment of suppressed laughter; Mrs. Jacobs awoke to the situation a second later, and the two women stood suddenly dumbfounded, petrified, with arms akimbo, staring at each other.

The wise, if apocryphal, Ecclesiasticus, sagely and pithily remarked, many centuries before modern civilization was invented: jest not with a rude man lest thy ancestors be disgraced. To this day the oriental methods of insult have survived in the Ghetto. The dead past is never allowed to bury its dead; the genealogical dust-heap is always liable to be raked up, and even innocuous ancestors may be traduced to the third and fourth generation.

Now it so happened that Mrs. Isaacs and Mrs. Jacobs were sisters. And when it dawned upon them into what dilemma their automatic methods of carte and tierce had inveigled them, they were frozen with confusion. They retired crestfallen to their respective parlours, and sported their oaks. The resources of repartee were dried up for the moment. Relatives are unduly handicapped in these verbal duels; especially relative same mother and father.

Presently Mrs. Isaacs reappeared. She had thought of something she ought to have said. She went up to her sister's closed door, and shouted into the key-hole: "None of my children ever had bandy-legs!"

Almost immediately the window of the front bedroom was flung up, and Mrs. Jacobs leant out of it waving what looked like an immense streamer.

"Aha," she observed, dangling it tantalizingly up and down. "Morry antique!"

The dress fluttered in the breeze. Mrs. Jacobs caressed the stuff between her thumb and forefinger.

"Aw-aw-aw-aw-aw-awl silk," she announced with a long ecstatic quaver.

Mrs. Isaacs stood paralyzed by the brilliancy of the repartee.

Mrs. Jacobs withdrew the moiré antique and exhibited a mauve gown. "Aw-aw-aw-aw-aw-awl silk."

The mauve fluttered for a triumphant instant, the next a puce and amber dress floated on the breeze.

"Aw-aw-aw-aw-aw-awl silk." Mrs. Jacobs's fingers smoothed it lovingly, then it was drawn within to be instantly replaced by a green dress. Mrs. Jacobs passed the skirt slowly through her fingers. "Aw-aw-aw-aw-aw-awl silk!" she quavered mockingly.

By this time Mrs. Isaacs's face was the colour of the latest flag of victory.

"The tallyman!" she tried to retort, but the words stuck in her throat. Fortunately just then she caught sight of her poor lamb playing with the other poor lamb. She dashed at her offspring, boxed its ears and crying, "You little blackguard, if I ever catch you playing with blackguards again, I'll wring your neck for you." She hustled the infant into the house and slammed the door viciously behind her.

Moses had welcomed this everyday scene, for it put off a few moments his encounter with the formidable Malka. As she had not appeared at door or window, he concluded she was in a bad temper or out of London; neither alternative was pleasant.

He knocked at the door of Milly's house where her mother was generally to be found, and an elderly char-woman opened it. There were some bottles of spirit, standing on a wooden side-table covered with a coloured cloth, and some unopened biscuit bags. At these familiar premonitory signs of a festival, Moses felt tempted to beat a retreat. He could not think for the moment what was up, but whatever it was he had no doubt the well-to-do persons would supply him with ice. The char-woman, with brow darkened by soot and gloom, told him that Milly was upstairs, but that her mother had gone across to her own house with the clothes-brush.

Moses's face fell. When his wife was alive; she had been a link of connection between 'The Family' and himself, her cousin having generously employed her as a char-woman. So Moses knew the import of the clothes-brush. Malka was very particular about her appearance and loved to be externally speckless, but somehow or other she had no clothes-brush at home. This deficiency did not matter ordinarily, for she practically lived at Milly's. But when she had words with Milly or her husband, she retired to her own house to sulk or *schmull,* as they called it. The carrying away of the clothes-brush was, thus, a sign that she considered the breach serious and hostilities likely to be protracted. Sometimes a whole week would go by without the two houses ceasing to stare sullenly across at each other, the situation in Milly's camp being aggravated by the lack of a clothes-brush. In such moments of irritation, Milly's husband was apt to declare that his mother-in-law had an abundance of clothes-brushes, for, he pertinently asked, how did she manage during her frequent business tours in the country? He gave it as his conviction that Malka merely took the clothes-brush away to afford herself a handle for returning. But then Ephraim Phillips was a graceless young fellow, the death of whose first wife was probably a judgment on his levity, and everybody except his second mother-in-law knew that he had a book of tickets for the Oxbridge Music Hall, and went there on Friday nights. Still, in spite of these facts, experience did show that whenever Milly's camp had outsulked Malka's, the old woman's surrender was always veiled under the formula of: "Oh Milly, I've brought you over your clothes-brush. I just noticed it, and thought you might be wanting it." After this, conversation was comparatively easy.

Moses hardly cared to face Malka in such a crisis of the clothes-brush. He turned away despairingly, and was going back through the small archway which led to the Ruins and the outside world, when a grating voice startled his ear.

"Well, Méshe, whither fliest thou? Has my Milly forbidden thee to see me?"

He looked back. Malka was standing at her house-door. He retraced his steps.

"N-n-o," he murmured. "I thought you still out with your stall."

That was where she should have been, at any rate, till half an hour ago. She did not care to tell herself, much less Moses, that she had been waiting at home for the envoy of peace from the filial camp summoning her to the ceremony of the Redemption of her grandson.

"Well, now thou seest me," she said, speaking Yiddish for his behoof, "thou lookest not outwardly anxious to know how it goes with me."

"How goes it with you?"

"As well as an old woman has the right to expect. The most High is good!" Malka was in her most amiable mood, to emphasize to outsiders the injustice of her kin in quarrelling with her. She was a tall woman of fifty, with a tanned equine gypsy face surmounted by a black wig, and decorated laterally by great gold earrings. Great black eyes blazed beneath great black eyebrows, and the skin between them was capable of wrinkling itself black with wrath. A gold chain was wound thrice round her neck, and looped up within her black silk bodice. There were numerous rings on her fingers, and she perpetually smelt of peppermint.

"*Nu*, stand not chattering there," she went on. "Come in. Dost thou wish me to catch my death of cold?"

Moses slouched timidly within, his head bowed as if in dread of knocking against the top of the door. The room was a perfect facsimile of Milly's parlour at the other end of the diagonal, save that instead of the festive bottles and paper bags on the small side table, there was a cheerless clothes-brush. Like Milly's, the room contained a round table, a chest of drawers with decanters on the top, and a high mantelpiece decorated with pendant green fringes, fastened by big-headed brass nails. Here cheap china dogs, that had had more than their day squatted amid lustres with crystal drops. Before the fire was a lofty steel guard, which, useful enough in Milly's household, had survived its function in Malka's, where no one was ever likely to tumble into the grate. In a corner of the room a little staircase began to go upstairs. There was oilcloth on the floor. In Zachariah Square anybody could go into anybody else's house and feel at home. There was no visible difference between one and another. Moses sat down awkwardly on a chair and refused a peppermint. In the end he accepted an apple, blessed God for creating the fruit of the tree, and made a ravenous bite at it.

"I must take peppermints," Malka explained. "It's for the spasms."

"But you said you were well," murmured Moses.

"And suppose? If I did not take peppermint I should have the spasms. My poor sister Rosina, peace be upon her, who died of typhoid, suffered greatly from spasms. It's in the family. She would have died of asthma if she had lived long enough. *Nu*, how goes it with thee?" she went on, suddenly remembering that Moses, too, had a right to be ill. At bottom, Malke felt a real respect for Moses, though he did not know it. It dated from the day he cut a chip of mahogany out of her best round table. He had finished cutting his nails, and wanted a morsel of wood to burn them in witness of his fulfilment of the pious custom. Malka raged, but in her inmost heart there was admiration for such unscrupulous sanctity.

"I have been out of work for three weeks," Moses answered, omitting to expound the state of his health in view of more urgent matters.

"Unlucky fool! What my silly cousin Gittel, peace be upon her, could see to marry in thee, I know not."

Moses could not enlighten her. He might have informed her that *olov hasholom*, "peace be upon him," was an absurdity when applied to a woman, but then he used the pious phrase himself, although aware of its grammatical shortcomings.

"I told her thou wouldst never be able to keep her, poor lamb," Malka went on. "But she was always an obstinate pig. And she kept her head high up, too, as if she had five pounds a week! Never would let her children earn money like other people's children. But thou oughtest not to be so obstinate. Thou shouldst have more sense, Méshe; thou belongest not to my family. Why can't Solomon go out with matches?"

"Gittel's soul would not like it."

"But the living have bodies! Thou rather seest thy children starve than work. There's Esther, an idle, lazy brat, always reading story-books; why doesn't she sell flowers or pull out bastings in the evening?"

"Esther and Solomon have their lessons to do."

"Lessons!" snorted Malka. "What's the good of lessons? It's English, not Judaism, they teach them in that Godless school. I could never read or write anything but Hebrew in all my life; but God be thanked, I have thriven without it. All they teach them in the school is English nonsense.

The teachers are a pack of heathens who eat forbidden things, but the good Yiddishkeit goes to the wall. I'm ashamed of thee, Méshe; thou dost not even send thy boys to a Hebrew class in the evening."

"I have no money, and they must do their English lesson, else, perhaps, their clothes will be stopped. Besides, I teach them myself every *Shabbos* afternoon and Sunday. Solomon translates into Yiddish the whole Pentateuch with Rashi."

"Yes, he may know *Térah*," said Malka not to be baffled. "But he'll never know *Gemorah* or *Mishnayis*." Malka herself knew very little of these abstruse subjects beyond their names, and the fact that they were studied out of minutely-printed folios by men of extreme sanctity.

"He knows a little *Gemorah*, too," said Moses. "I can't teach him at home because I haven't got a *Gemorah*, – it's so expensive, as you know. But he went with me to the *Beth-Medrash*, when the *Maggid* was studying it with a class free of charge, and we learnt the whole of the *Tractate Niddah*. Solomon understands very well all about the Divorce Laws, and he could adjudicate on the duties of women to their husbands."

"Ah, but he'll never know *Cabbulah*," said Malka, driven to her last citadel. "But then no one in England can study *Cabbulah* since the days of Rabbi Falk (the memory of the righteous for a blessing) any more than a born Englishman can learn Talmud. There's something in the air that prevents it. In my town there was a Rabbi who could do *Cabbulah*; he could call Abraham our father from the grave. But in this pig-eating country no one can be holy enough for the Name, blessed be It, to grant him the privilege. I don't believe the *Shochetim* kill the animals properly; the statutes are violated; even pious people eat *tripha* cheese and butter. I don't say thou dost, Méshe, but thou lettest thy children."

"Well, your own butter is not *kosher*," said Moses, nettled.

"My butter? What does it matter about my butter? I never set up for a purist. I don't come of a family of Rabbonim. I'm only a business woman. It's the *froom* people that I complain of; the people who ought to set an example, and are lowering the standard of *Froomkeit*. I caught a beadle's wife the other day washing her meat and butter plates in the same bowl of water. In time they will be frying steaks in butter, and they will end by eating *tripha* meat out of butter plates, and the judgment of God will come. But what is become of thine apple? Thou hast not gorged it already?" Moses nervously pointed to his trousers pocket, bulged out by the mutilated globe. After his first ravenous bite Moses had bethought himself of his responsibilities.

"It's for the *kinder*," he explained.

"*Nu*, the *kinder!*" snorted Malka disdainfully. "And what will they give thee for it? Verily, not a thank you. In my young days we trembled before the father and the mother, and my mother, peace be upon him, potched my face after I was a married woman. I shall never forget that slap – it nearly made me adhere to the wall. But now-a-days our children sit on our heads. I gave my Milly all she has in the world – a house, a shop, a husband, and my best bed-linen. And now when I want her to call the child Yosef, after my first husband, peace be on him, her own father, she would out of sheer vexatiousness, call it Yechezkel." Malka's voice became more strident than ever. She had been anxious to make a species of vicarious reparation to her first husband, and the failure of Milly to acquiesce in the arrangement was a source of real vexation.

Moses could think of nothing better to say than to inquire how her present husband was.

"He overworks himself," Malka replied, shaking her head. "The misfortune is that he thinks himself a good man of business, and he is always starting new enterprises without consulting me. If he would only take my advice more!"

Moses shook his head in sympathetic deprecation of Michael Birnbaum's wilfulness.

"Is he at home?" he asked.

"No, but I expect him back from the country every minute. I believe they have invited him for the *Pidyun Haben* today."

"Oh, is that today?"

"Of course. Didst thou not know?"

"No, no one told me."

"Thine own sense should have told thee. Is it not the thirty-first day since the birth? But of course he won't accept when he knows that my own daughter has driven me out of her house."

"You say not!" exclaimed Moses in horror.

"I do say," said Malka, unconsciously taking up the clothes-brush and thumping with it on the table to emphasize the outrage. "I told her that when Yeehezkel cried so much, it would be better to look for the pin than to dose the child for gripes. 'I dressed it myself, Mother,' says she. 'Thou art an obstinate cat's head, Milly,' says I. 'I say there is a pin.' 'And I know better,' says she. 'How canst thou know better than I' says I. 'Why, I was a mother before thou wast born.' So I unrolled the child's flannel, and sure enough underneath it just over the stomach I found –"

"The pin," concluded Moses, shaking his head gravely.

"No, not exactly. But a red mark where the pin had been pricking the poor little thing."

"And what did Milly say then?" said Moses in sympathetic triumph.

"Milly said it was a flea-bite! and I said, 'Gott in Himmel, Milly, dost thou want to swear my eyes away? My enemies shall have such a flea-bite.' And because Red Rivkah was in the room, Milly said I was shedding her blood in public, and she began to cry as if I had committed a crime against her in looking after her child. And I rushed out, leaving the two babies howling together. That was a week ago."

"And how is the child?"

"How should I know? I am only the grandmother. I only supplied the bed-linen it was born on."

"But is it recovered from the circumcision?"

"Oh, yes, all our family have good healing flesh. It's a fine child, *imbeshreer*. It's got my eyes and nose. It's a rare handsome baby, *imbeshreer*. Only it won't be its mother's fault if the Almighty takes it not back again. Milly has picked up so many ignorant Lane women who come in and blight the child, by admiring it aloud, not even saying *imbeshreer*. And then there's an old witch, a beggar-woman that Ephraim, my son-in-law, used to give a shilling a week to. Now he only gives her nine pence. She asked him 'why?' and he said, 'I'm married now. I can't afford more.' 'What!' she shrieked, 'you got married on my money!' And one Friday when the nurse had baby downstairs, the old beggar-woman knocked for her weekly allowance, and she opened the door, and she saw the child; and she looked at it with her Evil Eye! I hope to Heaven nothing will come of it."

"I will pray for Yechezkel," said Moses.

"Pray for Milly also, while thou art about it, that she may remember what is owing to a mother before the earth covers me. I don't know what's coming over children. Look at my Leah. She will marry that Sam Levine, though he belongs to a lax English family, and I suspect his mother was a proselyte. She can't fry fish anyway. I don't say anything against Sam, but still I do think my Leah might have told me before falling in love with him. And yet see how I treat them! My Michael made a *Missheberach* for them in synagogue the Sabbath after the engagement; not a common eighteen-penny benediction, but a guinea one, with half-crown blessings thrown in for his parents and the congregation, and a gift of five shillings to the ministry. That was of course in our own *Chevrah*, not reckoning the guinea my Michael *shnodared* at Duke's Plaizer Shool. You know we always keep two seats at Duke's Plaizer as well." Duke's Plaizer was the current distortion of Duke's Place.

"What magnanimity," said Moses overawed.

"I like to do everything with decorum," said Malka. "No one can say I have ever acted otherwise than as a fine person. I dare say thou couldst do with a few shillings thyself now."

Moses hung his head still lower. "You see my mother is so poorly," he stammered. "She is a very old woman, and without anything to eat she may not live long."

"They ought to take her into the Aged Widows' Home. I'm sure I gave her *my* votes."

"God shall bless you for it. But people say I was lucky enough to get my Benjamin into the Orphan Asylum, and that I ought not to have brought her from Poland. They say we grow enough poor old widows here."

"People say quite right – at least she would have starved in a Yiddishë country, not in a land of heathens."

"But she was lonely and miserable out there, exposed to all the malice of the Christians. And I was earning a pound a week. Tailoring was a good trade then. The few roubles I used to send her did not always reach her."

"Thou hadst no right to send her anything, nor to send for her. Mothers are not everything. Thou didst marry my cousin Gittel, peace be upon her, and it was thy duty to support her and her children. Thy mother took the bread out of the mouth of Gittel, and but for her my poor cousin might have been alive to-day. Believe me it was no *Mitzvah*."

Mitzvah is a "portmanteau-word." It means a commandment and a good deed, the two conceptions being regarded as interchangeable.

"Nay, thou errest there," answered Moses. "Gittel was not a phoenix which alone ate not of the Tree of Knowledge and lives for ever. Women have no need to live as long as men, for they have not so many *Mitzvahs* to perform as men; and inasmuch as" – here his tones involuntarily assumed the argumentative sing-song – "their souls profit by all the *Mitzvahs* performed by their husbands and children, Gittel will profit by the *Mitzvah* I did in bringing over my mother, so that even if she did die through it, she will not be the loser thereby. It stands in the Verse that man shall do the *Mitzvahs* and live by them. To live is a *Mitzvah*, but it is plainly one of those *Mitzvahs* that has to be done at a definite time, from which species women, by reason of their household duties, are exempt; wherefore I would deduce by another circuit that it is not so incumbent upon women to live as upon men. Nevertheless, if God had willed it, she would have been still alive. The Holy One, blessed be He, will provide for the little ones He has sent into the world. He fed Elijah the prophet by ravens, and he will never send me a black Sabbath."

"Oh, you are a saint, Méshe," said Malka, so impressed that she admitted him to the equality of the second person plural. "If everybody knew as much *Térah* as you, the Messiah would soon be here. Here are five shillings. For five shillings you can get a basket of lemons in the

Orange Market in Duke's Place, and if you sell them in the Lane at a halfpenny each, you will make a good profit. Put aside five shillings of your takings and get another basket and so you will, be able to live till the tailoring takes up a bit." Moses listened as if he had never heard of the elementary principles of barter.

"May the Name, blessed be It, bless you, and may you see rejoicings on your children's children."

So Moses went away and bought dinner, treating his family to some *beuglich,* or circular twist roles, in his joy. But on the morrow he repaired to the Market, thinking on the way of the ethical distinction between "duties of the heart" and "duties of the limbs," as expounded in choice Hebrew by Rabbenu Bachja, and he laid out the remnant in lemons. Then he stationed himself in Petticoat Lane, crying, in his imperfect English, "Lemans, verra good lemans, two a penny each, two a penny each!"

CHAPTER IV

The Redemption of the Son and the Daughter

Malka did not have long to wait for her liege lord. He was a fresh-coloured young man of thirty, rather good-looking, with side whiskers, keen, eager glance, and an air of perpetually doing business. Though a native of Germany, he spoke English as well as many Lane Jews, whose comparative impiety was a certificate of British birth. Michael Birnbaum was a great man in the local little synagogue if only one of the crowd at "Duke's Plaizer." He had been successively *Gabbai* and *Parnass*, or treasurer and president, and had presented the plush curtain, with its mystical decoration of intersecting triangles, woven in silk, that hung before the Ark in which the scrolls of the Law were kept. He was the very antithesis of Moses Ansell. His energy was restless. From hawking he had risen to a profitable traffic in gold lace and Brummagem jewellery, with a large clientèle all over the country, before he was twenty. He touched nothing which he did not profit by; and when he married, at twenty-three, a woman nearly twice his age, the transaction was not without the usual percentage. Very soon his line was diamonds – real diamonds. He carried a pocket-knife which was a combination of a corkscrew, a pair of scissors, a file, a pair of tweezers, a toothpick, and half a dozen other things, and which seemed an epitome of his character. His temperament was lively and, like Ephraim Phillips, he liked music-halls. Fortunately, Malka was too conscious of her charms to dream of jealousy.

Michael smacked her soundly on the mouth with his lips and said: "Well, mother!"

He called her mother, not because he had any children, but because she had, and it seemed a pity to multiply domestic nomenclature.

"Well, my little one," said Malka, hugging him fondly. "Have you made a good journey this time?"

"No, trade is so dull. People won't put their hands in their pockets. And here?"

"People won't take their hands out of their pockets, lazy dogs! Everybody is striking – Jews with them. Unheard-of things! The bootmakers, the capmakers, the furriers! And now they say the tailors are going to strike; more fools, too, when the trade is so slack. What with one thing and another (let me put your cravat straight, my little love), it's just the people who can't afford to buy new clothes that are hard up, so that they can't afford to buy second-hand clothes either. If the Almighty is not good to us, we shall come to the Board of Guardians ourselves."

"Not quite so bad as that, mother," laughed Michael, twirling the massive diamond ring on his finger. "How's baby? Is it ready to be redeemed?"

"Which baby?" said Malka, with well-affected agnosticism.

"Phew!" whistled Michael. "What's up now, mother?"

"Nothing, my pet, nothing."

"Well, I'm going across. Come along, mother. Oh, wait a minute. I want to brush this mud off my trousers. Is the clothes-brush here?"

"Yes, dearest one," said the unsuspecting Malka.

Michael winked imperceptibly, flicked his trousers and, without further parley, ran across the diagonal to Milly's house. Five minutes afterwards a deputation, consisting of a char-woman, waited upon Malka and said:

"Missus says will you please come over, as baby is a-cryin' for its grandma."

"Ah, that must be another pin," said Malka, with a gleam of triumph at her victory. But she did not budge. At the end of five minutes she rose solemnly, adjusted her wig and her dress in the mirror, put on her bonnet, brushed away a non-existent speck of dust from her left sleeve, put a peppermint in her mouth, and crossed the Square carrying the clothes-brush in her hand. Milly's door was half open, but she knocked at it and said to the char-woman:

"Is Mrs. Phillips in?"

"Yes, mum, the company's all upstairs."

"Oh, then I will go up and return her this myself."

Malka went straight through the little crowd of guests to Milly, who was sitting on a sofa with Ezekiel, quiet as a lamb and as good as gold, in her arms.

"Milly, my dear," she said. "I have come to bring you back your clothes-brush. Thank you so much for the loan of it."

"You know you're welcome, mother," said Milly, with unintentionally dual significance. The two ladies embraced. Ephraim Phillips, a sallow-looking, close-cropped Pole, also kissed his mother-in-law, and the gold chain that rested on Malka's bosom heaved with the expansion of domestic pride. Malka thanked God she was not a mother of barren or celibate children, which is only one degree better than personal unfruit-fulness, and testifies scarce less to the celestial curse.

"Is that pin-mark gone away yet, Milly, from the precious little thing?" said Malka, taking Ezekiel in her arms and disregarding the transforma-tion of face which in babies precedes a storm.

"Yes, it was a mere flea-bite," said Milly incautiously, adding hurriedly, "I always go through his flannels and things most carefully to see there are no more pins lurking about."

"That is right! Pins are like fleas – you never know where they get to," said Malka in an insidious spirit of compromise.

"Where is Leah?"

"She is in the back yard frying the last of the fish. Don't you smell it?"

"It will hardly have time to get cold."

"Well, but I did a dishful myself last night. She is only preparing a reserve in case the attack be too deadly."

"And where is the *Cohen?*"

"Oh, we have asked old Hyams across the Ruins. We expect him round every minute."

At this point the indications of Ezekiel's facial barometer were fulfilled, and a tempest of weeping shook him.

"*Na!* Go then! Go to the mother!" said Malka angrily. "All my children are alike. It's getting late. Hadn't you better send across again for old Hyams?"

"There's no hurry, mother," said Michael Birnbaum soothingly. "We must wait for Sam."

"And who's Sam?" cried Malka unappeased.

"Sam is Leah's *Chosan*," replied Michael ingenuously.

"Clever!" sneered Malka. "But my grandson is not going to wait for the son of a proselyte. Why doesn't he come?"

"He'll be here in one minute."

"How do you know?"

"We came up in the same train. He got in at Middlesborough. He's just gone home to see his folks, and get a wash and a brush-up. Considering he's coming up to town merely for the sake of the family ceremony, I think it would be very rude to commence without him. It's no joke, a long railway journey this weather. My feet were nearly frozen despite the foot-warmer."

"My poor lambkin," said Malka, melting. And she patted his side whiskers.

Sam Levine arrived almost immediately and Leah, fishfork in hand, flew out of the back-yard kitchen to greet him. Though a member of the tribe of Levi, he was anything but ecclesiastical in appearance, rather a representative of muscular Judaism. He had a pink and white complexion and a tawny moustache and bubbled over with energy and animal spirits. He could give most men thirty in a hundred in billiards, and fifty in anecdote. He was an advanced Radical in politics, and had a high opinion of the intelligence of his party. He paid Leah lip-fealty on his entry.

"What a pity it's Sunday!" was Leah's first remark when the kissing was done.

"No going to the play," said Sam ruefully, catching her meaning.

They always celebrated his return from a commercial round by going to the theatre – *the-etter* they pronounced it. They went to the pit of the West End houses rather than patronize the local dress circles for the same money. There were two strata of Ghetto girls, those who strolled in the Strand on Sabbath, and those who strolled in the Whitechapel Road. Leah was of the upper stratum. She was a tall lovely brunette, exuberant of voice and figure, with coarse red hands. She doted on ice-cream in the summer and hot chocolate in the winter, but her love of the theatre was a perennial passion. Both Sam and she had good ears, and were always first in the field with the latest comic opera tunes. Leah's healthy vitality was prodigious. There was a legend in the Lane of such a maiden having been chosen by a coronet; Leah was satisfied with Sam, who was just her match. On the heels of Sam came several other guests, notably Mrs. Jacobs (wife of "Reb" Shemuel), with her pretty daughter, Hannah. Mr. Hyams, the *Cohen*, came last – the Priest whose functions had so curiously dwindled since the times of the Temples. To be called first to the reading of the Law, to bless his brethren with symbolic spreadings of palms and fingers in a mystic incantation delivered, standing shoeless before the Ark of the Covenant at festival seasons, to redeem the mother's first-born son when neither parent was of priestly lineage – these privileges combined with a disability to be with or near the dead, differentiated his religious position from that of the Levite or the Israelite. Mendel Hyams was not puffed up about his tribal superiority, though if tradition were to be trusted, his direct descent from Aaron, the High Priest, gave him a longer genealogy than Queen Victoria's. He was a meek sexagenarian, with a threadbare black coat and a child-like smile. All the pride of the family seemed to be monopolised by his daughter Miriam, a girl whose very nose Heaven had fashioned scornful. Miriam had accompanied him out of contemptuous curiosity. She wore a stylish feather in her hat, and a boa round her throat, and earned thirty shillings a week, all told, as a school teacher. (Esther Ansell was in her class just now.) Probably her toilette had made old Hyams unpunctual.

His arrival was the signal for the commencement of the proceedings and the men hastened to assume their head-gear.

Ephraim Phillips cautiously took the swaddled-up infant from the bosom of Milly where it was suckling and presented it to old Hyams. Fortunately Ezekiel had already had a repletion of milk, and was drowsy and manifested very little interest in the whole transaction.

"This my first-born son," said Ephraim in Hebrew as he handed Ezekiel over – "is the first-born of his mother, and the Holy One, blessed be He, hath given command to redeem him as it is said, and those that are to be redeemed of them from a month old, shalt thou redeem according to thine estimation for the money of five shekels after the shekel of the sanctuary the shekel being twenty gerahs; and it is said, 'Sanctify unto me all the first-born, whatsoever openeth the womb among the children of Israel, both of man and of beast, it is mine.'"

Ephraim Phillips then placed fifteen shillings in silver before old Hyams, who thereupon inquired in Chaldaic: "Which wouldst thou rather – give me thy first-born son, the first-born of his mother, or redeem him for five selaim, which thou art bound to give according to the Law?"

Ephraim. replied in Chaldaic: "I am desirous rather to redeem my son, and here thou hast the value of his redemption, which I am bound to give according to the Law."

Thereupon Hyams took the money tendered, and gave back the child to his father, who blessed God for His sanctifying commandments, and thanked Him for His mercies; after which the old *Cohen* held the fifteen shillings over the head of the infant, saying: "This instead of that, this in exchange for that, this in remission of that. May this child enter into life, into the Law, and into the fear of Heaven. May it be God's will that even as he has been admitted to redemption, so may he enter into the Law, the nuptial canopy and into good deeds. Amen." Then, placing his hand in benediction upon the child's head, the priestly layman added: "God make thee as Ephraim and Manasseh. The Lord bless thee and keep thee. The Lord make His face to shine upon thee, and be gracious unto thee. The Lord turn His face to thee and grant thee peace. The Lord is thy guardian; the Lord is thy shade upon thy right hand. For length of days and years of life and peace shall they add to thee. The Lord shall guard thee from all evil. He shall guard thy soul."

"Amen," answered the company, and then there was a buzz of secular talk, general rapture being expressed at the. stolidness of Ezekiel's demeanour. Cups of tea were passed round by the lovely Leah, and the secrets of the paper bags were brought to light. Ephraim Phillips talked horses with Sam Levine, and old Hyams quarrelled with Malka over the disposal of the fifteen shillings. Knowing that Hyams was poor, Malka refused to take back the money retendered by him under pretence of a gift to the child. The Cohen, however, was a proud man, and under the eye of Miriam, a firm one. Ultimately it was agreed the money should be expended on a *Missheberach*, for the infant's welfare and the synagogue's. Birds of a feather flock together and Miriam forgathered with Hannah Jacobs, who also had a stylish feather in her hat, and was the most congenial of the company. Mrs. Jacobs was left to discourse of the ailments of childhood and the iniquities of servants with Mrs. Phillips.

Reb Shemuel's wife, commonly known as the Rebbitzin, was a tall woman with a bony nose and shrivelled cheeks, whereon the paths of the blood-vessels were scrawled in red. The same bones were visible beneath the plumper padding of Hannah's face. Mrs. Jacobs had escaped the temptation to fatness, which is the besetting peril of the Jewish matron. If Hannah could escape her mother's inclination to angularity she would be a pretty woman. She dressed with taste, which is half the battle, and for the present she was only nineteen.

"Do you think it's a good match?" said Miriam Hyams, indicating Sam Levine with a movement of the eyebrow.

A swift, scornful look flitted across Hannah's face. "Among the Jews," she said, "every match is a grand *Shidduch* before the marriage – after, we hear another tale."

"There is a good deal in that," admitted Miriam, thoughtfully. "The girl's family cries up the capture shamelessly. I remember when Clara

Emanuel was engaged, her brother Jack told me it was a splendid *Shidduck*. Afterwards I found he was a widower of fifty-five with three children."

"But that engagement went off," said Hannah.

"I know," said Miriam. "I'm only saying I can't fancy myself doing anything of the kind."

"What! breaking off an engagement?" said Hannah, with a cynical little twinkle about her eye.

"No, taking a man like that," replied Miriam. "I wouldn't look at a man over thirty-five, or with less than two hundred and fifty a year."

"You'll never marry a teacher, then," Hannah remarked.

"Teacher !" Miriam Hyams repeated, with a look of disgust. "How can one be respectable on three pounds a week? I must have a man in a good position." She tossed her piquant nose and looked almost handsome. She was five years older than Hannah, and it seemed an enigma why men did not rush to lay five pounds a week at her daintily shod feet.

"I'd rather marry a man with two pounds a week if I loved him," said Hannah in a low tone.

"Not in this century,", said Miriam, shaking her head incredulously. "We don't believe in that nonsense now-a-days. There was Alice Green – she used to talk like that – now look at her, riding about in a gig side-by-side with a bald monkey."

"Alice Green's mother," interrupted Malka, pricking up her ears, "married a son of Mendel Weinstein by his third wife, Dinah, who had ten pounds left her by her uncle Shloumi."

"No, Dinah was Mendel's second wife," corrected Mrs. Jacobs, cutting short a remark of Mrs. Phillips's in favour of the new interest.

"Dinah was Mendel's third wife," repeated Malka, her tanned cheeks reddening. "I know it because my Simon, God bless him, was breeched the same month."

Simon was Malka's eldest, now a magistrate in Melbourne.

"His third wife was Kitty Green, daughter of the yellow Melammed," persisted the Rebbitzin. "I know it for a fact, because Kitty's sister Annie was engaged for a week to my brother-in-law Nathaniel."

"His first wife," put in Malka's husband, with the air of arbitrating between the two, "was Shmool the publican's eldest daughter."

"Shmool the publican's daughter," said Malka, stirred to fresh indignation, "married Hyam Robins, the grandson of old Benjamin, who kept the cutlery shop at the corner of Little Eden Alley, there where the pickled cucumber store stands now."

"It was Shmool's sister that married Hyam Robins, wasn't it, mother?" asked Milly, incautiously.

"Certainly not," thundered Malka. "I knew old Benjamin well, and he sent me a pair of chintz curtains when I married your father."

"Poor old Benjamin! How long has he been dead?" mused Reb Shemuells wife.

"He died the year I was confined with my Leah."

"Stop! stop!" interrupted Sam Levine boisterously. "There's Leah getting as red as fire for fear you'll blab out her age."

"Don't be a fool, Sam," said Leah, blushing violently and looking the lovelier for it.

The attention of the entire company was now concentrated upon the question at issue, whatever it might be. Malka fixed her audience with her piercing eye, and said in a tone that scarce brooked contradiction: "Hyam Robins couldn't have married Shmool's sister because Shmool's sister was already the wife of Abraharn the fishmonger."

"Yes, but Shmool had two sisters," said Mrs. Jacobs, audaciously asserting her position as the rival genealogist.

"Nothing of the kind," replied Malka warmly.

"I'm quite sure," persisted Mrs. Jacobs. "There was Phoeby and there was Harriet."

"Nothing of the kind," repeated Malka. Shmool had three sisters. Only two were in the deaf and dumb home."

"Why, that wasn't Shmool at all," Milly forgot herself so far as to say, "that was Block the Baker."

"Of course!" said Malka in her most acid tone. "My *kinder* always know better than me."

There was a moment of painful silence. Malka's eye mechanically sought the clothes-brush. Then Ezekiel sneezed. It was a convulsive "atichoo," and agitated the infant to its most intimate flannel-roll.

"For thy Salvation do I hope, O Lord," murmured Malka, piously, adding triumphantly aloud, "There! the *kind* has sneezed to the truth of it. I knew I was right."

The sneeze of an innocent child silences everybody who is not a blasphemer. In the general satisfaction at the unexpected solution of the situation, no one even pointed out that the actual statement to which Ezekiel had borne testimony, was an assertion of the superior knowledge of Malka's children. Shortly afterwards the company trooped downstairs to partake of high tea, which in the Ghetto need not include anything more fleshly than fish. Fish was, indeed, the staple of the meal. Fried fish, and such fried fish! Only a great poet could sing the praises of the national dish, and the golden age of Hebrew poetry is over. Strange that Gebirol should have lived and died without the opportunity of the theme, and that the great Jehuda Halevi himself should have had to devote his genius merely to singing the glories of Jerusalem. "Israel is among the other nations," he sang, "as the heart among the limbs." Even so is the fried fish of Judæa to the fried fish of Christendom and Heathendom. With the audacity of true culinary genius, Jewish fried fish is always served cold. The skin is a beautiful brown, the substance firm and succulent. The very bones thereof are full of marrow, yea and charged with memories of the happy past. Fried fish binds Anglo-Judæa more than all the lip-professions of unity. Its savour is early known of youth, and the divine flavour, endeared by a thousand childish recollections, entwined with the most sacred associations, draws back the hoary sinner into the paths of piety. It is on fried fish, mayhap, that the Jewish matron grows fat. In the days of the Messiah, when the saints shall feed off the Leviathan; and the Sea Serpent shall be dished up for the last time, and the world and the silly season shall come to an end, in those days it is probable that the saints will prefer their Leviathan fried. Not that any physical frying will be necessary, for in those happy times (for whose coming every faithful Israelite prays three times a day), the Leviathan will have what taste the eater will. Possibly a few highly respectable saints, who were fashionable in their day and contrived to live in Kensington without infection of paganism, will take their Leviathan in conventional courses, and beginning with *hors d'oeuvres* may *will* him everything by turns and nothing long; making him soup and sweets, joint and *entrée*, and even ices and coffee, for in the millennium the harassing prohibition which bars cream after meat will fall through. But, however this be, it is beyond question that the bulk of the faithful will mentally fry him, and though the Christian saints, who shall be privileged to wait at table, hand them plate after plate, fried fish shall be all the fare. One suspects that Hebrews gained the taste in the Desert of Sinai, for the manna that fell there was not monotonous to the palate as the sciolist supposes, but likewise mutable under volition. It were incredible that Moses, who gave so many imperishable things to his people, did not also give them the knowledge of fried fish, so that they might obey his behest, and rejoice before the Lord. Nay, was it not because, while the manna fell, there could be no lack of fish to fry, that they lingered forty years in a dreary wilderness? Other delicious things there are in Jewish cookery – *Lockschen*, which are the apotheosis of vermicelli, *Ferfel*, which are *Lockschen* in an atomic state, and *Creplich*, which are triangular meat-pasties, and *Kuggol*, to which pudding has a far-away resemblance; and there is even *gefüllte Fisch*, which is stuffed fish without bones – but fried fish reigns above all in cold, unquestioned sovereignty. No other people possesses the recipe. As a poet of the commencement of the century sings:

> The Christians are ninnies, they can't fry Dutch plaice, Believe me, they can't tell a carp from a dace.

It was while discussing a deliciously brown oblong of the Dutch plaice of the ballad that Samuel Levine appeared to be struck by an idea. He threw down his knife and fork and exclaimed in Hebrew. "*Shemah beni!*"

Everyone looked at him.

"Hear, my son!"' he repeated in comic horror. Then relapsing into English, he explained. "I've forgotten to give Leah a present from her *chosan*."

"A-h-h!" Everybody gave a sigh of deep interest; Leah, whom the exigencies of service had removed from his side to the head of the table, half-rose from her seat in excitement.

Now, whether Samuel Levine had really forgotten, or whether he had chosen the most effective moment will never be known; certain it is that the Semitic instinct for drama was gratified within him as he drew a little folded white paper out of his waistcoat pocket, amid the keen expectation of the company.

"This," said he, tapping the paper as if he were a conjurer, "was purchased by me yesterday morning for my little girl. I said to myself, says I, look here, old man, you've got to go up to town for a day in honour of Ezekiel Phillips, and your poor girl, who had looked forward to your staying away till Passover, will want some compensation for her disappointment at seeing you earlier. So I thinks to myself, thinks I, now what is there that Leah would like? It must be something appropriate, of course, and it mustn't be of any value, because I can't afford it. It's a ruinous business getting engaged; the worst bit of business I ever did in all my born days." Here Sam winked facetiously at the company. "And I thought and thought of what was the cheapest thing I could get out of it with, and lo and behold I suddenly thought of a ring."

So saying, Sam, still with the same dramatic air, unwrapped the thick gold ring and held it up so that the huge diamond in it sparkled in the sight of all. A long "O-h-h" went round the company, the majority instantaneously pricing it mentally, and wondering at what reduction Sam had acquired it from a brother commercial. For that no Jew ever pays full retail price for jewellery is regarded as axiomatic. Even the engagement ring is not required to be first-hand – or should it be first-finger? – so long as it is solid; which perhaps accounts for the superiority of the Jewish marriage-rate. Leah rose entirely to her feet, the light of the diamond reflected in her eager eyes. She leant across the table, stretching out a finger to receive her lover's gift. Sam put the ring near her finger, then drew it away teasingly.

"Them as asks shan't have," he said, in high good humour.

"You're too greedy. Look at the number of rings you've got already." The fun of the situation diffused itself along the table.

"Give it me," laughed Miriam Hyams, stretching out her finger. "I'll say 'ta' so nicely."

"No," he said, "you've been naughty; I'm going to give it to the little girl who has sat quiet all the time. Miss Hannah Jacobs, rise to receive your prize."

Hannah, who was sitting two places to the left of him, smiled quietly, but went on carving her fish. Sam, growing quite boisterous under the appreciation of a visibly amused audience, leaned towards her, captured her right hand, and forcibly adjusted the ring on the second finger, exclaiming in Hebrew, with mock solemnity, "Behold, thou art consecrated unto me by this ring according to the Law of Moses and Israel."

It was the formal marriage speech he had learnt up for his approaching marriage. The company roared with laughter, and pleasure and enjoyment of the fun made Leah's lovely, smiling cheeks flush to a livelier crimson. Badinage flew about from one end of the table to the other; burlesque congratulations were showered on the couple, flowing over even unto Mrs. Jacobs, who appeared to enjoy the episode as much as if her daughter were really off her hands. The little incident added the last touch of high spirits to the company and extorted all their latent humour. Samuel excelled himself in vivacious repartee, and responded comically to the toast of his health as drunk in coffee. Suddenly, amid the hubbub of chaff and laughter and the clatter of cutlery, a still small voice made itself heard. It same from old Hyams, who had been sitting quietly with brow corrugated under his black velvet koppel.

"Mr. Levine," he said, in low grave tones. I have been thinking, and I am afraid that what you have done is serious."

The earnestness of his tones arrested the attention of the company. The laughter ceased.

"What do you mean?" said Samuel. He understood the Yiddish which old Hyams almost invariably used, though he did not speak it himself. Contrariwise, old Hyams understood much more English than he spoke.

"You have married Hannah Jacobs."

There was a painful silence, dim recollections surging in everybody's brain.

"Married Hannah Jacobs!" repeated Samuel incredulously.

"Yes," affirmed old Hyams. "What you have done constitutes a marriage according to Jewish law. You have pledged yourself to her in the presence of two witnesses."

There was another tense silence. Samuel broke it with a boisterous laugh.

"No, no, old fellow," he said; "you don't have me like that!"

The tension was relaxed. Everybody joined in the laugh with a feeling of indescribable relief. Facetious old Hyams had gone near scoring one. Hannah smilingly plucked off the glittering bauble from her finger and slid it on to Leah's. Hyams alone remained grave. "Laugh away!" he said. "You will soon find I am right. Such is our law."

"May be," said Samuel, constrained to seriousness despite himself. "But you forget that I am already engaged to Leah."

"I do not forget it," replied Hyams, "but it has nothing to do with the case. You are both single, or rather you were both single, for now you are man and wife."

Leah, who had been sitting pale and agitated, burst into tears. Hannah's face was drawn and white. Her mother looked the least alarmed of the company.

"Droll person!" cried Malka, addressing Sam angrily in jargon. "What hast thou done?"

"Don't let us all go mad," said Samuel, bewildered. "How can a piece of fun, a joke, be a valid marriage?"

"The law takes no account of jokes," said old Hyams solemnly.

"Then why didn't you stop me?" asked Sam, exasperated.

"It was all done in a moment. I laughed myself; I had no time to think."

Sam brought his fist down on the table with a bang.

"Well. I'll never believe this! If this is Judaism –!"

"Hush!" said Malka angrily. "These are your English Jews, who make mock of holy things. I always said the son of a proselyte was –"

"Look here, mother," put in Michael soothingly. "Don't let us make a fuss before we know the truth. Send for someone who is likely to know." He played agitatedly with his complex pocket-knife.

"Yes, Hannah's father, Reb Shemuel is just the man," cried Milly Phillips.

"I told you my husband was gone to Manchester for a day or two," Mrs. Jacobs reminded her.

"There's the *Maggid* of the Sons of the Covenant," said one of the company. "I'll go and fetch him."

The stooping, black-bearded *Maggid* was brought. When he arrived, it was evident from his look that he knew all and brought confirmation of their worst fears. He explained the law at great length, and cited precedent upon precedent. When he ceased, Leah's sobs alone broke the silence. Samuel's face was white. The merry gathering had been turned to a wedding party.

"You rogue!" burst forth Malka at last. "You planned all this – you thought my Leah didn't have enough money, and that Reb Shemuel will heap you up gold in the hands. But you don't take me in like this."

"May this piece of bread choke me if I had the slightest iota of intention!" cried Samuel passionately, for the thought of what Leah might think was like fire in his veins. He turned appealingly to the *Maggid*; "but there must be some way out of this, surely there must be some way out. I know you *Maggidim* can split hairs. Can't you make one of your clever distinctions even when there's more than a trifle concerned?" There was a savage impatience about the bridegroom which boded ill for the Law.

"Of course there's a way out," said the Maggid calmly. "Only one way, but a very broad and simple one."

"What's that?" everybody asked breathlessly.

"He must give her *Gett!*"

"Of course!" shouted Sam in a voice of thunder. "I divorce her at once." He guffawed hysterically; "What a pack of fools we are! Good old Jewish law!"

Leah's sobs ceased. Everybody except Mrs. Jacobs was smiling once more. Half a dozen hands grasped the *Maggid's*; half a dozen others thumped him on the back. He was pushed into a chair. They gave him a glass of brandy, they heaped a plate with fried fish. Verily the *Maggid*, who was in truth sore ahungered, was in luck's way. He blessed Providence and the Jewish Marriage Law.

"But you had better not reckon that a divorce," he warned them between two mouthfuls. "You had better go to Reb Shemuel, the maiden's father, and let him arrange the *Gett* beyond reach of cavil."

"But Reb Shemuel is away," said Mrs. Jacobs.

"And I must go away, too, by the first train tomorrow," said Sam. "However, there's no hurry. I'll arrange to run up to town again in a fortnight or so, and then Reb Shemuel shall see that we are properly untied. You don't mind being my wife for a fortnight, I hope, Miss Jacobs?" asked Sam, winking gleefully at Leah. She smiled back at him and they laughed together over the danger they had just escaped. Hannah laughed too, in contemptuous amusement at the rigidity of Jewish Law.

"I'll tell you what, Sam, can't you come back for next Saturday week?" said Leah.

"Why?" asked Sam. "What's on?"

"The Purim Ball at the Club. As you've got to come back to give Hannah *Gett*, you might as well come in time to take me to the ball."

"Right you are," said Sam cheerfully.

Leah clapped her hands. "Oh that will be jolly," she said.

"And we'll take Hannah with us," she added as an afterthought.

"Is that by way of compensation for losing my husband?" Hannah asked with a smile.

Leah gave a happy laugh, and turned the new ring on her finger in delighted contemplation.

"All's well that ends well," said Sam. "Through this joke Leah will be the belle of the Purim Ball. I think I deserve another piece of plaice, Leah, for that compliment. As for you, Mr. *Maggid*, you're a saint and a Talmud sage!"

The *Maggid's* face was brightened by a smile. He intoned the grace with unction when the meal ended, and everybody joined in heartily at the specifically vocal portions. Then the *Maggid* left, and the cards were brought out.

It is inadvisable to play cards before fried fish, because it is well known that you may lose, and losing may ruffle your temper, and you may call your partner an ass or your partner may call you an ass. Tonight the greatest good humour prevailed, though several pounds changed hands. They played Loo, "Klobbiyos," Napoleon, Vingt-et-un, and especially Brag. Solo whist had not yet come in to drive everything else out. Old Hyams did not spiel, because he could not afford to, and Hannah Jacobs because she did not care to. These and a few other guests left early. But the family party stayed late. On a warm green table, under a cheerful gas light, with brandy and whiskey and sweets and fruit to hand, with no trains or busses to catch, what wonder if the light-hearted assembly played far into the new day?

Meanwhile the Redeemed Son slept peacefully in his crib with his legs curled up, and his little fists clenched beneath the coverlet.

CHAPTER V

The Pauper Alien

Moses Ansell married mainly because all men are mortal. He knew he would die and he wanted an heir. Not to inherit anything, but to say *Kaddish* for him. *Kaddish* is the most beautiful and wonderful mourning prayer ever written. Rigidly excluding all references to death and grief, it exhausts itself in supreme glorification of the Eternal and in supplication for peace upon the House of Israel. But its significance has been gradually transformed; human nature, driven away with a pitchfork, has avenged itself by regarding the prayer as a mass, not without purgatorial efficacy, and so the Jew is reluctant to die without leaving some one qualified to say *Kaddish* after him every day for a year, and then one day a year. That is one reason why sons are of such domestic importance.

Moses had only a mother in the world when he married Gittel Silverstein, and he hoped to restore the balance of male relatives by this reckless measure. The result was six children, three girls and three *Kaddishim.* In Gittel, Moses found a tireless helpmate. During her lifetime the family always lived in two rooms, for she had various ways of supplementing the household income. When in London she chared for her cousin Malka at a shilling a day. Likewise she sewed underlinen and stitched slips of fur into caps in the privacy of home and midnight. For all Mrs. Ansell's industry, the family had been a typical group of wandering Jews, straying from town to town in search of better things. The congregation they left (every town which could muster the minimum of ten men for worship boasted its *Kehillah*) invariably paid their fare to the next congregation, glad to get rid of them so cheaply, and the new *Kehillah* jumped at the opportunity of gratifying their restless migratory instinct and sent them to a newer. Thus were they tossed about on the battledores of philanthropy, often reverting to their starting-point, to the disgust of the charitable committees. Yet Moses always made loyal efforts to find work. His versatility was marvellous. There was nothing he could not do badly. He had been glazier, synagogue beadle, picture-frame manufacturer, cantor, peddler, shoemaker in all branches, coat-seller, official executioner of fowls and cattle, Hebrew teacher, fruiterer, circumciser, professional corpse-watcher, and now he was a tailor out of work.

Unquestionably Malka was right in considering Moses a *Schlemihl* in comparison with many a fellow-immigrant, who brought indefatigable hand and subtle brain to the struggle for existence, and discarded the prop of charity as soon as he could, and sometimes earlier.

It was as a hawker that he believed himself most gifted, and he never lost the conviction that if he could only get a fair start, he had in him the makings of a millionaire. Yet there was scarcely anything cheap with which he had not tramped the country, so that when poor Benjamin, who profited by his mother's death to get into the Orphan Asylum, was asked to write a piece of composition on "The Methods of Travelling," he excited the hilarity of the classroom by writing that there were numerous ways of travelling, for you could travel with sponge, lemons, rhubarb, old clothes, jewellery, and so on, for a page of a copy book. Benjamin was a brilliant boy, yet he never shook off some of the misleading associations engendered by the parental jargon. For Mrs. Ansell had diversified her corrupt German by streaks of incorrect English, being of a much more energetic and ambitious temperament than the conservative Moses, who dropped nearly all his burden of English into her grave. For Benjamin, "to travel" meant to wander about selling goods, and when in his books he read of African travellers, he took it for granted that they were but exploiting the Dark Continent for small profits and quick returns.

And who knows? Perhaps of the two species, it was the old Jewish peddlers who suffered the more and made the less profit on the average. For the despised three-hatted scarecrow of Christian caricature, who shambled along snuffling "Old clo'," had a strenuous inner life, which might possibly have vied in intensity, elevation, and even sense of humour, with that of the best of the jeerers on the highway. To Moses, "travelling" meant straying forlornly in strange towns and villages, given over to the worship of an alien deity and ever ready to avenge his crucifixion; in a land of whose tongue he knew scarce more than the Saracen damsel married by legend to á Becket's father. It meant praying brazenly in crowded railway trains, winding the phylacteries sevenfold round his left arm and crowning his forehead with a huge leather bump of righteousness, to the bewilderment or irritation of unsympathetic fellow-passengers. It meant living chiefly on dry bread and drinking black tea out of his own cup, with meat and fish and the good things of life utterly banned by the traditional law, even if he were flush. It meant carrying the red rag of an obnoxious personality through a land of bulls. It meant passing months away from wife and children, in a solitude only occasionally alleviated by a Sabbath spent in a synagogue town. It meant putting up at low public houses and common lodging houses, where rowdy disciples of the Prince of Peace often sent him bleeding to bed, or shamelessly despoiled him of his merchandise, or bullied and blustered him out of his fair price, knowing he dared not resent. It meant being chaffed and gibed at in language of which he only understood that it was cruel, though certain trite facetiæ grew intelligible to him by repetition. Thus once, when he had been interrogated as to the locality of Moses when the light went out, he replied in Yiddish that the light could not go out, for "it stands in the verse, that round the head of Moses, our teacher, the great law-giver, was a perpetual halo." An old German happened to be smoking at the bar of the public house when the peddler gave his acute answer; he laughed heartily, slapped the Jew on the back and translated the repartee to the convivial crew. For once intellect told, and the rough drinkers, with a pang of shame, vied with one another in pressing bitter beer upon the temperate Semite. But, as a rule, Moses Ansell drank the cup of affliction instead of hospitality and bore his share to the full, without the remotest intention of being heroic, in the long agony of his race, doomed to be a byword and a mockery amongst the heathen. Assuredly, to die for a religion is easier than to live for it. Yet Moses never complained nor lost faith. To be spat upon was the very condition of existence of the modern Jew, deprived of Palestine and his Temple, a footsore mendicant, buffeted and reviled, yet the dearer to the Lord God who had chosen him from the nations. Bullies might break Moses's head in this world, but in the next he would sit on a gold chair in Paradise among the saints and sing exegetical acrostics to all eternity. It was some dim perception of these things that made Esther forgive her father when the Ansells waited weeks and weeks for a postal order and landlords were threatening to bundle them out neck and crop, and her mother's hands were worn to the bone slaving for her little ones.

Things improved a little just before the mother died, for they had settled down in London and Moses earned eighteen shillings a week as a machinist and presser and no longer roamed the country. But the interval of happiness was brief. The grandmother, imported from Poland, did not take kindly to her son's wife, whom she found wanting in the minutiae of ceremonial piety and godless enough to wear her own hair. There had been, indeed, a note of scepticism, of defiance, in Esther's mother, a hankering after the customs of the heathen, which her grandmother divined instinctively and resented for the sake of her son and the post-mundane existence of her grandchildren. Mrs. Ansell's scepticism based itself upon the uncleanliness which was so generally next to godliness in, the pious circles round them, and she had been heard to express contempt for the learned and venerable Israelite, who, being accosted by an acquaintance when the shadows of eve were beginning to usher in the Day of Atonement, exclaimed:

"For heaven's sake, don't stop me – I missed my bath last year."

Mrs. Ansell bathed her children from head to foot once a month, and even profanely washed them on the Sabbath, and had other strange, uncanny notions. She professed not to see the value to God, man or beast of the learned Rabbonim, who sat shaking themselves all day in the *Beth Hamidrash*, and said they would be better occupied in supporting their families, a view which, though mere surface blasphemy on the part of the good woman and primarily intended as a hint to Moses to study less and work longer, did not fail to excite lively passages of arms between the two women. But death ended these bickerings and the *Bube*, who had frequently reproached her son for bringing her into such an atheistic country, was left a drag the more upon the family deprived at once of a mother and a bread-winner. Old Mrs. Ansell was unfit for anything save grumbling, and so the headship naturally devolved upon Esther, whom her mother's death left a woman getting on for eight. The commencement of her reign coincided with a sad bisection of territory. Shocking as it may be to better regulated minds, these seven people lived in one room. Moses and the two boys slept in one bed and the grand-mother and the three girls in another. Esther had to sleep with her head on a supplementary pillow at the foot of the bed. But there can be much love in a little room.

The room was not, however, so very little, for it was of ungainly sprawling structure, pushing out an odd limb that might have been cut off with a curtain. The walls nodded fixedly to one another so that the ceiling was only half the size of the floor. The furniture comprised but the commonest necessities. This attic of the Ansells was nearer heaven than most earthly dwelling places, for there were four tall flights of stairs to mount before you got to it. No. 1 Royal Street had been in its time one of the great mansions of the Ghetto; pillars of the synagogue had quaffed kosher wine in its spacious reception rooms and its corridors had echoed with the gossip of portly dames in stiff brocades. It was stoutly built and its balusters were of carved oak. But now the threshold of the great street door, which was never closed, was encrusted with black mud, and a musty odour permanently clung to the wide staircase and blent subtly with far-away reminiscences of Mr. Belcovitch's festive turpentine. The Ansells had numerous housemates, for No. 1 Royal Street was a Jewish colony in itself and the resident population was periodically swollen by the "hands" of the Belcovitches and by the "Sons of the Covenant," who came to worship at their synagogue on the ground floor. What with Sugarman the *Shadchan*, on the first floor, Mrs. Simons and Dutch Debby on the second, the Belcovitches on the third, and the Ansells and Gabriel Hamburg, the great scholar, on the fourth, the door-posts twinkled with *Mezuzahs* – cases or cylinders containing sacred script with the word *Shaddai* (Almighty) peering out of a little glass eye at the centre. Even Dutch Debby, abandoned wretch as she was, had this protection against evil spirits (so it has come to be regarded) on her lintel, though she probably never touched the eye with her finger to kiss the place of contact after the manner of the faithful.

Thus was No. 1 Royal Street close packed with the stuff of human life, homespun and drab enough, but not altogether profitless, may be, to turn over and examine. So close packed was it that there was scarce breathing space. It was only at immemorial intervals that our pauper alien made a pun, but one day he flashed upon the world the pregnant remark that England was well named, for to the Jew it was verily the Enge-Land, which in German signifies the country without elbow room. Moses Ansell chuckled softly and beatifically when he emitted the remark that surprised all who knew him. But then it was the Rejoicing of the Law and the Sons of the Covenant had treated him to rum and currant cake. He often thought of his witticism afterwards, and it always lightened his unwashed face with a happy smile. The recollection usually caught him when he was praying.

For four years after Mrs. Ansell's charity funeral the Ansells, though far from happy, had no history to speak of, Benjamin accompanied Solomon to *Shool* morning and evening to say *Kaddish* for their mother till he passed into the Orphan Asylum and out of the lives of his relatives. Solomon and Rachel and Esther went to the great school and Isaac to the infant school, while the tiny Sarah, whose birth had cost Mrs. Ansell's life, crawled and climbed about in the garret, the grandmother coming in negatively useful as a safeguard against fire on the days when the grate was not empty. The *Bube's* own conception of her function as a safeguard against fire was quite other.

Moses was out all day working or looking for work, or praying or listening to *Droshes* by the *Maggid* or other great preachers. Such charities as brightened and warmed the Ghetto Moses usually came in for. Bread, meat and coal tickets, godsends from the Society for Restoring the Soul, made odd days memorable. Blankets were not so easy to get as in the days of poor Gittell's confinements.

What little cooking there was to do was done by Esther before or after school; she and her children usually took their midday meal with them in the shape of bread, occasionally made ambrosial by treacle. The Ansells had more fast days than the Jewish calendar, which is saying a good deal. Providence, however, generally stepped in before the larder had been bare twenty-four hours.

As the fast days of the Jewish calendar did not necessarily fall upon the Ansell fast days, they were an additional tax on Moses and his mother. Yet neither ever wavered in the scrupulous observance of them, not a crumb of bread nor a drop of water passing their lips. In the keen search for facts detrimental to the Ghetto it is surprising that no political economist has hitherto exposed the abundant fasts with which Israel has been endowed, and which obviously operate as a dole in aid of wages. So does the Lenten period of the "Three Weeks," when meat is prohibited in memory of the shattered Temples. The Ansells kept the "Three Weeks" pretty well all the year round. On rare occasions they purchased pickled Dutch herrings or brought home pennyworths of pea soup or of baked potatoes and rice from a neighbouring cook shop. For Festival days, if Malka had subsidized them with a half-sovereign, Esther sometimes compounded *Tzimmus*, a dainty blend of carrots, pudding and potatoes. She was prepared to write an essay on *Tzimmus* as a gastronomic ideal. There were other pleasing Polish combinations which were baked for twopence by the local bakers. *Tabechas*, or stuffed entrails, and liver, lights or milt were good substitutes for meat. A favourite soup was

Borsch, which was made with beet-root, fat taking the place of the more fashionable cream.

The national dish was seldom their lot; when fried fish came it was usually from the larder of Mrs. Simons, a motherly old widow, who lived in the second floor front, and presided over the confinements of all the women and the sicknesses of all the children in the neighbourhood. Her married daughter Dinah was providentially suckling a black-eyed boy when Mrs. Ansell died, so Mrs. Simons converted her into a foster mother of little Sarah, regarding herself ever afterwards as under special responsibilities toward the infant, whom she occasionally took to live with her for a week, and for whom she saw heaven encouraging a future alliance with the black-eyed foster brother. Life would have been gloomier still in the Ansell garret if Mrs. Simons had not been created to bless and sustain. Even old garments somehow arrived from Mrs. Simons to eke out the corduroys and the print gowns which were the gift of the school. There were few pleasanter events in the Ansell household than the falling ill of one of the children, for not only did this mean a supply of broth, port wine and other incredible luxuries from the charity doctor (of which all could taste), but it brought in its train the assiduous attendance of Mrs. Simons. To see the kindly brown face bending over it with smiling eyes of jet, to feel the soft, cool hand pressed to its forehead, was worth a fever to a motherless infant. Mrs. Simons was a busy woman and a poor withal, and the Ansells were a reticent pack, not given to expressing either their love or their hunger to outsiders; so altogether the children did not see so much Mrs. Simons or her bounties as they would have liked. Nevertheless, in a grave crisis she was always to be counted upon.

"I tell thee what, Méshe," said old Mrs. Ansell often, "that woman wants to marry thee. A blind man could see it."

"She cannot want it, mother," Moses would reply with infinite respect.

"What art thou saying? A wholly fine young man like thee," said his mother, fondling his side ringlets, "and one so *froom* too, and with such worldly wisdom. But thou must not have her, Méshe."

"What kind of idea thou stuffiest into my head! I tell thee she would not have me if I sent to ask."

"Talk not thyself thereinto. Who wouldn't like to catch hold of thy cloak to go to heaven by? But Mrs. Simons is too much of an Englishwoman for me. Your last wife had English ideas and made mock of pious men and God's judgment took her. What says the Prayer-book? For three things a woman dies in childbirth, for not separating the dough, for not lighting the Sabbath lamps and for not –"

"How often have I told thee she did do all these things!" interrupted Moses.

"Dost thou contradict the Prayer-book?" said the *Bube* angrily. "It would have been different if thon hadst let me pick a woman for thee. But this time thou wilt honour thy mother more. It must be a respectable, virtuous maiden, with the fear of heaven – not an old woman like Mrs. Simons, but one who can bear me robust grandchildren. The grandchildren thou hast given me are sickly, and they fear not the Most High. Ah! why did'st thou drag me to this impious country? Could'st thou not let me die in peace? Thy girls think more of English story books and lessons than of *Yiddishkeit*, and the boys run out under the naked sky with bare heads and are loth to wash their hands before meals, and they do not come home in the dinner hour for fear they should have to say the afternoon prayer. Laugh at me, Moses, as thou wilt, but, old as I am, I have eyes, and not two blotches of clay, in my sockets. Thou seest not how thy family is going to destruction. Oh, the abominations!"

Thus warned and put on his mettle, Moses would keep a keen look-out on his hopeful family for the next day, and the seed which the grandmother had sown came up in black and blue bruises on the family anatomy, especially on that portion of it which belonged to Solomon. For Moses's crumbling trousers were buckled with a stout strap, and Solomon was a young rogue who did his best to dodge the Almighty, and had never heard of Lowell's warning,

> "You've gut to git up airly,
> Ef you want to take in God."

Even if he had heard of it, he would probably have retorted that he usually got up early enough to take in his father, who was the more immediately terrible of the two. Nevertheless, Solomon learned many lessons at his father's knee, or rather, across it. In earlier days Solomon had had a number of confidential transactions, with his father's God, making bargains with Him according to his childish sense of equity. If, for instance, God would ensure he did his sums correctly, so that he should be neither caned nor "kept in", he would say his morning prayers without skipping the aggravating *Longë Verachum*, which bulked so largely on Mondays and Thursdays; otherwise he could not be bothered.

By the terms of the contract Solomon threw all the initiative on the Deity, and whenever the Deity undertook his share of the contract, Solomon honourably fulfilled his. Thus was his faith in Providence never shaken like that of some boys, who expect the Deity to follow their lead. Still, by declining to praise his Maker at extraordinary length, except in acknowledgment of services rendered, Solomon gave early evidence of his failure to inherit his father's business incapacity.

On days when things at the school went well, no one gabbled through the weary Prayer-book more conscientiously than he; he said all the things in large type and all the funny little bits in small type, and even some passages without vowels. Nay, he included the very preface, and was lured on and coaxed on and enticed by his father to recite the appendices, which shot up one after the other on the devotional horizon like the endless seeming terraces of a deceptive ascent; just another little bit, and now that little bit, and just that last bit, and one more very last little bit. It was like the infinite inclusiveness of a Chinese sphere, or the farewell performances of a distinguished singer.

For the rest, Solomon was a *Chine-ponim*, or droll, having that inextinguishable sense of humour which has made the saints of the Jewish Church human, has lit up dry technical Talmudic discussions with flashes of freakish fun, with Pun and jest and merry quibble, and has helped the race to survive (*pace* Dr. Wallace) by dint of a humorous acquiescence in the inevitable.

His *Chine* helped Solomon to survive synagogue, where the only drop of sweetness was in the beaker of wine for the sanctification service. Solomon was always in the van of the brave boys who volunteered to take part in the ceremonial quaffing of it. Decidedly, Solomon was not spiritual, he would not even kiss a Hebrew Pentateuch that he had dropped, unless his father was looking, and but for the personal supervision of the *Bube* the dirty white fringes of his "four-corners" might have got tangled and irredeemably invalidated for all he cared.

In the direst need of the Ansells, Solomon held his curly head high among his school-fellows, and never lacked personal possessions, though they were not negotiable at the pawnbroker's. He had a peep-show, made out of an old cocoa box, and representing the sortie from Plevna, a permit to view being obtainable for a fragment of slate pencil. For two pins he would let you look a whole minute. He also had bags of brass buttons, marbles, both commoners and alleys; nibs, beer bottle labels and cherry "hogs," besides bottles of liquorice water, vendible either by the sip or the teaspoonful, and he dealt in "assy-tassy," which consisted of little packets of acetic acid blent with brown sugar. The character of his stock varied according to the time of year, for nature and Belgravia are less stable in their seasons than the Jewish schoolboy, to whom buttons in March are as inconceivable as snow-balling in July.

On Purim Solomon always had nuts to gamble with, just as if he had been a banker's son, and on the Day of Atonement he was never without a little tin fusee box filled with savings of snuff. This, when the fast racked them most sorely, he would pass round among the old men with a grand manner. They would take a pinch and say, "May thy strength increase," and blow their delighted noses with great coloured handerchiefs, and Solomon would feel about fifty and sniff a few grains himself with the air of an aged connoisseur.

He took little interest in the subtle disquisitions of the Rabbis, which added their burden to his cross of secular learning. He wrestled but perfunctorily with the theses of the Bible commentators, for Moses Ansell was so absorbed in translating and enjoying the intellectual tangles, that Solomon had scarce more to do than to play the part of chorus. He was fortunate in that his father could not afford to send him to a *Chedar*, an insanitary institution that made Jacob a dull boy by cutting off his play-time and his oxygen, and delivering him over to the leathery mercies of an unintelligently learned zealot, scrupulously unclean.

The literature and history Solomon really cared for was not of the Jews. It was the history of Daredevil Dick and his congeners whose surpassing adventures, second-hand, in ink-stained sheets, were bartered to him for buttons, which shows the advantages of not having a soul above such. These deeds of derring-do (usually starting in a *Sturm und Drang* schoolroom period in which teachers were thankfully accepted as created by Providence for the sport of schoolboys) Solomon conned at all hours, concealing them under his locker when he was supposed to be studying the Irish question from an atlas, and even hiding them between the leaves of his dog-eared Prayer-book for use during the morning service. The only harm they did him was that inflicted through the medium of the educational rod, when his surreptitious readings were discovered and his treasures thrown to the flames amid tears copious enough to extinguish them.

CHAPTER VI

"Reb" Shemuel

"The Torah is greater than the priesthood and than royalty, seeing that royalty demands thirty qualifications, the priesthood twenty-four, while the Torah is acquired by forty-eight. And these are they: By audible study; by distinct pronunciation; by understanding and discernment of the heart; by awe, reverence, meekness, cheerfulness; by ministering to the sages; by attaching oneself to colleagues; by discussion with disciples; by sedateness; by knowledge of the Scripture and of the Mishnah; by moderation in business, in intercourse with the world, in pleasure, in sleep, in conversation, in laughter; by long suffering; by a good heart; by faith in the wise; by resignation under chastisement; by recognizing one's place, rejoicing in one's portion, putting a fence to one's words, claiming no merit for oneself; by being beloved, loving the All-present, loving mankind, loving just courses, rectitude and reproof, by keeping oneself far from honours, not boasting of one's learning, nor delighting in giving decisions; by bearing the yoke with one's fellow, judging him favourably and leading him to truth and peace; by being composed in one's study; by asking and answering, hearing and adding thereto (by one's own reflection); by learning with the object of teaching and learning with the object of practising, by making one's master wiser, fixing attention upon his discourse, and reporting a thing in the name of him who said it. So thou hast learnt. Whosoever reports a thing in the name of him that said it brings deliverance into the world, as it is said – And Esther told the King in the name of Mordecai." – (*Ethics of the Fathers*, Singer's translation.)

Moses Ansell only occasionally worshipped at the synagogue of "The Sons of the Covenant," for it was too near to make attendance a *Mitzvah*, pleasing in the sight of Heaven. It was like having the prayer-quorum brought to you, instead of your going to it. The pious Jew must speed to *Shool* to show his eagerness and return slowly, as with reluctant feet, lest Satan draw the attention of the Holy One to the laches of His chosen people. It was not easy to express these varying emotions on a few flights of stairs, and so Moses went farther afield. In subtle minutiæ like this Moses was *facile princeps*, being as Wellhausen puts it of the *virtuosi* of religion. If he put on his right stocking (or rather foot lappet, for he did not wear stockings) first, he made amends by putting on the left boot first, and if he had lace-up boots, then the boot put on second would have a compensatory precedence in the lacing. Thus was the divine principle of justice symbolized even in these small matters.

Moses was a great man in several of the more distant *Chevras*, among which he distributed the privilege of his presence. It was only when by accident the times of service did not coincide, that Moses favoured the "Sons of the Covenant," putting in an appearance either at the commencement or the fag end, for he was not above praying odd bits of the service twice over, and even sometimes prefaced or supplemented his synagogal performances by solo renditions of the entire ritual of a hundred pages at home. The morning services began at six in summer and seven in winter, so that the workingman might start his long day's work fortified.

At the close of the service at the Beth Hamidrash a few mornings after the Redemption of Ezekiel, Solomon went up to Reb Shemuel, who in return for the privilege of blessing the boy gave him a halfpenny. Solomon passed it on to his father, whom he accompanied.

"Well, how goes it, Reb Méshe?" said Reb Shemuel with his cheery smile, noticing Moses loitering. He called him "Reb" out of courtesy and in acknowledgment of his piety. The real "Reb" was a fine figure of a man, with matter, if not piety, enough for two Moses Ansells. Reb was a popular corruption of "Rav" or Rabbi.

"Bad," replied Moses. "I haven't had any machining to do for a month. Work is very slack at this time of year. But God is good."

"Can't you sell something?" said Reb Shemuel, thoughtfully caressing his long, grey-streaked black beard.

"I have sold lemons, but the four or five shillings I made went in bread for the children and in rent. Money runs through the fingers somehow, with a family of five and a frosty winter. When the lemons were gone I stood where I started."

The Rabbi sighed sympathetically and slipped half-a-crown into Moses's palm. Then he hurried out. His boy, Levi, stayed behind a moment to finish a transaction involving the barter of a pea-shooter for some of Solomon's buttons. Levi was two years older than Solomon, and was further removed from him by going to a "middle class school." His manner towards Solomon was of a corresponding condescension. But it took a great deal to overawe Solomon, who, with the rational humour, possessed the national *Chutzpah*, which is variously translated enterprise, audacity, brazen impudence and cheek.

"I say, Levi," he said, "we've got no school today. Won't you come round this morning and play I-spy-I in our street? There are some splendid corners for hiding, and they are putting up new buildings all round with lovely hoardings, and they're knocking down a pickle warehouse, and while you are hiding in the rubbish you sometimes pick up scrumptious bits of pickled walnut. Oh, golly, ain't they prime!"

Levi turned up his nose.

"We've got plenty of whole walnuts at home," he said.

Solomon felt snubbed. He became aware that this tall boy had smart black clothes, which would not be improved by rubbing against his own greasy corduroys.

"Oh, well," he said, "I can get lots of boys, and girls, too."

"Say," said Levi, turning back a little. "That little girl your father brought upstairs here on the Rejoicing of the Law, that was your sister, wasn't it?"

"Esther, d'ye mean?"

"How should I know? A little, dark girl, with a print dress, rather pretty – not a bit like you."

"Yes, that's our Esther – she's in the sixth standard and only eleven."

"We don't have standards in our school!" said Levi contemptuously. "Will your sister join in the I-spy-I?"

"No, she can't run," replied Solomon, half apologetically. "She only likes to read. She reads all my 'Boys of England' and things, and now she's got hold of a little brown book she keeps all to herself. I like reading, too, but I do it in school or in *Shool*, where there's nothing better to do."

"Has she got a holiday today, too?"

"Yes," said Solomon.

"But my school's open," said Levi enviously, and Solomon lost the feeling of inferiority, and felt avenged.

"Come, then, Solomon," said his father, who had reached the door. The two converted part of the half-crown into French loaves and carried them home to form an unexpected breakfast.

Meantime Reb Shemuel, whose full name was the Reverend Samuel Jacobs, also proceeded to breakfast. His house lay near the *Shool*, and was approached by an avenue of mendicants. He arrived in his shirt-sleeves.

"Quick, Simcha, give me my new coat. It is very cold this morning."

"You've given away your coat again!" shrieked his wife, who, though her name meant "Rejoicing," was more often upbraiding.

"Yes, it was only an old one, Simcha," said the Rabbi deprecatingly. He took off his high hat and replaced it by a little black cap which he carried in his tail pocket.

"You'll ruin me, Shemuel," moaned Simcha, wringing her hands. "You'd give away the shirt off your skin to a pack of good-for-nothing *Schnorrers*."

"Yes, if they had only their skin in the world. Why not?" said the old Rabbi, a pacific gleam in his large gazelle-like eyes. "Perhaps my coat may have the honour to cover Elijah the prophet."

"Elijah the prophet!" snorted Simcha. "Elijah has sense enough to stay in heaven and not go wandering about shivering in the fog and frost of this God-accursed country."

The old Rabbi answered, "Atschew!"

"For thy salvation do I hope, O Lord," murmured Simcha piously in Hebrew, adding excitedly in English, "Ah, you'll kill yourself, Shemuel." She rushed upstairs and returned with another coat and a new terror.

"Here, you fool, you've been and done a fine thing this time! All your silver was in the coat you've given away!"

"Was it?" said Reb Shemuel, startled. Then the tranquil look returned to his brown eyes. "No, I took it all out before I gave away the coat."

"God be thanked!" said Simcha fervently in Yiddish. "Where is it? I want a few shillings for grocery."

"I gave it away before, I tell you!"

Simcha groaned and fell into her chair with a crash that rattled the tray and shook the cups.

"Here's the end of the week coming," she sobbed, "and I shall have no fish for *Shabbos*."

"Do not blaspheme!" said Reb Shemuel, tugging a little angrily at his venerable beard. "The Holy One, blessed be He, will provide for our *Shabbos*."

Simcha made a sceptical mouth, knowing that it was she and nobody else whose economies would provide for the due celebration of the Sabbath. Only by a constant course of vigilance, mendacity and petty peculation at her husband's expense could she manage to support the family of four comfortably on his pretty considerable salary. Reb Shemuel went and kissed her on the sceptical mouth, because in another instant she would have him at her mercy. He washed his hands and durst not speak between that and the first bite.

He was an official of heterogeneous duties – he preached and taught and lectured. He married people and divorced them. He released bachelors from the duty of marrying their deceased brothers' wives. He superintended a slaughtering department, licensed men as competent killers, examined the sharpness of their knives that the victims might be put to as little pain as possible, and inspected dead cattle in the shambles, to see if they were perfectly sound and free from pulmonary disease. But his greatest function was *paskening*, or answering inquiries ranging from the simplest to the most complicated problems of ceremonial ethics and civil law. He had added a volume of *Shaaloth-u-Tshuvoth*, or "Questions and Answers" to the colossal casuistic literature of his race. His aid was also invoked as a *Shadchan*, though he forgot to take his commissions and lacked the restless zeal for the mating of mankind which animated Sugarman, the professional match-maker. In fine, he was a witty old fellow and everybody loved him. He and his wife spoke English with a strong foreign accent; in their more intimate causeries they dropped into Yiddish.

The Rebbitzin poured out the Rabbi's coffee and whitened it with milk drawn direct from the cow into her own jug. The butter and cheese were equally kosher, coming straight from Hebrew Hollanders and having passed through none but Jewish vessels. As the Reb sat himself down at the head of the table Hannah entered the room.

"Good morning, father," she said, kissing him. "What have you got your new coat on for? Any weddings today?"

"No, my dear," said Reb Shemuel, "marriages are falling off. There hasn't even been an engagement since Belcovitch's eldest daughter betrothed herself to Pesach Weingott."

"Oh, these Jewish young men!" said the Rebbitzin. "Look at my Hannah – as pretty a girl as you could meet in the whole Lane – and yet here she is wasting her youth."

Hannah bit her lip, instead of her bread and butter, for she felt she had brought the talk on herself. She had heard the same grumblings from her mother for two years. Mrs. Jacobs's maternal anxiety had begun when her daughter was seventeen. "When *I* was seventeen," she went on, "I was a married woman. Now-a-days the girls don't begin to get a *Chosan* till they're twenty."

"We are not living in Poland," the Reb reminded her.

"What's that to do with it? It's the Jewish young men who want to marry gold."

"Why blame them? A Jewish young man can marry several pieces of gold, but since Rabbenu Gershom he can only marry one woman," said the Reb, laughing feebly and forcing his humour for his daughter's sake.

"One woman is more than thou canst support," said the Rebbitzin, irritated into Yiddish, "giving away the flesh from off thy children's bones. If thou hadst been a proper father thou wouldst have saved thy money for Hannah's dowry, instead of wasting it on a parcel of vagabond *Schnorrers*. Even so I can give her a good stock of bedding and under-linen. It's a reproach and a shame that thou hast not yet found her a husband. Thou canst find husbands quick enough for other men's daughters!"

"I found a husband for thy father's daughter," said the Reb, with a roguish gleam in his brown eyes.

"Don't throw that up to me! I could have got plenty better. And my daughter wouldn't have known the shame of finding nobody to marry her. In Poland at least the youths would have flocked to marry her because she was a Rabbi's daughter, and they'd think it an honour to be a son-in-law of a Son of the Law. But in this godless country! Why in my village the Chief Rabbi's daughter, who was so ugly as to make one spit out, carried off the finest man in the district."

"But thou, my Simcha, hadst no need to be connected with Rabbonim!"

"Oh, yes; make mockery of me."

"I mean it. Thou art as a lily of Sharon."

"Wilt thou have another cup of coffee, Shemuel?"

"Yes, my life. Wait but a little and thou shalt see our Hannah under the *Chuppah*."

"Hast thou any one in thine eye?"

The Reb nodded his head mysteriously and winked the eye, as if nudging the person in it.

"Who is it, father?" said Levi. "I do hope it's a real swell who talks English properly."

"And mind you make yourself agreeable to him, Hannah," said the Rebbitzin. "You spoil all the matches I've tried to make for you by your stupid, stiff manner."

"Look here, mother!" cried Hannah, pushing aside her cup violently. "Am I going to have my breakfast in peace? I don't want to be married at all. I don't want any of your Jewish men coming round to examine me as if I were a horse, and wanting to know how much money you'll give them as a set-off. Let me be! Let me be single! It's my business, not yours."

The Rebbitzin bent eyes of angry reproach on the Reb.

"What did I tell thee, Shemuel? She's *meshugga* – quite mad! Healthy and fresh and mad!"

"Yes, you'll drive me mad," said Hannah savagely. "Let me be! I'm too old now to get a *Chosan*, so let me be as I am. I can always earn my own living."

"Thou seest, Shemuel?" said Simcha. "Thou seest my sorrows? Thou seest how impious our children wax in this godless country."

"Let her be, Simcha, let her be," said the Reb. "She is young yet. If she hasn't any inclination thereto –!"

"And what is *her* inclination? A pretty thing, forsooth! Is she going to make her mother a laughing-stock! Are Mrs. Jewell and Mrs. Abrahams to dandle grandchildren in my face, to gouge out my eyes with them! It isn't that she can't get young men. Only she is so high-blown. One would think she had a father who earned five hundred a year, instead of a man who scrambles half his salary among dirty *Schnorrers*."

"Talk not like an *Epicurean*," said the Reb. "What are we all but *Schnorrers*, dependent on the charity of the Holy One, blessed be He? What! Have we made ourselves? Rather fall prostrate and thank Him that His bounties to us are so great that they include the privilege of giving charity to others."

"But we work for our living!" said the Rebbitzin. "I wear my knees away scrubbing." External evidence pointed rather to the defrication of the nose.

"But, mother," said Hannah. "You know we have a servant to do the rough work."

"Yes, servants!" said the Rebbitzin, contemptuously. "If you don't stand over them as the Egyptian taskmasters over our forefathers, they don't do a stroke of work except breaking the crockery. I'd much rather sweep a room myself than see a *Shiksah* pottering about for an hour and end by leaving all the dust on the window-ledges and the corners of the mantelpiece. As for beds, I don't believe *Shiksahs* ever shake them! If I had my way I'd wring all their necks."

"What's the use of always complaining?" said Hannah, impatiently. "You know we must keep a *Shiksah* to attend to the *Shabbos* fire. The women or the little boys you pick up in the street are so unsatisfactory. When you call in a little barefoot street Arab and ask him to poke the fire, he looks at you as if you must be an imbecile not to be able to do it yourself. And then you can't always get hold of one."

The Sabbath fire was one of the great difficulties of the Ghetto. The Rabbis had modified the Biblical prohibition against having any fire whatever, and allowed it to be kindled by non-Jews. Poor women, frequently Irish, and known as *Shabbos-goyahs* or *fire-goyahs*, acted as stokers to the Ghetto at twopence a hearth. No Jew ever touched a match or a candle or burnt a piece of paper, or even opened a letter. The *Goyah*, which is literally heathen female, did everything required on the Sabbath. His grandmother once called Solomon Ansell a Sabbath-female merely for fingering the shovel when there was nothing in the grate.

The Reb liked his fire. When it sank on the Sabbath he could not give orders to the *Shiksah* to replenish it, but he would rub his hands and remark casually (in her hearing), "Ah, how cold it is!"

"Yes," he said now, "I always freeze on *Shabbos* when thou hast dismissed thy *Shiksah*. Thou makest me catch one cold a month."

"*I* make thee catch cold!" said the Rebbitzin. "When thou comest through the air of winter in thy shirt-sleeves! Thou'lt fall back upon me for poultices and mustard plasters. And then thou expectest me to have enough money to pay a *Shiksah* into the bargain! If I have any more of thy *Schnorrers* coming here I shall bundle them out neck and crop."

This was the moment selected by Fate and Melchitsedek Pinchas for the latter's entry.

CHAPTER VII

The Neo-Hebrew Poet

He came through the open street door, knocked perfunctorily at the door of the room, opened it and then kissed the *Mezuzah* outside the door. Then he advanced, snatched the Rebbitzin's hand away from the handle of the coffee-pot and kissed it with equal devotion. He then seized upon Hannah's hand and pressed his grimy lips to that, murmuring in German: "Thou lookest so charming this morning, like the roses of Carmel." Next he bent down and pressed his lips to the Reb's coat-tail. Finally he said, "Good morning, sir," to Levi, who replied very affably, "Good morning, Mr. Pinchas."

"Peace be unto you, Pinchas," said the Reb. "I did not see you in *Shool* this morning, though it was the New Moon."

"No, I went to the Great *Shool*," said Pinchas in German. "If you do not see me at your place you may be sure I'm somewhere else. Any one who has lived so long as I in the Land of Israel cannot bear to pray without a quorum. In the Holy Land I used to learn for an hour in the *Shool* every morning before the service began. But I am not here to talk about myself. I come to ask you to do me the honour to accept a copy of my new volume of poems: *Metatoron's Flames*. Is it not a beautiful title? When Enoch was taken up to heaven while yet alive, he was converted to flames of fire and became Metatoron, the great spirit of the Cabalah. So am I rapt up into the heaven of lyrical poetry and I become all fire and flame and light."

The poet was a slim, dark little man, with long, matted black hair. His face was hatchet-shaped and not unlike an Aztec's. The eyes were informed by an eager brilliance. He had a heap of little paper-covered books in one hand and an extinct cigar in the other. He placed the books upon the breakfast table.

"At last," he said. "See, I have got it printed – the great work which this ignorant English Judaism has left to moulder while it pays its stupid reverends thousands a year for wearing white ties."

"And who paid for it now, Mr. Pinchas?" said the Rebbitzin.

"Who? Wh-o-o?" stammered Melchitsedek. "Who but myself?"

"But you say you are blood-poor."

"True as the Law of Moses! But I have written articles for the jargon papers. They jump at me – there is not a man on the staff of them all who has the pen of a ready writer. I can't get any money out of them, my dear Rebbitzin, else I shouldn't be without breakfast this morning, but the proprietor of the largest of them is also a printer, and he has printed my little book in return. But I don't think I shall fill my stomach with the sales. Oh! the Holy One, blessed be He, bless you, Rebbitzin, of course I'll take a cup of coffee; I don't know any one else who makes coffee with such a sweet savour; it would do for a spice offering when the Almighty restores us our Temple. You are a happy mortal, Rabbi. You will permit that I seat myself at the table?"

Without awaiting permission he pushed a chair between Levi and Hannah and sat down; then he got up again and washed his hands and helped himself to a spare egg.

"Here is your copy, Reb Shemuel," he went on after an interval. "You see it is dedicated generally: 'To the Pillars of English Judaism.' "They are a set of donkey-heads, but one must give them a chance of rising to higher things. It is true that not one of them understands Hebrew, not even the Chief Rabbi, to whom courtesy made me send a copy. Perhaps he will be able to read my poems with a dictionary; he certainly can't write Hebrew without two grammatical blunders to every word. No, no, don't defend him, Reb Shemuel, because you're under him. He ought to be under you – only he expresses his ignorance in English and the fools think to talk nonsense in good English is to be qualified for the Rabbinate."

The remark touched the Rabbi in a tender place. It was the one worry of his life, the consciousness that persons in high quarters disapproved of him as a force impeding the Anglicization of the Ghetto. He knew his shortcomings, but could never quite comprehend the importance of becoming English. He had a latent feeling that Judaism had flourished before England was invented, and so the poet's remark was secretly pleasing to him.

"You know very well," went on Pinchas, "that I and you are the only two persons in London who can write correct Holy Language."

"No, no," said the Rabbi, deprecatingly.

"Yes, yes," said Pinchas, emphatically. "You can write quite as well as I. But just cast your eye now on the especial dedication which I have written to you in my own autograph. 'To the light of his generation, the great Gaon, whose excellency reaches to the ends of the earth, from whose lips all the people of the Lord seek knowledge, the never-failing well, the mighty eagle soars to heaven on the wings of understanding, to Rav Shemuel, may whose light never be dimmed, and in whose day may the Redeemer come unto Zion.' There, take it, honour me by taking it. It is the homage of the man of genius to the man of learning, the humble offering of the one Hebrew scholar in England to the other."

"Thank you," said the old Rabbi, much moved. "It is too handsome of you, and I shall read it at once and treasure it amongst my dearest books, for you know well that I consider that you have the truest poetic gift of any son of Israel since Jehuda Halevi."

"I have! I know it! I feel it! It burns me. The sorrow of our race keeps me awake at night – the national hopes tingle like electricity through me – I bedew my couch with tears in the darkness" – Pinchas paused to take another slice of bread and butter. "It is then that my poems are born. The words burst into music in my head and I sing like Isaiah the restoration of our land, and become the poet patriot of my people. But these English! They care only to make money and to stuff it down the throats of gorging reverends. My scholarship, my poetry, my divine dreams – what are these to a besotted, brutal congregation of Men-of-the-Earth? I sent Buckledorf, the rich banker, a copy of my little book, with a special dedication written in my own autograph in German, so that he might understand it. And what did he send me? A beggarly five shillings? Five shillings to the one poet in whom the heavenly fire lives! How can the heavenly fire live on five shillings? I had almost a mind to send it back. And then there was Gideon, the member of Parliament. I made one of the poems an acrostic on his name, so that he might be handed down to posterity. There, that's the one. No, the one on the paw you were just looking at. Yes, that's it, beginning:

> 'Great leader of our Israel's host,
> I sing thy high heroic deeds,
> Divinely gifted learned man.'

"I wrote his dedication in English, for he understands neither Hebrew nor German, the miserable, purse-proud, vanity-eaten Man-of-the-Earth."

"Why, didn't he give you anything at all? " said the Reb.

"Worse! He sent me back the book. But I'll be revenged on him. I'll take the acrostic out of the next edition and let him rot in oblivion. I have been all over the world to every great city where Jews congregate. In Russia, in Turkey, in Germany, in Romania, in Greece, in Morocco, in Palestine. Everywhere the greatest Rabbis have leaped like harts on the mountains with joy at my coming. They have fed and clothed me like a prince. I have preached at the synagogues, and everywhere people have said it was like the Wilna Gaon come again. From the neighbouring villages for miles and miles the pious have come to be blessed by me. Look at my testimonials from all the greatest saints and savants. But in England – in England alone – what is my welcome? Do they say: 'Welcome, Melchitsedek Pinchas, welcome as the bridegroom to the bride when the long day is done and the feast is o'er; welcome to you, with the torch of your genius, with the burden of your learning that is rich with the whole wealth of Hebrew literature in all ages and countries.

Here we have no great and wise men. Our Chief Rabbi is an idiot. Come thou and be our Chief Rabbi?' Do they say this? No! They greet me with scorn, coldness, slander. As for the Rev. Elkan Benjamin, who makes such a fuss of himself because he sends a wealthy congregation to sleep with his sermons, I'll expose him as sure as there's a Guardian of Israel. I'll let the world know about his four mistresses."

"Nonsense! Guard yourself against the evil tongue," said the Reb. "How do you know he has?"

"It's the Law of Moses," said the little poet. "True as I stand here. You ask Jacob Hermann. It was he who told me about it. Jacob Hermann said to me one day: 'That Benjamin has a mistress for every fringe of his four-corners.' And how many is that, eh? I do not know why he should be allowed to slander me and I not be allowed to tell the truth about him. One day I will shoot him. You know he said that when I first came to London I joined the *Meshumadim* in Palestine Place."

"Well, he had at least some foundation for that," said.Reb Shemuel.

"Foundation! Do you call that foundation – because I lived there for a week, hunting out their customs and their ways of ensnaring the souls of our brethren, so that I might write about them one day? Have I not already told you not a morsel of their food passed my lips and that the money which I had to take so as not to excite suspicion I distributed in charity among the poor Jews? Why not? From pigs we take bristles."

"Still, you must remember that if you had not been such a saint and such a great poet, I might myself have believed that you sold your soul for money to escape starvation. I know how these devils set their baits for the helpless immigrant, offering bread in return for a lip-conversion. They are grown so cunning now – they print their hellish appeals in Hebrew, knowing we reverence the Holy Tongue."

"Yes, the ordinary Man-of-the-Earth believes everything that's in Hebrew. That was the mistake of the Apostles – to write in Greek. But then they, too, were such Men-of-the Earth."

"I wonder who writes such good Hebrew for the missionaries," said Reb Shemuel.

"I wonder," gurgled Pinchas, deep in his coffee.

"But, father," asked Hannah, "don't you believe any Jew ever really believes in Christianity?"

"How is it possible?" answered Reb Shemuel. "A Jew who has the Law from Sinai, the Law that will never be changed, to whom God has given a sensible religion and common-sense, how can such a person believe in the farrago of nonsense that makes up the worship of the Christians! No Jew has ever apostatized except to fill his purse or his stomach or to avoid persecution. 'Getting grace' they call it in English; but with poor Jews it is always grace after meals. Look at the Crypto-Jews, the Marranos, who for centuries lived a double life, outwardly Christians, but handing down secretly from generation to generation the faith, the traditions, the observances of Judaism."

"Yes, no Jew was ever fool enough to turn Christian unless he was a clever man," said the poet paradoxically. "Have you not, my sweet, innocent young lady, heard the story of the two Jews in Burgos Cathedral?"

"No, what is it?" said Levi, eagerly.

"Well, pass my cup up to your highly superior mother who is waiting to fill it with coffee. Your eminent father knows the story – I can see by the twinkle in his learned eye."

"Yes, that story has a beard," said the Reb.

"Two Spanish Jews," said the poet, addressing himself deferentially to Levi, "who had got grace were waiting to be baptized at Burgos Cathedral. There was a great throng of Catholics and a special Cardinal was coming to conduct the ceremony, for their conversion was a great triumph. But the Cardinal was late and the Jews fumed and fretted at the delay. The shadows of evening were falling on vault and transept. At last one turned to the other and said, 'Knowest thou what, Moses? If the Holy Father does not arrive soon, we shall be too late to say *mincha*.'"

Levi laughed heartily; the reference to the Jewish afternoon prayer went home to him.

"That story sums up in a nutshell the whole history of the great movement for the conversion of the Jews. We dip ourselves in baptismal water and wipe ourselves with a *Talith*. We are not a race to be lured out of the fixed feelings of countless centuries by the empty spirituality of a religion in which, as I soon found out when I lived among the soul-dealers, its very professors no longer believe. We are too fond of solid things," said the poet, upon whom a good breakfast was beginning to produce a soothing materialistic effect. "Do you know that anecdote about the two Jews in the Transvaal?" Pinchas went on. "That's a real *Chine*."

"I don't think I know that *Maaseh*," said Reb Shemuel.

"Oh, the two Jews had made a *trek* and were travelling onwards exploring unknown country. One night they were sitting by their campfire playing cards when suddenly one threw up his cards, tore his hair and beat his breast in terrible agony. 'What's the matter?' cried the other. 'Woe, woe,' said the first. 'Today was the Day of Atonement! and we have eaten and gone on as usual.' 'Oh, don't take on so,' said his friend. After all, Heaven will take into consideration that we lost count of the Jewish calendar and didn't mean to be so wicked. And we can make up for it by fasting tomorrow.'

"'Oh, no! Not for me,' said the first. 'Today was the Day of Atonement.'"

All laughed, the Reb appreciating most keenly the sly dig at his race. He had a kindly sense of human frailty. Jews are very fond of telling stories against themselves – for their sense of humour is too strong not to be aware of their own foibles – but they tell them with closed doors, and resent them from the outside. They chastise themselves because they love themselves, as members of the same family insult one another. The secret is, that insiders understand the limitations of the criticism, which outsiders are apt to take in bulk. No race in the world possesses a richer anecdotal lore than the Jews – such pawky, even blasphemous humour, not understandable of the heathen, and to a suspicious mind Pinchas's overflowing cornucopia of such would have suggested a prior period of Continental wandering from town to town, like the *Minnesingers* of the middle ages, repaying the hospitality of his Jewish entertainers with a budget of good stories and gossip from the scenes of his pilgrimages.

"Do you know the story?" he went on, encouraged by Simcha's smiling face, "of the old Reb and the *Havdolah?* His wife left town for a few days and when she returned the Reb took out a bottle of wine, poured some into the consecration cup and began to recite the blessing. 'What art thou doing?' demanded his wife in amaze. 'I am making *Havdolah,*' replied the Reb. 'But it is not the conclusion of a festival tonight,' she said. 'Oh, yes, it is,' he answered. 'My Festival's over. You've come back.'"

The Reb laughed so much over this story that Simch's brow grew as the solid Egyptian darkness, and Pinchas perceived he had made a mistake.

"But listen to the end," he said with a creditable impromptu. "The wife said, 'No, you're mistaken. Your Festival's only beginning. You get no supper. It's the commencement of the Day of Atonement.'"

Simcha's brow cleared and the Reb laughed heartily.

"But I don't see the point, father," said Levi.

"Point! Listen, my son. First of all he was to have a Day of Atonement, beginning with no supper, for his sin of rudeness to his faithful wife. Secondly, dost thou not know that with us the Day of Atonement is called a festival, because we rejoice at the Creator's goodness in giving us the privilege of fasting? That's it, Pinchas, isn't it?"

"Yes, that's the point of the story, and I think the Rebbitzin had the best of it, eh?"

"Rebbitzins always have the last word," said the Reb. "But did I tell you the story of the woman who asked me a question the other day? She brought me a fowl in the morning and said that in cutting open the gizzard she had found a rusty pin which the fowl must have swallowed. She wanted to know whether the fowl might be eaten. It was a very difficult point, for how could you tell whether the pin had in any way contributed to the fowl's death? I searched the *Shass* and a heap of *Shaalothu-Tshuvos.* I went and consulted the *Maggid* and Sugarman the *Shadchan* and Mr. Karlkammer, and at last we decided that the fowl was *trifa* and could not be eaten. So the same evening I sent for the woman, and when I told her of our decision she burst into tears and wrung her hands. 'Do not grieve so,' I said, taking compassion upon her, 'I will buy thee another fowl.' But she wept on, uncomforted. 'O woe! woe!' she cried. 'We ate it all up yesterday.'"

Pinchas was convulsed with laughter. Recovering himself, he lit his half-smoked cigar without asking leave.

"I thought it would turn out differently," he said. "Like that story of the peacock. A man had one presented to him, and as this is such rare diet he went to the Reb to ask if it was *kosher*. The Rabbi said 'no' and confiscated the peacock. Later on the man heard that the Rabbi had given a banquet at which his peacock was the crowning dish. He went to his Rabbi and reproached him. "*I* may eat it," replied the Rabbi, "because my father considers it permitted and we may always go by what some eminent Son of the Law decides. But you unfortunately came to *me* for an opinion, and the permissibility of peacock is a point on which I have always disagreed with my father.'"

Hannah seemed to find peculiar enjoyment in the story.

"Anyhow," concluded Pinchas, "you have a more pious flock than the Rabbi of my native place, who, one day, announced to his congregation that he was going to resign. Startled, they sent to him a delegate, who asked, in the name of the congregation, why he was leaving them. 'Because,' answered the Rabbi, this is the first question any one has ever asked me!'"

"Tell Mr. Pinchas your repartee about the donkey," said Hannah, smiling.

"Oh, no, it's not worthwhile," said the Reb.

"Thou art always so backward with thine own," cried the Rebbitzin warmly. "Last Purim an impudent of face sent my husband a donkey made of sugar. My husband had a Rabbi baked in gingerbread and sent it in exchange to the donor, with the inscription 'A Rabbi sends a Rabbi.'"

Reb Shemuel laughed heartily, hearing this afresh at the lips of his wife. But Pinchas was bent double like a convulsive note of interrogation.

The clock on the mantelshelf began to strike nine. Levi jumped to his feet.

"I shall be late for school!" he cried, making for the door.

"Stop! stop!" shouted his father. "Thou hast not yet said grace."

"Oh, yes, I have, father. While you were all telling stories I was *benshing* quietly to myself."

"Is Saul also among the prophets, is Levi also among the story-tellers?" murmured Pinchas to himself. Aloud he said: "The child speaks truth; I saw his lips moving."

Levi gave the poet a grateful look, snatched up his satchel and ran off to No. 1 Royal Street. Pinchas followed him soon, inwardly upbraiding Reb Shemuel for meanness. He had only as yet had his breakfast for his book. Perhaps it was Simcha's presence that was to blame. She was the Reb's right hand and he did not care to let her know what his left was doing.

He retired to his study when Pinchas departed, and the Rebbitzin clattered about with a besom.

The study was a large square room lined with book-shelves and hung with portraits of the great continental Rabbis. The books were biblio-graphical monsters to which the Family Bibles of the Christian are mere pocket-books. They.were all printed purely with the consonants, the vowels being divined grammatically or known by heart. In each there was an island of text in a sea of commentary, itself lost in an ocean of super-commentary that was bordered by a continent of super-super-commentary. Reb Shemuel knew many of these immense folios – with all their tortuous windings of argument and anecdote – much as the child knows the village it was born in, the crooked by-ways and the field paths. Such and such a Rabbi gave such and such an opinion on such and such a line from the bottom of such and such a page – his memory of it was a visual picture. And just as the child does not connect its native village with the broader world without, does not trace its streets and turnings till they lead to the great towns, does not inquire as to its origins and its history, does not view it in relation to other villages, to the country, to the continent, to the world, but loves it for itself and in itself, so Reb Shemuel regarded and reverenced and loved these gigantic pages with their serried battalions of varied type. They were facts – absolute as the globe itself – regions of wisdom, perfect and self-sufficing. A little obscure here and there, perhaps, and in need of amplification or explication for inferior intellects – a half-finished manuscript commentary on one of the super-commentaries, to be called "The Garden of Lilies," was lying open on Reb Shemuel's own desk – but yet the only true encyclopædia of things terrestrial and divine. And, indeed, they were wonderful books. It was as difficult to say what was not in them as what was. Through them the old Rabbi held communion with his God whom he loved with all his heart and soul and thought of as a genial Father, watching tenderly over His froward children and chastising them because He loved them. Generations of saints and scholars linked Reb Shemuel with the marvels of Sinai. The infinite network of ceremonial never hampered his soul; it was his joyous privilege to obey his Father in all things and like the king who offered to reward the man who invented a new pleasure, he was ready to embrace the sage who could deduce a new commandment. He rose at four every morning to study, and snatched every odd moment he could during the day. Rabbi Meir, that ancient ethical teacher, wrote: "Whosoever labours in the Torah for its own sake, the whole world is indebted to him; he is called friend, beloved, a lover of the All-present, a lover of mankind; it clothes him in meekness and reverence; it fits him to become just, pious, upright and faithful; he becomes modest, long-suffering and forgiving of insult."

Reb Shemuel would have been scandalized if any one had applied these words to him.

At about eleven o'clock Hannah came into the room, an open letter in her hand.

"Father," she said, " I have just had a letter from Samuel Levine."

"Your husband?" he said, looking up with a smile.

"My husband," she replied, with a fainter smile.

"And what does he say?"

"It isn't a very serious letter; he only wants to reassure me that he is coming back by Sunday week to be divorced."

"All right; tell him it shall be done at cost price," he said, with the foreign accent that made him somehow seem more lovable to his daughter when he spoke English. "He shall only be charged for the scribe."

"He'll take that for granted," Hannah replied. "Fathers are expected to do these little things for their own children. But how much nicer it would be if you could give me the *Gett* yourself."

"I would marry you with pleasure," said Reb Shemuel, "but divorce is another matter. The Din has too much regard for a father's feelings to allow that."

"And you really think I am Sam Levine's wife?"

"How many times shall I tell you? Some authorities do take the *intention* into account, but the letter of the law is clearly against you. It is far safer to be formally divorced."

"Then if he were to die –"

"Save us and grant us peace," interrupted the Reb in horror.

"I should be his widow."

"Yes, I suppose you would. But what *Narrischkeit*! Why should he die? It isn't as if you were really married to him," said the Reb, his eye twinkling.

"But isn't it all absurd, father?"

"Do not talk so," said Reb Shemuel, resuming his gravity."Is it absurd that you should be scorched if you play with fire?"

Hannah did not reply to the question.

"You never told me how you got on at Manchester," she said. "Did you settle the dispute satisfactorily?"

"Oh, yes," said the Reb; "but it was very difficult. Both parties were so envenomed, and it seems that the feud has been going on in the congregation ever since the Day of Atonement, when the minister refused to blow the *Shofar* three minutes too early, as the President requested. The

Treasurer sided with the minister, and there has almost been a split."

"The sounding of the New Year trumpet seems often to be the signal for war," said Hannah, sarcastically.

"It is so," said the Reb, sadly.

"And how did you repair the breach?"

"Just by laughing at both sides. They would have turned a deaf ear to reasoning. I told them that Midrash about Jacob's journey to Laban."

"What is that?"

"Oh, it's an amplification of the Biblical narrative. The verse in Genesis says that he lighted on the place, and he put up there for the night because the sun had set, and he took of the stones of the place and he made them into pillows. But later on it says that he rose up in the morning and he took *the* stone which he had put as his pillows. Now what is the explanation?" Reb Shemuel's tone became momently more sing-song: "In the night the stones quarrelled for the honour of supporting the Patriarch's head, and so by a miracle they were turned into one stone to satisfy them all. Now you remember that when Jacob arose in the morning he said: 'How fearful is this place; this is none other than the House of God.' So I said to the wranglers: 'Why did Jacob say that? He said it because his rest had been so disturbed by the quarrelling stones that it reminded him of the House of God – the Synagogue.' I pointed out how much better it would be if they ceased their quarrellings and became one stone. And so I made peace again in the *Kehillah*."

"Till next year," said Hannah, laughing. "But, father, I have often wondered why they allow the ram's horn in the service. I thought all musical instruments were forbidden."

"It is not a musical instrument – in practice," said the Reb, with evasive facetiousness. And, indeed, the performers were nearly always incompetent, marring the solemnity of great moments by asthmatic wheezings and thin far-away tootlings.

"But it would be if we had trained trumpeters," persisted Hannah, smiling.

"If you really want the explanation, it is that since the fall of the second Temple we have dropped out of our worship all musical instruments connected with the old Temple worship, especially such as have become associated with Christianity. But the ram's horn on the New Year is an institution older than the Temple, and specially enjoined in the Bible."

"But surely there is something spiritualizing about an organ."

For reply the Reb pinched her ear. "Ah, you are a sad *Epikouros*," he said, half seriously. "If you loved God you would not want an organ to take your thoughts to heaven."

He released her ear and took up his pen, humming with unction a synagogue air full of joyous flourishes.

Hannah turned to go, then turned back.

"Father," she said nervously, blushing a little, "who was that you said you had in your eye?"

"Oh, nobody in particular," said the Reb, equally embarrassed and avoiding meeting her eye, as if to conceal the person in his.

"But you must have meant something by it," she said gravely. "You know I'm not going to be married off to please other people."

The Reb wriggled uncomfortably in his chair. "It was only a thought – an idea. If it does not come to you, too, it shall be nothing. I didn't mean anything serious – really, my dear, I didn't. To tell you the truth," he finished suddenly with a frank, heavenly smile, "the person I had mainly in my eye when I spoke was your mother."

This time his eye met hers, and they smiled at each other with the consciousness of the humours of the situation. The Rebbitzin's broom was heard banging viciously in the passage. Hannah bent down and kissed the ample forehead beneath the black skull-cap.

"Mr. Levine also writes insisting that I must go to the Purim ball with him and Leah," she said, glancing at the letter.

"A husband's wishes must be obeyed;" answered the Reb.

"No, I will treat him as if he were really my husband," retorted Hannah. "I will have my own way; I shan't go."

The door was thrown open suddenly.

"Oh yes thou wilt," said the Rebbitzin. "Thou art not going to bury thyself alive."

CHAPTER VIII

Esther and her Children

Esther Ansell did not welcome Levi Jacobs warmly. She had just cleared away the breakfast things and was looking forward to a glorious day's reading, and the advent of a visitor did not gratify her. And yet Levi Jacobs was a good-looking boy with brown hair and eyes, a dark glowing complexion and ruddy lips – a sort of reduced masculine edition of Hannah.

"I've come to play I-spy-I, Solomon," he said when he entered. "My, don't you live high up!"

"I thought you had to go to school," Solomon observed with a stare.

"Ours isn't a board school," Levi explained. "You might introduce a fellow to your sister."

"Garn! You know Esther right enough," said Solomon and began to whistle carelessly.

"How are you, Esther?" said Levi awkwardly.

"I'm very well, thank you," said Esther, looking up from a little brown-covered book and looking down at it again.

She was crouching on the fender trying to get some warmth at the little fire extracted from Reb Shemuel's half-crown. December continued grey; the room was dim and a spurt of flame played on her pale earnest face. It was a face that never lost a certain ardency of colour even at its palest: the hair was dark and abundant, the eyes were large and thoughtful, the nose slightly aquiline and the whole cast of the features betrayed the Polish origin. The forehead was rather low. Esther had nice teeth which accident had preserved white. It was an arrestive rather than a beautiful face, though charming enough when she smiled. If the grace and candour of childhood could have been disengaged from the face, it would have been easier to say whether it was absolutely pretty. It came nearer being so on Sabbaths and holidays when scholastic supervision was removed and the hair was free to fall loosely about the shoulders instead of being screwed up into the pendulous plait so dear to the educational eye. Esther could have earned a penny quite easily by sacrificing her tresses and going about with close-cropped head like a boy, for her teacher never failed thus to reward the shorn, but in the darkest hours of hunger she held on to her hair as her mother had done before her. The prospects of Esther's post-nuptial wig were not brilliant. She was not tall for a girl who is getting on for twelve; but some little girls shoot up suddenly and there was considerable room for hope.

Sarah and Isaac were romping noisily about and under the beds; Rachel was at the table, knitting a scarf for Solomon; the grandmother pored over a bulky enchiridion for pious women, written in jargon. Moses was out in search of work. No one took any notice of the visitor.

"What's that you're reading?" he asked Esther politely.

"Oh nothing," said Esther with a start, closing the book as if fearful he might want to look over her shoulder.

"I don't see the fun of reading books out of school," said Levi.

"Oh, but we don't read school books," said Solomon defensively.

"I don't care. It's stupid."

"At that rate you could never read books when you're grown up," said Esther contemptuously.

"No, of course not," admitted Levi. "Otherwise where would be the fun of being grown up? After I leave school I don't intend to open a book."

"No? Perhaps you'll open a shop," said Solomon.

"What will you do when it rains?" asked Esther crushingly.

"I shall smoke," replied Levi loftily.

"Yes, but suppose it's *Shabbos*," swiftly rejoined Esther.

Levi was nonplussed. "Well, it can't rain all day and there are only fifty-two *Shabbosim* in the year," he said lamely. "A man can always do something."

"I think there's more pleasure in reading than in doing something," remarked Esther.

"Yes, you're a girl," Levi reminded her, "and girls are expected to stay indoors. Look at my sister Hannah. She reads, too. But a man can be out doing what he pleases, eh, Solomon?"

"Yes, of course we've got the best of it," said Solomon. "The Prayer-book shows that. Don't I say every morning 'Blessed art Thou, O Lord our God, who hast not made me a woman'?"

"I don't know whether you do say it. You certainly have got to," said Esther witheringly.

"'Sh," said Solomon, winking in the direction of the grandmother.

"It doesn't matter," said Esther calmly. "She can't understand what I'm saying."

"I don't know," said Solomon dubiously. "She sometimes catches more than you bargain for."

"And then *you* catch more than you bargain for," said Rachel, looking up roguishly from her knitting.

Solomon stuck his tongue in his cheek and grimaced.

Isaac came behind Levi and gave his coat a pull and toddled off with a yell of delight.

"Be quiet, Ikey!" cried Esther. "If you don't behave better I shan't sleep in your new bed."

"Oh yeth, you mutht, Ethty," lisped Ikey, his elfish face growing grave. He went about depressed for some seconds.

"Kids are a beastly nuisance," said Levi, "don't you think so, Esther?"

"Oh no, not always," said the little girl. "Besides we were all kids once."

"That's what I complain of," said Levi. "We ought to be all born grown-up."

"But that's impossible!" put in Rachel.

"It isn't impossible at all," said Esther. "Look at Adam. and Eve!"

Levi looked at Esther gratefully instead. He felt nearer to her and thought of persuading her into playing Kiss-in-the-Ring. But he found it difficult to back out of his undertaking to play I-spy-I with Solomon; and in the end he had to leave Esther to her book.

She had little in common with her brother Solomon, least of all humour and animal spirits. Even before the responsibilities of headship had come upon her she was a preternaturally thoughtful little girl who had strange intuitions about things and was doomed to work out her own salvation as a metaphysician. When she asked her mother who made God, a slap in the face demonstrated to her the limits of human inquiry. The natural instinct of the child over-rode the long travail of the race to conceive an abstract Deity, and Esther pictured God as a mammoth cloud. In early years Esther imagined that the "body" that was buried when a person died was the corpse decapitated and she often puzzled herself to think what was done with the isolated head. When her mother was being tied up in grave-clothes, Esther hovered about with a real thirst for knowledge while the thoughts of all the other children were sensuously concentrated on the funeral and the glory of seeing a vehicle drive away from their own door. Esther was also disappointed at not seeing her mother's soul fly up to heaven though she watched vigilantly at the death-bed for the ascent of the long yellow hook-shaped thing. The genesis of this conception of the soul was probably to be sought in the pictorial representations of ghosts in the story-papers brought home by her eldest brother Benjamin. Strange shadowy conceptions of things more corporeal floated up from her solitary reading. Theatres she came across often, and a theatre was a kind of Babel plain or Vanity Fair in which performers and spectators were promiscuously mingled and wherein the richer folk clad in evening dress sat in thin deal boxes – the cases in Spitalfields market being Esther's main association with boxes. One of her day-dreams of the future was going to the theatre in a nightgown and being accommodated with an orange-box. Little rectification of such distorted views of life was to be expected from Moses Ansell, who went down to his grave without seeing even a circus, and had no interest in art apart from the "Police News" and his "Mizrach" and the synagogue decorations. Even when Esther's sceptical instinct drove her to inquire of her father how people knew that Moses got the Law on Mount Sinai, he could only repeat in horror that the Books of Moses said so, and could never be brought to see that his arguments travelled on round-abouts. She sometimes regretted that her brilliant brother Benjamin had been swallowed up by the orphan asylum, for she imagined she could have discussed many a knotty point with him. Solomon was both flippant and incompetent. But in spite of her theoretical latitudinari-anism, in practice she was pious to the point of fanaticism and could scarce conceive the depths of degradation of which she heard vague horror-struck talk. There were Jews about – grown-up men and women, not insane – who struck Lucifer matches on the Sabbath and housewives who carelessly mixed their butter-plates with their meat-plates even when they did not actually eat butter with meat. Esther promised herself that, please God, she would never do anything so wicked when she grew up. She at least would never fail to light the Sabbath candles nor to *kasher* the meat. Never was a child more alive to the beauty of duty, more open to the appeal of virtue, self-control, abnegation. She fasted till two o'clock on the Great White Fast when she was seven years old and accomplished the perfect feat at nine. When she read a simple little story in a prize-book, inculcating the homely moralities at which the cynic sneers, her eyes filled with tears and her breast with unselfish and dutiful determinations. She had something of the temperament of the stoic, fortified by that spiritual pride which does not look for equal goodness in others; and though she disapproved of Solomon's dodgings of duty, she did not sneak or preach, even gave him surreptitious crusts of bread before he had said his prayers, especially on Saturdays and Festivals when the praying took place in *Shool* and was liable to be prolonged till midday.

Esther often went to synagogue and sat in the ladies' compartment. The drone of the "Sons of the Convenant" downstairs was part of her consciousness of home, like the musty smell of the stairs, or Becky's young men through whom she had to plough her way when she went for the morning milk, or the odours of Mr. Belcovitch's rum or the whirr of his machines, or the bent, snuffy personality of the Hebrew scholar in the adjoining garret, or the dread of Dutch Debby's dog that was ultimately transformed to friendly expectation. Esther led a double life, just as she spoke two tongues. The knowledge that she was a Jewish child, whose people had had a special history, was always at the back of her consciousness; sometimes it was brought to the front by the scoffing rhymes of Christian children, who informed her that they had stuck a piece of pork upon a fork and given it to a member of her race.

But far more vividly did she realize that she was an English girl; far keener than her pride in Judas Maccabæus was her pride in Nelson and Wellington; she rejoiced to find that her ancestors had always beaten the French from the days of Cressy and Poictiers to the days of Waterloo, that Alfred the Great was the wisest of kings, and that Englishmen dominated the world and had planted colonies in every corner of it, that the English language was the noblest in the world and men speaking it had invented railway trains, steamships, telegraphs, and everything worth inventing. Esther absorbed these ideas from the school reading books. The experience of a month will overlay the hereditary bequest of a century. And yet, beneath all, the prepared plate remains most sensitive to the old impressions.

Sarah and Isaac had developed as distinct individualities as was possible in the time at their disposal. Isaac was just five and Sarah – who had never known her mother – just four. The thoughts of both ran strongly in the direction of sensuous enjoyment, and they preferred baked potatoes, especially potatoes touched with gravy, to all the joys of the kindergarten. Isaac's ambition ran in the direction of eider-down beds such as he had once felt at Malka's and Moses soothed him by the horizon-like prospect of such a new bed. Places of honour had already been conceded by the generous little chap to his father and brother. Heaven alone knows how he had come to conceive their common bed as his own peculiar property in which the other three resided at night on sufferance. He could not even plead it was his by right of birth in it. But Isaac was not after all wholly given over to worldly thoughts, for an intellectual problem often occupied his thoughts and led him to slap little Sarah's arms. He had been born on the fourth of December while Sarah had been born a year later on, the third.

"It ain't, it can't be," he would say. "Your birfday can't be afore mine."

"'Tis, Esty thays so," Sarah would reply.

"Esty's a liar," Isaac responded imperturbably.

"Ask *Tatah*."

"*Tatah* dunno. Ain't I five?"

"Yeth."

"And ain't you four?"

"Yeth."

"And ain't I older than you?"

"Courth."

"And wasn't I born afore you?"

"Yeth, Ikey."

"Then 'ow can your birfday come afore mine?"

"Cos it doth."

"Stoopid!"

"It doth, arx Esty," Sarah would insist.

"Than't teep in my new bed," Ikey would threaten.

"Thall if I like."

"Than't!"

Here Sarah would generally break down in tears and Isaac with premature economic instinct, feeling it wicked to waste a cry, would proceed to justify it by hitting her. Thereupon little Sarah would hit him back and develop a terrible howl.

"Hi, woe is unto me," she would wail in jargon, throwing herself on the ground in a corner and rocking herself to and fro like her far away ancestresses remembering Zion by the waters of Babylon.

Little Sarah's lamentations never ceased till she had been avenged by a higher hand. There were several great powers but Esther was the most trusty instrument of reprisal. If Esther was out little Sarah's sobs ceased speedily, for she, too, felt the folly of fruitless tears. Though she nursed in her breast the sense of injury, she would even resume her amicable romps with Isaac. But the moment the step of the avenger was heard on the stairs, little Sarah would betake herself to the corner and howl with the pain of Isaac's pummellings. She had a strong love of abstract justice and felt that if the wrong-doer were to go unpunished, there was no security for the constitution of things.

Today's holiday did not pass without an outbreak of this sort. It occurred about tea-time. Perhaps the infants were fractious because there was no tea. Esther had to economise her resources and a repast at seven would serve for both tea and supper. Among the poor, combination meals are as common as combination beds and chests. Esther had quieted Sarah by slapping Isaac, but as this made Isaac howl the gain was dubious. She had to put a fresh piece of coal on the fire and sing to them while their shadows contorted themselves grotesquely on the beds and then upwards along the sloping walls, terminating with twisted necks on the ceiling.

Esther usually sang melancholy things in minor keys. They seemed most attuned to the dim straggling room. There was a song her mother used to sing. It was taken from a *Purim-Spiel*, itself based upon a Midrash, one of the endless legends with which the People of One Book have broidered it, amplifying every minute detail with all the exuberance of oriental imagination and justifying their fancies with all the ingenuity of a race of lawyers. After his brethren sold Joseph to the Midianite merchants, the lad escaped from the caravan and wandered foot-sore and hungry to Bethlehem, to the grave of his mother, Rachel. And he threw himself upon the ground and wept aloud and sang to a heart-breaking melody in Yiddish.

> Und hei weh ist mir,
> Wie schlecht ist doch mir,
> Ich bin vertrieben geworen
> Junger heid voon dir.

Whereof the English runs:

> Alas! woe is me!
> How wretched to be
> Driven away and banished,
> Yet so young, from thee.

Thereupon the voice of his beloved mother Rachel was heard from the grave, comforting him and bidding him be of good cheer, for that his future should be great and glorious.

Esther could not sing this without the tears trickling down her cheeks. Was it that she thought of her own dead mother and applied the lines to herself? Isaac's ill-humour scarcely ever survived the anodyne of these mournful cadences. There was another melodious wail which Alte Belcovitch had brought from Poland. The chorus ran:

> Man nemt awek die chasanim voon die callohs
> Hi, hi, did-a-rid-a-ree!

> They tear away their lovers from the maidens,
> Hi, hi, did-a-rid-a-ree!

The air mingled the melancholy of Polish music with the sadness of Jewish and the words hinted of God knew what

> "Old unhappy far-off things
> And battles long ago."

And so over all the songs and stories was the trail of tragedy, under all the heart-ache of a hunted race. There are few more plaintive chants in the world than the recitation of the Psalms by the "Sons of the Covenant" on Sabbath afternoons amid the gathering shadows of twilight. Esther often stood in the passage to hear it, morbidly fascinated, tears of pensive pleasure in her eyes. Even the little jargon story-book which Moses Ansell read out that night to his *Kinder*, after tea-supper, by the light of the one candle, was prefaced with a note of pathos.

"These stories have we gathered together from the Gemorah and the Midrash, wonderful stories, and we have translated the beautiful stories, using the Hebrew alphabet so that every one, little or big, shall be able to read them, and shall know that there is a God in the world who forsaketh not His people Israel and who even for us will likewise work miracles and wonders and will send us the righteous Redeemer speedily in our days, Amen." Of this same Messiah the children heard endless tales. Oriental fancy had been exhausted in picturing him for the consolation of exiled and suffering Israel. Before his days there would be a wicked Messiah of the House of Joseph; later, a king with one ear deaf to hear good but acute to hear evil; there would be a scar on his forehead, one of his hands would be an inch long and the other three miles, apparently a subtle symbol of the persecutor. The jargon story-book among its "stories, wonderful stories," had also extracts from the famous romance, or diary, of Eldad the Danite, who professed to have discovered the lost Ten Tribes. Eldad's book appeared towards the end of the ninth century and became the Arabian Nights of the Jews, and it had filtered down through the ages into the Ansell garret, in common with many other tales from the rich storehouse of mediæval folklore in the diffusion of which the wandering Jew has played so great a part.

Sometimes Moses read to his charmed hearers the description of Heaven and Hell by Immanuel, the friend and contemporary of Dante, sometimes a jargon version of Robinson Crusoe. Tonight he chose Eldad's account of the tribe of Moses dwelling beyond the wonderful river, Sambatyon, which never flows on the Sabbath.

"There is also the tribe of Moses, our just master, which is called the tribe that flees, because it fled from idol worship and clung to the fear of God. A river flows round their land for a distance of four days' journey on every side. They dwell in beautiful houses provided with handsome towers, which they have built themselves. There is nothing unclean among them, neither in the case of birds, venison nor domesticated animals; there are no wild animals, no flies, no foxes, no vermin, no serpents, no dogs, and in general, nothing which does harm; they have only sheep and cattle, which bear twice a year. They sow and reap; there are all sorts of gardens, with all kinds of fruits and cereals, viz: beans, melons, gourds, onions, garlic, wheat and barley, and the seed grows a hundredfold. They have faith; they know the law, the Mishnah, the Talmud and the Agadah; but their Talmud is in Hebrew. They introduce their sayings in the name of the fathers, the wise men, who heard them from the mouth of Joshua, who himself heard them from the mouth of God. They have no knowledge of the Tanaim (doctors of the Mishnah) and Amoraim (doctors of the Talmud), who flourished during the time of the second Temple, which was, of course, not known to these tribes. They speak only Hebrew, and are very strict as regards the use of wine made by others than themselves, as well as the rules of slaughtering animals; in this respect the Law of Moses is much more rigorous than that of the Tribes. They do not swear by the name of God, for fear that their breath may leave them, and they become angry with those who swear; they reprimand them, saying, 'Woe, ye poor, why do you swear with the mention of the name of God upon your lips? Use your mouth for eating bread and drinking water. Do you not know that for the sin of swearing your children die young?' And in this way they exhort every one to serve God with fear and integrity of heart. 'Therefore, the children of Moses, the servant of God, live long, to the age of 100 or 120 years. No child, be it son or daughter, dies during the lifetime of its parent, but they reach a third and a fourth generation, and see grand-children and great-grandchildren with their offspring. They do all field work themselves, having no male or female servants; there are also merchants among them. They do not close their houses at night, for there is no thief nor any wicked man among them. Thus a little lad might go for days with his flock without fear of robbers, demons or danger of any other kind; they are, indeed, all holy and clean. These Levites busy themselves with the Law and with the commandments, and they still live in the holiness of our master, Moses; therefore, God has given them all this good. Moreover, they see nobody and nobody sees them, except the four tribes who dwell on the other side of the rivers of Cush; they see them and speak to them, but the river Sambatyon is between them, as it is said: 'That thou mayest say to prisoners, Go forth' (Isaiah xlix., 9). They have plenty of gold and silver; they sow flax and cultivate the crimson worm, and make beautiful garments. Their number is double or four times the number that went out from Egypt.

"The river Sambatyon is 200 yards broad – 'about as far as a bowshot' (Gen. xxi., 16), full of sand and stones, but without water; the stones make a great noise like the waves of the sea and a stormy wind, so that in the night the noise is heard at a distance of half a day's journey. There are sources of water which collect themselves in one pool, out of which they water the fields. There are fish in it, and all kinds of clean birds fly round it. And this river of stone and sand rolls during the six working days and rests on the Sabbath day. As soon as the Sabbath begins fire surrounds the river and the flames remain till the next evening, when the Sabbath ends. Thus no human being can reach the river for a distance of half a mile on either side; the fire consumes all that grows there. The four tribes, Dan, Naphtali, Gad and Asher, stand on the borders of the river. When shearing their flocks here, for the land is flat and clean without any thorns, if the children of Moses see them gathered together on the border they shout, saying, 'Brethren, tribes of Jeshurun, show us your camels, dogs and asses,' and they make their remarks about the length of the camel's neck and the shortness of the tail. Then they greet one another and go their way."

When this was done, Solomon called for Hell. He liked to hear about the punishment of the sinners; it gave a zest to life. Moses hardly needed a book to tell them about Hell. It had no secrets for him. The Old Testament has no reference to a future existence, but the poor Jew has no more been able to live without the hope of Hell than the poor Christian. When the wicked man has waxed fat and kicked the righteous skinny man, shall the two lie down in the same dust and the game be over? Perish the thought! One of the Hells was that in which the sinner was condemned to do over and over again the sins he had done in life.

"Why, that must be jolly!" said Solomon.

"No, that is frightful," maintained Moses Ansell. He spoke Yiddish, the children English.

"Of course, it is," said Esther. "Just fancy, Solomon, having to eat toffee all day."

"It's better than eating nothing all day," replied Solomon.

"But to eat it every day for ever and ever!" said Moses.

"There's no rest for the wicked."

"What! Not even on the Sabbath?" said, Esther.

"Oh, yes; of course, then. Like the river Sambatyon, even the flames of Hell rest on *Shabbos*."

"Haven't they got no fire-*goyas*?" inquired Ikey, and everybody laughed.

"*Shabbos* is a holiday in Hell," Moses explained to the little one. "So thou seest the result of thy making out Sabbath too early on Saturday night, thou sendest the poor souls back to their tortures before the proper time."

Moses never lost an opportunity of enforcing the claims of the ceremonial law. Esther had a vivid picture flashed upon her of poor, yellow hook-shaped souls floating sullenly back towards the flames.

Solomon's chief respect for his father sprang from the halo of military service encircling Moses ever since it leaked out through the lips of the *Bube*, that he had been a conscript in Russia and been brutally treated by the sergeant. But Moses could not be got to speak of his exploits. Solomon pressed him to do so, especially when his father gave symptoms of inviting him to the study of Rashi's Commentary. Tonight Moses brought out a Hebrew tome, and said, "Come, Solomon. Enough of stories. We must learn a little."

"Today is a holiday," grumbled Solomon.

"It is never a holiday for the study of the Law."

"Only this once, father; let's play draughts."

Moses weakly yielded. Draughts was his sole relaxation and when Solomon acquired a draught board by barter his father taught him the game. Moses played the Polish variety, in which the men are like English kings that leap backwards and forwards and the kings shoot diagonally across like bishops at chess. Solomon could not withstand these gigantic grasshoppers, whose stopping places he could never anticipate. Moses won every game tonight and was full of glee and told the *Kinder* another story. It was about the Emperor Nicholas and is not to be found in the official histories of Russia.

"Nicholas was a wicked king, who oppressed the Jews and made their lives sore and bitter. And one day he made it known to the Jews that if a million roubles were not raised for him in a month's time they should be driven from their homes. Then the Jews prayed unto God and besought him to help them for the merits of the forefathers, but no help came. Then they tried to bribe the officials, but the officials pocketed their gold and the Emperor still demanded his tax. Then they went to the great Masters of Cabalah, who, by pondering day and night on the name and its transmutations, had won the control of all things, and they said, 'Can ye do naught for us?' Then the Masters of Cabalah took counsel together and at midnight they called up the spirits of Abraham our father, and Isaac and Jacob, and Elijah the prophet, who wept to hear of their children's sorrows. And Abraham our father, and Isaac and Jacob, and Elijah the prophet took the bed whereon Nicholas the Emperor slept and transported it to a wild place. And they took Nicholas the Emperor out of his warm bed and whipped him soundly so that he yelled for mercy. Then they asked: 'Wilt thou rescind the edict against the Jews?' And he said 'I will.' But in the morning Nicholas the Emperor woke up and called for the chief of the bed-chamber and said, 'How darest thou allow my bed to be carried out in the middle of the night into the forest?' And the chief of the bed-chamber grew pale and said that the Emperor's guards had watched all night outside the door, neither was there space for the bed to pass out. And Nicholas the Emperor, thinking he had dreamed, let the man go unhung. But the next night lo! the bed was transported again to the wild place and Abraham our father, and Isaac and Jacob, and Elijah the prophet drubbed him doubly and again he promised to remit the tax. So in the morning the chief of the bed-chamber was hanged and at night the guards were doubled. But the bed sailed away to the wild place and Nicholas the Emperor was trebly whipped. Then Nicholas the Emperor annulled the edict and the Jews rejoiced and fell at the knees of the Masters of Cabalah."

"But why can't they save the Jews altogether?" queried Esther.

"Oh," said Moses mysteriously. "Cabalah is a great force and must not be abused. The Holy Name must not he made common. Moreover one might lose one's life."

"Could the Masters make men?" inquired Esther, who had recently come across Frankenstein.

"Certainly," said Moses. "And what is more, it stands written that Reb Chanina and Reb Osheya fashioned a fine fat calf on Friday and enjoyed it on the Sabbath."

"Oh, father!" said Solomon, piteously, "don't you know Cabalah?"

CHAPTER IX

Dutch Debby

A year before we got to know Esther Ansell she got to know Dutch Debby and it changed her life. Dutch Debby was a tall, sallow ungainly girl who lived in the wee back room on the second floor behind Mrs. Simons and supported herself and her dog by needle-work. Nobody ever came to see her, for it was whispered that her parents had cast her out when she presented them with an illegitimate grandchild. The baby was fortunate enough to die, but she still continued to incur suspicion by keeping a dog, which is an un-Jewish trait. Bobby often squatted on the stairs guarding her door and, as it was very dark on the staircase, Esther suffered great agonies lest she should tread on his tail and provoke reprisals. Her anxiety led her to do so one afternoon and Bobby's teeth just penetrated through her stocking. The clamour brought out Dutch Debby, who took the girl into her room and soothed her. Esther had often wondered what uncanny mysteries lay behind that dark dog-guarded door and she was rather more afraid of Debby than of Bobby.

But that afternoon saw the beginning of a friendship which added one to the many factors which were moulding the future woman. For Debby turned out a very mild bogie, indeed, with a good English vocabulary and a stock of old *London Journals*, more precious to Esther than mines of Ind. Debby kept them under the bed, which, as the size of the bed all but coincided with the area of the room, was a wise arrangement. And on the long summer evenings and the Sunday afternoons when her little ones needed no looking after and were traipsing about playing "whoop!" and pussy-cat in the street downstairs, Esther slipped into the wee back room, where the treasures lay, and there, by the open window, overlooking the dingy back yard and the slanting perspectives of sun-flecked red tiles where cats prowled and dingy sparrows hopped, in an atmosphere laden with whiffs from a neighbouring dairyman's stables, Esther lost herself in wild tales of passion and romance. She frequently read them aloud for the benefit of the sallow-faced needle-woman, who had found romance square so sadly with the realities of her own existence. And so all a summer afternoon, Dutch Debby and Esther would be rapt away to a world of brave men and fair women, a world of fine linen and purple, of champagne and wickedness and cigarettes, a world where nobody worked or washed shirts or was hungry or had holes in boots, a world utterly ignorant of Judaism and the heinousness of eating meat with butter. Not that Esther for her part correlated her conception of this world with facts. She never realized that it was an actually possible world – never indeed asked herself whether it existed outside print or not. She never thought of it in that way at all, any more than it ever occurred to her that people once spoke the Hebrew she learned to read and translate. "Bobby" was often present at these readings, but he kept his thoughts to himself, sitting on his hind legs with his delightfully ugly nose tilted up inquiringly at Esther. For the best of all this new friendship was that Bobby was not jealous. He was only a sorry dun-coloured mongrel to outsiders, but Esther learned to see him almost through Dutch Debby's eyes. And she could run up the stairs freely, knowing that if she trod on his tail now, he would take it as a mark of *camaraderie*.

"I used to pay a penny a week for the *London Journal*," said Debby early in their acquaintanceship, "till one day I discovered I had a dreadful bad memory."

"And what was the good of that?" said Esther.

"Why, it was worth shillings and shillings to me. You see I used to save up all the back numbers of the *London Journal* because of the answers to correspondents, telling you how to do your hair and trim your nails and give yourself a nice complexion. I used to bother my head about that sort of thing in those days, dear; and one day I happened to get reading a story in a back number only about a year old and I found I was just as interested as if I had never read it before and I hadn't the slightest remembrance of it. After that I left off buying the Journal and took to reading my big heap of back numbers. I get through them once every two years." Debby interrupted herself with a fit of coughing, for lengthy monologue is inadvisable for persons who bend over needle-work in dark back rooms. Recovering herself, she added, "And then I start afresh. You couldn't do that, could you?"

"No," admitted Esther, with a painful feeling of inferiority. "I remember all I've ever read."

"Ah, you will grow up a clever woman!" said Debby, patting her hair.

"Oh, do you think so?" said Esther, her dark eyes lighting up with pleasure.

"Oh yes, you're always first in your class, ain't you?"

"Is that what you judge by, Debby?" said Esther, disappointed. "The other girls are so stupid and take no thought for anything but their hats and their frocks. They would rather play gobs or shuttlecock or hopscotch than read about the 'Forty Thieves.' They don't mind being kept a whole year in one class but I – oh, I feel so mad at getting on so slow. I could easily learn the standard work in three months. I want to know everything – so that I can grow up to be a teacher at our school."

"And does your teacher know everything?"

"Oh yes! She knows the meaning of every word and all about foreign countries."

"And would you like to be a teacher?"

"If I could only be clever enough!" sighed Esther. "But then you see the teachers at our school are real ladies and they dress, oh, so beautifully! With fur tippets and six-button gloves. I could never afford it, for even when I was earning five shillings a week I should have to give most of it to father and the children."

"But if you're very good – I dare say some of the great ladies like the Rothschilds will buy you nice clothes. I have heard they are very good to clever children."

"No, then the other teachers would know I was getting charity! And they would mock at me. I heard Miss Hyams make fun of a teacher because she wore the same dress as last winter. I don't think I should like to be a teacher after all, though it is nice to be able to stand with your back to the fire in the winter. The girls would know –" Esther stopped and blushed.

"Would know what, dear?"

"Well, they would know father," said Esther in low tones. "They would see him selling things in the Lane and they wouldn't do what I told them."

"Nonsense, Esther. I believe most of the teachers' fathers are just as bad – I mean as poor. Look at Miss Hyams's own father."

"Oh Debby! I do hope that's true. Besides when I was earning five shillings a week, I could buy father a new coat, couldn't I? And then there would be no need for him to stand in the Lane with lemons or 'four-corner fringes,' would there?"

"No, dear. You shall be a teacher, I prophesy, and who knows? Some day you may be Head Mistress!"

Esther laughed a startled little laugh of delight, with a suspicion of a sob in it. "What! Me! Me go round and make all the teachers do their work. Oh, wouldn't I catch them gossiping! I know their tricks!"

"You seem to look after your teacher well. Do you ever call her over the coals for gossiping?" inquired Dutch Debby, amused.

"No, no," protested Esther quite seriously. "I like to hear them gossiping. When my teacher and Miss Davis, who's in the next room, and a few other teachers get together, I learn – Oh such a lot! – from their conversation."

"Then they do teach you after all," laughed Debby.

"Yes, but it's not on the Time Table," said Esther, shaking her little head sapiently. "It's mostly about young men. Did you ever have a young man, Debby?"

"Don't – don't ask such questions, child!" Debby bent over her needle-work.

"Why not?" persisted Esther. "If I only had a young man when I grew up, I should be proud of him. Yes, you're trying to turn your head away. I'm sure you had. Was he nice like Lord Eversmonde or Captain Andrew Sinclair? Why you're crying, Debby!"

"Don't be a little fool, Esther! A tiny fly has just flown into my eye – poor little thing! He hurts me and does himself no good."

"Let me see, Debby," said Esther. "Perhaps I shall be in time to save him."

"No, don't trouble."

"Don't be so cruel, Debby. You're as bad as Solomon, who pulls off flies' wings to see if they can fly without them."

"He's dead now. Go on with 'Lady Ann's Rival;' we've been wasting the whole afternoon talking. Take my advice, Esther, and don't stuff your head with ideas about young men. You're too young. Now, dear, I'm ready. Go on."

"Where was I? Oh yes. 'Lord Eversmonde folded the fair young form to his manly bosom and pressed kiss after kiss upon her ripe young lips, which responded passionately to his own. At last she recovered herself and cried reproachfully, Oh Sigismund, why do you persist in coming here, when the Duke forbids it?' – Oh, do you know, Debby, father said the other day I oughtn't to come here?"

"Oh no, you must," cried Debby impulsively. "I couldn't part with you now."

"Father says people say you are not good," said Esther candidly.

Debby breathed painfully. "Well!" she whispered.

"But I said people were liars. You *are* good!"

"Oh, Esther, Esther!" sobbed Debby, kissing the earnest little face with a vehemence that surprised the child.

"I think father only said that," Esther went on, "because he fancies I neglect Sarah and Isaac when he's at *Shool* and they quarrel so about their birthdays when they're together. But they don't slap one another hard. I'll tell you what! Suppose I bring Sarah down here!"

"Well, but won't she cry and be miserable here, if you read, and with no Isaac to play with?"

"Oh no," said Esther confidently. "She'll keep Bobby company."

Bobby took kindly to little Sarah also. He knew no other dogs and in such circumstances a sensible animal falls back on human beings. He had first met Debby herself quite casually and the two lonely beings took to each other. Before that meeting Dutch Debby was subject to wild temptations. Once she half starved herself and put aside ninepence a week for almost three months and purchased one-eighth of a lottery ticket from Sugarman the *Shadchan*, who recognized her existence for the occasion. The fortune did not come off.

Debby saw less and less of Esther as the months crept on again towards winter, for the little girl feared her hostess might feel constrained to offer her food, and the children required more soothing. Esther would say very little about her home life, though Debby got to know a great deal about her school-mates and her teacher.

One summer evening after Esther had passed into the hands of Miss Miriam Hyams she came to Dutch Debby with a grave face and said: "Oh, Debby, Miss Hyams is not a heroine."

"No?" said Debby, amused. "You were so charmed with her at first."

"Yes, she is very pretty and her hats are lovely. But she is not a heroine."

"Why, what's happened?"

"You know what lovely weather it's been all day?"

"Yes."

"Well, this morning all in the middle of the Scripture lesson, she said to us, 'What a pity, girls, we've got to stay cooped up here this bright weather' – you know she chats to us so nicely – 'in some schools they have half-holidays on Wednesday afternoons in the summer. Wouldn't it be nice if we could have them and be out in the sunshine in Victoria Park?' 'Hoo, yes, teacher, wouldn't that be jolly?' we all cried. Then teacher said: 'Well, why not ask the Head Mistress for a holiday this afternoon? You're the highest standard in the school —I daresay if you ask for it, the whole school will get a holiday. Who will be spokeswoman?' Then all the girls said I must be because I was the first girl in the class and sounded all my h's, and when the Head Mistress came into the room I up and curtseyed and asked her if we could have a holiday this afternoon on account of the beautiful sunshine. Then the Head Mistress put on her eye-glasses and her face grew black and the sunshine seemed to go out of the room. And she said 'What! After all the holidays we have here, a month at New Year and a fortnight at Passover, and all the fast-days! I am surprised that you girls should be so lazy and idle and ask for more. Why don't you take example by your teacher? Look at Miss Hyams.' We all looked at Miss Hyams, but she was looking for some papers in her desk. 'Look how Miss Hyams works!' said the Head Mistress. '*She* never grumbles, *she* never asks for a holiday!' We all looked again at Miss Hyams, but she hadn't yet found the papers. There was an awful silence; you could have heard a pin drop. There wasn't a single cough or rustle of a dress. Then the Head Mistress turned to me and she said: 'And you, Esther Ansell, whom I always thought so highly of, I'm surprised at your being the ringleader in such a disgraceful request. You ought to know better. I shall bear it in mind, Esther Ansell.' With that she sailed out, stiff and straight as a poker, and the door closed behind her with a bang."

"Well, and what did Miss Hyams say then?" asked Debby, deeply interested.

"She said: 'Selina Green, and what did Moses do when the Children of Israel grumbled for water?' She just went on with the Scripture lesson, as if nothing had happened."

"I should tell the Head Mistress who sent me on," cried Debby indignantly.

"Oh, no," said Esther shaking her head. "That would be mean. It's a matter for her own conscience. Oh, but I do wish," she concluded, "we had had a holiday. It would have been so lovely out in the Park."

Victoria Park was *the* Park to the Ghetto. A couple of miles off, far enough to make a visit to it an excursion, it was a perpetual blessing to the Ghetto. On rare Sunday afternoons the Ansell family minus the *Bube* toiled there and back *en masse*, Moses carrying Isaac And Sarah by turns upon his shoulder. Esther loved the Park in all weathers, but best of all in the summer, when the great lake was bright and busy with boats, and the birds twittered in the leafy trees and the lobelias and calceolarias were woven into wonderful patterns by the gardeners. Then she would throw herself down on the thick grass and look up in mystic rapture at the brooding blue sky and forget to read the book she had brought with her, while the other children chased one another about in savage delight. Only once on a Saturday afternoon when her father was not with them, did she get Dutch Debby to break through her retired habits and accompany them, and then it was not summer but late autumn. There was an indefinable melancholy about the sere landscape. Russet refuse strewed the paths and the gaunt trees waved flesh-less arms in the breeze. The November haze rose from the moist ground and dulled the blue of heaven with smoky clouds amid which the sun, a red sailless boat, floated at anchor among golden and crimson furrows and glimmering far-dotted fleeces. The small lake was slimy, reflecting the trees on its borders as a network of dirty branches. A solitary swan ruffled its plumes and elongated its throat, doubled in quivering outlines beneath the muddy surface. All at once the splash of oars was heard and the sluggish waters were stirred by the passage of a boat in which a heroic young man was rowing a no less heroic young woman.

Dutch Debby burst into tears and went home. After that she fell back entirely on Bobby and Esther and the *London Journal* and never even saved up nine shillings again.

CHAPTER X

A Silent Family

Sugarman the *Shadchan* arrived one evening a few days before Purim at the tiny two-storied house in which Esther's teacher lived, with little Nehemiah tucked under his arm. Nehemiah wore shoes and short red socks. The rest of his legs was bare. Sugarman always carried him so as to demonstrate this fact. Sugarman himself was rigged out in a handsome manner, and the day not being holy, his blue bandanna peeped out from his left coat-tail, instead of being tied round his trouser band.

"Good morning, marm," he said cheerfully.

"Good morning, Sugarman," said Mrs. Hyams.

She was a little careworn old woman of sixty with white hair. Had she been more pious her hair would never have turned grey. But Miriam had long since put her veto on her mother's black wig. Mrs. Hyams was a meek, weak person and submitted in silence to the outrage on her deepest instincts. Old Hyams was stronger, but not strong enough. He, too, was a silent person.

"P'raps you're surprised," said Sugarman, "to get a call from me in my sealskin vest-coat. But de fact is, marm, I put it on to call on a lady. I only dropped in here on my vay."

"Won't you take a chair?" said Mrs. Hyams. She spoke English painfully and slowly, having been schooled by Miriam.

"No, I'm not tired. But I vill put Nechemyah down on one, if you permit. Dere! Sit still or I *potch* you! P'raps you could lend me your corkscrew."

"With pleasure," said Mrs. Hyams.

"I dank you. You see my boy, Ebenezer, is *Barmitzvah* next *Shabbos* a veek, and I may not be passing again. You vill come?"

"I don't know," said Mrs. Hyams hesitatingly. She was not certain whether Miriam considered Sugarman on their visiting list.

"Don't say dat. I expect to open dirteen bottles of lemonade! You must come, you and Mr. Hyams and the whole family."

"Thank you, I will tell Miriam and Daniel and my husband."

"Dat's right. Nechemyah, don't dance on de good lady's chair. Did you hear, Mrs. Hyams, of Mrs. Jonas's luck?"

"No."

"I won her eleven pounds on the lottery."

"How nice," said Mrs. Hyams, a little fluttered.

"I would let you have half a ticket for two pounds."

"I haven't the money."

"Veil, dirty-six shillings! Dere! I have to pay dat myself."

"I would if I could, but I can't."

"But you can have an eighth for nine shillings."

Mrs. Hyams shook her head hopelessly.

"How is your son Daniel?" Sugarman asked.

"Pretty well, thank you. How is your wife?"

"Tank Gawd"

"And your Bessie?"

"Tank Gawd! Is your Daniel in?"

"Yes."

"Tank Gawd! I mean, can I see him?"

"It won't do any good."

"No, not dat," said Sugarman. "I should like to ask him to de Confirmation myself."

"Daniel!" called Mrs. Hyams.

He came from the back yard in rolled-up shirt-sleeves, soap-suds drying on his arms. He was a pleasant-faced, flaxen-haired young fellow, the junior of Miriam by eighteen months. There was will in the lower part of the face and tenderness in the eyes.

"Good morning, sir," said Sugarman. "My Ebenezer is *Barmitzvah* next *Shabbos* week; vill you do me the honour to drop in wid your moder and fader after *Shool*?"

Daniel crimsoned suddenly. He had "No" on his lips, but suppressed it and ultimately articulated it in some polite periphrasis. His mother noticed the crimson. On a blonde face it tells.

"Don't say dat," said Sugarman. "I expect to open dirteen bottles of lemonade. I have lent your good moder's corkscrew."

"I shall be pleased to send Ebenezer a little present, but I can't come, I really can't. You must excuse me." Daniel turned away.

"Veil," said Sugarman, anxious to assure him he bore no malice. "If you send a present I reckon it de same as if you come."

"That's all right," said Daniel with strained heartiness.

Sugarman tucked Nehemiah under his arm but lingered on the threshold. He did not know how to broach the subject. But the inspiration came.

"Do you know I have summonsed Morris Kerlinski?"

"No," said Daniel. "What for?"

"He owes me dirty shillings. I found him a very fine maiden, but, now he is married, he says it was only worth a suvran. He offered it me but I vouldn't take it. A poor man he vas, too, and got ten pun from a marriage portion society."

"Is it worthwhile bringing a scandal on the community for the sake of ten shillings? It will be in all the papers, and *Shadchan* will be spelt shatcan, shodkin, shatkin, chodcan, shotgun, and goodness knows what else."

"Yes, but it isn't ten shillings," said Sugarman. "It's dirty shillings."

"But you, say he offered you a sovereign."

"So he did. He arranged for two pun ten. I took the suvran – but not in full payment."

"You ought to settle it before the Beth-din," said Daniel vehemently, "or get some Jew to arbitrate. You make the Jews a laughing-stock. It is true all marriages depend on money," he added bitterly, "only it is the fashion of police court reporters to pretend the custom is limited to the Jews."

"Veil, I did go to Reb Shemuel," said Sugarman. "I dought he'd be the very man to arbitrate."

"Why?" asked Daniel.

"Vy? Hasn't he been a *Shadchan* himself? From who else shall we look for sympaty?"

"I see," said Daniel smiling a little. "And apparently you got none."

"No," said Sugarman, growing wroth at the recollection. "He said ve are not in Poland."

"Quite true."

"Yes, but I gave him an answer he didn't like," said Sugarman. "I said, and ven ve are not in Poland mustn't ve keep none of our religion?"

His tone changed from indignation to insinuation.

"Vy vill you not let me get *you* a vife, Mr. Hyams? I have several extra fine maidens in my eye. Come now, don't look so angry. How much commission vill you give me if I find you a maiden vid a hundred pound?"

"The maiden!" thundered Daniel. Then it dawned upon him that he had said a humorous thing and he laughed. There was merriment as well as mysticism in Daniel's blue eyes.

But Sugarman went away, down-hearted. Love is blind, and even marriage-brokers may be myopic. Most people not concerned knew that Daniel Hyams was "sweet on" Sugarman's Bessie. And it was so. Daniel loved Bessie, and Bessie loved Daniel. Only Bessie did not speak because she was a woman and Daniel did not speak because he was a man. They were a quiet family – the Hyamses. They all bore their crosses in a silence unbroken even at home. Miriam herself, the least reticent, did not give the impression that she could not have husbands for the winking. Her demands were so high – that was all. Daniel was proud of her and her position and her cleverness and was confident she would marry as well as she dressed. He did not expect her to contribute towards the expenses of the household – though she did – for he felt he had broad shoulders. He bore his father and mother on those shoulders, semi-invalids both. In the bold bad years of shameless poverty, Hyams had been a wandering metropolitan glazier, but this open degradation became intolerable as Miriam's prospects improved. It was partly for her sake that Daniel ultimately supported his parents in idleness and refrained from speaking to Bessie. For he was only an employé in a fancy-goods warehouse, and on forty-five shillings a week you cannot keep up two respectable establishments.

Bessie was a bonnie girl and could not in the nature of things be long uncaught. There was a certain night on which Daniel did not sleep – hardly a white night as our French neighbours say; a tear-stained night rather. In the morning he was resolved to deny himself Bessie. Peace would be his instead. If it did not come immediately he knew it was on the way. For once before he had struggled and been so rewarded. That was in his eighteenth year when he awoke to the glories of free thought, and knew himself a victim to the Moloch of the Sabbath, to which fathers' sacrifice their children. The proprietor of the fancy goods was a Jew, and moreover closed on Saturdays. But for this anachronism of keeping Saturday holy when you had Sunday also to laze on, Daniel felt a hundred higher careers would have been open to him. Later, when free thought waned (it was after Daniel had met Bessie), although he never returned to his father's narrowness, he found the abhorred Sabbath sanctifying his life. It made life a conscious voluntary sacrifice to an ideal, and the reward was a touch of consecration once a week. Daniel could not have described these things, nor did he speak of them, which was a pity. Once and once only in the ferment of free thought he had uncorked his soul, and it had run over with much froth, and thenceforward old Mendel Hyams and Beenah, his wife, opposed more furrowed foreheads to a world too strong for them. If Daniel had taken back his words and told them he was happier for the ruin they had made of his prospects, their gait might not have been so listless. But he was a silent man.

"You will go to Sugarman's, mother," he said now. "You and father. Don't mind that I'm not going. I have another appointment for the afternoon."

It was a superfluous lie for so silent a man.

"He doesn't like to be seen with us," Beenah Hyams thought. But she was silent.

"He has never forgiven my putting him to the fancy goods," thought Mendel Hyams when told. But he was silent.

It was of no good discussing it with his wife. Those two had rather halved their joys than their sorrows. They had been married forty years and had never had an intimate moment. Their marriage had been a matter of contract. Forty years ago, in Poland, Mendel Hyams had awoke one morning to find a face he had never seen before on the pillow beside his. Not even on the wedding-day had he been allowed a glimpse of his bride's countenance. That was the custom of the country and the time. Beenah bore her husband four children, of whom the elder two died; but the marriage did not beget affection, often the inverse offspring of such unions. Beenah was a dutiful housewife and Mendel Hyams supported her faithfully so long as his children would let him. Love never flew out of the window for he was never in the house. They did not talk to each other much. Beenah did the housework unaided by the sprig of a servant who was engaged to satisfy the neighbours. In his enforced idleness Mendel fell back on his religion, almost a profession in itself. They were a silent couple.

At sixty there is not much chance of a forty-year-old silence being broken on this side of the grave. So far as his personal happiness was concerned, Mendel had only one hope left in the world – to die in Jerusalem. His feeling for Jerusalem was unique. All the hunted Jew in him combined with all the battered man to transfigure Zion with the splendour of sacred dreams and girdle it with the rainbows that are builded of bitter tears. And with it all a dread that if he were buried elsewhere, when the last trump sounded he would have to roll under the earth and under the sea to Jerusalem, the rendezvous of resurrection.

Every year at the Passover table he gave his hope voice: "Next year in Jerusalem." In her deepest soul Miriam echoed this wish of his. She felt she could like him better at a distance. Beenah Hyams had only one hope left in the world – to die.

CHAPTER XI

The Purim Ball

Sam Levine duly returned for the Purim ball. Malka was away and so it was safe to arrive on the Sabbath. Sam and Leah called for Hannah in a cab, for the pavements were unfavourable to dancing shoes, and the three drove to the "Club," which was not a sixth of a mile off.

"The Club" was the People's Palace of the Ghetto; but that it did not reach the bed-rock of the inhabitants was sufficiently evident from the fact that its language was English. The very lowest stratum was of secondary formation – the children of immigrants – while the highest touched the lower middle-class, on the mere fringes of the Ghetto. It was a happy place where young men and maidens met on equal terms and similar subscriptions, where billiards and flirtations and concerts and laughter and gay gossip were always on, and lemonade and cakes never off; a heaven where marriages were made, books borrowed and newspapers read. Muscular Judaism was well to the fore at "the Club," – and entertainments were frequent. The middle classes of the community, overflowing with artistic instinct, supplied a phenomenal number of reciters, vocalists and instrumentalists ready to oblige, and the greatest favourites of the London footlights were pleased to come down, partly because they found such keenly appreciative audiences, and partly because they were so much mixed up with the race, both professionally and socially. There were serious lectures now and again, but few of the members took them seriously; they came to the Club not to improve their minds but to relax them. The Club was a blessing without disguise to the daughters of Judah, and certainly kept their brothers from harm. The ballroom, with its decorations of evergreens and winter blossoms, was a gay sight. Most of the dancers were in evening dress, and it would have been impossible to tell the ball from a Belgravian gathering, except by the preponderance of youth and beauty. Where could you match such a bevy of brunettes, where find such blondes? They were anything but lymphatic, these oriental blondes, if their eyes did not sparkle so intoxicatingly as those of the darker majority. The young men had carefully curled moustaches and ringlets oiled like the Assyrian bull, and figure-six noses, and studs glittering on their creamy shirt-fronts. How they did it on their wages was one of the many miracles of Jewish history. For socially, and even in most cases financially, they were only on the level of the Christian artisan. These young men in dress-coats were epitomes of one aspect of Jewish history. Not in every respect improvements on the "Sons of the Covenant," though; replacing the primitive manners and the piety of the foreign Jew by a veneer of cheap culture and a laxity of ceremonial observance. It was a merry party, almost like a family gathering, not merely because most of the dancers knew one another, but because "all Israel are brothers" – and sisters. They danced very buoyantly, not boisterously; the square dances symmetrically executed, every performer knowing his part; the waltzing full of rhythmic grace. When the music was popular they accompanied it on their voices. After supper their heels grew lighter, and the laughter and gossip louder, but never beyond the bounds of decorum. A few Dutch dancers tried to introduce the more gymnastic methods in vogue in their own clubs, where the kangaroo is dancing master, but the sentiment of the floor was against them. Hannah danced little, a voluntary wallflower, for she looked radiant in tussore silk, and there was an air of refinement about the slight, pretty girl that attracted the beaux of the Club. But she only gave a duty dance to Sam, and a waltz to Daniel Hyams, who had been brought by his sister, though he did not boast a swallow-tail to match her flowing draperies. Hannah caught a rather unamiable glance from pretty Bessie Sugarman, whom poor Daniel was trying hard not to see in the crush.

"Is your sister engaged yet?" Hannah asked, for want of something to say.

"You would know it if she was," said Daniel, looking so troubled that Hannah reproached herself for the meaningless remark.

"How well she dances!" she made haste to say. ·

"Not better than you," said Daniel, gallantly.

"I see compliments are among the fancy goods you deal in. Do you reverse?" she added, as they came to an awkward corner.

"Yes – but not my compliments," he said smiling. "Miriam taught me."

"She makes me think of Miriam dancing by the Red Sea," she said, laughing at the incongruous idea.

"She played a timbrel, though, didn't she?" he asked. "I confess I don't quite know what a timbrel is."

"A sort of tambourine, I suppose," said Hannah merrily, "and she sang because the children of Israel were saved."

They both laughed heartily, but when the waltz was over they returned to their individual gloom. Towards supper-time, in the middle of a square dance, Sam, suddenly noticing Hannah's solitude, brought her a tall bronzed gentlemanly young man in a frock coat, mumbled an introduction and rushed back to the arms of the exacting Leah.

"Excuse me, I am not dancing tonight," Hannah said coldly in reply to the stranger's demand for her programme.

"Well, I'm not half sorry," he said, with a frank smile. "I had to ask you, you know. But I should feel quite out of place bumping such a lot of swells."

There was something unusual about the words and the manner which impressed Hannah agreeably, in spite of herself. Her face relaxed a little as she said:

"Why, haven't you been to one of these affairs before?"

"Oh yes, six or seven years ago, but the place seems quite altered. They've rebuilt it, haven't they? Very few of us sported dress-coats here in the days before I went to the Cape. I only came back the other day and somebody gave me a ticket and so I've looked in for auld lang syne."

An unsympathetic hearer would have detected a note of condescension in the last sentence. Hannah detected it, for the announcement that the young man had returned from the Cape froze all her nascent sympathy. She was turned to ice again. Hannah knew him well – the young man from the Cape. He was a higher and more disagreeable development of the young man in the dress-coat. He had put South African money in his purse – whether honestly or not, no one inquired – the fact remained he had put it in his purse. Sometimes the law confiscated it, pretending he had purchased diamonds illegally, or what not, but then the young man did *not* return from the Cape. But, to do him justice, the secret of his success was less dishonesty than the opportunities for initiative energy in unexploited districts. Besides, not having to keep up appearances, he descended to menial occupations and toiled so long and terribly that he would probably have made just as much money at home, if he had had the courage. Be this as it may, there the money was; and, armed with it, the young man set sail literally for England, home and beauty; resuming his cast-off gentility with several extra layers of superciliousness. Pretty Jewesses pranked in their prettiest clothes, hastened, metaphorically speaking, to the port to welcome the wanderer; for they knew it was from among them he would make his pick. There were several varieties of him – marked by financial ciphers – but whether he married in his old station or higher up the scale, he was always faithful to the sectarian tradition of the race, and this less from religious motives than from hereditary instinct. Like the young man in the dress-coat, he held the Christian girl to be cold of heart, and unsprightly of temperament. He laid it down that all Yiddishë girls possessed that warmth and *chic* which, among Christians, were the birthright of a few actresses and music-hall artistes – themselves, probably, Jewesses! And on things theatrical this young man spoke as one having authority. Perhaps, though he was scarce conscious of it, at the bottom of his repulsion was the certainty that the Christian girl could not fry fish. She might be delightful for flirtation of all degrees, but had not been formed to make him permanently happy. Such was the conception which Hannah had formed for herself of the young man from the Cape. This latest specimen of the genus was prepossessing into the bargain. There was no denying he was well built, with a shapely head and a lovely moustache. Good looks alone were vouchers for insolence and conceit, but, backed by the aforesaid purse–! She turned her head away and stared at the evolutions of the "Lancers" with much interest.

"They've got some pretty girls in that set," he observed admiringly. Evidently the young man did not intend to go away.

Hannah felt very annoyed. "Yes," she said, sharply, "which would you like?"

"I shouldn't care to make invidious distinctions," he replied with a little laugh.

"Odious prig!" thought Hannah. "He actually doesn't see I'm sitting on him!" Aloud she said, "No? But you can't marry them all."

"Why should I marry any?" he asked in the same light tone, though there was a shade of surprise in it.

"Haven't you come back to England to get a wife? Most young men do, when they don't have one exported to them in Africa."

He laughed with genuine enjoyment and strove to catch the answering gleam in her eyes, but she kept them averted. They were standing with their backs to the wall and he could only see the profile and note the graceful poise of the head upon the warm-coloured neck that stood out against the white bodice. The frank ring of his laughter mixed with the merry jingle of the fifth figure –

"Well, I'm afraid I'm going to be an exception," he said.

"You think nobody good enough, perhaps," she could not help saying.

"Oh! Why should you think that?"

"Perhaps you're married already."

"Oh no, I'm not," he said earnestly. "You're not, either, are you?"

"Me?" she asked; then, with a barely perceptible pause, she said, "Of course I am."

The thought of posing as the married woman she theoretically was, flashed upon her suddenly and appealed irresistibly to her sense of fun. The recollection that the nature of the ring on her finger was concealed by her glove afforded her supplementary amusement.

"Oh!" was all he said. "I didn't catch your name exactly."

"I didn't catch yours," she replied evasively.

"David Brandon," he said readily.

"It's a pretty name," she said, turning smilingly to him. The infinite possibilities of making fun of him latent in the joke quite warmed her towards him. "How unfortunate for me I have destroyed my chance of getting it."

It was the first time she had smiled, and he liked the play of light round the curves of her mouth, amid the shadows of the soft dark skin, in the black depths of the eyes.

"How unfortunate for me!" he said, smiling in return.

"Oh yes, of course!" she said with a little toss of her head. "There is no danger in saying that now."

"I wouldn't care if there was."

"It is easy to smooth down the serpent when the fangs are drawn," she laughed back.

"What an extraordinary comparison!" he exclaimed. "But where are all the people going? It isn't all over, I hope."

"Why, what do you want to stay for? You're not dancing."

"That is the reason. Unless I dance with you."

"And then you would want to go?" she flashed with mock resentment.

"I see you're too sharp for me," he said lugubriously. "Roughing it among the Boers makes a fellow a bit dull in compliments."

"Dull indeed!" said Hannah, drawing herself up with great seriousness. "I think you're more complimentary than you have a right to be to a married woman."

His face fell. "Oh, I didn't mean anything," he said apologetically.

"So I thought," retorted Hannah.

The poor fellow grew more red and confused than ever. Hannah felt quite sympathetic with him now, so pleased was she at the humiliated condition to which she had brought the young man from the Cape.

"Well, I'll say good-bye," he said awkwardly. "I suppose I mustn't ask to take you down to supper. I dare say your husband will want that privilege."

"I dare say," replied Hannah smiling. "Although husbands do not always appreciate their privileges."

"I shall be glad if yours doesn't," he burst forth.

"Thank you for your good wishes for my domestic happiness," she said severely.

"Oh, why will you misconstrue everything I say?" he pleaded. "You must think me an awful *Shlemihl*, putting my foot into it so often. Anyhow I hope I shall meet you again somewhere."

"The world is very small," she reminded him.

"I wish I knew your husband," he said ruefully.

"Why?" said Hannah, innocently.

"Because I could call on him," he replied, smiling.

"Well, you do know him," she could not help saying.

"Do I? Who is it? I don't think I do," he exclaimed.

"Well, considering he introduced you to me!"

"Sam!" cried David startled.

"Yes."

"But –" said David, half incredulously, half in surprise. He certainly had never credited Sam with the wisdom to select or the merit to deserve a wife like this.

"But what?" asked Hannah with charming *naïveté*.

"He said – I – I – at least I think he said – I – I – understood that he introduced me to Miss Solomon, as his intended wife."

Solomon was the name of Malka's first husband, and so of Leah.

"Quite right," said Hannah simply.

"Then – what – how?" he stammered.

"She was his intended wife," explained Hannah as if she were telling the most natural thing in the world. "Before he married me, you know."

"I – I beg your pardon if I seemed to doubt you. I really thought you were joking."

"Why, what made you think so?"

"Well," he blurted out. "He didn't mention he was married, and seeing him dancing with her the whole time –"

"I suppose he thinks he owes her some attention," said Hannah indifferently. "By way of compensation probably. I shouldn't be at all surprised if he takes her down to supper instead of me."

"There he is, struggling towards the buffet. Yes, he has her on his arm."

"You speak as if she were his phylacteries," said Hannah, smiling. "It would be a pity to disturb them. So, if you like, *you* can have me on your arm, as you put it."

The young man's face lit up with pleasure, the keener that it was unexpected.

"I am very glad to have such phylacteries on my arm, as you put it," he responded. "I fancy I should be a good deal *froomer* if my phylacteries were like that."

"What, aren't you *froom?*" she said, as they joined the hungry procession in which she noted Bessie Sugarman on the arm of Daniel Hyams.

"No, I'm a regular wrong'un," he replied. "As for phylacteries, I almost forget how to lay them."

"That is bad," she admitted, though he could not ascertain her own point of view from the tone.

"Well, everybody else is just as bad," he said cheerfully. "All the old piety seems to be breaking down. It's Purim, but how many of us have been to hear the – the what do you call it? – the *Megillah* read? There is actually a minister here tonight bare-headed. And how many of us are going to wash our hands before supper or *bensh* afterwards, I should like to know. Why, it's as much as can be expected if the food's *kosher*, and there's no ham sandwiches on the dishes. Lord! how my old dad, God rest his soul, would have been horrified by such a party as this!"

"Yes, it's wonderful how ashamed Jews are of their religion outside a synagogue," said Hannah rousingly. "My father, if he were here, would put on his hat after supper and *bensh*, though there wasn't another man in the room to follow his example."

"And I should admire him for it," said David, earnestly, "though I admit I shouldn't follow his example myself. I suppose he's one of the old school."

"He is Reb Shemuel," said Hannah, with dignity.

"Oh, indeed!" he exclaimed, not without surprise, "I know him well. He used to bless me when I was a boy, and it used to cost him a halfpenny a time. Such a jolly fellow!"

"I'm so glad you think so," said Hannah flushing with pleasure.

"Of course I do. Does he still have all those *Greeners* coming to ask him questions?"

"Oh, yes. Their piety is just the same as ever."

"They're poor," observed David. "It's always those poorest in worldly goods who are richest in religion."

"Well, isn't that a compensation?" returned Hannah, with a little sigh. "But from my father's point of view, the truth is rather that those who have most pecuniary difficulties have most religious difficulties."

"Ah, I suppose they come to your father as much to solve the first as the second."

"Father is very good," she said simply.

They had by this time obtained something to eat, and for a minute or so the dialogue became merely dietary.

"Do you know," he said in the course of the meal, "I feel I ought not to have told you what a wicked person I am? I put my foot into it there, too."

"No, why?"

"Because you are Reb Shemuel's daughter."

"Oh, what nonsense! I like to hear people speak their minds. Besides, you mustn't fancy I'm as *froom* as my father."

"I don't fancy that. Not quite," he laughed. "I know there's some blessed old law or other by which women haven't got the same chance of distinguishing themselves that way as men. I have a vague recollection of saying a prayer thanking God for not having made me a woman."

"Ah, that must have been a long time ago," she said slyly.

"Yes, when I was a boy," he admitted. Then the oddity of the premature thanksgiving struck them both and they laughed.

"You've got a different form provided for you, haven't you?" he said.

"Yes, I have to thank God for having made me according to His will."

"You don't seem satisfied for all that," he said, struck by something in the way she said it.

"How can a woman be satisfied?" she asked, looking up frankly. "She has no voice in her destinies. She must shut her eyes and open her mouth and swallow what it pleases God to send her."

"All right, shut your eyes," he said, and putting his hand over them he gave her a titbit and restored the conversation to a more flippant level.

"You mustn't do that," she said. "Suppose my husband were to see you."

"Oh, bother!" he said. "I don't know why it is, but I don't seem to realise you're a married woman."

"Am I playing the part so badly as all that?"

"Is it a part?" he cried eagerly.

She shook her head. His face fell again. She could hardly fail to note the change.

"No, it's a stern reality," she said. "I wish it wasn't."

It seemed a bold confession, but it was easy to understand. Sam had been an old school-fellow of his, and David had not thought highly of him. He was silent a moment.

"Are you not happy?" he said gently.

"Not in my marriage."

"Sam must be a regular brute!" he cried indignantly. "He doesn't know how to treat you. He ought to have his head punched the way he's going on with that fat thing in red."

"Oh, don't run her down," said Hannah, struggling to repress her emotions, which were not purely of laughter. "She's my dearest friend."

"They always are," said David oracularly. "But how came you to marry him?"

"Accident," she said indifferently.

"Accident!" he repeated, open-eyed.

"Ah, well, it doesn't matter," said Hannah, meditatively conveying a spoonful of trifle to her mouth. "I shall be divorced from him tomorrow. Be careful! You nearly broke that plate."

David stared at her, open-mouthed.

"Going to be divorced from him tomorrow?"

"Yes, is there anything odd about it?"

"Oh," he said, after staring at her impassive face for a full minute. "Now I'm sure you've been making fun of me all along."

"My dear Mr. Brandon, why will you persist in making me out a liar?"

He was forced to apologise again and became such a model of perplexity and embarrassment that Hannah's gravity broke down at last and her merry peal of laughter mingled with the clatter of plates and the hubbub of voices.

"I must take pity on you and enlighten you," she said, "but promise me it shall go no further. It's only our own little circle that knows about it and I don't want to be the laughing-stock of the Lane."

"Of course I will promise," he said eagerly.

She kept his curiosity on the *qui vive* to amuse herself a little longer, but ended by telling him all, amid frequent exclamations of surprise.

"Well, I never!" he said when it was over. "Fancy a religion in which only two per cent of the people who profess it have ever heard of its laws. I suppose we're so mixed up with the English, that it never occurs to us we've got marriage laws of our own – like the Scotch. Anyhow I'm real glad and I congratulate you."

"On what?"

"On not being really married to Sam."

"Well, you're a nice friend of his, I must say. I don't congratulate myself, I can tell you."

"You don't?" he said in a disappointed tone.

She shook her head silently.

"Why not?" he inquired anxiously.

"Well, to tell the truth, this forced marriage was my only chance of getting a husband who wasn't pious. Don't look so puzzled. I wasn't shocked at your wickedness – you mustn't be at mine. You know there's such a lot of religion in our house that I thought if I ever did get married I'd like a change."

"Ha! ha! ha! So you're as the rest of us. Well, it's plucky of you to admit it."

"Don't see it. My living doesn't depend on religion, thank Heaven. Father's a saint, I know, but he swallows everything he sees in his books just as he swallows everything mother and I put before him in his plate – and in spite of it all –" She was about to mention Levi's shortcomings but checked herself in time. She had no right to unveil anybody's soul but her own and she didn't know why she was doing that.

"But you don't mean to say your father would forbid you to marry a man you cared for, just because he wasn't *froom*."

"I'm sure he would."

"But that would be cruel."

"He wouldn't think so. He'd think he was saving my soul, and you must remember he can't imagine anyone who has been taught to see its beauty not loving the yoke of the Law. He's the best father in the world – but when religion is concerned, the best-hearted of mankind are liable to become hard as stone. You don't know my father as I do. But apart from that, I wouldn't marry a man, myself, who might hurt my father's position. I should have to keep a *kosher* house or look how people would talk!"

"And wouldn't you if you had your own way?"

"I don't know what I would do. It's so impossible, the idea of my having my own way. I think I should probably go in for a change, I'm so tired – so tired of this eternal ceremony. Always washing up plates and dishes. I dare say it's all for our good, but I am so tired."

"Oh, I don't see much difficulty about *Koshers*. I always eat *kosher* meat myself when I can get it, providing it's not so beastly tough as it has a knack of being. Of course it's absurd to expect a man to go without meat when he's travelling up country, just because it hasn't been killed with a knife instead of a pole-axe. Besides, don't we know well enough that the folks who are most particular about those sort of things don't mind swindling and setting their houses on fire and all manner of abominations? I wouldn't be a Christian for the world, but I should like to see a little more common-sense introduced into our religion; it ought to he more up-to-date. If ever I marry, I should like my wife to be a girl who wouldn't want to keep anything but the higher parts of Judaism. Not out of laziness, mind you, but out of conviction."

David stopped suddenly, surprised at his own sentiments, which he learned for the first time. However vaguely they might have been simmering in his brain, he could not honestly accuse himself of having ever bestowed any reflection on "the higher parts of Judaism" or even on the religious convictions apart from the racial aspects of his future wife. Could it be that Hannah's earnestness was infecting him?

"Oh, then you would marry a Jewess!" said Hannah.

"Oh, of course," he said in astonishment. Then as he looked at her pretty, earnest face the amusing recollection that she was married already came over him with a sort of shock, not wholly comical. There was a minute of silence, each pursuing a separate train of thought. Then David wound up, as if there had been no break, with an elliptical, "wouldn't you?"

Hannah shrugged her shoulders and elevated her eyebrows in a gesture that lacked her usual grace.

"Not if I had only to please myself," she added.

"Oh, come! Don't say that," he said anxiously. "I don't believe mixed marriages are a success. Really, I don't. Besides, look at the scandal!"

Again she shrugged her shoulders, defiantly this time.

"I don't suppose I shall ever get married," she said. "I never could marry a man father would approve of, so that a Christian would be no worse than an educated Jew."

David did not quite grasp the sentence; he was trying to, when Sam and Leah passed them. Sam winked in a friendly if not very refined manner.

"I see you two are getting on all right," he said.

"Good gracious!" said Hannah, starting up with a blush. "Everybody's going back. They *will* think us greedy. What a pair of fools we are to have got into such serious conversation at a ball."

"Was it serious?" said David with a retrospective air. "Well, I never enjoyed a conversation so much in my life."

"You mean the supper," Hannah said lightly.

"Well, both. It's your fault that we don't behave more appropriately."

"How do you mean?"

"You won't dance."

"Do you want to?"

"Rather."

"I thought you were afraid of all the swells."

"Supper has given me courage."

"Oh, very well if you want to, that's to say if you really can waltz."

"Try me, only you must allow for my being out of practice. I didn't get many dances at the Cape, I can tell you."

"The Cape!" Hannah heard the words without making her usual grimace. She put her hand lightly on his shoulder, he encircled her waist with his arm and they surrendered themselves to the intoxication of the slow, voluptuous music.

CHAPTER XII

The Sons of the Covenant

The "Sons of the Covenant" sent no representatives to the club balls, wotting neither of waltzes nor of dress-coats, and preferring death to the embrace of a strange dancing woman. They were the congregation of which Mr. Belcovitch was President and their synagogue was the ground floor of No. 1 Royal Street – two large rooms knocked into one, and the rear partitioned off for the use of the bewigged, heavy-jawed women who might not sit with the men lest they should fascinate their thoughts away from things spiritual. Its furniture was bare benches, a raised platform with a reading desk in the centre and a wooden curtained ark at the end containing two parchment scrolls of the Law, each with a silver pointer and silver bells and pomegranates. The scrolls were in manuscript, for the printing press has never yet sullied the sanctity of the synagogue editions of the Pentateuch. The room was badly ventilated and what little air there was was generally sucked up by a greedy company of wax candles, big and little, struck in brass holders. The back window gave on the yard and the contiguous cow-sheds, and "moos" mingled with the impassioned supplications of the worshippers, who came hither two and three times a day to batter the gates of heaven and to listen to sermons more exegetical than ethical. They dropped in, mostly in their work-a-day garments and grime, and rumbled and roared and chorused prayers with a zeal that shook the window-panes, and there was never lack of *minyan* – the congregational quorum of ten. In the West End, synagogues are built to eke out the income of poor *minyan-men* or professional congregants; in the East End rooms are tricked up for prayer. This synagogue was all of luxury many of its Sons could boast. It was their *salon* and their lecture-hall. It supplied them not only with their religion but their art and letters, their politics and their public amusements. It was their home as well as the Almighty's, and on occasion they were familiar and even a little vulgar with Him. It was a place in which they could sit in their slippers, metaphorically that is; for though they frequently did so literally, it was by way of reverence, not ease. They enjoyed themselves in this *Shool* of theirs; they shouted and skipped and shook and sang, they wailed and moaned; they clenched their fists and thumped their breasts and they were not least happy when they were crying. There is an apocryphal anecdote of one of them being in the act of taking a pinch of snuff when the "Confession" caught him unexpectedly.

"We have trespassed," he wailed mechanically, as he spasmodically put the snuff in his bosom and beat his nose with his clenched fist.

They prayed metaphysics, acrostics, angelology, Cabalah, history, exegetics, Talmudical controversies, *menus,* recipes, priestly prescriptions, the canonical books, psalms, love-poems, an undigested hotch-potch of exalted and questionable sentiments, of communal and egoistic aspirations of the highest order. It was a wonderful liturgy, as grotesque as it was beautiful – like an old cathedral in all styles of architecture, stored with shabby antiquities and side-shows and overgrown with moss and lichen – a heterogeneous blend of historical strata of all periods, in which gems of poetry and pathos and spiritual fervour glittered and pitiful records of ancient persecution lay petrified. And the method of praying these things was equally complex and uncouth, equally the bond-slave of tradition; here a rising and there a bow, now three steps backwards and now a beating of the breast, this bit for the congregation and that for the minister, variants of a page, a word, a syllable, even a vowel, ready for every possible contingency. Their religious consciousness was largely a musical box – the thrill of the ram's horn, the cadenza of psalmic phrase, the jubilance of a festival "Amen" and the sobriety of a work-a-day "Amen," the Passover melodies and the Pentecost, the minor keys of Atonement and the hilarious rhapsodies of Rejoicing, the plain chant of the Law and the more ornate intonation of the Prophets – all this was known and loved and was far more important than the meaning of it all or its relation to their real lives; for page upon page was gabbled off at rates that could not be excelled by automata. But if they did not always know what they were saying they always meant it. If the service had been more intelligible it would have been less emotional and edifying. There was not a sentiment, however incomprehensible, for which they were not ready to die or to damn.

"All Israel are brethren," and indeed there was a strange antique clannishness about these "Sons of the Covenant" which in the modern world, where the ends of the ages meet, is Socialism. They prayed for one another while alive, visited one another's bedsides when sick, buried one another when dead. No mercenary hands poured the yolks of eggs over their dead faces and arrayed their corpses in their praying-shawls. No hired masses were said for the sick or the troubled, for the psalm-singing services of the "Sons of the Covenant" were always available for petitioning the Heavens, even though their brother had been arrested for buying stolen goods, and the service might be an invitation to Providence to compound a felony. Little charities of their own they had, too – a Sabbath Meal Society, and a Marriage Portion Society to buy the sticks for poor couples – and when a pauper countryman arrived from Poland, one of them boarded him and another lodged him and a third taught him a trade. Strange exotics in a land of prose carrying with them through the paven highways of London the odour of Continental Ghettos and bearing in their eyes through all the shrewdness of their glances the eternal mysticism of the Orient, where God was born! Hawkers and peddlers, tailors and cigar-makers, cobblers and furriers, glaziers and cap-makers – this was in sum their life. To pray much and to work long, to beg a little and to cheat a little, to eat not over-much and to "drink" scarce at all, to beget annual children by chaste wives (disallowed them half the year), and to rear them not over-well, to study the

Law and the Prophets and to reverence the Rabbinical tradition and the chaos of commentaries expounding it, to abase themselves before the "Life of Man" and Joseph Caro's "Prepared Table" as though the authors had presided at the foundation of the earth, to wear phylacteries and fringes, to keep the beard unshaven, and the corners of the hair uncut, to know no work on Sabbath and no rest on week-day. It was a series of recurrent landmarks, ritual and historical, of intimacy with God so continuous that they were in danger of forgetting His existence as of the air they breathed. They ate unleavened bread in Passover and blessed the moon and counted the days of the *Omer* till Pentecost saw the synagogue dressed with flowers in celebration of an Asiatic fruit harvest by a European people divorced from agriculture; they passed to the terrors and triumphs of the New Year (with its domestic symbolism of apple and honey and its procession to the river) and the revelry of repentance on the Great White Fast, when they burned long candles and whirled fowls round their heads and attired themselves in grave-clothes and saw from their seats in synagogue the long fast-day darken slowly into dusk, while God was scaling the decrees of life and death; they passed to Tabernacles when they ran up rough booths in back yards draped with their bed-sheets and covered with greenery, and bore through the streets citrons in boxes and a waving combination of myrtle, and palm and willow branches, wherewith they made a pleasant rustling in the synagogue; and thence to the Rejoicing of the Law when they danced and drank rum in the House of the Lord and scrambled sweets for the little ones, and made a sevenfold circuit with the two scrolls, supplemented by toy flags and children's candles stuck in hollow carrots; and then on again to Dedication with its celebration of the Maccabaean deliverance and the miracle of the unwaning oil in the Temple, and to Purim with its masquerading and its execration of Haman's name by the banging of little hammers; and so back to Passover. And with these larger cycles, epicycles of minor fasts and feasts, multiplex, not to be overlooked, from the fast of the ninth of Ab – fatal day for the race – when they sat on the ground in shrouds, and wailed for the destruction of Jerusalem, to the feast of the Great Hosannah when they whipped away willow leaves on the *Shool* benches in symbolism of forgiven sins, sitting up the whole of the night before in a long paroxysm of prayer mitigated by coffee and cakes; from the period in which nuts were prohibited to the period in which marriages were commended.

And each day, too, had its cycles of religious duty, its comprehensive and cumbrous ritual with accretions of commentary and tradition.

And every contingency of the individual life was equally provided for, and the writings that regulated all this complex ritual are a marvellous monument of the patience, piety and juristic genius of the race – and of the persecution which threw it back upon its sole treasure, the Law.

Thus they lived and died, these Sons of the Covenant, half-automata, sternly disciplined by voluntary and involuntary privation, hemmed and mewed in by iron walls of form and poverty, joyfully ground under the perpetual rotary wheel of ritualism, good-humoured withal and casuistic like all people whose religion stands much upon ceremony; inasmuch as a ritual law comes to count one equally with a moral, and a man is not half bad who does three-fourths of his duty.

And so the stuffy room with its guttering candles and its chameleon-coloured ark curtain was the pivot of their barren lives. Joy came to bear to it the offering of its thanksgiving and to vow sixpenny bits to the Lord, prosperity came in a high hat to chaffer for the holy privileges, and grief came with rent garments to lament the beloved dead and glorify the name of the Eternal.

The poorest life is to itself the universe and all that therein is, and these humble products of a great and terrible past, strange fruits of a motley-flowering secular tree whose roots are in Canaan and whose boughs overshadow the earth, were all the happier for not knowing that the fulness of life was not theirs.

And the years went rolling on, and the children grew up and here and there a parent.

* * * * *

The elders of the synagogue were met in council.

"He is greater than a Prince," said the Shalotten *Shammos*.

"If all the Princes of the Earth were put in one scale," said Mr. Belcovitch, "and our *Maggid*, Moses, in the other, he would outweigh them all. He is worth a hundred of the Chief Rabbi of England, who has been seen bareheaded."

"From Moses to Moses there has been none like Moses," said old Mendel Hyams, interrupting the Yiddish with a Hebrew quotation.

"Oh no," said the Shalotten *Shammos*, who was a great stickler for precision, being, as his nickname implied, a master of ceremonies. "I can't admit that. Look at my brother Nachmann."

There was a general laugh at the Shalotten *Shammos's* bull; the proverb dealing only with Moseses.

"He has the true gift," observed *Froom* KarIkammer, shaking the flames of his hair pensively. "For the letters of his name have the same numerical value as those of the great Moses da Leon."

Froom Karlkammer was listened to with respect, for he was an honorary member of the committee, who paid for two seats in a larger congregation and only worshipped with the Sons of the Covenant on special occasions. The Shalotten *Shammos*, however, was of contradictory temperament – a born dissentient, upheld by a steady consciousness of highly superior English, the drop of bitter in Belcovitch's presidential cup. He was a long thin man, who towered above the congregation, and was as tall as the bulk of them even when he was bowing his acknowledgments to his Maker.

"How do you make that out?" he asked Karlkammer. "Moses of course adds up the same as Moses – but while the other part of the *Maggid's* name makes seventy-three, da Leon's makes ninety-one."

"Ah, that's because you're ignorant of *Gematriyah*," said little Karlkammer, looking up contemptuously at the cantankerous giant. "You reckon all the letters on the same system, and you omit to give yourself the license of deleting the ciphers."

In philology it is well known that all consonants are interchangeable and vowels don't count; in *Gematriyah* any letter may count for anything, and the total may he summed up anyhow.

Karlkammer was, one of the curiosities of the Ghetto. In a land of *froom* men he was the *froomest*. He had the very genius of fanaticism. On the Sabbath he spoke nothing but Hebrew whatever the inconvenience and however numerous the misunderstandings, and if he perchance paid a visit he would not perform the "work" of lifting the knocker. Of course he had his handkerchief girt round his waist to save him from carrying it, but this compromise being general was not characteristic of Karlkammer any more than his habit of wearing two gigantic sets of phylacteries where average piety was content with one of moderate size.

One of the walls of his room had an unpapered and unpainted scrap in mourning for the fall of Jerusalem. He walked through the streets to synagogue attired in his praying-shawl and phylacteries, and knocked three times at the door of God's house when he arrived. On the Day of Atonement he walked in his socks, though the heavens fell, wearing his grave-clothes. On this day he remained standing in synagogue from 6 a.m. to 7 p.m. with his body bent at an angle of ninety degrees; it was to give him bending space that he hired two seats. On Tabernacles, not having any ground whereon to erect a booth, by reason of living in an attic, he knocked a square hole in the ceiling, covered it with branches through which the free air of heaven played, and hung a quadrangle of sheets from roof to floor; he bore to synagogue the tallest *Lulav* of palm-branches that could be procured and quarrelled with a rival pietist for the last place in the floral procession, as being the lowliest and meekest man in Israel – an ethical pedestal equally claimed by his rival. He insisted on bearing a corner of the biers of all the righteous dead. Almost every other day was a fast-day for Karlkammer, and he had a host of supplementary ceremonial observances which are not for the vulgar. Compared with him Moses Ansell and the ordinary "Sons of the Covenant" were mere heathens. He was a man of prodigious distorted mental activity. He had read omnivorously amid the vast stores of Hebrew literature, was a great authority on Cabalah, understood astronomy, and, still more, astrology, was strong on finance, and could argue coherently on any subject outside religion. His letters to the press on specifically Jewish subjects were the most hopeless, involved, incomprehensible and protracted puzzles ever penned, bristling with Hebrew quotations from the most varying, the most irrelevant and the most mutually incongruous sources and peppered with the dates of birth and death of every Rabbi mentioned.

No one had ever been known to follow one of these argumentations to the bitter end. They were written in good English modified by a few peculiar terms used in senses unsuspected by dictionary-makers; in a beautiful hand, with the t's uncrossed, but crowned with the side-stroke, so as to avoid the appearance of the symbol of Christianity, and with the dates expressed according to the Hebrew Calendar, for Karlkammer refused to recognize the chronology of the Christian. He made three copies of every letter, and each was exactly like the others in every word and every line. His bill for midnight oil must have been extraordinary, for he was a business man and had to earn his living by day. Kept within the limits of sanity by a religion without apocalyptic visions, he was saved from predicting the end of the world by mystic calculations, but he used them to prove everything else and fervently believed that endless meanings were deducible from the numerical value of Biblical words, that not a curl at the tail of a letter of any word in any sentence but had its supersubtle significance. The elaborate cipher with which Bacon is alleged to have written Shakspeare's plays was mere child's play compared with the infinite revelations which in Karlkammer's belief the Deity left latent in writing the Old Testament from Genesis to Malachi and in inspiring the Talmud and the holier treasures of Hebrew literature. Nor were these ideas of his own origination. His was an eclectic philosophy and religionism, of which all the elements were discoverable in old Hebrew books; scraps of Alexandrian philosophy inextricably blent with Aristotelian, Platonic, mystic.

He kept up a copious correspondence with scholars in other countries and was universally esteemed and pitied.

"We haven't come to discuss the figures of the *Maggid's* name, but of his salary," said Mr. Belcovitch, who prided himself on his capacity for conducting public business.

"I have examined the finances," said Karlkammer, "and I don't see how we can possibly put aside more for our preacher than the pound a week."

"But he is not satisfied," said Mr. Belcovitch.

"I don't see why he shouldn't be," said the Shalotten *Shammos*. "A pound a week is luxury for a single man."

The Sons of the Covenant did not know that the poor consumptive *Maggid* sent half his salary to his sisters in Poland to enable them to buy back their husbands from military service; also they had vague unexpressed ideas that he was not mortal, that Heaven would look after his larder, that if the worst came to the worst he could fall back on Cabalah and engage himself with the mysteries of food-creation.

"I have a wife and family to keep on a pound a week," grumbled Greenberg the *Chazan*.

Besides being Reader, Greenberg blew the horn and killed cattle and circumcised male infants and educated children and discharged the functions of beadle and collector. He spent a great deal of his time in avoiding being drawn into the contending factions of the congregation and in steering equally between Belcovitch and the Shalotten *Shammos*. The Sons only gave him fifty a year for all his trouble, but they eked it out by allowing him to be on the Committee, where on the question of a rise in the Reader's salary he was always an ineffective minority of one. His other grievance was that for the High Festivals the Sons temporarily engaged a finer voiced Reader and advertised him at raised prices to repay themselves out of the surplus congregation. Not only had Greenberg to play second fiddle on these grand occasions, but he had to iterate "Pom" as a sort of musical accompaniment in the pauses of his rival's vocalization.

"You can't compare yourself with the *Maggid*," the Shalotten *Shammos* reminded him consolingly. "There are hundreds of you in the market.

There are several *morceaux* of the service which you do not sing half so well as your predecessor; your horrid blowing cannot compete with Freedman's of the Fashion Street *Chevrah*, nor can you read the Law as quickly and accurately as Prochintski. I have told you over and over again you confound the air of the Passover *Yigdal* with the New Year ditto. And then your preliminary flourish to the Confession of Sin – it goes 'Ei, Ei, Ei, Ei, Ei, Ei, Ei'" (he mimicked Greenberg's melody) "whereas it should be 'Oi, Oi, Oi, Oi, Oi, Oi.'"

"Oh no," interrupted Belcovitch. "All the *Chazanim* I've ever heard do it 'Ei, Ei, Ei.'"

"You are not entitled to speak on this subject, Belcovitch," said the Shalotten *Shammos* warmly. "You are a Man-of-the-Earth. I have heard every great *Chazan* in Europe."

"What was good enough for my father is good enough for me," retorted Belcovitch. "The *Shool* he took me to at home had a beautiful *Chazan*, and he always sang it 'Ei, Ei, Ei.'"

"I don't care what you heard at home. In England every *Chazan* sings 'Oi, Oi, Oi.'"

"We can't take our tune from England," said Karlkammer reprovingly. "England is a polluted country by reason of the Reformers whom we were compelled to excommunicate."

"Do you mean to say that my father was an Epicurean?" asked Belcovitch indignantly. "The tune was as Greenberg sings it. That there are impious Jews who pray bareheaded and sit in the synagogue side by side with the women has nothing to do with it."

The Reformers did neither of these things, but the Ghetto to a man believed they did, and it would have been countenancing their blasphemies to pay a visit to their synagogues and see. It was an extraordinary example of a myth flourishing in the teeth of the facts, and as such should be useful to historians sifting "the evidence of contemporary writers."

The dispute thickened; the synagogue hummed with "Eis" and "Ois" not in concord.

"Shah!" said the President at last. "Make an end, make an end!"

"You see he knows I'm right," murmured the Shalotten *Shammos* to his circle.

"And if you are!" burst forth the impeached Greenberg, who had by this time thought of a retort. "And if I do sing the Passover *Yigdal* instead of the New Year, have I not reason seeing I have *no bread in the house?* With my salary I have Passover all the year round."

The *Chazan's* sally made a good impression on his audience if not on his salary. It was felt that he had a just grievance, and the conversation was hastily shifted to the original topic.

"We mustn't forget the *Maggid* draws crowds here every Saturday and Sunday afternoon," said Mendel Hyams. "Suppose he goes over to a *Chevrah* that will pay him more!"

"No, he won't do that," said another of the Committee. "He will remember that we brought him out of Poland."

"Yes, but we shan't have room for the audiences soon," said Belcovitch. "There are so many outsiders turned away every time that I think we ought to let half the applicants enjoy the first two hours of the sermon and the other half the second two hours."

"No, no, that would be cruel," said Karlkammer. "He will have to give the Sunday sermons at least in a larger synagogue. My own *Shool*, the German, will be glad to give him facilities."

"But what if they want to take him altogether at a higher salary?" said Mendel.

"No, I'm on the Committee, I'll see to that," said Karlkammer reassuringly.

"Then do you think we shall tell him we can't afford to give him more?" asked Belcovitch.

There was a murmur of assent with a fainter mingling of dissent. The motion that the *Maggid's* application be refused was put to the vote and carried by a large majority.

It was the fate of the *Maggid* to be the one subject on which Belcovitch and the Shalotten *Shammos* agreed. They agreed as to his transcendent merits and they agreed as to the adequacy of his salary.

"But he's so weakly," protested Mendel Hyams, who was in the minority. "He coughs blood."

"He ought to go to a sunny place for a week," said Belcovitch, compassionately.

"Yes, he must certainly have that," said Karlkammer. "Let us add as a rider that although we cannot pay him more per week, he must have a week's holiday in the country. The Shalotten *Shammos* shall write the letter to Rothschild."

Rothschild was a magic name in the Ghetto; it stood next to the Almighty's as a redresser of grievances and a friend of the poor, and the Shalotten *Shammos* made a large part of his income by writing letters to it. He charged twopence halfpenny per letter, for his English vocabulary was larger than any other scribe's in the Ghetto, and his words were as much longer than theirs as his body. He also filled up printed application forms for Soup or Passover cakes, and had a most artistic sense of the proportion of orphans permissible to widows and a correct instinct for the plausible duration of sicknesses.

The Committee agreed *nem. con.* to the grant of a seaside holiday, and the Shalotten *Shammos* with a gratified feeling of importance waived his twopence halfpenny. He drew up a letter forthwith, not of course in the name of the Sons of the Covenant, but in the *Maggid's* own.

He took the magniloquent sentences to the *Maggid* for signature. He found the *Maggid* walking up and down Royal Street waiting for the verdict. The *Maggid* walked with a stoop that was almost a permanent bow, so that his long black beard reached well towards his baggy knees. His curved eagle nose was grown thinner, his long coat shinier, his look more haggard, his corkscrew earlocks were more matted, and when he spoke his voice was a tone more raucous. He wore his high hat – a tall cylinder that reminded one of a weather-beaten turret.

The Shalotten *Shammos* explained briefly what he had done.

"May thy strength increase!" said the *Maggid* in the Hebrew formula of gratitude.

"Nay, thine is more important," replied the Shalotten *Shammos* with hilarious heartiness, and he proceeded to read the letter as they walked along together, giant and doubled-up wizard.

"But I haven't got a wife and six children;" said the Maggid, for whom one or two phrases stood out intelligible. "My wife is dead and I never was blessed with a *Kaddish*." ·

"It sounds better so," said the Shalotten *Shammos* authoritatively. "Preachers are expected to have heavy families dependent upon them. It would sound lies if I told the truth."

This was an argument after the *Maggid's* own heart, but it did not quite convince him.

"But they will send and make inquiries," he murmured.

"Then your family are in Poland; you send your money over there."

"That is true," said the *Maggid* feebly. "But still it likes me not."

"You leave it to me," said the Shalotten *Shammos* impressively. "A shamefaced man cannot learn, and a passionate man cannot teach. So said Hillel. When you are in the pulpit I listen to you; when I have my pen in hand, do you listen to me. As the proverb says, if I were a Rabbi the town would burn. But if you were a scribe the letter would burn. I don't pretend to be a *Maggid*, don't you set up to be a letter writer."

"Well, but do you think it's honourable?"

"Hear, O Israel" cried the Shalotten Shammos, spreading out his palms impatiently. "Haven't I written letters for twenty years?"

The Maggid was silenced. He walked on brooding. "And what is this place, Burnmud, I ask to go to?" he inquired.

"Bournemouth," corrected the other. "It is a place on the South coast where all the most aristocratic consumptives go."

"But it must be very dear," said the poor *Maggid* affrighted.

"Dear? Of course it's dear," said the Shalotten *Shammos* pompously. "But shall we consider expense where your health is concerned?"

The *Maggid* felt so grateful he was almost ashamed to ask whether he could eat *kosher* there, but the Shalotten *Shammos*, who had the air of a tall encyclopædia, set his soul at rest on all points.

CHAPTER XIII

Sugarman's Bar-mitzvah Party

The day of Ebenezer Sugarman's *Bar-mitzvah* duly arrived. All his sins would henceforth be on his own head and everybody rejoiced. By the Friday evening so many presents had arrived – four breastpins, two rings, six pocket-knives, three sets of *Machzorim* or Festival Prayer-books, and the like – that his father barred up the door very carefully and in the middle of the night, hearing a mouse scampering across the floor, woke up in a cold sweat and threw open the bedroom window and cried "Ho! Buglers!" But the "Buglers" made no sign of being scared, everything was still and nothing purloined, so Jonathan took a reprimand from his disturbed wife and curled himself up again in bed.

Sugarman did things in style and through the influence of a client the confirmation ceremony was celebrated in "Duke's Plaizer Shool." Ebenezer, who was tall and weak-eyed, with lank black hair, had a fine new black cloth suit and a beautiful silk praying-shawl with blue stripes, and a glittering watch-chain and a gold ring and a nice new Prayer-book with gilt edges, and all the boys under thirteen made up their minds to grow up and be responsible for their sins as quick as possible. Ebenezer walked up to the Reading Desk with a dauntless stride and intoned his Portion of the Law with no more tremor than was necessitated by the musical roulades, and then marched upstairs, as bold as brass, to his mother, who was sitting up in the gallery, and who gave him a loud smacking kiss that could be heard in the four corners of the synagogue, just as if she were a real lady.

Then there was the *Bar-mitzvah* breakfast, at which Ebenezer deliv-ered an English sermon and a speech, both openly written by the Shalotten *Shammos*, and everybody commended the boy's beautiful senti-ments and the beautiful language in which they were couched. Mrs. Sugarman forgot all the trouble Ebenezer had given her in the face of his assurances of respect and affection and she wept copiously. Having only one eye she could not see what her Jonathan saw, and what was spoiling his enjoyment of Ebenezer's effusive gratitude to his dear parents for having trained him up in lofty principles.

It was chiefly male cronies who had been invited to breakfast, and the table had been decorated with biscuits and fruit and sweets not apper-taining to the meal, but provided for the refreshment of the less-favoured visitors – such as Mr. and Mrs. Hyams – who would be dropping in during the day. Now, nearly every one of the guests had brought a little boy with him, each of whom stood like a page behind his father's chair.

Before starting on their prandial fried fish, these trencher-men took from the dainties wherewith the ornamental plates were laden and gave thereof to their offspring. Now this was only right and proper, because it is the prerogative of children to "*nash*" on these occasions. But as the meal progressed, each father from time to time, while talking briskly to his neighbour, allowed his hand to stray mechanically into the plates and thence negligently backwards into the hand of his infant, who stuffed the treasure into his pockets. Sugarman fidgeted about uneasily; not one surreptitious seizure escaped him, and every one pricked him like a needle. Soon his soul grew punctured like a pin-cushion. The Shalotten *Shammos* was among the worst offenders, and he covered his back-handed proceedings with a ceaseless flow of complimentary conversation.

"Excellent fish, Mrs. Sugarman," he said, dexterously slipping some almonds behind his chair.

"What?" said Mrs. Sugarman, who was hard of hearing.

"First-class plaice," shouted the Shalotten *Shammos*, negligently conveying a bunch of raisins.

"So they ought to be," said Mrs. Sugarman in her thin tinkling accents, "they were all alive in the pan."

"Ah, did they twitter?" said Mr. Belcovitch, pricking up his ears.

"No," Bessie interposed. "What do you mean?"

"At home in my town," said Mr. Belcovitch impressively, "a fish made a noise in the pan one Friday."

"Well? and suppose?" said the Shalotten *Shammos*, passing a fig to the rear, "the oil frizzles."

"Nothing of the kind," said Belcovitch angrily. "A real living noise. The woman snatched it out of the pan and ran with it to the Rabbi. But he did not know what to do. Fortunately there was staying with him for the Sabbath a travelling Saint from the far city of Ridnik, a *Chasid*, very skilful in plagues and purifications, and able to make clean a creeping thing by a hundred and fifty reasons. He directed the woman to wrap the fish in a shroud and give it honourable burial as quickly as possible. The funeral took place the same afternoon and a lot of people went in solemn procession to the woman's back garden and buried it with all seemly rites, and the knife with which it had been cut was buried in the same grave, having been defiled by contact with the demon. One man said it should be burned, but that was absurd because the demon would be only too glad to find itself in its native element, but to prevent Satan from rebuking the woman any more its mouth was stopped with furnace ashes. There was no time to obtain Palestine earth, which would have completely crushed the demon."

"The woman must have committed some *Avirah*," said Karlkammer.

"A true story!" said the Shalotten *Shammos*, ironically. "That tale has been over Warsaw this twelvemonth."

"It occurred when I was a boy," affirmed Belcovitch indignantly. "I remember it quite well. Some people explained it favourably. Others were of opinion that the soul of the fishmonger had transmigrated into the fish, an opinion borne out by the death of the fishmonger a few days before. And the Rabbi is still alive to prove it – may his light continue to shine – though they write that he has lost his memory."

The Shalotten *Shammos* sceptically passed a pear to his son. Old Gabriel Hamburg, the scholar, came compassionately to the raconteur's assistance.

"Rabbi Solomon Maimon," he said, "has left it on record that he witnessed a similar funeral in Posen."

"It was well she buried it," said Karlkarnmer. "It was an atonement for a child, and saved its life."

The Shalotten *Shammos* laughed outright.

"Ah, laugh not," said Mrs. Belcovitch. "Or you might laugh with blood. It isn't for my own sins that I was born with ill-matched legs."

"I must laugh when I hear of God's fools burying fish anywhere but in their stomach," said the Shalotten *Shammos*, transporting a Brazil nut to the rear, where it was quickly annexed by Solomon Ansell, who had sneaked in uninvited and ousted the other boy from his coign of vantage.

The conversation was becoming heated; Breckeloff turned the topic.

"My sister has married a man who can't play cards," he said lugubriously.

"How lucky for her," answered several voices.

"No, it's just her black luck," he rejoined. "For he will play."

There was a burst of laughter and then the company remembered that Breckeloff was a *Badchan* or jester.

"Why, your sister's husband is a splendid player," said Sugarman with a flash of memory, and the company laughed afresh.

"Yes," said Breckeloff. "But he doesn't give me the chance of losing to him now, he's got such a stuck-up *Kotzon*. He belongs to Duke's Plaizer *Shool* and comes there very late, and when you ask him his birthplace he forgets he was a *Pullack* and says he comes from 'behind Berlin.'"

These strokes of true satire occasioned more merriment and were worth a biscuit to Solomon Ansell *vice* the son of the Shalotten *Shammos*.

Among the inoffensive guests were old Gabriel Hamburg, the scholar, and young Joseph Strelitski, the student, who sat together. On the left of the somewhat seedy Strelitski pretty Bessie in blue silk presided over the coffee-pot. Nobody knew whence Bessie had stolen her good looks; probably some remote ancestress! Bessie was in every way the most agreeable member of the family, inheriting some of her father's brains, but wisely going for the rest of herself to that remote ancestress.

Gabriel Hamburg and Joseph Strelitski had both had relations with . No. 1 Royal Street for some time, yet they had hardly exchanged a word and their meeting at this breakfast table found them as great strangers as though they had never seen each other. Strelitski came because he boarded with the Sugarmans, and Hamburg came because he sometimes consulted Jonathan Sugarman about a Talmudical passage. Sugarman was charged with the oral traditions of a chain of Rabbis, like an actor who knows all the "business" elaborated by his predecessors, and even a scientific scholar like Hamburg found him occasionally and fortuitously illuminating. Even so Karlkammer's red hair was a pillar of fire in the trackless wilderness of Hebrew literature. Gabriel Hamburg was a mighty savant who endured all things for the love of knowledge and the sake of six men in Europe who followed his work and profited by its results. Verily, fit audience though few. But such is the fate of great scholars whose readers are sown throughout the lands more sparsely than monarchs. One by one Hamburg grappled with the countless problems of Jewish literary history, settling dates and authors, disinte-grating the Books of the Bible into their constituent parts, now inserting a gap of centuries between two halves of the same chapter, now flashing the light of new theories upon the development of Jewish theology. He lived at Royal Street and the British Museum, for he spent most of his time groping among the folios and manuscripts, and had no need for more than the little back bedroom, behind the Ansells, stuffed with mouldy books. Nobody (who was anybody) had heard of him in England, and he worked on, unencumbered by patronage or a full stomach. The Ghetto, itself, knew little of him, for there were but few with whom he found intercourse satisfying. He was not "orthodox" in belief though eminently so in practice – which is all the Ghetto demands

– not from hypocrisy but from ancient prejudice. Scholarship had not shrivelled up his humanity, for he had a genial fund of humour and a gentle play of satire and loved his neighbours for their folly and narrow-mindedness. Unlike Spinoza, too, he did not go out of his way to inform them of his heterodox views, content to comprehend the crowd rather than be misunderstood by it. He knew that the bigger soul includes the smaller and that the smaller can never circumscribe the bigger. Such money as was indispensable for the endowment of research he earned by copying texts and hunting out references for the numerous scholars and clergymen who infest the Museum and prevent the general reader from having elbow room. In person he was small and bent and snuffy. Superficially more intelligible, Joseph Strelitski was really a deeper mystery than Gabriel Hamburg. He was known to be a recent arrival on English soil, yet he spoke English fluently. He studied at Jews' College by day and was preparing for the examinations at the London University. None of the other students knew where he lived nor a bit of his past history. There was a vague idea afloat that he was an only child whose parents had been hounded to penury and death by Russian persecution, but who launched it nobody knew. His eyes were sad and earnest, a curl of raven hair fell forwards on his high brow; his clothing was shabby and darned in places by his own hand. Beyond accepting the gift of education at the hands of dead men he would take no help. On several distinct occasions, the magic name, Rothschild, was appealed to on his behalf by well-wishers, and through its avenue of almoners it responded with its eternal quenchless unquestioning generosity to students. But Joseph Strelitski always quietly sent back these bounties. He made enough to exist upon by touting for a cigar-firm in the evenings. In the streets he walked with tight-pursed lips, dreaming no one knew what.

And yet there were times when his tight-pursed lips unclenched themselves and he drew in great breaths even of Ghetto air with the huge contentment of one who has known suffocation. "One can breathe here," he seemed to be saying. The atmosphere, untainted by spies, venal officials, and jeering soldiery, seemed fresh and sweet. Here the ground was stable, not mined in all directions; no arbitrary ukase – veritable sword of Damocles – hung over the head and darkened the sunshine. In such a country, where faith was free and action untrammelled, mere living was an ecstasy when remembrance came over one, and so Joseph Strelitski sometimes threw back his head and breathed in liberty. The voluptuousness of the sensation cannot be known by born freemen.

When Joseph Strelitski's father was sent to Siberia, he took his nine-year old boy with him in infringement of the law which prohibits exiles from taking children above five years of age. The police authorities, however, raised no objection, and they permitted Joseph to attend the public school at Kansk, Yeniseisk province, where the Strelitski family resided. A year or so afterwards the Yeniseisk authorities accorded the family permission to reside in Yeniseisk, and Joseph, having given proof of brilliant abilities, was placed in the Yeniseisk gymnasium. For nigh three years the boy studied here, astonishing the gymnasium with his extraordinary ability, when suddenly the Government authorities ordered the boy to return at once "to the place where he was born." In vain the directors of the gymnasium, won over by the poor boy's talent and enthusiasm for study, petitioned the Government. The Yeniseisk authorities were again ordered to expel him. No respite was granted and the thirteen-year-old lad was sent to Sokolk in the Government of Grodno at the other extreme of European Russia, where he was quite alone in the world. Before he was sixteen, he escaped to England, his soul branded by terrible memories, and steeled by solitude to a stern strength.

At Sugarman's he spoke little and then mainly with the father on scholastic points. After meals he retired quickly to his business or his sleeping den, which was across the road. Bessie loved Daniel Hyams, but she was a woman and Strelitski's neutrality piqued her. Even today it is possible he might not have spoken to Gabriel Hamburg if his other neighbour had not been Bessie. Gabriel Hamburg was glad to talk to the youth, the outlines of whose English history were known to him.

Strelitski seemed to expand under the sunshine of a congenial spirit; he answered Hamburg's sympathetic inquiries about his work without reluctance and even made some remarks on his own initiative.

And as they spoke, an undercurrent of pensive thought was flowing in the old scholar's soul and his tones grew tenderer and tenderer. The echoes of Ebenezer's effusive speech were in his ears and the artificial notes rang strangely genuine. All round him sat happy fathers of happy children, men who warmed their hands at the home-fire of life, men who lived while he was thinking. Yet he, too, had had his chance far back in the dim and dusty years, his chance of love and money with it. He had let it slip away for poverty and learning, and only six men in Europe cared whether he lived or died. The sense of his own loneliness smote him with a sudden aching desolation. His gaze grew humid; the face of the young student was covered with a veil of mist and seemed to shine with the radiance of an unstained soul. If he had been as other men he might have had such a son. At this moment Gabriel Hamburg was speaking of paragoge in Hebrew grammar, but his voice faltered and in imagination he was laying hands of paternal benediction on Joseph Strelitski's head. Swayed by an overmastering impulse he burst out at last.

"An idea strikes me!"

Strelitski looked up in silent interrogation at the old man's agitated face.

"You live by yourself. I live by myself. We are both students. Why should we not live together as students, too?"

A swift wave of surprise traversed Strelitski's face, and his eyes grew soft. For an instant the one solitary soul visibly yearned towards the other; he hesitated.

"Do not think I am too old," said the great scholar, trembling all over. "I know it is the young who chum together, but still I am a student. And you shall see how lively and cheerful I will be." He forced a smile that hovered on tears. "We shall be two rackety young students, every night raising a thousand devils. *Gaudeamus igitur.*" He began to hum in his cracked hoarse voice the *Burschen-lied* of his early days at the Berlin Gymnasium.

But Strelitski's face had grown dusky with a gradual flush and a deepening gloom; his black eyebrows were knit and his lips set together and his eyes full of sullen ire. He suspected a snare to assist him.

He shook his head. "Thank you," he said slowly. "But I prefer to live alone."

And he turned and spoke to the astonished Bessie, and so the two strange lonely vessels that had hailed each other across the darkness drifted away and apart forever in the waste of waters.

But Jonathan Sugarman's eye was on more tragic episodes. Gradually the plates emptied, for the guests openly followed up the more substantial elements of the repast by dessert, more devastating even than the rear manœuvres. At last there was nothing but an aching china blank. The men looked round the table for something else to "*nash,*" but everywhere was the same depressing desolation. Only in the centre of the table towered in awful intact majesty the great *Bar-mitzvah* cake, like some mighty sphinx of stone surveying the ruins of empires, and the least reverent shrank before its austere gaze. But at last the Shalotten *Shammos* shook off his awe and stretched out his hand leisurely towards the cake, as became the master of ceremonies. But when Sugarman the *Shadchan* beheld his hand moving like a creeping flame forward, he sprang towards him, as the tigress springs when the hunter threatens her cub. And speaking no word he snatched the great cake from under the hand of the spoiler and tucked it under his arm, in the place where he carried Nehemiah, and sped therewith from the room. Then consternation fell upon the scene till Solomon Ansell, crawling on hands and knees in search of windfalls, discovered a basket of apples stored under the centre of the table, and the Shalotten *Shammos's* son told his father thereof ere Solomon could do more than secure a few for his brother and sisters. And the Shalotten *Shammos* laughed joyously, "Apples," and dived under the table, and his long form reached to the other side and beyond, and greybearded men echoed the joyous cry and scrambled an the ground like schoolboys.

"*Leolom tikkach* – always take," quoted the Badchan gleefully.

When Sugarman returned, radiant, he found his absence had been fatal.

"Piece of fool! Two-eyed lump of flesh," said Mrs. Sugarman in a loud whisper. "Flying out of the room as if thou hadst the ague."

"Shall I sit still like thee while our home is eaten up around us?" Sugarman whispered back. "Couldst thou not look to the apples? Plaster image! Leaden fool! See, they have emptied the basket, too."

"Well, dost thou expect luck and blessing to crawl into it? Even five shillings' worth of *nash* cannot last for ever. May ten ammunition wagons of black curses be discharged on thee!" replied Mrs. Sugarman, her one eye shooting fire.

This was the last straw of insult added to injury. Sugarman was exasperated beyond endurance. He forgot that he had a wider audience than his wife; he lost all control of himself, and cried aloud in a frenzy of rage, "What a pity thou hadst not a fourth uncle!"

Mrs. Sugarman collapsed, speechless.

"A greedy lot, marm," Sugarman reported to Mrs. Hyams on the Monday. "I was very glad you and your people didn't come; dere was noding left except de prospectuses of the Hamburg lottery vich I left laying all about for de guests to take. Being *Shabbos* I could not give dem out."

"We were sorry not to come, but neither Mr. Hyams nor myself felt well," said the white-haired broken-down old woman with her painfully slow enunciation. Her English words rarely went beyond two syllables.

"Ah!" said Sugarman. "But I've come to give you back your corkscrew."

"Why, it's broken," said Mrs. Hyams, as she took it.

"So it is, marm," he admitted readily. "But if you taink dat I ought to pay for de damage you're mistaken. If you lend me your cat" – here he began to make the argumentative movement with his thumb, as though scooping out imaginary *kosher* cheese with it; "if you lend me your cat to kill my rat," his tones took on the strange Talmudic singsong – "and my rat instead kills your cat, then it is the fault of your cat and not the fault of my rat."

Poor Mrs. Hyams could not meet this argument. If Mendel had been at home, he might have found a counter analogy. As it was, Sugarman re-tucked Nehemiah under his arm and departed triumphant, almost consoled for the raid on his provisions by the thought of money saved. In the street he met the Shalotten *Shammos.*

"Blessed art thou who comest," said the giant, in Hebrew; then relapsing into Yiddish he cried: "I've been wanting to see you. What did you mean by telling your wife you were sorry she had not a fourth uncle?"

"Soorka knew what 1 meant," said Sugarman with a little croak of victory. "I have told her the story before. When the Almighty *Shadchan* was making marriages in Heaven, before we were yet born, the name of my wife was coupled with my own. The spirit of her eldest uncle hearing this flew up to the Angel who made the proclamation and said: 'Angel! thou art making a mistake. The man of whom thou makest mention will be of a lower status than this future niece of mine.' Said the Angel: 'Sh! It is all right. She will halt on one leg.' Came then the spirit of her second uncle and said: 'Angel, what blazonest thou? A niece of mine marry a man of such family?' Says the Angel: 'Sh! It is all right. She will be blind in one eye.' Came the spirit of her third uncle and said: 'Angel, hast thou not erred? Surely thou canst not mean to marry my future niece into such a humble family.' Said the Angel: 'Sh! It is all right. She will be deaf in one ear.' Now, do you see? If she had only had a fourth uncle, she would have been dumb into the bargain; there is only one mouth and my life would have been a happy one. Before I told Soorka that history she used to throw up her better breeding and finer family to me. Even in public she would shed my blood. Now she does not do it even in private."

Sugarman the *Shadchan* winked, readjusted Nehemiah and went his way.

CHAPTER XIV

The Hope of the Family

It was a cold, bleak Sunday afternoon, and the Ansells were spending it as usual. Little Sarah was with Mrs. Simons, Rachel had gone to Victoria Park with a party of school-mates, the grandmother was asleep on the bed, covered with one of her son's old coats (for there was no fire in the grate), with her pious vade mecum in her hand; Esther had prepared her lessons and was reading a little brown book at Dutch Debby's, not being able to forget the *London Journal* sufficiently; Solomon had not prepared his and was playing "rounder" in the street, Isaac being permitted to "feed" the strikers, in return for a prospective occupation of his new bed; Moses Ansell was at *Shool*, listening to a *Hesped* or funeral oration at the German Synagogue, preached by Reb Shemuel over one of the lights of the Ghetto, prematurely gone out – no other than the consumptive *Maggid*, who had departed suddenly for a less fashionable place than Bournemouth. "He has fallen," said the Reb, "not laden with age, nor sighing for release because the grasshopper was a burden. But He who holds the keys said: 'Thou hast done thy share of the work; it is not thine to complete it. It was in thy heart to serve Me, from Me thou shalt receive thy reward.'"

And all the perspiring crowd in the black-draped hall shook with grief, and thousands of working men followed the body, weeping, to the grave, walking all the way to the great cemetery in Bow.

A slim, black-haired, handsome lad of about twelve, dressed in a neat black suit, with a shining white Eton collar, stumbled up the dark stairs of No. 1 Royal Street, with an air of unfamiliarity and disgust. At Dutch Debby's door he was delayed by a brief altercation with Bobby. He burst open the door of the Ansell apartment without knocking, though he took off his hat involuntarily. as he entered. Then he stood still with an air of disappointment. The room seemed empty.

"What dost thou want, Esther?" murmured the grandmother rousing herself sleepily.

The boy looked towards the bed with a start. He could not make out what the grandmother was saying. It was four years since he had heard Yiddish spoken, and he had almost forgotten the existence of the dialect. The room, too, seemed chill and alien, so unspeakably poverty-stricken.

"Oh, how are you, grandmother?" he said, going up to her and kissing her perfunctorily. "Where's everybody?"

"Art thou Benjamin?" said the grandmother, her stern, wrinkled face shadowed with surprise and doubt.

Benjamin guessed what she was asking and nodded.

"But how richly they have dressed thee! Alas, I suppose they have taken away thy Judaism instead. For four whole years – is it not – thou hast been with English folk. Woe! Woe! If thy father had married a pious woman, she would have been living still and thou wouldst have been able to live happily in our midst instead of being exiled among strangers, who feed thy body and starve thy soul. If thy father had left me in Poland, I should have died happy and my old eyes would never have seen the sorrow. Unbutton thy waistcoat, let me see if thou wearest the 'four-corners' at least." Of this harangue, poured forth at the rate natural to thoughts running ever in the same groove, Benjamin understood but a word here and there. For four years he had read and read and read English books, absorbed himself in English composition, heard nothing but English spoken about him. Nay, he had even deliberately put the jargon out of his mind at the commencement as something degrading and humiliating. Now it struck vague notes of old outgrown associations but called up no definite images.

"Where's Esther?" he said.

"Esther," grumbled the grandmother, catching the name. "Esther is with Dutch Debby. She's always with her. Dutch Debby pretends to love her like a mother – and why? Because she wants to *be* her mother. She aims at marrying my Moses. But not for us. This time we shall marry the woman I select. No person like that who knows as much about Judaism as the cow of Sunday, nor like Mrs. Simons, who coddles our little Sarah because she thinks my Moses will have her. It's plain as the eye in her head what she wants. But the Widow Finkelstein is the woman we're going to marry. She is a true Jewess, shuts up her shop the moment *Shabbos* comes in, not works right into the Sabbath like so many, and goes to *Shool* even on Friday nights. Look how she brought up her Avromkely, who intoned the whole Portion of the Law and the Prophets in *Shool* before he was six years old. Besides she has money and has cast eyes upon him."

The boy, seeing conversation was hopeless, murmured something inarticulate and ran down the stairs to find some traces of the intelligible members of his family. Happily Bobby, remembering their former alter-cation, and determining to have the last word, barred Benjamin's path with such pertinacity that Esther came out to quiet him and leapt into her brother's arms with a great cry of joy, dropping the book she held full on Bobby's nose.

"O Benjy – Is it really you? Oh, I am so glad. I am so glad. I knew you would come some day. O Benjy! Bobby, you bad dog, this is Benjy, my brother. Debby, I'm going upstairs. Benjamin's come back. Benjamin's come back."

"All right, dear," Debby called out. "Let me have a look at him soon. Send me in Bobby if you're going away." The words ended in a cough.

Esther hurriedly drove in Bobby, and then half led, half dragged Benjamin upstairs. The grandmother had fallen asleep again and was snoring peacefully.

"Speak low, Benjy," said Esther. "Grandmother's asleep."

"All right, Esther. I don't want to wake her, I'm sure. I was up here just now, and couldn't make out a word she was jabbering."

"I know. She's losing all her teeth, poor thing."

"No, it isn't that. She speaks that beastly Yiddish – I made sure she'd have learned English by this time. I hope *you* don't speak it, Esther."

"I must, Benjy. You see father and grandmother never speak anything else at home, and only know a few words of English. But I don't let the children speak it except to them. You should hear little Sarah speak English. It's beautiful. Only when she cries she says 'Woe is me' in Yiddish. I have had to slap her for it – but that makes her cry 'Woe is me' all the more. Oh, how nice you look, Benjy, with your white collar, just like the pictures of little Lord Launceston in the Fourth Standard Reader. I wish I could show you to the girls! Oh, my, what'll Solomon say when he sees you! He's always wearing his corduroys away at the knees."

"But where is everybody? And why is there no fire?" said Benjamin impatiently. "It's beastly cold."

"Father hopes to get a bread, coal and meat ticket tomorrow, dear."

"Well, this is a pretty welcome for a fellow!" grumbled Benjamin.

"I'm so sorry, Benjy! If I'd only known you were coming I might have borrowed some coals from Mrs. Belcovitch. But just stamp your feet a little if they freeze. No, do it outside the door; grandmother's asleep. Why didn't you write to me you were coming?"

"I didn't know. Old Four-Eyes – that's one of our teachers – was going up to London this afternoon, and he wanted a boy to carry some parcels, and as I'm the best boy in my class he let me come. He let me run up and see you all and I'm to meet him at London Bridge Station at seven o'clock. You're not much altered, Esther."

"Ain't I?" she said, with a little pathetic smile. "Ain't I bigger?"

"Not four years bigger. For a moment I could fancy I'd never been away. How the years slip by! I shall be *Bar-mitzvah* soon."

"Yes, and now I've got you again I've so much to say I don't know where to begin. That time father went to see you I couldn't get much out of him about you, and your own letters have been so few."

"A letter costs a penny, Esther. Where am I to get pennies from?"

"I know, dear. I know you would have liked to write. But now you shall tell me everything. Have you missed us very much?"

"No, I don't think so," said Benjamin.

"Oh, not at all?" asked Esther in disappointed tones.

"Yes, I missed *you*, Esther, at first," he said, soothingly. "But there's such a lot to do and to think about. It's a new life."

"And have you been happy, Benjy?"

"Oh yes. Quite. Just think! Regular meals, with oranges and sweets and entertainments every now and then, a bed all to yourself, good fires, a mansion with a noble staircase and hall, a field to play in, with balls and toys –"

"A field!" echoed Esther. "Why it must be like going to Greenwich every day."

"Oh, better than Greenwich where they take you girls for a measly day's holiday once a year."

"Better than the Crystal Palace, where they take the boys?"

"Why, the Crystal Palace is quite near. We can see the fireworks every Thursday night in the season."

Esther's eyes opened wider. "And have you been inside?"

"Lots of times."

"Do you remember the time you didn't go?" Esther said softly.

"A fellow doesn't forget that sort of thing," he grumbled. "I so wanted to go – I had heard such a lot about it from the boys who had been. When the day of the excursion came my *Shabbos* coat was in pawn, wasn't it?"

"Yes," said Esther, her eyes growing humid. "I was so sorry for you, dear. You didn't want to go in your corduroy coat and let the boys know you didn't have a best coat. It was quite right, Benjy."

"I remember mother gave me a treat instead," said Benjamin with a comic grimace. "She took me round to Zachariah Square and let me play there while she was scrubbing Malka's floor. I think Milly gave me a penny, and I remember Leah let me take a couple of licks from a glass of ice cream she was eating on the Ruins. It was a hot day – I shall never forget that ice cream. But fancy parents pawning a chap's only decent coat." He smoothed his well-brushed jacket complacently.

"Yes, but don't you remember mother took it out the very next morning before school with the money she earnt at Malka's."

"But what was the use of that? I put it on of course when I went to school and told the teacher I was ill the day before, just to show the boys I was telling the truth. But it was too late to take me to the Palace."

"Ah, but it came in handy – don't you remember, Benjy, how one of the Great ladies died suddenly the next week!"

"Oh yes! Yoicks! Tallyho!" cried Benjamin, with sudden excitement. "We went down on hired omnibuses to the cemetery ever so far into the country, six of the best boys in each class, and I was on the box seat next to the driver, and I thought of the old mail coach days and looked out for highwaymen. We stood along the path in the cemetery and the sun was shining and the grass was so green and there were such lovely flowers on the coffin when it came past with the gentlemen crying behind it and then we had lemonade and cakes on the way back. Oh, it was just beautiful! I went to two other funerals after that, but that was the one I enjoyed most. Yes, that coat did come in useful after all for a day in the country."

Benjamin evidently did not think of his own mother's interment as a funeral. Esther did and she changed the subject quickly.

"Well, tell me more about your place."

"Well, it's like going to funerals every day. It's all country all round about, with trees and flowers and birds. Why, I've helped to make hay in the autumn."

Esther drew a sigh of ecstasy. "It's like a book," she said.

"Books!" he said. "We've got hundreds and hundreds, a whole library – Dickens, Mayne Reid, George Eliot, Captain Marryat, Thackeray – I've read them all."

"Oh, Benjy!" said Esther, clasping her hands in admiration, both of the library and her brother. "I wish I were you."

"Well, you could be me easily enough."

"How?" said Esther, eagerly.

"Why, we have a girls' department, too. You're an orphan as much as me. You get father to enter you as a candidate."

"Oh, how could I, Benjy?" said Esther, her face falling. "What would become of Solomon and Ikey and little Sarah?"

"They've got a father, haven't they? and a grandmother?"

"Father can't do washing and cooking, you silly boy! And grandmother's too old."

"Well, I call it a beastly shame. Why can't father earn a living and give out the washing? He never has a penny to bless himself with."

"It isn't his fault, Benjy. He tries hard. I'm sure he often grieves that he's so poor that he can't afford the railway fare to visit you on visiting days. That time he did go he only got the money by selling a work-box I had for a prize. But he often speaks about you."

"Well, I don't grumble at his not coming," said Benjamin. "I forgive him that because – you know he's not very presentable, is he, Esther?"

Esther was silent. "Oh, well, everybody knows he's poor. They don't expect father to be a gentleman."

"Yes, but he might look decent. Does he still wear those two beastly little curls at the side of his head? Oh, I did hate it when I was at school here, and he used to come to see the master about something. Some of the boys had such respectable fathers, it was quite a pleasure to see them come in and overawe the teacher. Mother used to be as bad, coming in with a shawl over her head."

"Yes, Benjy, but she used to bring us in bread and butter when there had been none in the house at breakfast-time. Don't you remember, Benjy?"

"Oh, yes, I remember. We've been through some beastly bad times, haven't we, Esther? All I say is you wouldn't like father coming in before all the girls in your class, would you, now?"

Esther blushed. "There is no occasion for him to come," she said evasively.

"Well, I know what I shall do," said Benjamin decisively; "I'm going to be a very rich man –"

"Are you, Benjy?" inquired Esther.

"Yes, of course. I'm going to write books – like Dickens and those fellows. Dickens made a pile of money, just by writing down plain everyday things going on around."

"But you can't write!"

Benjamin laughed a superior laugh. "Oh, can't I? What about *Our Own*, eh?"

"What's that?"

"That's our journal. I edit it. Didn't I tell you about it? Yes, I'm running a story through it, called 'The Soldier's Bride,' all about life in Afghanistan."

"Oh, where could I get a number?"

"You can't get a number. It ain't printed, stupid. It's all copied by hand, and we've only got a few copies. If you came down, you could see it."

"Yes, but I can't come down," said Esther, with tears in her eyes.

"Well, never mind. You'll see it some day. Well, what was I telling you? Oh, yes! About my prospects. You see, I'm going in for a scholarship in a few months, and everybody says I shall get it. Then, perhaps I might go to a higher school, perhaps to Oxford or Cambridge!"

"And row in the boat-race!" said Esther, flushing with excitement.

"No, bother the boat-race. I'm going in for Latin and Greek. I've begun to learn French already. So I shall know three foreign languages."

"Four!" said Esther, "you forget Hebrew!"

"Oh, of course, Hebrew. I don't reckon Hebrew. Everybody knows Hebrew. Hebrew's no good to anyone. What I want is something that'll get me on in the world and enable me to write my books."

"But Dickens – did he know Latin or Greek?" asked Esther.

"No, he didn't," said Benjamin proudly. "That's just where I shall have the pull of him. Well, when I've got rich I shall buy father a new suit of clothes and a high hat – it *is* so beastly cold here, Esther, just feel my hands, like ice! – and I shall make him live with grandmother in a decent room, and give him an allowance so that he can study beastly big books all day long – does he still take a week to read a page? And Sarah and Isaac and Rachel shall go to a proper boarding school, and Solomon – how old will he be then?"

Esther looked puzzled. "Oh, but suppose it takes you ten years getting famous! Solomon will be nearly twenty."

"It can't take me ten years. But never mind! We shall see what is to be done with Solomon when the time comes. As for you –"

"Well, Benjy," she said, for his imagination was breaking down.

"I'll give you a dowry and you'll get married. See!" he concluded triumphantly.

"Oh, but suppose I shan't want to get married?"

"Nonsense – every girl wants to get married. I overheard Old Four-Eyes say all the teachers in the girls' department were dying to marry him. I've got several sweethearts already, and I dare say you have." He looked at her quizzingly.

"No, dear," she said earnestly. "There's only Levi Jacobs, Reb Shemuel's son, who's been coming round sometimes to play with Solomon, and brings me almond-rock. But I don't care for him – at least not in that way. Besides, he's quite above us."

"*Oh*, is he? Wait till I write my novels."

"I wish you'd write them now. Because then I should have something to read – Oh!"

"What's the matter?"

"I've lost my book. What have I done with my little brown book?"

"Didn't you drop it on that beastly dog?"

"Oh, did I? People'll tread on it on the stairs. Oh dear! I'll run down and get it. But don't call Bobby beastly, please."

"Why not? Dogs are beasts, aren't they?"

Esther puzzled over the retort as she flew downstairs, but could find no reply. She found the book, however, and that consoled her.

"What have you got hold of?" replied Benjamin, when she returned.

"Oh, nothing! It wouldn't interest you."

"All books interest me," announced Benjamin with dignity.

Esther reluctantly gave him the book. He turned over the pages carelessly, then his face grew serious and astonished.

"Esther!" he said, "how did you come by this?"

"One of the girls gave it me in exchange for a stick of slate pencil. She said she got it from the missionaries – she went to their night-school for a lark and they gave her it and a pair of boots as well."   .

"And you have been reading it?"

"Yes, Benjy," said Esther meekly.

"You naughty girl! Don't you know the New Testament is a wicked book? Look here! There's the word 'Christ' on nearly every page, and the word 'Jesus' on every other. And you haven't even scratched them out! Oh, if anyone was to catch you reading this book!"

"I don't read it in school hours," said the little girl deprecatingly.

"But you have no business to read it at all!"

"Why not?" she said doggedly. "I like it. It seems just as interesting as the Old Testament, and there are more miracles to the page."

"You wicked girl!" said her brother, overwhelmed by her audacity. "Surely you know that all these miracles were false?"

"Why were they false?" persisted Esther.

"Because miracles left off after the Old Testament! There are no miracles now-a-days, are there?"

"No," admitted Esther.

"Well, then," he said triumphantly, "if miracles had gone overlapping into New Testament times we might just as well expect to have them now."

"But why shouldn't we have them now?"

"Esther, I'm surprised at you. I should like to set Old Four-Eyes on to you. He'd soon tell you why. Religion all happened in the past. God couldn't be always talking to His creatures."

"I wish I'd lived in the past, when Religion was happening," said Esther ruefully. "But why do Christians all reverence this book? I'm sure there are many more millions of them than of Jews!"

"Of course there are, Esther. Good things are scarce. We are so few because we are God's chosen people."

"But why do I feel good when I read what Jesus said?"

"Because you are so bad," he answered, in a shocked tone.

"Here, give me the book, I'll burn it."

"No, no!" said Esther. "Besides there's no fire."

"No, hang it," he said, rubbing his hands. "Well, it'll never do if you have to fall back on this sort of thing. I'll tell you what I'll do. Ill send you *Our Own.*"

"Oh, will you Benjy? That is good of you," she said joyfully, and was kissing him when Solomon and Isaac came romping in and woke up the grandmother.

"How are you, Solomon?" said Benjamin. "How are you, my little man," he added, patting Isaac on his curly head. Solomon was overawed for a moment. Then he said, "Hullo, Benjy, have you got any spare buttons?"

But Isaac was utterly ignorant who the stranger could be and hung back with his finger in his mouth.

"That's your brother Benjamin, Ikey," said Solomon.

"Don't want no more brovers," said Ikey.

"Oh, but I was here before you," said Benjamin laughing.

"Does oor birfday come before mine, then?"

"Yes, if I remember."

Isaac looked tauntingly at the door. "See!" he cried to the absent Sarah. Then turning graciously to Benjamin he said, "I thant kiss oo, but I'll lat oo teep in my new bed."

"But you *must* kiss him," said Esther, and saw that he did it before she left the room to fetch little Sarah from Mrs. Simons.

When she came back Solomon was letting Benjamin inspect his Plevna peep-show without charge and Moses Ansell was back, too. His eyes were red with weeping, but that was on account of the *Maggid.* His nose was blue with the chill of the cemetery.

"He was a great man," he was saying to the grandmother. "He could lecture for four hours together on any text and he would always manage to get back to the text before the end. Such exegetics, such homiletics! He was greater than the Emperor of Russia. Woe! Woe!"

"Woe! Woe!" echoed the grandmother. "If women were allowed to go to funerals, I would gladly have followed him. Why did he come to England? In Poland he would still have been alive. And why did I come to England? Woe! Woe!"

Her head dropped back on the pillow and her sighs passed gently into snores. Moses turned again to his eldest born, feeling that he was secondary in importance only to the *Maggid*, and proud at heart of his genteel English appearance.

"Well, you'll soon be *Bar-mitzvah*, Benjamin," he said, with clumsy geniality blent with respect, as he patted his boy's cheeks with his discoloured fingers.

Benjamin caught the last two words and nodded his head.

"And then you'll be coming back to us. I suppose they will apprentice you to something."

"What does he say, Esther?" asked Benjamin, impatiently.

Esther interpreted.

"Apprentice me to something!" he repeated, disgusted. "Father's ideas are so beastly humble. He would like everybody to dance on him. Why he'd be content to see me a cigar-maker or a presser. Tell him I'm not coming home, that I'm going to win a scholarship and to go to the University."

Moses's eyes dilated with pride. "Ah, you will become a Rav," he said, and lifted up his boy's chin and looked lovingly into the handsome face.

"What's that about a Rav, Esther?" said Benjamin. "Does he want me to become a Rabbi – Ugh! Tell him I'm going to write books."

"My blessed boy! A good commentary on the Song of Songs is much needed. Perhaps you will begin by writing that."

"Oh, it's no use talking to him, Esther. Let him be. Why can't he speak English?"

"He can – but you'd understand even less," said Esther with a sad smile.

"Well, all I say is it's a beastly disgrace. Look at the years he's been in England – just as long as we have." Then the humour of the remark dawned upon him and he laughed. "I suppose he's out of work, as usual," he added.

Moses's ears pricked up at the syllables "out-of-work," which to him was a single word of baneful meaning.

"Yes," he said in Yiddish. "But if I only had a few pounds to start with I could work up a splendid business."

"Wait! He shall have a business," said Benjamin when Esther interpreted.

"Don't listen. to him," said Esther. "The Board of Guardians has started him again and again. But he likes to think he is a man of business."

Meantime Isaac had been busy explaining Benjamin to Sarah, and pointing out the remarkable confirmation of his own views as to birthdays. This will account for Esther's next remark being, "Now, dears, no fighting today. We must celebrate Benjy's return. We ought to kill a fatted calf – like the man in the Bible."

"What are you talking about, Esther?" said Benjamin suspiciously.

"I'm so sorry, nothing, only foolishness," said Esther. "We really must do something to make a holiday of the occasion. Oh, I know; we'll have tea before you go, instead of waiting till supper-time. Perhaps Rachel'll be back from the Park. You haven't seen her yet."

"No, I can't stay," said Benjy. "It'll take me three-quarters of an hour getting to the station. And you've got no fire to make tea with either."

"Nonsense, Benjy. You seem to have forgotten everything; we've got a loaf and a penn'uth of tea in the cupboard. Solomon, fetch a farthing's worth of boiling water from the Widow Finkelstein."

At the words "Widow Finkelstein" the grandmother awoke and sat up.

"No, Im too tired," said Solomon. "Isaac can go."

"No," said Isaac. "Let Estie go."

Esther took a jug and went to the door.

"Méshe," said the grandmother. "Go thou to the Widow Finkelstein."

"But Esther can go," said Moses.

"Yes, I'm going," said Esther.

"Méshe!" repeated the *Bube* inexorably. "Go thou to the Widow Finkelstein."

Moses went.

"Have you said the afternoon prayer, boys?" the old woman asked.

"Yes," said Solomon. "While you were asleep."

"Oh-h-h!" said Esther under her breath. And she looked reproachfully at Solomon.

"Well, didn't you say we must make a holiday today?" he whispered back.

CHAPTER XV

The Holy Land League

"Oh, these English Jews!" said Melchitsedek Pinchas, in German. "What have they done to you now?" said Guedalyah, the greengrocer, in Yiddish.

The two languages are relatives and often speak as they pass by.

"I have presented my book to every one of them, but they have paid me scarce enough to purchase poison for them all," said the little poet scowling. The cheekbones stood out sharply beneath the tense bronzed skin. The black hair was tangled and unkempt and the beard untrimmed, the eyes darted venom.

"One of them – Gideon, M. P., the stockbroker, engaged me to teach his son for his *Bar-mitzvah*. But the boy is so stupid! So stupid! Just like his father. I have no doubt he will grow up to be a Rabbi. I teach him his Portion – I sing the words to him with a most beautiful voice, but he has as much ear as soul. Then I write him a speech – a wonderful speech for him to make to his parents and the company at the breakfast, and in it, after he thanks them for their kindness, I make him say how, with the blessing of the Almighty, he will grow up to be a good Jew, and munificently support Hebrew literature and learned men like his revered teacher, Melchitsedek Pinchas. And he shows it to his father, and his father says it is not written in good English, and that another scholar has already written him a speech. Good English! Gideon has as much knowledge of style as the Rev. Elkan Benjamin of decency. Ah, I will shoot them both. I know I do not speak English like a native – but what language under the sun is there I cannot write? French, German, Spanish, Arabic – they flow from my pen like honey from a rod. As for Hebrew, you know, Guedalyah, I and you are the only two men in England who can write Holy Language grammatically. And yet these miserable stockbrokers, Men-of-the-Earth, they dare to say I cannot write English, and they have given me the sack. I, who was teaching the boy true Judaism and the value of Hebrew literature."

"What! They didn't let you finish teaching the boy his Portion because you couldn't write English?"

"No; they had another pretext – one of the servant girls said I wanted to kiss her – lies and falsehood. I was kissing my finger after kissing the *Mezuzah*, and the stupid abomination thought I was kissing my hand to her. It sees itself that they don't kiss the *Mezuzahs* often in that house – the impious crew. And what will be now? The stupid boy will go home to breakfast in a bazaar of costly presents, and he will make the stupid speech written by the fool of an Englishman, and the ladies will weep. But where will be the Judaism in all this? Who will vaccinate him against free-thinking as I would have done? Who will infuse into him the true patriotic fervour, the love of his race, the love of Zion, the land of his fathers?"

"Ah, you are, verily a man after my own heart!" said Guedalyah, the greengrocer, overswept by a wave of admiration. "Why should you not come with me to my *Beth-Hamidrash* tonight, to the meeting for the foundation of the Holy Land League? That cauliflower will be four-pence, mum."

"Ah, what is that?" said Pinchas.

"I have an idea; a score of us meet tonight to discuss it."

"Ah, yes! You have always ideas. You are a sage and a saint, Guedalyah. The Beth-Hamidrash which you have established is the only centre of real orthodoxy and Jewish literature in London. The ideas you expound in the Jewish papers for the amelioration of the lot of our poor brethren are most statesmanlike. But these donkey-head English rich people – what help can you expect from them? They do not even understand your plans. They have only sympathy with needs of the stomach."

"You are right! You are right, Pinchas!" said Guedalyal, the green-grocer, eagerly. He was a tall, loosely-built man, with a pasty complexion capable of shining with enthusiasm. He was dressed shabbily, and in the intervals of selling cabbages projected the regeneration of Judah.

"That is just what is beginning to dawn upon me, Pinchas," he went on. "Our rich people give plenty away in charity; they have good hearts but not Jewish hearts. As the verse says – A bundle of rhubarb and two pounds of Brussels sprouts and threepence halfpenny change. Thank you. Much obliged. – Now I have bethought myself why should we not work out our own salvation? It is the poor, the oppressed, the perse-cuted, whose souls pant after the Land of Israel as the hart after the water-brooks. Let us help ourselves. Let us put our hands in our own pockets. With our *Groschen* let us rebuild Jerusalem and our Holy Temple. We will collect a fund slowly but surely – from all parts of the East End and the provinces the pious will give. With the first fruits we will send out a little party of persecuted Jews to Palestine; and then another; and another. The movement will grow like a sliding snowball that becomes an avalanche."

"Yes, then the rich will come to you," said Pinchas, intensely excited. "Ah! it is a great idea, like all yours. Yes, I will come, I will make a mighty speech, for my lips, like Isaiah's, have been touched with the burning coal. I will inspire all hearts to start the movement at once. I will write its Marseillaise this very night, bedewing my couch with a poet's tears. We shall no longer be dumb – we shall roar like the lions of Lebanon. I shall be the trumpet to call the dispersed together from the four corners of the earth – yea, I shall be the Messiah himself," said Pinchas, rising on the wings of his own eloquence, and forgetting to puff at his cigar.

"I rejoice to see you so ardent; but mention not the word Messiah, for I fear some of our friends will take alarm and say that these are not Messianic times, that neither Elias, nor Gog, King of Magog, nor any of the portents have yet appeared. Kidneys or regents, my child?"

"Stupid people! Hillel said more wisely: 'If I help not myself who will help me?' Do they expect the Messiah to fall from heaven? Who knows but I am the Messiah? Was I not born on the ninth of Ab?"

"Hush, hush!" said Guedalyah, the greengrocer. "Let us be practical. We are not yet ready for Marsellaises or Messiahs. The first step is to get funds enough to send one family to Palestine."

"Yes, yes," said Pinchas, drawing vigorously at his cigar to rekindle it. "But we must look ahead. Already I see it all. Palestine in the hands of the Jews – the Holy Temple rebuilt, a Jewish state, a President who is equally accomplished with the sword and the pen – the whole campaign stretches before me. I see things like Napoleon, general and dictator alike."

"Truly we wish that," said the greengrocer cautiously. "But tonight it is only a question of a dozen men founding a collecting society."

"Of course, of course, that I understand. You're right – people about here say Guedalyah the greengrocer is always right. I will come before-hand to supper with you to talk it over, and you shall see what I will write for the *Mizpeh* and the *Arbeiter-freund*. You know all these papers jump at me – their readers are the class to which you appeal – in them will I write my burning verses and leaders advocating the cause. I shall be your Tyrtacus, your Mazzini, your Napoleon. How blessed that I came to England just now. I have lived in the Holy Land – the genius of the soil is blent with mine. I can describe its beauties as none other can. I am the very man at the very hour. And yet I will not go rashly – slow and sure – my plan is to collect small amounts from the poor to start by sending one family at a time to Palestine. That is how we must do it. How does that strike you, Guedalyah. You agree?"

"Yes, yes. That is also my opinion."

"You see I am not a Napoleon only in great ideas. I understand detail, though as a poet I abhor it. Ah, the Jew is king of the world. He alone conceives great ideas and executes them by petty means. The heathen are so stupid, so stupid! Yes, you shall see at supper how practically I will draw up the scheme. And then I will show you, too, what I have written about Gideon, M. P., the dog of a stockbroker – a satirical poem have I written about him, in Hebrew – an acrostic with his name for the mockery of posterity. Stocks and shares have I translated into Hebrew, with new words which will at once be accepted by the Hebraists of the world and added to the vocabulary of modern Hebrew. Oh! I am terrible in satire. I sting like the hornet; witty as Immanuel, but mordant as his friend Dante. It will appear in the *Mizpeh* tomorrow. I will show this Anglo-Jewish community that I am a man to be reckoned with. I will crush it – not it me."

"But they don't see the *Mizpeh* and couldn't read it if they did."

"No matter. I send it abroad – I have friends, great Rabbis, great scholars, everywhere, who send me their learned manuscripts, their commentaries, their ideas, for revision and improvement. Let the Anglo-Jewish community hug itself in its stupid prosperity – but I will make it the laughing-stock of Europe and Asia. Then some day it will find out its mistake; it will not have ministers like the Rev. Elkan Benjamin, who keeps four mistresses, it will depose the lump of flesh who reigns over it and it will seize the hem of my coat and beseech me to be its Rabbi."

"We should have a more orthodox Chief Rabbi, certainly," admitted Guedalyah.

"Orthodox? Then and only then shall we have true Judaism in London and a burst of literary splendour far exceeding that of the much overpraised Spanish School, none of whom had that true lyrical gift which is like the carol of the bird in the pairing season. O why have I not the bird's privileges as well as its gift of song? Why can I not pair at will? Oh the stupid Rabbis who forbade polygamy. Verily as the verse says: The Law of Moses is perfect, enlightening the eyes – marriage, divorce, all is regulated with the height of wisdom. Why must we adopt the stupid customs of the heathen? At present I have not even one mate – but I love – ah Guedalyah! I love! The women are so beautiful. You love the women, hey?"

"I love my Rivkah," said Guedalyah. "A penny on each gingerbeer bottle."

"Yes, but why haven't *I* got a wife? Eh?" demanded the little poet fiercely, his black eyes glittering. "I am a fine tall well-built good-looking man. In Palestine and on the Continent all the girls would go about sighing and casting sheep's eyes at me, for there the Jews love poetry and literature. But here! I can go into a room with a maiden in it and she makes herself unconscious of my presence. There is Reb Shemuel's daughter – a fine beautiful virgin. I kiss her hand – and it is ice to my lips. Ah, if I only had money! And money I should have, if these English Jews were not so stupid and if they elected me Chief Rabbi. Then I would marry – one, two, three maidens."

"Talk not such foolishness," said Guedalyah, laughing, for he thought the poet jested. Pinchas saw his enthusiasm had carried him too far, but his tongue was the most reckless of organs and often slipped into the truth. He was a real poet with an extraordinary faculty for language and a gift of unerring rhythm. He wrote after the medieval model – with a profusion of acrostics and double rhyming – not with the bald duplications of primitive Hebrew poetry. Intellectually he divined things like a woman – with marvellous rapidity, shrewdness and inaccuracy. He saw into people's souls through a dark refracting suspiciousness. The same bent of mind, the same individuality of distorted insight made him overflow with ingenious explanations of the Bible and the Talmud, with new views and new lights on history, philology, medicine – anything, everything. And he believed in his ideas because they were his and in himself because of his ideas. To himself his stature sometimes seemed to expand till his head touched the sun – but that was mostly after wine – and his brain retained a permanent glow from the contact.

"Well, peace be with you!" said Pinchas. "I will leave you to your customers who besiege you as I have been besieged by the maidens. But what you have just told me has gladdened my heart. I always had an affection for you, but now I love you like a woman. We will found this Holy Land League, you and I. You shall be President – I waive all claims in your favour – and I will be Treasurer. Hey?"

"We shall see; we shall see," said Guedalyah the greengrocer.

"No, we cannot leave it to the mob, we must settle it beforehand. Shall we say done?"

He laid his finger cajolingly to the side of his nose.

"We shall see," repeated Guedalyah the greengrocer, impatiently.

"No, say! I love you like a brother. Grant me this favour and I will never ask anything of you so long as I live."

"Well, if the others –" began Guedalyah feebly.

· "Ah! You are a Prince in Israel," Pinchas cried enthusiastically. "If I could only show you my heart, how it loves you."

He capered off at a sprightly trot, his head haloed by huge volumes of smoke. Guedalyah the greengrocer bent over a bin of potatoes. Looking up suddenly he was startled to see the head fixed in the open front of the shop window. It was a narrow dark bearded face distorted with an insinuative smile. A dirty-nailed forefinger was laid on the right of the nose.

"You won't forget," said the head coaxingly.

"Of course I won't forget," cried the greengrocer querulously.

The meeting took place at ten that night at the Beth Hamidrash founded by Guedalyah, a large unswept room rudely fitted up as a synagogue and approached by reeking staircases, unsavoury as the neighbourhood. On one of the black benches a shabby youth with very long hair and lank fleshless limbs shook his body violently to and fro while he vociferated the sentences of the Mishnah in the traditional argumentative singsong. Near the central raised platform was a group of enthusiasts, among whom *Froom* Karlkammer, with his thin ascetic body and the mass of red hair that crowned his head like the light of a pharos, was a conspicuous figure.

"Peace be to you, Karlkammer!" said Pinchas to him in Hebrew.

"To you be peace, Pinchas!" replied Karlkammer.

"Ah!" went on Pinchas. "Sweeter than honey it is to me, yea than fine honey, to talk to a man in the Holy Tongue. Woe, the speakers are few in these latter days. I and thou, Karlkammer, are the only two people who can speak the Holy Tongue grammatically on this isle of the sea. Lo, it is a great thing we are met to do this night – I see Zion laughing on her mountains and her fig trees skipping for joy. I will be the treasurer of the fund, Karlkrammer – do thou vote for me, for so our society shall flourish as the green bay tree."

Karlkammer grunted vaguely, not having humour enough to recall the usual associations of the simile, and Pinchas passed on to salute Hamburg. To Gabriel Hamburg, Pinchas was occasion for half-respectful amusement. He could not but reverence the poet's genius even while he laughed at his pretensions to omniscience, and at the daring and unscientific guesses which the poet offered as plain prose. For when in their arguments Pinchas came upon Jewish ground, he was in presence of a man who knew every inch of it.

"Blessed art thou who arrivest," he said when he perceived Pinchas. Then dropping into German he continued – "did not know you would join in the rebuilding of Zion."

"Why not?" inquired Pinchas.

"Because you have written so many poems thereupon."

"Be not so foolish," said Pinchas, annoyed. "Did not King David fight the Philistines as well as write the Psalms?"

"Did he write the Psalms?" said Hamburg quietly, with a smile.

"No – not so loud! Of course he didn't! The Psalms were written by Judas Maccabæus, as I proved in the last issue of the Stuttgard *Zeitschrift*. But that only makes my analogy more forcible. You shall see how I will gird on sword and armour, and I shall yet see even you in the forefront of the battle. I will be treasurer, you shall vote for me, Hamburg, for I and you are the only two people who know the Holy Tongue grammatically, and we must work shoulder to shoulder and see that the balance sheets are drawn up in the language of our fathers."

"In like manner did Melchitsedek Pinchas approach Hiram Lyons and Simon Gradkoski, the former a poverty-stricken pietist who added day by day to a furlong of crabbed manuscript, embodying a useless commentary on the first chapter of Genesis; the latter the portly fancy-goods dealer in whose warehouse Daniel Hyams was employed. Gradkoski rivalled Reb Shemuel in his knowledge of the exact *loci* of Talmudical remarks – page this, and line that – and secretly a tolerant latitudinarian, enjoyed the reputation of a bulwark of orthodoxy too well to give it up. Gradkoski passed easily from writing an invoice to writing a learned article on Hebrew astronomy. Pinchas ignored Joseph Strelitski whose raven curl floated wildly over his forehead like a pirate's flag, though Hamburg, who was rather surprised to see the taciturn young man at a meeting, strove to draw him into conversation. The man to whom Pinchas ultimately attached himself was only a man in the sense of having attained his religious majority. He was a Harrow boy named Raphael Leon, a scion of a wealthy family. The boy had manifested a strange premature interest in Jewish literature and had often seen Gabriel Hamburg's name in learned footnotes and, discovering that he was in England, had just written to him. Hamburg had replied; they had met that day for the first time and at the lad's own request the old scholar brought him on to this strange meeting. The boy grew to be Hamburg's one link with wealthy England, and though he rarely saw Leon again, the lad came in a shadowy way to take the place he had momentarily designed for Joseph Strelitski. Tonight it was Pinchas who assumed the paternal manner, but he mingled it with a subtle obsequiousness that made the shy simple lad uncomfortable, though when he came to read the poet's lofty sentiments which arrived (with an acrostic dedication) by the first post next morning, he conceived an enthusiastic admiration for the neglected genius.

The rest of the "remnant" that were met to save Israel looked more commonplace – a furrier, a slipper-maker, a locksmith, an ex-glazier (Mendel Hyams), a confectioner, a *Melammed* or Hebrew teacher, a carpenter, a presser, a cigar-maker, a small shopkeeper or two, and last and least, Moses Ansell. They were of many birthplaces – Austria, Holland, Poland, Russia, Germany, Italy, Spain – yet felt themselves of no country and of one. Encircled by the splendours of modern Babylon, their hearts turned to the East, like passion-flowers seeking the sun. Palestine, Jerusalem, Jordan, the Holy Land were magic syllables to them, the sight of a coin struck in one of Baron Edmund's colonies filled their eyes with tears; in death they craved no higher boon than a handful of Palestine earth sprinkled over their graves.

But Guedalyah the greengrocer was not the man to encourage idle hopes. He explained his scheme lucidly – without high-falutin. They were to rebuild Judaism as the coral insect builds its reefs – not as the prayer went, "speedily and in our days."

They had brought themselves up to expect more and were disappointed. Some protested against peddling little measures – like Pinchas they were for high, heroic deeds. Joseph Strelitski student and cigar commission agent, jumped to his feet and cried passionately in German: "Everywhere Israel groans and travails – must we indeed wait and wait till our hearts are sick and strike never a decisive blow? It is nigh two thousand years since across the ashes of our Holy Temple we were driven into the Exile, clanking the chains of Pagan conquerors. For nigh two thousand years have we dwelt on alien soils, a mockery and a byword for the nations, hounded out from every worthy employ and persecuted for turning to the unworthy, spat upon and trodden under foot, suffusing the scroll of history with our blood and illuminating it with the lurid glare of the fires to which our martyrs have ascended gladly for the Sanctification of the Name. We who twenty centuries ago were a mighty nation, with a law and a constitution and a religion which have been the key-notes of the civilization of the world, we who sat in judgment by the gates of great cities, clothed in purple and fine linen, are the sport of peoples who were then roaming wild in woods and marshes clothed in the skins of the wolf and the bear. Now in the East there gleams again a star of hope – why shall we not follow it? Never has the chance of the Restoration flamed so high as today. Our capitalists rule the markets of Europe, our generals lead armies, our great men sit in the Councils of every State. We are everywhere – a thousand thousand stray rivulets of power that could be blent into a mighty ocean. Palestine is one if we wish the whole house of Israel has but to speak with a mighty unanimous voice. Poets will sing for us, journalists write for us, diplomatists haggle for us, millionaires pay the price for us. The sultan would restore our land to us tomorrow, did we but essay to get it. There are no obstacles –

but ourselves. It is not the heathen that keeps us out of our land – it is the Jews, the rich and prosperous Jews – Jeshurun grown fat and sleepy, dreaming the false dream of assimilation with the people of the pleasant places in which their lines have been cast. Give us back our country; this alone will solve the Jewish question. Our paupers shall become agricul-
· turists, and like Antaeus, the genius of Israel shall gain fresh strength by contact with mother earth. And for England it will help to solve the Indian question – Between European Russia and India there will be planted a people, fierce, terrible, hating Russia for her wild-beast deeds. Into the Exile we took with us of all our glories, only a spark of the fire by which our Temple, the abode of our great One was engirdled, and this little spark kept us alive while the towers of our enemies crumbled to dust, and this spark leaped into celestial flame and shed light upon the faces of the heroes of our race and inspired them to endure the horrors of the Dance of Death and the tortures of the *Auto-da-fé*. Let us fan the spark again till it leap up and become a pillar of flame going before us and showing us the way to Jerusalem, the City of our sires. And if gold will not buy back our land we must try steel. As the National Poet of Israel, Naphtali Herz Imber, has so nobly sung (here he broke into the Hebrew *Wacht Am Rhein*, of which an English version would run thus):

THE WATCH ON THE JORDAN

I

"Like the crash of the thunder
Which splitteth asunder
    The flame of the cloud,
On our ears ever falling.
A voice is heard calling
    From Zion aloud:
'Let your spirits' desires
For the land of your sires
    Eternally burn.
From the foe to deliver
Our own holy river,

To Jordan return.'
Where the soft flowing stream
Murmurs low as in dream,
    There set we our watch.
Our watchword, 'The sword
Of our land and our Lord' –
    By the Jordan then set we our watch.

II

"Rest in peace, lovèd land,
For we rest not, but stand,
    Off shaken our sloth.
When the bolts of war rattle
To shirk not the battle,
    We make thee our oath.
As we hope for a Heaven,
Thy chains shall be riven,
    Thine ensign unfurled.
And in pride of our race
We will fearlessly face
    The might of the world.
When our trumpet is blown,
And our standard is flown,
    Then set we our watch.
Our watchword, 'The sword
Of our land and our Lord' –
    By Jordan then set we our watch.

III

"Yea, as long as there be
Birds in air, fish in sea,
    And blood in our veins;
And the lions in might,
Leaping down from the height,
    Shake, roaring, their manes;
And the dew nightly laves
The forgotten old graves
    Where Juda's sires sleep, –
We swear, who are living,

To rest not in striving,
    To pause not to weep.
Let the trumpet be blown,
Let the standard be flown,
    Now set we our watch.
Our watchword, 'The sword
Of our land and our Lord' –
    In Jordan Now set we our watch."

He sank upon the rude, wooden bench, exhausted, his eyes glittering, his raven hair dishevelled by the wildness of his gestures. He had said. For the rest of the evening he neither moved nor spake. The calm, good-humoured tones of Simon Gradkoski followed like a cold shower.

"We must be sensible," he said, for he enjoyed the reputation of a shrewd conciliatory man of the world as well as of a pillar of orthodoxy. "The great people will come to us, but not if we abuse them. We must flatter them up and tell them they are the descendants of the Maccabees. There is much political kudos to be got out of leading such a movement – this, too, they will see. Rome was not built in a day, and the Temple will not be rebuilt in a year. Besides, we are not soldiers now. We must recapture our land by brain, not sword. Slow and sure and the blessing of God over all."

After such wise Simon Gradkoski. But Gronovitz, the Hebrew teacher, crypto-atheist and overt revolutionary, who read a Hebrew edition of the "Pickwick Papers" in synagogue on the Day of Atonement, was with Strelitski, and a bigot whose religion made his wife and children wretched was with the cautious Simon Gradkoski. Froom Karlkammer followed, but his drift was uncertain. He apparently looked forward to miraculous interpositions. Still he approved of the movement from one point of view. The more Jews lived in Jerusalem the more would be enabled to die there – which was the aim of a good Jew's life. As for the Messiah, he would come assuredly – in God's good time. Thus Karlkammer at enormous length with frequent intervals of unintelligibility and huge chunks of irrelevant quotation and much play of

Cabalistic conceptions. Pinchas, who had been fuming throughout this speech, for to him Karlkammer stood for the archetype of all donkeys, jumped up impatiently when Karlkammer paused for breath and denounced as an interruption that gentleman's indignant continuance of his speech. The sense of the meeting was with the poet and Karlkammer was silenced. Pinchas was dithyrambic, sublime, with audacities which only genius can venture on. He was pungently merry over Imber's pretensions to be the National Poet of Israel, declaring that his prosody, his vocabulary, and even his grammar were beneath contempt. He, Pinchas, would write Judæa a real Patriotic Poem, which should be sung from the slums of Whitechapel to the *Veldts* of South Africa, and from the *Mellah* of Morocco to the *Yudengassen* of Germany, and should gladden the hearts and break from the mouths of the poor immigrants saluting the Statue of Liberty in New York Harbour. When he, Pinchas, walked in Victoria Park of a Sunday afternoon and heard the band play, the sound of a cornet always seemed to him, said he, like the sound of Bar Cochba's trumpet calling the warriors to battle. And when it was all over and the band played "God save the Queen," it sounded like the paean of victory when he marched, a conqueror, to the gates of Jerusalem. Wherefore he, Pinchas, would be their leader. Had not the Providence, which concealed so many revelations in the letters of the Torah, given him the name Melchitsedek Pinchas, whereof one initial stood for Messiah and the other for Palestine. Yes, he would be their Messiah. But money now-a-days was the sinews of war and the first step to Messiahship was the keeping of the funds. The Redeemer must in the first instance be the treasurer. With this anti-climax Pinchas wound up, his childishness and *naïveté* conquering his cunning.

Other speakers followed but in the end Guedalyah the greengrocer prevailed. They appointed him President and Simon Gradkoski, Treasurer, collecting twenty-five shillings on the spot, ten from the lad Raphael Leon. In vain Pinchas reminded the President they would need Collectors to make house-to-house calls; three other members were chosen to trisect the Ghetto. All felt the incongruity of hanging money bags at the saddle-bow of Pegasus. Whereupon Pinchas re-lit his cigar and muttering that they were all fool-men betook himself unceremoniously without.

Gabriel Hamburg looked on throughout with something like a smile on his shrivelled features. Once while Joseph Strelitski was holding forth he blew his nose violently. Perhaps he had taken too large a pinch of snuff. But not a word did the great scholar speak. He would give up his last breath to promote the Return (provided the Hebrew manuscripts were not left behind in alien museums); but the humours of the enthusiasts were part of the great comedy in the only theatre he cared for. Mendel Hyams was another silent member. But he wept openly under Strelitski's harangue.

When the meeting adjourned, the lank unhealthy swaying creature in the corner, who had been mumbling the tractate Baba Kama out of courtesy, now burst out afresh in his quaint argumentative recitative.

"What then does it refer to? To his stone or his knife or his burden which he has left on the highway and it injured a passer-by. How is this? If he gave up his ownership, whether according to Rav or according to Shemuel, it is a pit, and if he retained his ownership, if according to Shemuel, who holds that all are derived from 'his pit,' then it is 'a pit,' and if according to Rav, who holds that all are derived from 'his ox,' then it is 'an ox,' therefore the derivatives of 'an ox' are the same as 'an ox' itself."

He had been at it all day, and he went on far into the small hours, shaking his body backwards and forwards without remission.

CHAPTER XVI

The Courtship of Shosshi Shmendrik

Meckisch was a *Chasid*, which in the vernacular is a saint, but in the actual a member of the sect of the *Chasidim* whose centre is Galicia. In the eighteenth century Israel Baal Shem, "the Master of the Name," retired to the mountains to meditate on philosophical truths. He arrived at a creed of cheerful and even stoical acceptance of the Cosmos in all its aspects and a conviction that the incense of an enjoyed pipe was grateful to the Creator. But it is the inevitable misfortune of religious founders to work apocryphal miracles and to raise up an army of disciples who squeeze the teaching of their master into their own mental moulds and are ready to die for the resultant distortion. It is only by being misunderstood that a great man can have any influence upon his kind. Baal Shem was succeeded by an army of thaumaturgists, and the wonder-working Rabbis of Sadagora who are in touch with all the spirits of the air enjoy the revenue of princes and the reverence of Popes. To snatch a morsel of such a Rabbi's Sabbath *Kuggol*, or pudding, is to insure Paradise, and the scramble is a scene to witness. *Chasidism* is the extreme expression of Jewish optimism. The *Chasidim* are the Corybantes or Salvationists of Judaism. In England their idiosyncrasies are limited to noisy jubilant services in their *Chevrah*, the worshippers dancing or leaning or standing or writhing or beating their heads against the wall as they will, and frisking like happy children in the presence of their Father.

Meckisch also danced at home and sang "Tiddy, riddy, roi, toi, toi toi, ta," varied by "Rom, pom, pom" and "Bim, bom" in a quaint melody to express his personal satisfaction with existence. He was a weazened little widower with a deep yellow complexion, prominent cheek bones, a hook nose and a scrubby, straggling little beard. Years of professional practice as a mendicant had stamped his face with an anguished suppliant concil- iatory grin, which he could not now erase even after business hours. It might perhaps have yielded to soap and water but the experiment had not been tried. On his head he always wore a fur cap with lappets for his ears. Across his shoulders was strung a lemon-basket filled with grimy, gritty bits of sponge which nobody ever bought. Meckisch's merchandise was quite other. He dealt in sensational spectacle. As he shambled along with extreme difficulty and by the aid of a stick, his lower limbs which were crossed in odd contortions appeared half paralyzed, and, when his strange appearance had attracted attention, his legs would give way and he would find himself with his back on the pavement, where he waited to he picked up by sympathetic spectators shedding silver and copper. After an indefinite number of performances Meckisch would hurry home in the darkness to dance and sing "Tiddy, riddy, roi, toi, bim, bom."

Thus Meckisch lived at peace with God and man, till one day the fatal thought came into his head that he wanted a second wife. There was no difficulty in getting one – by the aid of his friend, Sugarman the *Shadchan* – and soon the little man found his household goods increased by the possession of a fat, Russian giantess. Meckisch did not call in the authorities to marry him.

He had a "still wedding," which cost nothing. An artificial canopy made out of a sheet and four broomsticks was erected in the chimney corner and nine male friends sanctified the ceremony by their presence. Meckisch and the Russian giantess fasted on their wedding morn and everything was in honourable order.

But Meckisch's happiness and economies were short-lived. The Russian giantess turned out a tartar. She got her claws into his savings and decorated herself with Paisley shawls and gold necklaces. Nay more!

She insisted that Meckisch must give her "Society" and keep open house. Accordingly the bed-sitting room which they rented was turned into a *salon* of reception, and hither one Friday night came Peleg Shmendrik and his wife and Mr. and Mrs. Sugarman. Over the Sabbath meal the current of talk divided itself into masculine and feminine freshets. The ladies discussed bonnets and the gentlemen Talmud. All the three men dabbled, pettily enough, in stocks and shares, but nothing in the world would tempt them to transact any negotiation or discuss the merits of a prospectus on the Sabbath, though they were all fluttered by the allurements of the Sapphire Mines Limited, as set forth in a whole page of advertisement in the *Jewish Chronicle*, the organ naturally perused for its religious news on Friday evenings. The share-list would close at noon on Monday.

"But when Moses, our teacher, struck the rock," said Peleg Shmendrik, in the course of the discussion, "he was right the first time but wrong the second, because as the Talmud points out, a child may be chastised when it is little, but as it grows up it should be reasoned with."

"Yes," said Sugarman the *Shadchan*, quickly; "but if his rod had not been made of sapphire he would have split that instead of the rock."

"Was it made of sapphire?" asked Meckisch, who was rather a Man-of-the-Earth.

"Of course it was – and a very fine thing, too," answered Sugarman.

"Do you think so?" inquired Peleg Shmendrik eagerly.

"The sapphire is a magic stone," answered Sugarman. "It improves the vision and makes peace between foes. Issachar, the studious son of Jacob, was represented on the Breast-plate by the sapphire. Do you not know that the mist-like centre of the sapphire symbolizes the cloud that enveloped Sinai at the giving of the Law?"

"I did not know that," answered Peleg Shmendrik, "but I know that Moses's Rod was created in the twilight of the first Sabbath and God did everything after that with this sceptre."

"Ah, but we are not all strong enough to wield Moses's Rod; it weighed forty seahs," said Sugarman.

"How many seahs do you think one could safely carry?" said Meckisch.

"Five or six seahs – not more," said Sugarman. "You see one might drop them if he attempted more and even sapphire may break – the First Tables of the Law were made of sapphire, and yet from a great height they fell terribly, and were shattered to pieces."

"Gideon, the M. P., may be said to desire a Rod of Moses, for his secretary told me he will take forty," said Shmendrik.

"Hush! what are you saying!" said Sugarman. "Gideon is a rich man, and then he is a director."

"It seems a good lot of directors," said Meckisch.

"Good to look at. But who can tell?" said Sugarman, shaking his head. "The Queen of Sheba probably brought sapphires to Solomon, but she was not a virtuous woman."

"Ah, Solomon!" sighed Mrs. Shmendrik, pricking up her ears and interrupting this talk of stocks and stones, "If he'd had a thousand daughters instead of a thousand wives, even his treasury couldn't have held out. I had only two girls, praised be He, and yet it nearly ruined me to buy them husbands. A dirty *Greener* comes over, without a shirt to his skin, and nothing else but he must have two hundred pounds in the hand. And then you've got to stick to his back to see that he doesn't take his breeches in his hand and off to America. In Poland he would have been glad to get a maiden, and would have said thank you."

"Well, but what about your own son?" said Sugarman. "Why haven't you asked me to find Shosshi a wife? It's a sin against the maidens of Israel. He must be long past the Talmudical age."

"He is twenty-four," replied Peleg Shmendrik.

"Tu, tu, tu, tu, tu!" said Sugarman, clacking his tongue in horror, "have you perhaps an objection to his marrying?"

"Save us and grant us peace!" said the father in deprecatory horror. "Only Shosshi is so shy. You are aware, too, he is not handsome. Heaven alone knows whom he takes after."

"Peleg, I blush for you," said Mrs. Shmendrik. "What is the matter with the boy? Is he deaf, dumb, blind, unprovided with legs? If Shoshi is backward with the women, it is because he 'learns' so hard when he's not at work. He earns a good living by his cabinet-making and it is quite time he set up a Jewish household for himself. How much will you want for finding him a *Calloh*?"

"Hush!" said Sugarman sternly, "do you forget it is the Sabbath? Be assured I shall not charge more than last time, unless the bride has an extra good dowry."

On Saturday night immediately after *Havdalah*, Sugarman went to Mr. Belcovitch, who was just about to resume work, and informed him he had the very *Chosan* for Becky. "I know," he said, "Becky has a lot of young men after her, but what are they but a pack of bare-backs? How much will you give for a solid man?"

After much haggling Belcovitch consented to give twenty pounds immediately before the marriage ceremony and another twenty at the end of twelve months.

"But no pretending you haven't got it about you, when we're at the *Shool*, no asking us to wait till we get home," said Sugarman, "or else I withdraw my man, even from under the *Chuppah* itself. When shall I bring him for your inspection?"

"Oh, tomorrow afternoon, Sunday, when Becky will be out in the park with her young men. It's best I shall see him first!"

Sugarman now regarded Shoshi as a married man! He rubbed his hands and went to see him. He found him in a little shed in the back yard where he did extra work at home. Shoshi was busy completing little wooden articles – stools and wooden spoons and money boxes for sale in Petticoat Lane next day. He supplemented his wages that way.

"Good evening, Shoshi," said Sugarman.

"Good evening," murmured Shoshi, sawing away.

Shoshi was a gawky young man with a blotched sandy face ever ready to blush deeper with the suspicion that conversations going on at a distance were all about him. His eyes were shifty and catlike; one shoulder overbalanced the other, and when he walked, he swayed loosely to and fro. Sugarman was rarely remiss in the offices of piety and he was nigh murmuring the prayer at the sight of monstrosities, "Blessed art Thou who variest the creatures." But resisting the temptation he said aloud, "I have something to tell you."

Shosshi looked up suspiciously.

"Don't bother; I am busy," he said, and applied his plane to the leg of a stool.

"But this is more important than stools. How would you like to get married?"

Shosshils face became like a peony.

"Don't make laughter," he said.

"But I mean it. You are twenty-four years old and ought to have a wife and four children by this time."

"But I don't want a wife and four children," said Shosshi.

"No, of course not. I don't mean a widow. It is a maiden I have in my eye."

"Nonsense, what maiden would have me?" said Shosshi, a note of eagerness mingling with the diffidence of the words.

"What maiden? *Gott in Himmel!* A hundred. A fine, strong, healthy young man like you, who can make a good living!"

Shosshi put down his plane and straightened himself. There was a moment of silence. Then his frame collapsed again into a limp mass. His head drooped over his left shoulder. "This is all foolishness you talk, the maidens make mock."

"Be not a piece of clay! I know a maiden who has you quite in affection!"

The blush which had waned mantled in a full flood. Shosshi stood breathless, gazing half suspiciously, half credulously at his strictly honourable Mephistopheles.

It was about seven o'clock and the moon was a yellow crescent in the frosty heavens. The sky was punctured with clear-cut constellations. The back yard looked poetic with its blend of shadow and moonlight.

"A beautiful fine maid," said Sugarman ecstatically, "with pink cheeks and black eyes and forty pounds dowry."

The moon sailed smilingly along. The water was running into the cistern with a soothing, peaceful sound. Shosshi consented to go and see Mr. Belcovitch.

Mr. Belcovitch made no parade. Everything was as usual. On the wooden table were two halves of squeezed lemons, a piece of chalk, two cracked cups and some squashed soap. He was not overwhelmed by Shosshi, but admitted he was solid. His father was known to be pious, and both his sisters had married reputable men. Above all, he was not a Dutchman. Shosshi left No. 1 Royal Street, Belcovitch's accepted son-in-law. Esther met him on the stairs and noted the radiance on his pimply countenance. He walked with his head erect. Shosshi was indeed very much in love and felt that all that was needed for his happiness was a sight of his future wife.

But he had no time to go and see her except on Sunday afternoon and then she was always out. Mrs. Belcovitch, however, made amends by paying him considerable attention. The sickly-looking little woman chatted to him for hours at a time about her ailments and invited him to taste her medicine, which was a compliment Mrs. Belcovitch passed only to her most esteemed visitors. By and by she even wore her night-cap in his presence as a sign that he had become one of the family. Under this encouragement Shosshi grew confidential and imparted to his future mother-in-law the details of his mother's disabilities. But he could mention nothing which Mrs. Belcovitch could not cap, for she was a woman extremely catholic in her maladies. She was possessed of considerable imagination, and once when Fanny selected a bonnet for her in a milliner's window, the girl had much difficulty in persuading her it was not inferior to what turned out to be the reflection of itself in a side mirror.

"I'm so weak upon my legs," she would boast to Shosshi. "I was born with ill-matched legs. One is a thick one and one is a thin one, and so one goes about."

Shosshi expressed his sympathetic admiration and the courtship proceeded apace. Sometimes Fanny and Pesach Weingott would be at home working, and they were very affable to him. He began to lose something of his shyness and his lurching gait, and he quite looked forward to his weekly visit to the Belcovitches. It was the story of Cymon and Iphigenia over again. Love improved even his powers of conversation, for when Belcovitch held forth at length Shosshi came in several times with "So?" and sometimes in the right place. Mr. Belcovitch loved his own voice and listened to it, the arrested press-iron in his hand. Occasionally in the middle of one of his harangues it would occur to him that some one was talking and wasting time, and then he would say to the room, "Shah! Make an end, make an end," and dry up. But to Shosshi he was especially polite, rarely interrupting himself when his son-in-law elect was hanging on his words. There was an intimate tender tone about these *causeries*.

"I should like to drop down dead suddenly," he would say with the air of a philosopher, who had thought it all out. "I shouldn't care to lie up in bed and mess about with medicine and doctors. To make a long job of dying is so expensive."

"So?" said Shosshi.

"Don't worry, Bear! I dare say the devil will seize you suddenly," interposed Mrs. Belcovitch drily.

"It will not be the devil," said Mr. Belcovitch, confidently and in a confidential manner. "If I had died as a young man, Shosshi, it might have been different."

Shosshi pricked up his ears to listen to the tale of Bear's wild cubhood.

"One morning," said Belcovitch, "in Poland, I got up at four o'clock to go to Supplications for Forgiveness. The air was raw and there was no sign of dawn! Suddenly I noticed a black pig trotting behind me. I quickened my pace and the black pig did likewise. I broke into a run and I heard the pig's paws patting furiously upon the hard frozen ground. A cold sweat broke out all over me. I looked over my shoulder and saw the pig's eyes burning like red-hot coals in the darkness. Then I knew that the Not Good One was after me. 'Hear, O Israel,' I cried. I looked up to the heavens but there was a cold mist covering the stars. Faster and faster I flew and faster and faster flew the demon pig. At last the *Shool* came in sight. I made one last wild effort and fell exhausted upon the holy threshold and the pig vanished."

"So?" said Shosshi, with a long breath.

"Immediately after *Shool* I spake with the Rabbi and he said 'Bear, are thy *Tephillin* in order?' So I said 'Yea, Rabbi, they are very large and I bought them of the pious scribe, Naphtali, and I look to the knots weekly.' But he said, 'I will examine them.' So I brought them to him and he opened the head-phylactery and lo! in place of the holy parchment he found bread crumbs."

"Hoi, hoi," said Shosshi in horror, his red hands quivering.

"Yes," said Bear mournfully, "I had worn them for ten years and moreover the leaven had defiled all my Passovers."

Belcovitch also entertained the lover with details of the internal politics of the "Sons of the Covenant."

Shosshi's affection for Becky increased weekly under the stress of these intimate conversations with her family. At last his passion was rewarded, and Becky, at the violent instance of her father, consented to disappoint one of her young men and stay at home to meet her future husband. She put off her consent till after dinner though, and it began to rain immediately before she gave it.

The moment Shosshi came into the room he divined that a change had come over the spirit of the dream. Out of the corners of his eyes he caught a glimpse of an appalling beauty standing behind a sewing machine. His face fired up, his legs began to quiver, he wished the ground would open and swallow him as it did Korah.

"Becky," said Mr. Belcovitch, "this is Mr. Shosshi Shmendrik."

Shosshi put on a sickly grin and nodded his head affirmatively, as if to corroborate the statement, and the round felt hat he wore slid back till the broad rim rested on his ears. Through a sort of mist a terribly fine maid loomed.

Becky stared at him haughtily and curled her lip. Then she giggled.

Shosshi held out his huge red hand limply. Becky took no notice of it.

"*Nu*, Becky!" breathed Belcovitch, in a whisper that could have been heard across the way.

"How are you? All right?" said Becky, very loud, as if she thought deafness was among Shosshi's disadvantages.

Shosshi grinned reassuringly.

There was another silence.

Shosshi wondered whether the *convenances* would permit him to take his leave now. He did not feel comfortable at all. Everything had been going so delightfully, it had been quite a pleasure to him to come to the house. But now all was changed. The course of true love never does run smooth, and the advent of this new personage into the courtship was distinctly embarrassing.

The father came to the rescue.

"A little rum?" he said.

"Yes," said Shosshi.

"Chayah! *nu*. Fetch the bottle!"

Mrs. Belcovitch went to the chest of drawers in the corner of the room and took from the top of it a large decanter. She then produced two glasses without feet and filled them with the home-made rum, handing one to Shosshi and the other to her husband. Shosshi muttered a blessing over it, then he leered vacuously at the company and cried, "To life!"

"To peace!" replied the older man, gulping down the spirit. Shosshi was doing the same, when his eye caught Becky. He choked for five minutes, Mrs. Belcovitch thumping him maternally on the back. When he was comparatively recovered the sense of his disgrace rushed upon him and overwhelmed him afresh. Becky was still giggling behind the sewing machine. Once more Shosshi felt that the burden of the conversation was upon him. He looked at his boots and not seeing anything there, looked up again and grinned encouragingly at the company as if to waive his rights. But finding the company did not respond, he blew his nose enthusiastically as a lead off to the conversation.

Mr. Belcovitch saw his embarrassment, and, making a sign to Chayah, slipped out of the room followed by his wife. Shosshi was left alone with the terribly fine maid.

Becky stood still, humming a little air and looking up at the ceiling, as if she had forgotten Shosshi's existence. With her eyes in that position it was easier for Shosshi to look at her He stole side-long glances at her, which, growing bolder and bolder, at length fused into an uninterrupted steady gaze. How fine and beautiful she was! His eyes began to glitter, a smile of approbation overspread his face. Suddenly she looked down and their eyes met. Shosshi's smile hurried off and gave way to a sickly sheepish look and his legs felt weak. The terribly fine maid gave a kind of snort and resumed her inspection of the ceiling. Gradually Shosshi found himself examining her again. Verily Sugarman had spoken truly of her charms. But – overwhelming thought – had not Sugarman also said she loved him? Shosshi knew nothing of the ways of girls, except what he had learned from the Talmud. Quite possibly Becky was now occupied in expressing ardent affection. He shuffled towards her, his heart beating violently. He was near enough to touch her. The air she was humming throbbed in his cars. He opened his mouth to speak – Becky becoming suddenly aware of his proximity fixed him with a basilisk glare – the words were frozen on his lips. For some seconds his mouth remained open, then the ridiculousness of shutting it again without speaking spurred him on to make some sound, however meaningless. He made a violent effort and there burst from his lips in Hebrew:

"Happy are those who dwell in thy house, ever shall they praise thee, Selah!" It was not a compliment to Becky. Shosshi's face lit up with joyous relief. By some inspiration he had started the afternoon prayer. He felt that Becky would understand the pious necessity. With fervent gratitude to the Almighty he continued the Psalm: "Happy are the people whose lot is thus, etc." Then he turned his back on Becky, with his face to the East wall, made three steps forwards and commenced the silent delivery of the *Amidah*. Usually he gabbled off the "Eighteen Blessings" in five minutes. Today they were prolonged till he heard the footsteps of the returning parents. Then he scurried through the relics of the service at lightning speed. When Mr. and Mrs. Belcovitch re-entered the room they saw by his happy face that all was well and made no opposition to his instant departure.

He came again the next Sunday and was rejoiced to find that Becky was out, though he had hoped to find her in. The courtship made great strides that afternoon, Mr. and Mrs. Belcovitch being more amiable than ever to compensate for Becky's private refusal to entertain the addresses of such a *Shmuck*. There had been sharp domestic discussions during the week, and Becky had only sniffed at her parents' commendations of Shosshi as a "very worthy youth." She declared that it was "remission of sins merely to look at him."

Next Sabbath Mr. and Mrs. Belcovitch paid a formal visit to Shosshi's parents to make their acquaintance, and partook of tea and cake. Becky was not with them; moreover she defiantly declared she would never be at home on a Sunday till Shosshi was married. They circumvented her by getting him up on a weekday. The image of Becky had been so often in his thoughts now that by the time he saw her the second time he was quite habituated to her appearance. He had even imagined his arm round her waist, but in practice he found he could go no further as yet than ordinary conversation.

Becky was sitting sewing buttonholes when Shosshi arrived. Everybody was there – Mr. Belcovitch pressing coats with hot irons; Fanny shaking the room with her heavy machine; Pesach Weingott cutting a piece of chalk-marked cloth; Mrs. Belcovitch carefully pouring out tablespoonfuls of medicine. There were even some outside "hands," work being unusually plentiful, as from the manifestos of Simon Wolf, the labour-leader, the slop manufacturers anticipated a strike.

Sustained by their presence, Shosshi felt a bold and gallant wooer. He determined that this time he would not go without having addressed at least one remark to the object of his affections. Grinning amiably at the company generally, by way of salutation, he made straight for Becky's corner. The terribly fine lady snorted at the sight of him, divining that she had been out-manœuvred. Belcovitch surveyed the situation out of the corners of his eyes, not pausing a moment in his task.

"*Nu*, how goes it, Becky?" Shosshi murmured.

Becky said, "All right, how are you?"

"God be thanked, I have nothing to complain of," said Shosshi, encouraged by the warmth of his welcome. "My eyes are rather weak, still, though much better than last year."

Becky made no reply, so Shosshi continued: "But my mother is always a sick person. She has to swallow bucketsful of cod liver oil. She cannot be long for this world."

"Nonsense, nonsense," put in Mrs. Belcovitch, appearing suddenly behind the lovers. "My children's children shall never be any worse; it's all fancy with her, she coddles herself too much."

"Oh, no, she says she's much worse than you," Shosshi blurted out, turning round to face his future mother-in-law.

"Oh, indeed!" said Chayah angrily. "My enemies shall have my maladies! If your mother had my health, she would be lying in bed with it. But I go about in a sick condition. I can hardly crawl around. Look at my legs – has your mother got such legs? One a thick one and one a thin one."

Shosshi grew scarlet; he felt he had blundered. It was the first real shadow on his courtship – perhaps the little rift within the lute. He turned back to Becky for sympathy. There was no Becky. She had taken advantage of the conversation to slip away. He found her again in a moment though, at the other end of the room. She was seated before a machine. He crossed the room boldly and bent over her.

"Don't you feel cold, working?"

Br-r-r-r-r-r-h!

It was the machine turning. Becky had set the treadle going madly and was pushing a piece of cloth under the needle. When she paused, Shosshi said:

"Have you heard Reb Shemuel preach? He told a very amusing allegory last –"

Br-r-r-r-r-r-h!

Undaunted, Shosshi recounted the amusing allegory at length, and as the noise of her machine prevented Becky hearing a word she found his conversation endurable. After several more monologues, accompanied on the machine by Becky, Shosshi took his departure in high feather, promising to bring up specimens of his handiwork for her edification.

On his next visit he arrived with his arms laden with choice morsels of carpentry. He laid them on the table for her admiration.

They were odd knobs and rockers for Polish cradles! The pink of Becky's cheeks spread all over her face like a blot of red ink on a piece of porous paper. Shosshi's face reflected the colour in even more ensanguined dyes. Becky rushed from the room and Shosshi heard her giggling madly on the staircase. It dawned upon him that he had displayed bad taste in his selection.

"What have you done to my child?" Mrs. Belcovitch inquired.

"N-n-othing," he stammered; "I only brought her some of my work to see."

"And is this what one shows to a young girl?" demanded the mother indignantly.

"They are only bits of cradles," said Shosshi deprecatingly. "I thought she would like to see what nice workmanly things I turned out. See how smoothly these rockers are carved! There is a thick one, and there is a thin one!"

"Ah! Shameless droll! Dost thou make mock of my legs, too?" said Mrs. Belcovitch. "Out, impudent face, out with thee!"

Shosshi gathered up his specimens in his arms and fled through the door. Becky was still in hilarious eruption outside. The sight of her made confusion worse confounded. The knobs and rockers rolled thunderously down the stairs; Shosshi stumbled after them, picking them up on his course and wishing himself dead.

All Sugarman's strenuous efforts to patch up the affair failed. Shosshi went about broken-hearted for several days. To have been so near the goal – and then not to arrive after all! What made failure more bitter was that he had boasted of his conquest to his acquaintances, especially to the two who kept the stalls to the right and left of him on Sundays in Petticoat Lane. They made a butt of him as it was; he felt he could never stand between them for a whole morning now, and have Attic salt put upon his wounds. He shifted his position, arranging to pay sixpence a time for the privilege of fixing himself outside Widow Finkelstein's shop, which stood at the corner of a street, and might be presumed to intercept two streams of pedestrians. Widow Finkelstein's shop was a chandler's, and she did a large business in farthing-worths of boiling water. There was thus no possible rivalry between her ware and Shosshi's, which consisted of wooden candlesticks, little rocking chairs, stools, ashtrays, etc., piled up artistically on a barrow.

But Shosshi's luck had gone with the change of *locus*. His *clientèle* went to the old spot but did not find him. He did not even make a hansel. At two o'clock he tied his articles to the barrow with a complicated arrangement of cords. Widow Finkelstein waddled out and demanded her sixpence. Shosshi replied that he had not taken sixpence, that the coign was not one of vantage. Widow Finkelstein stood up for her rights, and even hung on to the barrow for them. There was a short, sharp argument, a simultaneous jabbering, as of a pair of monkeys. Shosshi Shmendrik's pimply face worked with excited expostulation. Widow Finkelstein's cushion-like countenance was agitated by waves of righteous indignation. Suddenly Shosshi darted between the shafts and made a dash off with the barrow down the side street. But Widow Finkelstein pressed it down with all her force, arresting the motion like a drag. Incensed by the laughter of the spectators, Shosshi put forth all his strength at the shafts, jerked the widow off her feet and see-sawed her skywards, huddled up spherically like a balloon, but clinging as grimly as ever to the defalcating barrow. Then Shosshi started off at a run, the carpentry rattling, and the dead weight of his living burden making his muscles ache.

Right to the end of the street he dragged her, pursued by a hooting crowd. Then he stopped, worn out.

"Will you give me that sixpence, you *Gonof!*"

"No, I haven't got it. You'd better go back to your shop, else you'll suffer from worse thieves."

It was true. Widow Finkelstein smote her wig in horror and hurried back to purvey treacle.

But that night when she shut up the shutters, she hurried off to Shosshi's address, which she had learned in the interim. His little brother opened the door and said Shosshi was in the shed.

He was just nailing the thicker of those rockers on to the body of a cradle. His soul was full of bitter-sweet memories. Widow Finkelstein suddenly appeared in the moonlight. For a moment Shosshi's heart beat wildly. He thought the buxom figure was Becky's.

"I have come for my sixpence."

Ah! The words awoke him from his dream. It was only the Widow Finkelstein.

And yet –! Verily, the widow, too, was plump and agreeable; if only her errand had been pleasant, Shosshi felt she might have brightened his back yard. He had been moved to his depths latterly and a new tenderness and a new boldness towards women shone in his eyes.

He rose and put his head on one side and smiled amiably and said, "Be not so foolish. I did not take a copper. I am a poor young man. You have plenty of money in your stocking."

"How know you that?" said the widow, stretching forward her right foot meditatively and gazing at the strip of stocking revealed.

"Never mind," said Shosshi, shaking his head sapiently.

"Well, it's true," she admitted. "I have two hundred and seventeen golden sovereigns besides my shop. But for all that why should you keep my sixpence?" She asked it with the same good-humoured smile.

The logic of that smile was unanswerable. Shosshi's mouth opened, but no sound issued from it. He did not even say the Evening Prayer. The moon sailed slowly across the heavens. The water flowed into the cistern with a soft soothing sound.

Suddenly it occurred to Shosshi that the widow's waist was not very unlike that which he had engirdled imaginatively. He thought he would just try if the sensation was anything like what he had fancied. His arm strayed timidly round her black-beaded mantle. The sense of his audacity was delicious. He was wondering whether he ought to say *Shehechyoni* – the prayer over a new pleasure. But the Widow Finkelstein stopped his mouth with a kiss. After that Shosshi forgot his pious instincts.

Except old Mrs. Ansell, Sugarman was the only person scandalized. Shosshi's irrepressible spirit of romance had robbed him of his commission. But Meckisch danced with Shosshi Shmendrik at the wedding, while the *Calloh* footed it with the Russian giantess. The men danced in one-half of the room, the women in the other.

CHAPTER XVII

The Hyams's Honeymoon

"BEENAH, hast thou heard aught about our Daniel?" There was a note of anxiety in old Hyams's voice.

"Naught, Mendel."

"Thou hast not heard talk of him and Sugarman's daughter?"

"No, is there aught between them?" The listless old woman spoke a little eagerly.

"Only that a man told me that his son saw our Daniel pay court to the maiden."

"Where?"

"At the Purim Ball."

"The man is a fool; a youth must dance with some maiden or other."

Miriam came in, fagged out from teaching. Old Hyams dropped from Yiddish into English.

"You are right, he must."

Beenah replied in her slow painful English.

"Would he not have told us?"

Mendel repeated: – "Would he not have told us?"

Each avoided the other's eye. Beenah dragged herself about the room, laying Miriam's tea.

"Mother, I wish you wouldn't scrape your feet along the floor so. It gets on my nerves and I *am* so worn out. Would he not have told you what? And who's he?"

Beenah looked at her husband.

"I heard Daniel was engaged," said old Hyams jerkily.

Miriam started and flushed.

"To whom?" she cried, in excitement.

"Bessie Sugarman."

"Sugarman's daughter?" Miriam's voice was pitched high.

"Yes."

Miriam's voice rose to a higher pitch.

"Sugarman the *Shadchan's* daughter?"

"Yes."

Miriam burst into a fit of incredulous laughter.

"As if Daniel would marry into a miserable family like that!"

"It is as good as ours," said Mendel, with white lips.

His daughter looked at him astonished. "I thought your children had taught you more self-respect than that," she said quietly. "Mr. Sugarman is a nice person to be related to!"

"At home, Mrs. Sugarman's family was highly respected," quavered old Hyams.

"We are not at home now," said Miriam witheringly. "We're in England. A bad-tempered old hag!"

"That is what she thinks me," thought Mrs. Hyams. But she said nothing.

"Did you not see Daniel with her at the ball?" said Mr. Hyams, still visibly disquieted.

"I'm sure I didn't notice," Miriam replied petulantly. "I think you must have forgot the sugar, mother, or else the tea is viler than usual. Why don't you let Jane cut the bread and butter instead of lazing in the kitchen?"

"Jane has been washing all day in the scullery," said Mrs. Hyams apologetically.

"H'm!" snapped Miriam, her pretty face looking peevish and careworn. "Jane ought to have to manage sixty-three girls whose ignorant parents let them run wild at home, and haven't the least idea of discipline. As for this chit of a Sugarman, don't you know that Jews always engage every fellow and girl that look at each other across the street, and make fun of them and discuss their united prospects before they are even introduced to each other."

She finished her tea, changed her dress and went off to the theatre with a girl friend. The really harassing nature of her work called for some such recreation. Daniel came in a little after she had gone out, and ate his supper, which was his dinner saved for him and warmed up in the oven. Mendel sat studying from an unwieldy folio which he held on his lap by the fireside and bent over. When Daniel had done supper and was standing yawning and stretching himself, Mendel said suddenly as if trying to bluff him:

"Why don't you ask your father to wish you *Mazzoltov?*"

"*Mazzoltov?* What for?" asked Daniel puzzled.

"On your engagement."

"My engagement!" repeated Daniel, his heart thumping against his ribs.

"Yes – to Bessie Sugarman."

Mendel's eye, fixed scrutinizingly on his boy's face, saw it pass from white to red and from red to white. Daniel caught hold of the mantel as if to steady himself.

"But it is a lie!" he cried hotly. "Who told you that?"

"No one; a man hinted as much."

"But I haven't even been in her company."

"Yes – at the Purim Ball."

Daniel bit his lip.

"Damned gossips!" he cried. "I'll never speak to the girl again."

There was a tense silence for a few seconds, then old Hyams said:

"Why not? You love her."

Daniel stared at him, his heart palpitating painfully. The blood in his ears throbbed mad sweet music.

"You love her," Mendel repeated quietly. "Why do you not ask her to marry you? Do you fear she would refuse?"

Daniel burst into semi-hysterical laughter. Then seeing his father's half-reproachful, half-puzzled look he said shamefacedly:

"Forgive me, father, I really couldn't help it. The idea of your talking about love! The oddity of it came over me all of a heap."

"Why should I not talk about love?"

"Don't be so comically serious, father," said Daniel, smiling afresh. "What's come over you? What have you to do with love? One would think you were a romantic young fool on the stage. It's all nonsense about love. I don't love anybody, least of all Bessie Sugarman, so don't you go worrying your old head about my affairs. You get back to that musty book of yours there. I wonder if you've suddenly come across anything about love in that, and don't forget to use the reading glasses and not your ordinary spectacles, else it'll be a sheer waste of money. By the way, mother, remember to go to the Eye Hospital on Saturday to be tested. I feel sure it's time you had a pair of specs, too."

"Don't I look old enough already?" thought Mrs. Hyams. But she said, "Very well, Daniel," and began to clear away his supper.

"That's the best of being in the fancy," said Daniel cheerfully. "There's no end of articles you can get at trade prices."

He sat for half an hour turning over the evening paper, then went to bed. Mr. and Mrs. Hyams's eyes sought each other involuntarily but they said nothing. Mrs. Hyams fried a piece of *Wurst* for Miriam's supper and put it into the oven to keep hot, then she sat down opposite Mendel to stitch on a strip of fur, which had got unripped on one of Miriam's jackets. The fire burnt briskly, little flames leaped up with a crackling sound, the clock ticked quietly.

Beenah threaded her needle at the first attempt.

"I can still see without spectacles," she thought bitterly. But she said nothing.

Mendel looked up furtively at her several times from his book. The meagreness of her parchment flesh, the thickening mesh of wrinkles, the snow-white hair struck him with almost novel force. But he said nothing. Beenah patiently drew her needle through and through the fur, ever and anon glancing at Mendel's worn spectacled face, the eyes deep in the sockets, the forehead that was bent over the folio furrowed painfully beneath the black *Koppel*, the complexion sickly. A lump seemed to be rising in her throat. She bent determinedly over her sewing, then suddenly looked up again. This time their eyes met. They did not droop them; a strange subtle flash seemed to pass from soul to soul. They gazed at each other, trembling on the brink of tears.

"Beenah." The voice was thick with suppressed sobs.

"Yes, Mendel."

"Thou hast heard?"

"Yes, Mendel."

"He says he loves her not."

"So he says."

"It is lies, Beenah."

"But wherefore should he lie?"

"Thou askest with thy mouth, not thy heart. Thou knowest that he wishes us not to think that he remains single for our sake. All his money goes to keep up this house we live in. It is the law of Moses. Sawest thou not his face when I spake of Sugarman's daughter?"

Beenah rocked herself to and fro, crying: "My poor Daniel, my poor lamb! Wait a little. I shall die soon. The All-High is merciful. Wait a little."

Mendel caught Miriam's jacket which was slipping to the floor and laid it aside.

"It helps not to cry," said he said gently, longing to cry with her. "This cannot be. He must marry the maiden whom his heart desires. Is it not enough that he feels that we have crippled his life for the sake of our Sabbath? He never speaks of it, but it smoulders in his veins."

"Wait a little!" moaned Beenah, still rocking to and fro.

"Nay, calm thyself." He rose and passed his horny hand tenderly over her white hair. "We must not wait. Consider how long Daniel has waited."

"Yes, my poor lamb, my poor lamb!" sobbed the old woman.

"If Daniel marries," said the old man, striving to speak firmly, "we have not a penny to live upon. Our Miriam requires all her salary.

Already she gives us more than she can spare. She is a lady, in a great position. She must dress finely. Who knows, too, but that we are in the way of a gentleman marrying her? We are not fit to mix with high people. But above all, Daniel must marry and I must earn your and my living as I did when the children were young."

"But what wilt thou do?" said Beenah, ceasing to cry and looking up with affrighted face. "Thou canst not go glaziering. Think of Miriam. What canst thou do, what canst thou do? Thou knowest no trade!"

"No, I know no trade," he said bitterly. "At home, as thou art aware, I was a stone-mason, but here I could get no work without breaking the Sabbath, and my hand has forgotten its cunning. Perhaps I shall get my hand back." He took hers in the meantime. It was limp and chill, though so near the fire. "Have courage," he said. "There is naught I can do here that will not shame Miriam. We cannot even go into an almshouse without shedding her blood. But the Holy One, blessed be He, is good. I will go away."

"Go away!" Beenah's clammy hand tightened her clasp of his, "Thou wilt travel with ware in the country?"

"No. If it stands written that I must break with my children, let the gap be too wide for repining. Miriam will like it better. I will go to America."

"To America!" Beenah's heart beat wildly. "And leave me?" A strange sense of desolation swept over her.

"Yes – for a little, anyhow. Thou must not face the first hardships. I shall find something to do. Perhaps in America there are more Jewish stone-masons to get work from. God will not desert us. There I can sell ware in the streets – do as I will. At the worst I can always fall back upon glaziering. Have faith, my dove."

The novel word of affection thrilled Beenah through and through.

"I shall send thee a little money; then as soon as I can see my way clear I shall send for thee and thou shalt come out to me and we will live happily together and our children shall live happily here."

But Beenah burst into fresh tears.

"Woe! Woe!" she sobbed. "How wilt thou, an old man, face the sea and the strange faces all alone? See how sorely thou art racked with rheumatism. How canst thou go glaziering? Thou liest often groaning all the night. How shalt thou carry the heavy crate on thy shoulders?"

"God will give me strength to do what is right." The tears were plain enough in his voice now and would not be denied. His words forced themselves out in a husky wheeze.

Beenah threw her arms round his neck. "No! No!" she cried hysterically. "Thou shalt not go! Thou shalt not leave me!"

"I must go," his parched lips articulated. He could not see that the snow of her hair had drifted into her eyes and was scarce whiter than her cheeks. His spectacles were a blur of mist.

"No, no," she moaned incoherently. "I shall die soon. God is merciful. Wait a little, wait a little. He will kill us both soon. My poor lamb, my poor Daniel! Thou shalt not leave me."

The old man unlaced her arms from his neck.

"I must. I have heard God's word in the silence."

"Then I will go with thee. Wherever thou goest I will go."

"No, no; thou shalt not face the first hardships. I will front them alone; I am strong, I am a man."

"And thou hast the heart to leave me?" She looked piteously into his face, but hers was still hidden from him in the mist. But through the darkness the flash passed again. His hand groped for her waist, he drew her again towards him and put the arms he had unlaced round his neck and stooped his wet cheek to hers. The past was a void, the forty years of joint housekeeping, since the morning each had seen a strange face on the pillow, faded to a point. For fifteen years they had been drifting towards each other, drifting nearer, nearer in dual loneliness; driven together by common suffering and growing alienation from the children they had begotten in common; drifting nearer, nearer in silence, almost in unconsciousness. And now they had met. The supreme moment of their lives had come. The silence of forty years was broken. His withered lips sought hers and love flooded their souls at last.

When the first delicious instants were over, Mendel drew a chair to the table and wrote a letter in Hebrew script and posted it and Beenah picked up Miriam's jacket. The crackling flames had subsided to a steady glow, the clock ticked on quietly as before, but something new and sweet and sacred had come into her life, and Beenah no longer wished to die.

When Miriam came home, she brought a little blast of cold air into the room. Beenah rose and shut the door and put out Miriam's supper; she did not drag her feet now.

"Was it a nice play, Miriam?" said Beenah softly.

"The usual stuff and nonsense," said Miriam peevishly. "Love and all that sort of thing, as if the world never got any older."

At breakfast next morning old Hyams received a letter by the first post. He carefully took his spectacles off and donned his reading-glasses to read it, throwing the envelope carelessly into the fire. When he had scanned a few lines he uttered an exclamation of surprise and dropped the letter.

"What's the matter, father?" said Daniel, while Miriam tilted her snub nose curiously.

"Praised be God!" was all the old man could say.

"Well, what is it? Speak!" said Beenah, with unusual animation, while a flush of excitement lit up Miriam's face and made it beautiful.

"My brother in America has won a thousand pounds on the lottery and he invites me and Beenah to come and live with him."

"Your brother in America!" repeated his children staring.

"Why, I didn't know you had a brother in America," added Miriam.

"No, while he was poor, I didn't mention him," replied Mendel, with unintentional sarcasm. "But I've heard from him several times. We both came over from Poland together, but the Board of Guardians sent him and a lot of others on to New York."

"But you won't go, father!" said Daniel.

"Why not? I should like to see my brother before I die. We were very thick as boys."

"But a thousand pounds isn't so very much," Miriam could not refrain from saying.

Old Hyams had thought it boundless opulence and was now sorry he had not done his brother a better turn.

"It will be enough for us all to live upon, he and Beenah and me. You see his wife died and he has no children."

"You don't really mean to go?" gasped Daniel, unable to grasp the situation suddenly sprung upon him. "How will you get the money to travel with?"

"Read here!" said Mendel, quietly passing him the letter. "He offers to send it."

"But it's written in Hebrew!" cried Daniel, turning it upside down hopelessly.

"You can read Hebrew writing surely," said his father.

"I could, years and years ago. I remember you taught me the letters. But my Hebrew correspondence has been so scanty" He broke off with a laugh and handed the letter to Miriam, who surveyed it with mock comprehension. There was a look of relief in her eyes as she returned it to her father.

"He might have sent something to his nephew and his niece," she said half seriously.

"Perhaps he will when I get to America and tell him how pretty you are," said Mendel oracularly. He looked quite joyous and even ventured to pinch Miriam's flushed cheek roguishly, and she submitted to the indignity without a murmur.

"Why *you're* looking as pleased as Punch too, mother," said Daniel, in half-rueful amazement. "You seem delighted at the idea of leaving us."

"I always wanted to see America," the old woman admitted with a smile. "I also shall renew an old friendship in New York." She looked meaningly at her husband, and in his eye was an answering love-light.

"Well, that's cool!" Daniel burst forth. "But she doesn't mean it, does she, father?"

"I mean it," Hymas answered.

"But it can't be true," persisted Daniel, in ever-growing bewilderment. "I believe it's all a hoax."

Mendel hastily drained his coffee-cup.

"A hoax!" he murmured, from behind the cup.

"Yes, I believe some one is having a lark with you."

"Nonsense!" cried Mendel vehemently, as he put down his coffee-cup and picked up the letter from the table. "Don't I know my own brother Yankov's writing. Besides, who else would know all the little things he writes about?"

Daniel was silenced, but lingered on after Miriam had departed to her wearisome duties.

"I shall write at once, accepting Yankov's offer," said his father. "Fortunately we took the house by the week, so you can always move out if it is too large for you and Miriam. I can trust you to look after Miriam, I know, Daniel." Daniel expostulated yet further, but Mendel answered:

"He is so lonely. He cannot well come over here by himself because he is half paralyzed. After all, what have I to do in England? And the mother naturally does not care to leave me. Perhaps I shall get my brother to travel with me to the land of Israel, and then we shall all end our days in Jerusalem, which you know has always been my heart's desire."

Neither mentioned Bessie Sugarman.

"Why do you make so much bother?" Miriam said to Daniel in the evening. "It's the best thing that could have happened. Who'd have dreamed at this hour of the day of coming into possession of a relative who might actually have something to leave us. It'll be a good story to tell, too."

After *Shool* next morning Mendel spoke to the President.

"Can you lend me six pounds?" he asked.

Belcovitch staggered.

"Six pounds!" he repeated, dazed.

"Yes. I wish to go to America with my wife. And I want you moreover to give your hand as a countryman that you will not breathe a word of this, whatever you hear. Beenah and I have sold a few little trinkets which our children gave us, and we have reckoned that with six pounds more we shall be able to take steerage passages and just exist till I get work."

"But six pounds is a very great sum – without sureties," said Belcovitch, rubbing his time-worn workaday high hat in his agitation.

"I know it is!" answered Mendel, "but God is my witness that I mean to pay you. And if I die before I can do so I vow to send word to my son Daniel, who will pay you the balance. You know my son Daniel. His word is an oath."

"But where shall I get six pounds from?" said Bear helplessly. "I am only a poor tailor, and my daughter gets married soon. It is a great sum. By my honourable word, it is. I have never lent so much in my life, nor even been security for such an amount."

Mendel dropped his head. There was a moment of anxious silence. Bear thought deeply.

"I tell you what I'll do," said Bear at last. "I'll lend you five if you can manage to come out with that."

Mendel gave a great sigh of relief. "God shall bless you," he said. He wrung the sweater's hand passionately. "I dare say we shall find another sovereign's-worth to sell." Mendel clinched the borrowing by standing the lender a glass of rum, and Bear felt secure against the graver shocks of doom. If the worst come to the worst now, he had still had something for his money.

And so Mendel and Beenah sailed away over the Atlantic. Daniel accompanied them to Liverpool, but Miriam said she could not get a day's holiday – perhaps she remembered the rebuke Esther Ansell had drawn down on herself, and was chary of asking.

At the dock in the chill dawn, Mendel Hyams kissed his son Daniel on the forehead and said in a broken voice:

"Good-bye. God bless you." He dared not add and God bless your Bessie, my daughter-in-law to be; but the benediction was in his heart.

Daniel turned away heavy-hearted, but the old man touched him on the shoulder and said in a low tremulous voice:

"Won't you forgive me for putting you into the fancy goods?"

"Father! What do you mean?" said Daniel choking. "Surely you are not thinking of the wild words I spoke years and years ago. I have long forgotten them."

"Then you will remain a good Jew," said Mendel, trembling all over, "even when we are far away?"

"With God's help," said Daniel. And then Mendel turned to Beenah and kissed her, weeping, and the faces of the old couple were radiant behind their tears.

Daniel stood on the clamorous hustling wharf, watching the ship move slowly from her moorings towards the open river, and neither he nor any one in the world but the happy pair knew that Mendel and Beenah were on their honeymoon.

*　　*　　*　　*　　*

Mrs. Hyams died two years after her honeymoon, and old Hyams laid a lover's kiss upon her sealed eyelids. Then, being absolutely alone in the world, he sold off his scanty furniture, sent the balance of the debt with a sovereign of undemanded interest to Bear Belcovitch, and girded up his loins for the journey to Jerusalem, which had been the dream of his life.

But the dream of his life had better have remained a dream.

Mendel saw the hills of Palestine and, the holy Jordan and Mount Moriah, the site of the Temple, and the tombs of Absalom and Melchitsedek, and the gate of Zion and the aqueduct built by Solomon, and all that he had longed to see from boyhood. But somehow it was not *his* Jerusalem – scarce more than his London Ghetto transplanted, only grown filthier and narrower and more ragged, with cripples for beggars and lepers in lieu of hawkers. The magic of his dream-city was not here. This was something prosaic, almost sordid. It made his heart sink as he thought of the sacred splendours of the Zion he had imaged in his suffering soul. The rainbows builded of his bitter tears did not span the firmament of this dingy Eastern city, set amid sterile hills. Where were the roses and lilies, the cedars and the fountains? Mount Moriah was here indeed, but it bore the Mosque of Omar, and the Temple of

Jehovah was but one ruined wall. The Shechinah, the Divine Glory, had faded into cold sunshine. "Who shall go up into the Mount of Jehovah." Lo, the Moslem worshipper and the Christian tourist. Barracks and convents stood on Zion's hill. His brethren, rulers by divine right of the soil they trod, were lost in the chaos of populations – Syrians, Armenians, Turks, Copts, Abyssinians, Europeans – as their synagogues were lost amid the domes and minarets of the Gentiles. The city was full of venerated relics of the Christ his people had lived – and died – to deny, and over all flew the crescent flag of the Mussulman.

And so every Friday, heedless of scoffing on-lookers, Mendel Hyams kissed the stones of the Wailing Place, bedewing their barrenness with tears; and every year at Passover, until he was gathered to his fathers, he continued to pray: "Next year – in Jerusalem!"

CHAPTER XVIII

The Hebrew's Friday Night

"Ah, the Men-of-the-Earth!" said Pinchas to Reb Shemuel, "ignorant fanatics, how shall a movement prosper in their hands? They have not the poetic vision, their ideas are as the mole's; they wish to make Messiahs out of half-pence. What inspiration for the soul is there in the sight of snuffy collectors that have the air of *Schnorrers*? with Karlkammer's red hair for a flag and the sound of Gradkoski's nose blowing for a trumpet-peal. But I have written an acrostic against Guedalyah the greengrocer, virulent as serpent's gall. He the Redeemer, indeed, with his diseased potatoes and his flat ginger-beer! Not thus did the great prophets and teachers in Israel figure the Return. Let a great signal-fire be lit in Israel and lo! the beacons will leap up on every mountain and tongue of flame shall call to tongue. Yea, I, even I, Melchitsedek Pinchas, will light the fire forthwith."

"Nay, not today," said Reb Shemuel, with his humorous twinkle; "it is the Sabbath."

The Rabbi was returning from synagogue and Pinchas was giving him his company on the short homeward journey. At their heels trudged Levi and on the other side of Reb Shemuel walked Eliphaz Chowchoski, a miserable-looking Pole whom Reb Shemuel was taking home to supper. In those days Reb Shemuel was not alone in taking to his hearth "the Sabbath guest" – some forlorn starveling or other – to sit at the table in like honour with the master. It was an object lesson in equality and fraternity for the children of many a well-to-do household, nor did it fail altogether in the homes of the poor. "All Israel are brothers," and how better honour the Sabbath than by making the lip-babble a reality?

"You will speak to your daughter?" said Pinchas, changing the subject abruptly. "You will tell her that what I wrote to her is not a millionth part of what I feel – that she is my sun by day and my moon and stars by night, that I must marry her at once or die, that I think of nothing in the world but her, that I can do, write, plan, nothing without her, that once she smiles on me I will write her great love-poems, greater than Byron's, greater than Heine's – the real Song of Songs, which is Pinchas's – that I will make her immortal as Dante made Beatrice, as Petrarch made Laura, that I walk about wretched, bedewing the pavements with my tears, that I sleep not by night nor eat by day – you will tell her this?" He laid his finger pleadingly on his nose.

"I will tell her," said Reb Shemuel. "You are a son-in-law to gladden the heart of any man. But I fear the maiden looks but coldly on wooers. Besides you are fourteen years older than she."

"Then I love her twice as much as Jacob loved Rachel – for it is written 'seven years were but as a day in his love for her.' To me fourteen years are but as a day in my love for Hannah."

The Rabbi laughed at the quibble and said.

"You are like the man who when he was accused of being twenty years older than the maiden he desired, replied 'but when I look at her I shall become ten years younger, and when she looks at me she will become ten years older, and thus we shall be even.'"

Pinchas laughed enthusiastically in his turn, but replied:

"Surely you will plead my cause, you whose motto is the Hebrew saying – 'the husband help the housewife, God help the bachelor.'"

"But have you the wherewithal to support her?"

"Shall my writings not suffice? If there are none to protect literature in England, we will go abroad – to your birthplace, Reb Shmuel, the cradle of great scholars."

The poet spoke yet more, but in the end his excited stridulous accents fell on Reb Shemuel's ears as a storm without on the ears of the slippered reader by the fireside. He had dropped into a delicious reverie – tasting in advance the Sabbath peace. The work of the week was over. The faithful Jew could enter on his rest – the narrow, miry streets faded before the brighter image of his brain. *"Come, my beloved, to meet the Bride, the face of the Sabbath let us welcome."*

Tonight his sweetheart would wear her Sabbath face, putting off the mask of the shrew, which hid not from him the angel countenance. Tonight he could in very truth call his wife (as the Rabbi in the Talmud did) "not wife, but home." Tonight she would be in very truth *Simcha* – rejoicing. A cheerful warmth glowed at his heart, love for all the wonderful Creation dissolved him in tenderness. As he approached the door, cheerful lights gleamed on him like a heavenly smile. He invited Pinchas to enter, but the poet in view of his passion thought it prudent to let others plead for him and went off with his finger to his nose in final reminder. The Reb kissed the *Mezuzah* on the outside of the door and his daughter, who met him, on the inside. Everything was as he had pictured it – the two tall wax candles in quaint heavy silver candlesticks, the spotless tablecloth, the dish of fried fish made picturesque with sprigs of parsley, the Sabbath loaves shaped like boys' tip-cats, with a curious plait of crust from point to point and thickly sprinkled with a drift of poppy-seed, and covered with a velvet cloth embroidered with Hebrew words; the flask of wine and the silver goblet. The sight was familiar yet it always struck the simple old Reb anew, with a sense of special blessing.

"Good *Shabbos*, Simcha," said Reb Shemuel.

"Good *Shabbos*, Shemuel," said Simcha. The light of love was in her eyes, and in her hair her newest comb. Her sharp features shone with peace and good-will and the consciousness of having duly lit the Sabbath candles and thrown the morsel of dough into the fire. Shemuel kissed her, then he laid his hands upon Hannah's head and murmured:

"May God make thee as Sarah, Rebecca, Rachel, and Leah," and upon Levi's, murmuring. "May God make thee as Ephraim and Manasseh."

Even the callous Levi felt the breath of sanctity in the air and had a vague restful sense of his Sabbath Angel hovering about and causing him to cast two shadows on the wall while his Evil Angel shivered impotent on the door-step.

Then Reb Shemuel repeated three times a series of sentences commencing: "*Peace be unto you, ye ministering Angel,*" and thereupon the wonderful picture of an ideal woman from Proverbs, looking affectionately at Simcha the while. "A woman of worth, whoso findeth her, her price is far above rubies. The heart of her husband trusteth in her; good and not evil will she do him all the days of her life; she riseth, while it is yet night, giveth food to her household and a task to her maidens. She putteth her own hands to the spindle; she stretcheth out her hand to the poor – strength and honour are her clothing and she looketh forth smilingly to the morrow; she openeth her mouth with wisdom and the law of kindness is on her tongue – she looketh well to the ways of her household and eateth not the bread of idleness. Deceitful is favour and vain is beauty, but the woman that feareth the Lord, *she* shall be praised."

Then, washing his hands with the due benediction, he filled the goblet with wine, and while every one reverently stood he "made Kiddish," in a traditional joyous recitative "...blessed art thou, O Lord, our God! King of the Universe, Creator of the fruit of the vine, who doth sanctify us with His commandments and hath delight in us . . .Thou hast chosen and sanctified us above all peoples and with love and favour hast made us to inherit Thy holy Sabbath..."

And all the household, and the hungry Pole, answered "Amen," each sipping of the cup in due gradation, then eating a special morsel of bread cut by the father and dipped in salt; after which the good wife served the fish, and cups and saucers clattered and knives and forks rattled. And after a few mouthfuls, the Pole knew himself a Prince in Israel and felt he must forthwith make choice of a maiden to grace his royal Sabbath board. Soup followed the fish; it was not served direct from the saucepan but transferred by way of a large tureen; since any creeping thing that might have got into the soup would have rendered the plateful in which it appeared not legally potable, whereas if it were detected in the large tureen, its polluting powers would be dissipated by being diffused over such a large mass of fluid. For like religious reasons, another feature of the etiquette of the modern fashionable table had been anticipated by many centuries – the eaters washed their hands in a little bowl of water after their meal. The Pollack was thus kept by main religious force in touch with a liquid with which he had no external sympathy.

When supper was over, grace was chanted and then the *Zemiroth* was sung – songs summing up in light and jingling metre the very essence of holy joyousness – neither riotous nor ascetic – the note of spiritualized common sense which has been the key-note of historical Judaism. For to feel "the delight of Sabbath" is a duty and to take three meals thereon a religious obligation – the sanctification of the sensuous by a creed to which everything is holy. The Sabbath is the hub of the Jew's universe; to protract it is a virtue, to love it a liberal education. It cancels all mourning – even for Jerusalem. The candles may gutter out at their own greasy will – unsnuffed, untended – is not Sabbath its own self-sufficient light?

> This is the sanctified rest-day;
> Happy the man who observes it,
> Thinks of it over the wine-cup,
> Feeling no pang at his heart-strings
> For that his purse-strings are empty,
> Joyous, and if he must borrow
> God will repay the good lender,
> Meat, wine and fish in profusion –
> See no delight is deficient.
> Let but the table be spread well,
> Angels of God answer "Amen!"
> So when a soul is in dolour,
> Cometh the sweet restful Sabbath,
> Singing and joy in its footsteps,
> Rapidly floweth Sambatyon,
> Till that, of God's love the symbol,
> Sabbath, the holy, the peaceful,
> Husheth its turbulent waters.

THE HEBREW'S FRIDAY NIGHT

*   *   *   *   *

Bless Him, O constant companions,
Rock from whose stores we have eaten,
Eaten have we and have left, too,
Just as the Lord hath commanded
Father and Shepherd and Feeder.
His is the bread we have eaten.
His is the wine we have drunken,
Wherefore with lips let us praise Him,
Lord of the land of our fathers.
Gratefully, ceaselessly chaunting
None like Jehovah is holy."

*   *   *   *   *

Light and rejoicing to Israel,
Sabbath, the soother of sorrows,
Comfort of down-trodden Israel,
Healing the hearts that were broken!
Banish despair! Here is Hope come,
What! A soul crushed! Lo a stranger
Bringeth the balsamous Sabbath.
Build, O rebuild thou, Thy Temple,
Fill again Zion, Thy city,
Clad with delight will we go there,
Other and new songs to sing there,
Merciful One and All-Holy,
Praisèd for ever and ever.

During the meal the Pollack began to speak with his host about the persecution in the land whence he had come, the bright spot in his picture being the fidelity of his brethren under trial, only a minority deserting and those already tainted with Epicureanism – students wishful of University distinction and such like. Orthodox Jews are rather surprised when men of (secular) education remain in the fold.

Hannah took advantage of a pause in their conversation to say in German:

"I am so glad, father, thou didst not bring that man home."

"What man?" said Reb Shemuel.

"The dirty monkey-faced little man who talks so much."

The Reb considered.

"I know none such."

"Pinchas she means," said her mother. "The poet!"

Reb Shemuel looked at her gravely. This did not sound promising.

"Why dost thou speak so harshly of thy fellow-creatures?" he said. "The man is a scholar and a poet, such as we have too few in Israel."

"We have too many *Schnorrers* in Israel already," retorted Hannah.

"Sh!" whispered Reb Shemuel reddening and indicating his guest with a slight movement of the eye.

Hannah bit her lip in self-humiliation and hastened to load the lucky Pole's plate with an extra piece of fish.

"He has written me a letter," she went on.

"He has told me so," he answered. "He loves thee with a great love."

"What nonsense, Shemuel!" broke in Simcha, setting down her coffee-cup with work-a-day violence. "The idea of a man who has not a penny to bless himself with marrying our Hannah! They would be on the Board of Guardians in a month."

"Money is not everything. Wisdom and learning outweigh much. And as the Midrash says: 'As a scarlet ribbon becometh a black horse, so poverty becometh the daughter of Jacob.' The world stands on the Torah, not on gold; as it is written: 'Better is the Law of Thy mouth to me than thousands of gold or silver.' He is greater than I, for he studies the law for nothing like the fathers of the Mishna while I am paid a salary."

"Methinks thou art little inferior," said Simcha, "for thou retainest little enough thereof. Let Pinchas get nothing for himself, 'tis his affair, but, if he wants my Hannah, he must get something for her. Were the fathers of the Mishna also fathers of families?"

"Certainly; is it not a command – 'Be fruitful and multiply'?"

"And how did their families live?"

"Many of our sages were artisans."

"Aha!" snorted Simcha triumphantly.

"And says not the Talmud," put in the Pole as if he were on the family council, "'Flay a carcass in the streets rather than be under an obligation'?" This with supreme unconsciousness of any personal application. "Yea, and said not Rabban Gamliel, the son of Rabbi Judah the Prince, 'it is commendable to join the study of the Law with worldly employment'? Did not Moses our teacher keep sheep?"

"Truth," replied the host. "I agree with Maimonides that man should first secure a living, then prepare a residence and after that seek a wife; and that they are fools who invert the order. But Pinchas works also with his pen. He writes articles in the papers. But the great thing, Hannah, is that he loves the Law."

"H'm!" said Hannah. "Let him marry the Law, then."

"He is in a hurry," said Reb Shemuel with a flash of irreverent facetiousness. "And he cannot become the Bridegroom of the Law till *Simchath Torah.*"

All laughed. The Bridegroom of the Law is the temporary title of the Jew who enjoys the distinction of being "called up" to the public reading of the last fragment of the Pentateuch, which is got through once a year.

Under the encouragement of the laughter, the Rabbi added:

"But he will know much more of his Bride than the majority of the Law's Bridegrooms."

Hannah took advantage of her father's pleasure in the effect of his jokes to show him Pinchas's epistle, which he deciphered laboriously. It commenced:

> **H**ebrew Hebe
> **A**ll-fair Maid,
> **N**ext to Heaven
> **N**ightly laid
> **A**h, I love you
> **H**alf afraid.

The Pole, looking a different being from the wretch who had come empty, departed invoking Peace on the household; Simcha went into the kitchen to superintend the removal of the crockery thither; Levi slipped out to pay his respects to Esther Ansell, for the evening was yet young, and father and daughter were left alone.

Reb Shmuel was already poring over a Pentateuch in his Friday night duty of reading the Portion twice in Hebrew and once in Chaldaic.

Hannah sat opposite him, studying the kindly furrowed face, the massive head set on founded shoulders, the shaggy eyebrows, the long whitening beard moving with the mumble of the pious lips, the brown peering eyes held close to the sacred tome, the high forehead crowned with the black skullcap.

She felt a moisture gathering under her eyelids as she looked at him.

"Father," she said at last, in a gentle voice.

"Did you call me, Hannah?" he asked, looking up.

"Yes, dear. About this man, Pinchas."

"Yes, Hannah."

"I am sorry I spoke harshly of him."

"Ah, that is right, my daughter. If he is poor and ill-clad we must only honour him the more. Wisdom and learning must be respected if they appear in rags. Abraham entertained God's messengers though they came as weary travellers."

"I know, father. It is not because of his appearance that I do not like him. If he is really a scholar and a poet, I will try to admire him as you do."

"Now you speak like a true daughter of Israel"

"But about my marrying him – you are not really in earnest?"

"*He* is," said Reb Shemuel, evasively.

"Ah, I knew you were not," she said, catching the lurking twinkle in his eye. "You know I could never marry a man like that."

"Your mother could," said the Reb.

"Dear old goose," she said, leaning across to pull his beard. "You are not a bit like that – you know a thousand times more, you know you do."

The old Rabbi held up his hands in comic deprecation.

"Yes, you do," she persisted. "Only you let him talk so much; you let everybody talk and bamboozle you."

Reb Shemuel drew the hand that fondled his beard in his own, feeling the fresh warm skin with a puzzled look.

"The hands are the hands of Hannah," he said, "but the voice is the voice of Simcha."

Hannah laughed merrily.

"All right, dear, I won't scold you any more. I'm so glad it didn't really enter your great stupid, clever old head that I was likely to care for Pinchas."

"My dear daughter, Pinchas wished to take you to wife, and I felt pleased. It is a union with a son of the Torah, who has also the pen of a ready writer. He asked me to tell you and I did."

"But you would not like me to marry anyone I did not like."

"God forbid! My little Hannah shall marry whomever she pleases."

A wave of emotion passed over the girl's face.

"You don't mean that, father," she said, shaking her head.

"True as the Torah! Why should I not?"

"Suppose," she said slowly, "I wanted to marry a Christian?"

Her heart beat painfully as she put the question.

Reb Shemuel laughed heartily.

"My Hannah would have made a good Talmudist. Of course, I don't mean it in that sense."

"Yes, but if I was to marry a very *link* Jew, you'd think it almost as bad."

"No, no!" said the Reb, shaking his head. "That's a different thing altogether; a Jew is a Jew, and a Christian a Christian."

"But you can't always distinguish between them," argued Hannah. "There are Jews who behave as if they were Christians, except, of course, they don't believe in the Crucified One."

Still the old Reb shook his head.

"The worst of Jews cannot put off his Judaism. His unborn soul undertook the yoke of the Torah at Sinai."

"Then you really wouldn't mind if I married a *link* Jew!"

He looked at her, startled, a suspicion dawning in his eyes.

"I should mind," he said slowly. "But if you loved him he would become a good Jew."

The simple conviction of his words moved her to tears, but she kept them back.

"But if he wouldn't?"

"I should pray. While there is life there is hope for the sinner in Israel."

She fell back on her old question.

"And you would really not mind whom I married?"

"Follow your heart, my little one," said Reb Shemuel. "It is a good heart and it will not lead you wrong."

Hannah turned away to hide the tears that could no longer be stayed. Her father resumed his reading of the Law. But he had got through very few verses ere he felt a soft warm arm round his neck and a wet cheek laid close to his.

"Father, forgive me," whispered the lips. "I am so sorry. I thought that – that I – that you – oh father, father! I feel as if I had never known you before tonight."

"What is it, my daughter?" said Reb Shemuel, stumbling into Yiddish in his anxiety. "What hast thou done?"

"I have betrothed myself," she answered, unwittingly adopting his dialect. "I have betrothed myself without telling thee or mother."

"To whom?" he asked anxiously.

"To a Jew," she hastened to assure him. "But he is neither a Talmud-sage nor pious. He is newly returned from the Cape."

"Ah, they are a *link* lot," muttered the Reb anxiously.

"Where didst thou first meet him?"

"At the Club," she answered. "At the Purim Ball – the night before Sam Levine came round here to be divorced from me."

He wrinkled his great brow. "Thy mother would have thee go," he said. "Thou didst not deserve I should get thee the divorce. What is his name?"

"David Brandon. He is not like other Jewish young men; I thought he was and did him wrong and mocked at him when first he spoke to me, so that afterwards I felt tender towards him. His conversation is agreeable, for he thinks for himself, and deeming thou wouldst not hear of such a match and that there was no danger, I met him at the Club several times in the evening, and – and – thou knowest the rest."

She turned away her face, blushing, contrite, happy, anxious.

Her love-story was as simple as her telling of it. David Brandon was not the shadowy Prince of her maiden dreams, nor was the passion exactly as she had imagined it; it was both stronger and stranger, and the sense of secrecy and impending opposition instilled into her love a poignant sweetness.

The Reb stroked her hair silently.

"I would not have said 'Yea' so quick, father," she went on, "but David had to go to Germany to take a message to the aged parents of his Cape chum, who died in the gold-fields. David had promised the dying man to go personally as soon as he returned to England – I think it was a request for forgiveness and blessing – but after meeting me he delayed going, and when I learned of it I reproached him, but he said he could not tear himself away, and he would not go till I had confessed I loved him. At last I said if he would go home the moment I said it and not bother about getting me a ring or anything, but go off to Germany the first thing the next morning, I would admit I loved him a little bit. Thus did it occur. He went off last Wednesday. Oh, isn't it cruel to think, father, that he should be going with love and joy in his heart to the parents of his dead friend!"

Her father's head was bent. She lifted it up by the chin and looked pleadingly into the big brown eyes.

"Thou art not angry with me, father?

"No, Hannah. But thou shouldst have told me from the first."

"I always meant to, father. But I feared to grieve thee."

"Wherefore? The man is a Jew. And thou lovest him, dost thou not?"

"As my life, father."

He kissed her lips.

"It is enough, my Hannah. With thee to love him, he will become pious. When a man has a good Jewish wife like my beloved daughter, who will keep a good Jewish house, he cannot be long among the sinners. The light of a true Jewish home will lead his footsteps back to God."

Hannah pressed her face to his in silence. She could not speak. She had not strength to undeceive him further, to tell him she had no care for trivial forms. Besides, in the flush of gratitude and surprise at her father's tolerance, she felt stirrings of responsive tolerance to his religion. It was not the moment to analyze her feelings or to enunciate her state of mind regarding religion. She simply let herself sink in the sweet sense of restored confidence and love, her head resting against his.

Presently Reb Shemuel put his hands on her head and murmured again: "May God make thee as Sarah, Rebecca, Rachel and Leah."

Then he added: "Go now, my daughter, and make glad the heart of thy mother."

Hannah suspected a shade of satire in the words, but was not sure.

*   *   *   *   *

The roaring Sambatyon of life was at rest in the Ghetto; on thousands of squalid homes the light of Sinai shone. The Sabbath Angels whispered words of hope and comfort to the foot-sore hawker and the aching machinist, and refreshed their parched souls with celestial anodyne and made them kings of the hour, with leisure to dream of the golden chairs that awaited them in Paradise.

The Ghetto welcomed the Bride with proud song and humble feast and sped her parting with optimistic symbolisms of fire and wine, of spice and light and shadow. All around their neighbours sought distraction in the blazing public-house and their tipsy bellowings resounded through the streets and mingled with the Hebrew hymns. Here and there the voice of a beaten woman rose on the air. But no Son of the Covenant was among the revellers or the wife-beaters; the Jews remained a chosen race, a peculiar people, faulty enough, but redeemed at least from the grosser vices, a little human islet won from the waters of animalism by the genius of ancient engineers. For while the genius of the Greek or the Roman, the Egyptian or the Phoenician, survives but in word. and stone, the Hebrew word alone was made flesh.

CHAPTER XIX

With the Strikers

"Ignorant donkey-heads!" cried Pinchas next Friday morning. "Him they make a Rabbi and give him the right of answering questions and he know no more of Judaism," the patriotic poet paused to take a bite out of his ham-sandwich, "than a cow of Sunday. I lof his daughter and I tell him so and he tells me she lof another. But I haf held him up on the point of my pen to the contempt of posterity. I haf written an acrostic on him; it is terrible. Her vill I shoot."

"Ah, they are a bad lot, these Rabbis," said Simon Wolf, sipping his sherry. The conversation took place in English and the two men were seated in a small private room in a public house, awaiting the advent of the Strike Committee.

"Dey are like de rest of de Community. I vash my hands of dem," said the poet, waving his cigar in a fiery crescent.

"I have long since washed my hands of them," said Simon Wolf, though the fact was not obvious. "We can trust neither our Rabbis nor our philanthropists. The Rabbis engrossed in the hypocritical endeavour to galvanize the corpse of Judaism into a vitality that shall last at least their own lifetime, have neither time nor thought for the great labour question. Our philanthropists do but scratch the surface. They give the working-man with their right hand what they have stolen from him with the left."

Simon Wolf was the great Jewish labour leader. Most of his cronies were rampant atheists, disgusted with the commercialism of the believers. They were clever young artisans from Russia and Poland with

a smattering of education, a feverish receptiveness for all the icono-
clastic ideas that were in the London air, a hatred of capitalism and
strong social sympathies. They wrote vigorous jargon for the *Friend of
Labour* and compassed the extreme proverbial limits of impiety by
"eating pork on the Day of Atonement." This was done partly to vindi-
cate their religious opinions whose correctness was demonstrated by the
non-appearance of thunderbolts, partly to show that nothing one way or
the other was to be expected from Providence or its professors.

"The only way for our poor brethren to be saved from their slavery,"
went on Simon Wolf, "is for them to combine against the sweaters and to
let the West-End Jews go and hang themselves."

"Ah, dat is mine policee," said Pinchas, "dat was mine policee ven I
founded de Holy Land League. Help yourselves and Pinchas vill help
you. You muz combine, and den I vill be de Moses to lead you out of de
land of bondage. Nein, I vill be more dan Moses, for he had not de gift
of eloquence."

"And he was the meekest man that ever lived," added Wolf.

"Yes, he was a fool-man," said Pinchas imperturbably. "I agree with
Goethe – *nur Lumpen sind bescheiden,* only clods are modaist. I am not
modaist. Is the Almighty modaist? I know, I feel vat I am, vat I can do."

"Look here, Pinchas, you're a very clever fellow, I know, and I'm very
glad to have you with us – but remember I have organized this
movement for years, planned it out as I sat toiling in Belcovitch's
machine-room, written on it till I've got the cramp, spoken on it till I was
hoarse, given evidence before innumerable Commissions. It is I who
have stirred up the East-End Jews and sent the echo of their cry into
Parliament, and I will not be interfered with. Do you hear?"

"Yes, I hear. Vy you not listen to me? You no understand vat I mean!"

"Oh, I understand you well enough. You want to oust me from my
position."

"Me? Me?" repeated the poet in an injured and astonished tone. "Vy
midout you de movement vould crumble like a mummy in de air: be not
such a fool-man. To everybody I haf said – ah, dat Simon Wolf he is a

great man, a vair great man; he is de only man among de English Jews who can save de East-End; it is he that should be member for Vitechapel – not that fool-man Gideon. Be not such a fool-man! Haf anoder glaz sherry and some more ham-sandwiches." The poet had a simple child-like delight in occasionally assuming the host.

"Very well, so long as I have your assurance," said the mollified labour-leader, mumbling the conclusion of the sentence into his wine-glass. "But you know how it is! After I have worked the thing for years, I don't want to see a drone come in and take the credit."

"Yes, *sic vos non vobis*, as the Talmud says. Do you know I haf proved that Virgil stole all his ideas from the Talmud?"

"First there was Black and then there was Cohen – now Gideon, M.P., sees he can get some advertisement out of it in the press, he wants to preside at the meetings. Members of Parliament are a bad lot!"

"Yes – but dey shall not take de credit from you. I will write and expose dem – the world shall know what humbugs dey are, how de whole wealthy West-End stood idly by with her hands in de working-men's pockets while you vere building up de great organization. You know all de jargon – papers jump at vat I write, dey sign my name in vair large type – Melchitsedek Pinchas – under everyting, and I am so pleased with deir homage, I do not ask for payment, for dey are vair poor. By dis time I am famous everywhere, my name has been in de evening papers, and ven I write about you to de *Times*, you vill become as famous as me. And den you vill write about me – ve vill put up for Vitechapel at de elections, ve vill both become membairs of Parliament, I and you, eh?"

"I'm afraid there's not much chance of that," sighed Simon Wolf.

"Vy not? Dere are two seats. Vy should you not haf de oder?"

"Ain't you forgetting about election expenses, Pinchas?"

"*Nein!*" repeated the poet emphatically. "I forgets noding. Ve vill start a fund."

"We can't start funds for ourselves."

"Be not a fool-man; of course not. You for me, I for you."

"You won't get much," said Simon, laughing ruefully at the idea.

"Tink not? Praps not. But *you* vill for me. Ven I am in Parliament, de load vill be easier for us both. Besides I vill go to de Continent soon to give avay de rest of de copies of my book. I expect to make dousands of pounds by it – for dey know how to honour scholars and poets abroad. Dere dey haf not stupid-head stockbrokers like Gideon, M.P., ministers like the Reverend Elkan Benjamin who keep four mistresses, and Rabbis like Reb Shemuel vid long white beards outside and emptiness vidin who sell deir daughters."

"I don't want to look so far ahead," said Simon Wolf. "At present, what we have to do is to carry this strike through. Once we get our demands from the masters a powerful blow will have been struck for the emancipation of ten thousand workingmen. They will have more money and more leisure, a little less of hell and a little more of heaven. The coming Passover would, indeed, be an appropriate festival even for the most heterodox among them if we could strike off their chains in the interim. But it seems impossible to get unity among them – a large section appears to mistrust me, though I swear to you, Pinchas, I am actuated by nothing but an unselfish desire for their good. May this morsel of sandwich choke me if I have ever been swayed by anything but sympathy with their wrongs. And yet you saw that malicious pamphlet that was circulated against me in Yiddish – silly, illiterate scribble."

"Oh, no!" said Pinchas. "It was vair beautiful; sharp as de sting of de hornet. But vat can you expect? Christ suffered. An great benefactors suffer. Am *I* happy? But it is only your own foolishness that you must tank if dere is dissension in de camp. De *Gamorah* says ve muz be vize, *chocham*; ve muz haf tact. See vat you haf done. You haf frighten avay de ortodox fool-men. Dey are oppressed, dey sweat – but dey tink deir God make dem sweat. Why you tell dem, no? Vat mattairs? Free dem from hunger and tirst first, den freedom from deir fool-superstitions vill come of itself. Jeshurun vax fat and kick? Hey? You go de wrong vay."

"Do you mean I'm to pretend to be *froom*," said Simon Wolf.

"And ven? Vat mattairs? You are a fool, man. To get to de goal one muz go crooked vays. Ah, you have no stadesmanship. You frighten dem.

You lead processions vid bands and banners on *Shabbos* to de *Shools*. Many who vould be glad to be delivered by you tremble for de heavenly lightning. Dey go not in de procession. Many go when deir head is on fire – afterwards, dey take flight and beat deir breasts. Vat vill happen? De ortodox are de majority; in time dere vill come a leader who vill be, or pretend to be, ortodox as vell as socialist. Den vat become of you? You are left vid von, two, tree ateists not enough to make *Minyan*. No, ve muz be *chocham*, ve muz take de men as ve find dem. God has made two classes of men – vise-men and fool-men. Dere is one vise-man to a million fool-men – and he sits on deir head and dey support him. If dese fool-men vant to go to *Shool* and to fast on *Yom Kippur*, vat for you make a feast of a pig and shock dem, so dey not believe in your socialism? Ven you vant to eat pig, you do it here, like ve do now, in private. In public, ve spit out ven ve see pig. Ah, you are a fool-man. I am a stadesman, a politician. I vill be de Machiavelli of de movement."

"Ah, Pinchas, you are a devil of a chap," said Wolf, laughing. "And yet you say you are the poet of patriotism and Palestine."

"Vy not? Vy should ve lif here in captivity? Vy ve shall not have our own state – and our own President, a man who combine deep politic vid knowledge of Hebrew literature and de pen of a poet. No, let us fight to get back our country – ve vill not hang our harps on the villows of Babylon and veep – ve vill take our swords vid Ezra and Judas Maccabaeus, and –"

"One thing at a time, Pinchas," said Simon Wolf. "At present, we have to consider how to distribute these food-tickets. The committee-men are late; I wonder if there has been any fighting at the centres, where they have been addressing meetings."

"Ah, dat is anoder point," said Pinchas. "Vy you no let me address meetings – not de little ones in de street, but de great ones in de hall of de Club? Dere my vords vould rush like de moundain dorrents, sweeping avay de corruptions. But you let all dese fool-men talk. You know, Simon, I and you are de only two persons in de East-End who speak Ainglish properly."

"I know. But these speeches must be in Yiddish."

"*Gewiss.* But who speak her like me and you? You muz gif me a speech tonight."

"I can't; really not," said Simon. "The programme's arranged. You know they're all jealous of me already. I dare not leave one out."

. " Ah, no; do not say dat!" said Pinchas, laying his finger pleadingly on the side of his nose.

"I must."

"You tear my heart in two. I lof you like a brother – almost like a voman. Just von!" There was an appealing smile in his eye.

"I cannot. I shall have a hornet's nest about my ears."

"Von leedle von, Simon Wolf." Again his finger was on his nose.

"It is impossible."

"You haf not considair how my Yiddish shall make kindle every heart, strike tears from every eye, as Moses did from de rock."

"I have. I know. But what am I to do?"

"Jus dis leedle favour; and I vill be gradeful to you all mine life."

"You know I would if I could."

Pinchas's finger was laid more insistently on his nose.

"Just dis vonce. Grant me dis, and I vill nevair ask anyding of you in all my life."

"No, no. Don't bother, Pinchas. Go away now," said Wolf, getting annoyed. "I have lots to do."

"I vill never gif you mine ideas again!" said the poet, flashing up, and he went out and banged the door.

The labour-leader settled to his papers with a sigh of relief.

The relief was transient. A moment afterwards the door was slightly opened, and Pinchas's head was protruded through the aperture. The poet wore his most endearing smile, the finger was laid coaxingly against the nose.

"Just von leedle speech, Simon. Tink how I lof you."

"Oh, well, go away. I'll see," replied Wolf, laughing amid all his annoyance.

The poet rushed in and kissed the hem of Wolf's coat.

"Oh, you be a great man!" he said. Then he walked out, closing the door gently. A moment afterwards, a vision of the dusky head, with the carneying smile and the finger on the nose, reappeared.

"You von't forget your promise," said the head.

"No, no. Go to the devil. I won't forget."

Pinchas walked home through streets thronged with excited strikers, discussing the situation with oriental exuberance of gesture, with any one who would listen. The demands of these poor slop-hands (who could only count upon six hours of the twenty-four for themselves, and who, by the help of their wives and little ones in finishing, might earn a pound a week) were moderate enough – hours from eight to eight, with an hour for dinner and half an hour for tea, two shillings from the government contractors for making a policeman's great-coat instead of one and ninepence halfpenny, and so on and so on. Their intentions were strictly peaceful. Every face was stamped with the marks of intellect and ill-health – the hue of a muddy pallor relieved by the flash of eyes and teeth. Their shoulders stooped, their chests were narrow, their arms flabby. They came in their hundreds to the hall at night. It was square-shaped with a stage and galleries, for a jargon-company sometimes thrilled the Ghetto with tragedy and tickled it with farce. Both species were playing tonight, and in jargon to boot. In real life you always get your drama mixed, and the sock of comedy galls the buskin of tragedy. It was an episode in the pitiful tussle of hunger and greed, yet its humours were grotesque enough.

Full as the Hall was, it was not crowded, for it was Friday night and a large contingent of strikers refused to desecrate the Sabbath by attending the meeting. But these were the zealots – Moses Ansell among them, for he, too, had struck. Having been out of work already he had nothing to lose by augmenting the numerical importance of the agitation. The moderately pious argued that there was no financial business to transact and attendance could hardly come under the denomination of work. It was rather analogous to attendance at a lecture – they would simply have to listen to speeches. Besides it would be but a black Sabbath at home with a barren larder, and they had already been to synagogue. Thus degenerates ancient piety in the stress of modern social problems. Some of the men had not even changed their everyday face for their Sabbath countenance by washing it. Some wore collars, and shiny threadbare garments of dignified origin, others were unaffectedly poverty-stricken with dingy shirt-cuffs peeping out of frayed sleeve edges and unhealthily coloured scarfs folded complexly round their necks. A minority belonged to the Free-thinking party, but the majority only availed themselves of Wolf's services because they were indispensable. For the moment he was the only possible leader, and they were sufficiently Jesuitic to use the Devil himself for good ends.

Though Wolf would not give up a Friday-night meeting – especially valuable, as permitting of the attendance of tailors who had not yet struck – Pinchas's politic advice had not failed to make an impression. Like so many reformers who have started with blatant atheism, he was beginning to see the insignificance of irreligious dissent as compared with the solution of the social problem, and Pinchas's seed had fallen on ready soil. As a labour-leader, pure and simple, he could count upon a far larger following than as a preacher of militant impiety. He resolved to keep his atheism in the background for the future and devote himself to the enfranchisement of the body before tampering with the soul. He was too proud ever to acknowledge his indebtedness to the poet's suggestion, but he felt grateful to him all the same.

"My brothers," he said in Yiddish, when his turn came to speak. "It pains me much to note how disunited we are. The capitalists, the Belcovitches, would rejoice if they but knew all that is going on. Have we not enemies enough that we must quarrel and split up into little factions among ourselves? (Hear, hear.) How can we hope to succeed unless we are thoroughly organized? It has come to my ears that there are men who insinuate things even about me and before I go on further tonight I wish to put this question to you." He paused and there was a breathless silence. The orator threw his chest forwards and gazing fearlessly at the assembly cried in a stentorian voice:

"*Sind sie zufrieden mit ihrer Chairman?*" (Are you satisfied with your chairman?)

His audacity made an impression. The discontented cowered timidly in their places.

"*Yes*," rolled back from the assembly, proud of its English monosyllables.

"*Nein*," cried a solitary voice from the topmost gallery.

Instantly the assembly was on its legs, eyeing the dissentient angrily. "Get down! Go on the platform! " mingled with cries of "order" from the Chairman, who in vain summoned him on to the stage. The dissentient waved a roll of paper violently and refused to modify his standpoint. He was evidently speaking, for his jaws were making movements, which in the din and uproar could not rise above grimaces. There was a battered high hat on the back of his head, and his hair was uncombed, and his face unwashed. At last silence was restored and the tirade became audible.

"Cursed sweaters – capitalists – stealing men's brains – leaving us to rot and starve in darkness and filth. Curse them! Curse them!" The speaker's voice rose to a hysterical scream, as he rambled on.

Some of the men knew him and soon there flew from lip to lip, "Oh, it's only *Meshuggene Dovid.*"

Mad Davy was a gifted Russian university student, who had been mixed up with nihilistic conspiracies and had fled to England where the struggle to find employ for his clerical talents had addled his brain. He had a gift for chess and mechanical invention, and in the early days had saved himself from starvation by the sale of some ingenious patents to a swaggering co-religionist who owned race-horses and a music-hall, but he sank into squaring the circle and inventing perpetual motion. He lived now on the casual crumbs of indigent neighbours, for the charitable organizations had marked him "dangerous." He was a man of infinite loquacity, with an intense jealousy of Simon Wolf or any such uninstructed person who assumed to lead the populace, but when the assembly accorded him his hearing he forgot the occasion of his rising in a burst of passionate invective against society.

When the irrelevancy of his remarks became apparent, he was rudely howled down and his neighbours pulled him into his seat, where he gibbered and mowed inaudibly.

Wolf continued his address.

"*Sind sie zufrieden mit ihrer Secretary?*"

This time there was no dissent. The "*Yes*" came like thunder.

"*Sind sie zufrieden mit ihrer Treasurer?*"

Yeas and *nays* mingled. The question of the retention of the functionary was put to the vote. But there was much confusion, for the East-End Jew is only slowly becoming a political animal. The ayes had it, but Wolf was not yet satisfied with the satisfaction of the gathering. He repeated the entire batch of questions in a new formula so as to drive them home.

"*Hot aner etwas zu sagen gegen mir?*" Which is Yiddish for "has any one anything to say against me?"

"*No!*" came in a vehement roar.

"*Hot aner etwas zu sagen gegen dem secretary?*"

"*No!*"

"*Hat aner etwas zu sagen gegen dem treasurer?*"

Having thus shown his grasp of logical exhaustiveness in a manner unduly exhausting to the more intelligent, Wolf consented to resume his oration. He had scored a victory, and triumph lent him added eloquence. When he ceased he left his audience in a frenzy of resolution and loyalty. In the flush of conscious power and freshly added influence, he found a niche for Pinchas's oratory.

"Brethren in exile," said the poet in his best Yiddish. Pinchas spoke German which is an outlandish form of Yiddish and scarce understanded of the people, so that to be intelligible he had to divest himself of sundry inflections, and to throw gender to the winds and to say "wet" for "wird" and mix hybrid Hebrew and ill-pronounced English with his vocabulary. There was some cheering as Pinchas tossed his dishevelled locks and addressed the gathering, for everybody to whom he had ever spoken knew that he was a wise and learned man and a great singer in Israel.

"Brethren in exile," said the poet. "The hour has come for laying the sweaters low. Singly we are sand-grains, together we are the simoom. Our great teacher, Moses, was the first Socialist. The legislation of the Old Testament – the land laws, the jubilee regulations, the tender care for the poor, the subordination of the rights of property to the interests of the working-men – all this is pure Socialism!"

The poet paused for the cheers which came in a mighty volume. Few of those present knew what Socialism was, but all knew the word as a shibboleth of salvation from sweaters. Socialism meant shorter hours and higher wages and was obtainable by marching with banners and brass bands – what need to inquire further?

"In short," pursued the poet, "Socialism is Judaism and Judaism is Socialism, and Karl Marx and Lassalle, the founders of Socialism, were Jews. Judaism does not bother with the next world. It says, 'Eat, drink and be satisfied and thank the Lord, thy God, who brought thee out of Egypt from the land of bondage.' But we have nothing to eat, we have nothing to drink, we have nothing to be satisfied with, we are still in the land of bondage." (Cheers.) "My brothers, how can we keep Judaism in a land where there is no Socialism? We must become better Jews, we must bring on Socialism, for the period of Socialism on earth and of peace and plenty and brotherly love is what all our prophets and great teachers meant by Messiah-times."

A little murmur of dissent rose here and there, but Pinchas went on.

"When Hillel the Great summed up the law to the would-be proselyte while standing on one leg, how did he express it? 'Do not unto others what you would not have others do unto you.' This is Socialism in a nut-shell. Do not keep your riches for yourself, spread them abroad. Do not fatten on the labour of the poor, but share it. Do not eat the food others have earned, but earn your own. Yes, brothers, the only true Jews in England are the Socialists. Phylacteries, praying-shawls – all nonsense.

Work for Socialism – that pleases the Almighty. The Messiah will be a Socialist."

There were mingled sounds, men asking, each other dubiously, "What says he?" They began to sniff brimstone. Wolf, shifting uneasily on his chair, kicked the poet's leg in reminder of his own warning. But Pinchas's head was touching the stars again. Mundane considerations were left behind somewhere in the depths of space below his feet.

"But how is the Messiah to redeem his people?" he asked. "Not now-a-days by the sword but by the tongue. He will plead the cause of Judaism, the cause of Socialism, in Parliament. He will not come with mock miracle like Bar Cochba or Zevi. At the general election, brothers, I will stand as the candidate for Whitechapel. I, a poor man, one of yourselves, will take my stand in that mighty assembly and touch the hearts of the legislators. They shall bend before my oratory as the bulrushes of the Nile when the wind passes. They will make me Prime Minister like Lord Beaconsfield, only he was no true lover of his people, he was not the Messiah. To hell with the rich bankers and the stockbrokers – we want them not. We will free ourselves."

The extraordinary vigour of the poet's language and gestures told. Only half comprehending, the majority stamped and huzzahed. Pinchas swelled visibly. His slim, lithe form, five and a quarter feet high, towered over the assembly. His complexion was as burnished copper, his eyes flashed flame.

"Yes, brethren," he resumed. "These Anglo-Jewish swine trample unheeding on the pearls of poetry and scholarship, they choose for Ministers men with four mistresses, for Chief Rabbis hypocrites who cannot even write the holy tongue grammatically, for *Dayanim* men who sell their daughters to the rich, for Members of Parliament stockbrokers who cannot speak English, for philanthropists greengrocers who embezzle funds. Let us have nothing to do with these swine – Moses our teacher forbade it. (Laughter.) I will be the Member for Whitechapel. See, my name Melchitsedek Pinchas already makes M. P. – it was foreordained. If every letter of the Torah has its special meaning, and none was put by chance, why should the finger of heaven not have written my name thus: M. P. – Melchitsedek Pinchas. Ah, our brother Wolf speaks truth – wisdom issues from his lips. Put aside your petty quarrels and unite in working for my election to Parliament. Thus and thus only shall you be redeemed from bondage, made from beasts of burden into men, from slaves to citizens, from false Jews to true Jews. Thus and thus only shall you eat, drink and be satisfied, and thank me for bringing you out of the land of bondage. Thus and thus only shall Judaism cover the world as the waters cover the sea."

The fervid peroration overbalanced the audience, and from all sides except the platform, applause warmed the poet's ears. He resumed his seat, and as he did so he automatically drew out a match and a cigar, and lit the one with the other. Instantly the applause dwindled, died; there was a moment of astonished silence, then a roar of execration. The bulk of the audience, as Pinchas, sober, had been shrewd enough to see, was still orthodox. This public desecration of the Sabbath by smoking was intolerable. How should the God of Israel aid the spread of Socialism and the shorter hours movement and the rise of prices a penny on a coat, if such devil's incense were borne to His nostrils? Their vague admiration of Pinchas changed into definite distrust. "*Epikouros, Epikouros, Meshumad,*" resounded from all sides. The poet looked wonderingly about him, failing to grasp the situation. Simon Wolf saw his opportunity. With an angry jerk he knocked the glowing cigar from between the poet's teeth. There was a yell of delight and approbation.

Wolf jumped to his feet. "Brothers," he roared, "you know I am not *froom*, but I will not have anybody else's feelings trampled upon." So saying, he ground the cigar under his heel.

Immediately an abortive blow from the poet's puny arm swished the air. Pinchas was roused, the veins on his forehead swelled, his heart thumped rapidly in his bosom. Wolf shook his knobby fist laughingly at the poet, who made no further effort to use any other weapon of offence but his tongue.

"Hypocrite!" he shrieked. "Liar! Machiavelli! Child of the separation!

A black year on thee! An evil spirit in thy bones and in the bones of thy father and mother. Thy father was a proselyte and thy mother an abomination. The curses of Deuteronomy light on thee. Mayest thou become covered with boils like job! And you," he added, turning on the audience, "pack of Men-of-the-earth! Stupid animals! How much longer will you bend your neck to the yoke of superstition while your bellies are empty? Who says I shall not smoke? Was tobacco known to Moses our teacher? If so he would have enjoyed it on the *Shabbos*. He was a wise man like me. Did the Rabbis know of it? No, fortunately, else they were so stupid they would have forbidden it. You are all so ignorant that you think not of these things. Can any one show me where it stands that we must not smoke on *Shabbos*? Is not *Shabbos* a day of rest, and how can we rest if we smoke not? I believe with the Baal-Shem that God is more pleased when I smoke my cigar than at the prayers of all the stupid Rabbis. How dare you rob me of my cigar – is that keeping *Shabbos*?" He turned back to Wolf, and tried to push his foot from off the cigar. There was a brief struggle. A dozen men leaped on the platform and dragged the poet away from his convulsive clasp of the labour-leader's leg. A few opponents of Wolf on the platform cried, "Let the man alone, give him his cigar," and thrust themselves amongst the invaders. The hall was in tumult. From the gallery the voice of Mad Davy resounded again:

"Cursed sweaters – stealing men's brains – darkness and filth – curse them! Blow them up! as we blew up Alexander. Curse them!"

Pinchas was carried, shrieking hysterically, and striving to bite the arms of his bearers, through the tumultuous crowd, amid a little ineffective opposition, and deposited outside the door.

Wolf made another speech, sealing the impression he had made. Then the poor narrow-chested pious men went home through the cold air to recite the Song of Solomon, in their stuffy backrooms and garrets. "Behold thou art fair, my love,"they intoned in a strange chant. "Behold thou art fair, thou hast doves' eyes. Behold thou art fair, my beloved, yea pleasant; also our couch is green. The beams of our house are cedar and our rafters are fir. For lo, the winter is past, the rain is over and gone; the flowers appear upon the earth; the time of the singing of birds is come and the voice of the turtle is heard in our land. Thy plants are an orchard of pomegranates, with pleasant fruits, calamus, cinnamon with all trees of frankincense; myrrh and aloe with all the chief spices; a fountain of gardens; a well of living waters and streams from Lebanon. Awake, O north wind and come thou south, blow upon my garden that the spices thereof may flow out."

CHAPTER XX

The Hope Extinct

The strike came to an end soon after. To the delight of Melchitsedek Pinchas, Gideon, M. P., intervened at the eleventh hour, unceremoniously elbowing Simon Wolf out of his central position. A compromise was arranged and jubilance and tranquillity reigned – for some months, till the corruptions of competitive human nature brought back the old state of things – for employers have quite a diplomatic reverence for treaties and the brotherly love of employees breaks down under the strain of supporting families. Rather to his own surprise Moses Ansell found himself in work at least three days a week, the other three being spent in hanging round the workshop waiting for it. It is an uncertain trade, is the manufacture of slops, which was all Moses was fitted for, but if you are not at hand you may miss the "work" when it does come.

It never rains but it pours, and so more luck came to the garret of No. 1 Royal Street. Esther won five pounds at school. It was the Henry Goldsmith prize, a new annual prize for general knowledge, instituted by a lady named Mrs. Henry Goldsmith who had just joined the committee, and the semi-divine person herself – a surpassingly beautiful radiant being, like a princess in a fairy tale – personally congratulated her upon her success. The money was not available for a year, but the neighbours hastened to congratulate the family on its rise to wealth. Even Levi Jacob's visits became more frequent, though this could scarcely be ascribed to mercenary motives.

The Belcovitches recognized their improved status so far as to send to borrow some salt; for the colony of No. 1 Royal Street carried on an extensive system of mutual accommodation, coals, potatoes, chunks of bread, saucepans, needles, wood-choppers, all passing daily to and fro. Even garments and jewellery were lent on great occasions, and when that dear old soul Mrs. Simons went to a wedding she was decked out in contributions from a dozen wardrobes. The Ansells themselves were too proud to borrow though they were not above lending.

It was early morning and Moses in his big phylacteries was droning his orisons. His mother had had an attack of spasms and so he was praying at home to be at hand in case of need. Everybody was up, and Moses was superintending the household even while he was gabbling psalms. He never minded breaking off his intercourse with Heaven to discuss domestic affairs, for he was on free and easy terms with the powers that be, and there was scarce a prayer in the liturgy which he would not interrupt to reprimand Solomon for lack of absorption in the same. The exception was the *Amidah* or eighteen Blessings, so-called because there are twenty-two. This section must be said standing and inaudibly and when Moses was engaged upon it, a message from an earthly monarch would have extorted no reply from him. There were other sacred silences which Moses would not break save of dire necessity and then only by talking Hebrew; but the *Amidah* was the silence of silences. This was why the utterly unprecedented arrival of a telegraph boy did not move him. Not even Esther's cry of alarm when she opened the telegram had any visible effect upon him, though in reality he whispered off his prayer at a record-beating rate and duly danced three times on his toes with spasmodic celerity at the finale.

"Father," said Esther, the never before received species of letter trembling in her hand, "we must go at once to see Benjy. He is very ill."

"Has he written to say so?"

"No, this is a telegram. I have read of such. Oh! perhaps he is dead. It is always so in books. They break the news by saying the dead are still alive." Her tones died away in a sob. The children clustered round her – Rachel and Solomon fought for the telegram in their anxiety to read it.

Ikey and Sarah stood grave and interested. The sick grandmother sat up in bed excited.

"He never showed me his 'four corners,'" she moaned. "Perhaps he did not wear the fringes at all."

"Father, dost thou hear?" said Esther, for Moses Ansell was fingering the russet envelope with a dazed air. "We must go to the Orphanage at once."

"Read it! What stands in the letter?" said Moses Ansell.

She took the telegram from the hands of Solomon. "It stands, 'Come up at once. Your son Benjamin very ill.'"

"Tu! Tu! Tu!" clucked Moses. "The poor child. But how can we go up? Thou canst not walk there. It will take me more than three hours."

His praying-shawl slid from his shoulders in his agitation.

"Thou must not walk, either!" cried Esther excitedly. "We must get to him at once! Who knows if he will be alive when we come? We must go by train from London Bridge the way Benjy came that Sunday. Oh, my poor Benjy!"

"Give me back the paper, Esther,'" interrupted Solomon, taking it from her limp hand. "The boys have never seen a telegram."

"But we cannot spare the money," urged Moses helplessly.

"We have just enough money to get along with today. Solomon, go on with thy prayers; thou seizest every excuse to interrupt them. Rachel, go away from him. Thou art also a disturbing Satan to him. I do not wonder his teacher flogged him black and blue yesterday – he is a stubborn and rebellious son who should be stoned, according to Deuteronomy."

"We must do without dinner," said Esther impulsively.

Sarah sat down on the floor and howled "Woe is me! Woe is me!"

"I didden touch 'er," cried Ikey in indignant bewilderment.

"Tain't Ikey!" sobbed Sarah. "Little Tharah wants 'er dinner."

"Thou hearest?" said Moses pitifully. "How can we spare the money?"

"How much is it?" asked Esther.

"It will be a shilling each there and back," replied Moses, who from his long periods of peregrination was a connoisseur in fares. "How can we afford it when I lose a morning's work into the bargain?"

"No, what talkest thou?" said Esther. "Thou art looking a few months ahead – thou deemest perhaps, I am already twelve. It will be only sixpence for me."

Moses did not disclaim the implied compliment to his rigid honesty but answered:

"Where is my head? Of course thou goest half-price. But even so where is the eighteenpence to come from?"

"But it is not eighteenpence!" ejaculated Esther with a new inspiration. Necessity was sharpening her wits to extraordinary acuteness. "We need not take return tickets. We can walk back."

"But we cannot be so long away from the mother – both of us," said Moses. "She, too, is ill. And how will the children do without thee? I will go by myself."

"No, I must see Benjy!" Esther cried.

"Be not so stiff-necked, Esther! Besides, it stands in the letter that I am to come – they do not ask thee. Who knows that the great people will not be angry if I bring thee with me? I dare say Benjamin will soon be better. He cannot have been ill long."

"But, quick, then, father, quick!" cried Esther, yielding to the complex difficulties of the position. "Go at once."

"Immediately, Esther. Wait only till I have finished my prayers. I am nearly done."

"No! No!" cried Esther agonized. "Thou prayest so much – God will let thee off a little bit just for once. Thou must go at once and ride both ways, else how shall we know what has happened? I will pawn my new prize and that will give thee money enough."

"Good!" said Moses. "While thou art pledging the book I shall have time to finish *davening*." He hitched up his *Talith* and commenced to gabble off, "Happy are they who dwell in Thy house; ever shall they praise Thee, Selah," and was already saying, "And a Redeemer shall come unto Zion," by the time Esther rushed out through the door with the pledge. It was a gaudily bound volume called "Treasures of Science," and Esther knew it almost by heart, having read it twice from gilt cover to gilt cover. All the same, she would miss it sorely. The pawnbroker lived only round the corner, for like the publican he springs up wherever the conditions are favourable. He was a Christian; by a curious anomaly the Ghetto does not supply its own pawnbrokers, but sends them out to the provinces or the West End. Perhaps the business instinct dreads the solicitation of the racial.

Esther's pawnbroker was a rubicund portly man. He knew the fortunes of a hundred families by the things left with him or taken back. It was on his stuffy shelves that poor Benjamin's coat had lain compressed and packed away when it might have had a beautiful airing in the grounds of the Crystal Palace. It was from his stuffy shelves that Esther's mother had redeemed it – a day after the fair – soon to be herself compressed and packed away in a pauper's coffin, awaiting in silence whatsoever Redemption might be. The best coat itself had long since been sold to a ragman, for Solomon, upon whose back it devolved, when Benjamin was so happily translated, could never be got to keep a best coat longer than a year, and when a best coat is degraded to everyday wear its attrition is much more than six times as rapid.

"Good mornen, my little dear," said the rubicund man. "You're early this mornen." The apprentice had, indeed, only just taken down the shutters. "What can I do for you today? You look pale, my dear; what's the matter?"

"A have a bran-new seven and sixpenny book," she answered hurriedly, passing it to him.

He turned instinctively to the fly-leaf.

"Bran-new book!" he said contemptuously. Esther Ansell "'For improvement!' When a book's spoiled like that, what can you expect for it?"

"Why, it's the inscription that makes it valuable," said Esther tearfully.

"Maybe," said the rubicund man gruffly. "But d'yer suppose I should just find a buyer named Esther Ansell? Do you suppose everybody in the world's named Esther Ansell or is capable of improvement?"

"No," breathed Esther dolefully. "But I shall take it out myself soon."

"In this world," said the rubicund man, shaking his head sceptically, "there ain't never no knowing. Well, how much d'yer want?"

"I only want a shilling," said Esther, "and threepence," she added as a happy thought.

"All right," said the rubicund man softened. "I won't 'aggle this mornen. You look quite knocked up. Here you are!" and Esther darted out of the shop with the money clasped tightly in her palm.

Moses had folded his phylacteries with pious primness and put them away in a little bag, and he was hastily swallowing a cup of coffee.

"Here is the shilling," she cried. And twopence extra for the bus to London Bridge. Quick! She put the ticket away carefully among its companions in a discoloured leather purse her father had once picked up in the street, and hurried him off. When his steps ceased on the stairs, she yearned to run after him and go with him, but Ikey was clamouring for breakfast and the children had to run off to school. She remained at home herself, for the grandmother groaned heavily. When the other children had gone off she tidied up the vacant bed and smoothed the old woman's pillows. Suddenly Benjamin's reluctance to have his father exhibited before his new companions recurred to her; she hoped Moses would not be needlessly obtrusive and felt that if she had gone with him she might have supplied tact in this direction. She reproached herself for not having made him a bit more presentable. She should have spared another halfpenny for a new collar, and seen that he was washed; but in the rush and alarm all thoughts of propriety had been submerged. Then her thoughts went off at a tangent and she saw her classroom, where new things were being taught, and new marks gained. It galled her to think she was missing both. She felt so lonely in the company of her grandmother, she could have gone downstairs and cried on Dutch Debby's musty lap. Then she strove to picture the room where Benjy was lying, but her imagination lacked the data. She would not let herself think the brilliant Benjamin was dead, that he would be sewn up in a shroud just like his poor mother, who had no literary talent whatever, but she wondered whether he was groaning like the grand-mother. And so, half distracted, pricking up her ears at the slightest creak on the stairs, Esther waited for news of her Benjy. The hours dragged on and on, and the children coming home at one found dinner ready but Esther still waiting. A dusty sunbeam streamed in through the garret window as though to give her hope.

Benjamin had been beguiled from his books into an unaccustomed game of ball in the cold March air. He had taken off his jacket and had got very hot with his unwonted exertions. A reactionary chill followed. Benjamin had a slight cold, which being ignored, developed rapidly into a heavy one, still without inducing the energetic lad to ask to be put upon the sick list. Was not the publishing day of *Our Own* at hand?

The cold became graver with the same rapidity, and almost as soon as the boy had made complaint he was in a high fever, and the official doctor declared that pneumonia had set in. In the night Benjamin was delirious, and the nurse summoned the doctor, and next morning his condition was so critical that his father was telegraphed for. There was little to be done by science – all depended on the patient's constitution. Alas! the four years of plenty and country breezes had not counteracted the eight and three-quarter years of privation and foul air, especially in a lad more intent on emulating Dickens and Thackeray than on profiting by the advantages of his situation.

When Moses arrived he found his boy tossing restlessly in a little bed, in a private little room away from the great dormitories. "The matron" – a sweet-faced young lady – was bending tenderly over him, and a nurse sat at the bedside. The doctor stood – waiting – at the foot of the bed. Moses took his boy's hand. The matron silently stepped aside. Benjamin stared at him with wide, unrecognizing eyes.

"*Nu*, how goes it, Benjamin?" cried Moses in Yiddish, with mock heartiness.

"Thank you, old Four-Eyes. It's very good of you to come. I always said there mustn't be any hits at you in the paper. I always told the fellows you were a very decent chap."

"What says he?" asked Moses, turning to the company. "I cannot understand English."

They could not understand his own question, but the matron guessed it. She tapped her forehead and shook her head for reply. Benjamin closed his eyes and there was silence. Presently he opened them and looked straight at his father. A deeper crimson mantled on the flushed cheek as Benjamin beheld the dingy stooping being to whom he owed birth. Moses wore a dirty red scarf below his untrimmed beard, his clothes were greasy, his face had not yet been washed, and – for a climax – he had not removed his hat, which other considerations than those of etiquette should have impelled him to keep out of sight.

"I thought you were old Four-Eyes," the boy murmured in confusion "Wasn't he here just now?"

"Go and fetch Mr. Coleman," said the matron to the nurse, half-smiling through tears at her own knowledge of the teacher's nickname and wondering what endearing term she was herself known by.

"Cheer up, Benjamin," said his father, seeing his boy had become sensible of his presence. "Thou wilt be all right soon. Thou hast been much worse than this."

"What does he say?" asked Benjamin, turning his eyes towards the matron.

"He says he is sorry to see you so bad," said the matron, at a venture.

"But I shall be up soon, won't I? I can't have *Our Own* delayed," whispered Benjamin.

"Don't worry about *Our Own*, my poor boy," murmured the matron, pressing his forehead. Moses respectfully made way for her.

"What says he?" he asked. The matron repeated the words, but Moses could not understand the English.

Old Four-Eyes arrived – a mild spectacled young man. He looked at the doctor, and the doctor's eye told him all.

"Ah, Mr. Coleman," said Benjamin, with joyous huskiness, "you'll see that *Our Own* comes out this week as usual. Tell Jack Simmonds he must not forget to rule black lines around the page containing Bruno's epitaph. Bony-nose – I – I mean Mr. Bernstein, wrote it for us in dog-Latin. Isn't it a lark? Thick, black lines, tell him. He was a good dog and only bit one boy in his life."

"All, right. I'll see to it," old Four-Eyes assured him with answering huskiness.

"What says he?" helplessly inquired Moses, addressing himself to the newcomer.

"Isn't it a sad case, Mr. Coleman?" said the matron, in a low tone. "They can't understand each other."

"You ought to keep an interpreter on the premises," said the doctor, blowing his nose. Coleman struggled with himself. He knew the jargon to perfection, for his parents spoke it still, but he had always posed as being ignorant of it.

"Tell my father to go home, and not to bother; I'm all right – only a little weak," whispered Benjamin.

Coleman was deeply perturbed. He was wondering whether he should plead guilty to a little knowledge, when a change of expression came over the wan face on the pillow. The doctor came and felt the boy's pulse.

"No, I don't want to hear that *Maaseh*," cried Benjamin. "Tell me about the Sambatyon, father, which refuses to flow on *Shabbos*."

He spoke Yiddish, grown a child again. Moses's face lit up with joy. His eldest born had returned to intelligibility. There was hope still then. A sudden burst of sunshine flooded the room. In London the sun would not breakthrough the clouds for somehours. Moses leaned over the pillow, his face working with blended emotions. He let a hot tear fall on his boy's upturned face.

"Hush, hush, my little Benjamin, don't cry," said Benjamin, and began to sing in his mother's jargon:

"Sleep, little father, sleep,
Thy father shall be a Ray,
Thy mother shall bring little apples,
Blessings on thy little head."

Moses saw his dead Gittel lulling his boy to sleep. Blinded by his tears, he did not see that they were falling thick upon the little white face.

"Nay, dry thy tears, I tell thee, my little Benjamin," said Benjamin, in tones more tender and soothing, and launched into the strange wailing melody:

> "Alas, woe is me!
> How wretched to be
> Driven away and banished,
> Yet so young, from thee."

"And Joseph's mother called to him from the grave: Be comforted, my son, a great future shall be thine."

"The end is near," old Four-Eyes whispered to the father in jargon.

Moses trembled from head to foot. "My poor lamb! My poor Benjamin," he wailed. "I thought thou wouldst say *Kaddish* after me, not I for thee." Then he began to recite quietly the Hebrew prayers. The hat he should have removed was appropriate enough now.

Benjamin sat up excitedly in bed: "There's mother, Esther!" he cried in English. "Coming back with my coat. But what's the use of it now?"

His head fell back again. Presently a look of, yearning came over the face so full of boyish beauty. "Esther," he said. "Wouldn't you like to be in the green country today? Look how the sun shines."

It shone, indeed, with deceptive warmth, bathing in gold the green country that stretched beyond, and dazzling the eyes of the dying boy. The birds twittered outside the window. "Esther!" he said, wistfully, "do you think there'll be another funeral soon?"

The matron burst into tears and turned away.

"Benjamin," cried the father, frantically, thinking the end had come, "say the *Shemang*."

The boy stared at him, a clearer look in his eyes.

"Say the *Shemang*!" said Moses peremptorily. The word *Shemang*, the old authoritative tone, penetrated the consciousness of the dying boy.

"Yes, father, I was just going to," he grumbled, submissively.

They repeated the last declaration of the dying Israelite together. It was in Hebrew. "Hear, O Israel, the Lord our God, the Lord is one." Both understood that.

Benjamin lingered on a few more minutes, and died in a painless torpor.

"He is dead," said the doctor.

"Blessed be the true judge," said Moses. He rent his coat, and closed the staring eyes. Then he went to the toilet table and turned the looking-glass to the wall, and opened the window and emptied the jug of water upon the green sunlit grass.

CHAPTER XXI

The Jargon Players

"No, don't stop me, Pinchas," said Gabriel Hamburg. "I'm packing up, and I shall spend my Passover in Stockholm. The Chief Rabbi there has discovered a manuscript which I am anxious to see, and as I have saved up a little money I shall speed thither."

"Ah, he pays well, that boy-fool, Raphael Leon," said Pinchas, emitting a lazy ring of smoke.

"What do you mean?" cried Gabriel, flushing angrily. "Do you mean, perhaps, that *you* have been getting money out of him?"

"Precisely. That is what I *do* mean," said the poet naively. "What else?"

"Well, don't let me hear you call him a fool. He *is* one to send you money, but then it is for others to call him so. That boy will be a great man in Israel. The son of rich English Jews – a Harrow-boy, yet he already writes Hebrew almost grammatically."

Pinchas was aware of this fact; had he not written to the lad (in response to a crude Hebrew eulogium and a crisp Bank of England note): "I and thou are the only two people in England who write the Holy Tongue grammatically."

He replied now: "It is true; soon he will vie with me and you."

The old scholar took snuff impatiently. The humours of Pinchas were beginning to pall upon him. "Goodbye," he said again.

"No, wait yet a little," said Pinchas, buttonholing him resolutely. "I want to show you my acrostic on Simon Wolf; ah! I will shoot him, the miserable labour-leader, the wretch who embezzles the money of the Socialist fools who trust him. Aha! it will sting like Juvenal, that acrostic."

"I haven't time," said the gentle savant, beginning to lose his temper.

"Well, have I time? I have to compose a three-act comedy by tomorrow at noon. I expect I shall have to sit up all night to get it done in time." Then, anxious to complete the conciliation of the old snuff-and-pepper-box, as he mentally christened him for his next acrostic, he added: "If there is anything in this manuscript that you cannot decipher or understand, a letter to me, care of Reb Shemuel, will always find me. Somehow I have a special genius for filling up *lacunæ* in manuscripts. You remember the famous discovery that I made by rewriting the six lines torn out of the first page of that Midrash I discovered in Cyprus."

"Yes, those six lines proved it thoroughly," sneered the savant.

"Aha! You see!" said the poet, a gratified smile pervading his dusky features. "But I must tell you of this comedy – it will be a satirical picture (in the style of Molière, only sharper) of Anglo-Jewish Society. The Rev. Elkan Benjamin, with his four mistresses, they will all be there, and Gideon, the Man-of-the-Earth, M. P., – ah, it will be terrible. If I could only get them to see it performed, they should have free passes."

"No, shoot them first; it would be more merciful. But where is this comedy to be played?" asked Hamburg curiously.

"At the Jargon Theatre, the great theatre in Prince's Street, the only real national theatre in England. The English stage – Drury Lane – pooh! It is not in harmony with the people; it does not express them."

Hamburg could not help smiling. He knew the wretched little hall, since tragically famous for a massacre of innocents, victims to the fatal cry of fire – more deadly than fiercest flame.

"But how will your audience understand it?" he asked.

"Aha!" said the poet, laying his finger on his nose and grinning. "They will understand. They know the corruptions of our society. All this conspiracy to crush me, to hound me out of England so that ignoramuses may prosper and hypocrites wax fat – do you think it is not the talk of the Ghetto? What! Shall it be the talk of Berlin, of Constantinople, of Mogadore, of Jerusalem, of Paris, and here it shall not be known? Besides, the leading actress will speak a prologue. Ah! she is beautiful, beautiful as Lilith, as the Queen of Sheba, as Cleopatra! And how she acts! She and Rachel – both Jewesses! Think of it! Ah, we are a great people. If I could tell you the secrets of her eyes as she looks at me – but no, you are dry as dust, a creature of prose! And there will be an orchestra, too, for Pesach Weingott has promised to play the overture on his fiddle. How he stirs the soul! It is like David playing before Saul."

"Yes, but it won't be javelins the people will throw," murmured Hamburg, adding aloud: "I suppose you have written the music of this overture."

"No, I cannot write music," said Pinchas.

"Good heavens! You don't say so?" gasped Gabriel Hamburg. "Let that be my last recollection of you! No! Don't say another word! Don't spoil it! Goodbye." And he tore himself away, leaving the poet bewildered.

"Mad! mad!" said Pinchas, tapping his brow significantly; "mad, the old snuff-and-pepper-box." He smiled at the recollection of his latest phrase. "These scholars stagnate so. They see not enough of the women. Ha! I will go and see my actress."

He threw out his chest, puffed out a volume of smoke, and took his way to Petticoat Lane. The compatriot of Rachel was wrapping up a scrag of mutton. She was a butcher's daughter and did not even wield the chopper, as Mrs. Siddons is reputed to have flourished the domestic table-knife. She was a simple, amiable girl, who had stepped into the position of lead in the stock jargon company as a way of eking out her pocket-money, and because there was no one else who wanted the post. She was rather plain except when be-rouged and be-pencilled. The company included several tailors and tailoresses of talent, and the low comedian was a Dutchman who sold herrings. They all had the gift of improvisation more developed than memory, and consequently availed themselves of the faculty that worked easier. The repertory was written by goodness knew whom, and was very extensive. It embraced all the species enumerated by Polonius, including comic opera, which was not known to the Danish saw-monger. There was nothing the company would not have undertaken to play or have come out of with a fair measure of success. Some of the plays were on Biblical subjects, but only a minority. There were also plays in rhyme, though Yiddish knows not blank verse. Melchitsedek accosted his interpretess and made sheep's-eyes at her. But an actress who serves in a butcher's shop is doubly accustomed to such, and being busy the girl paid no attention to the poet, though the poet was paying marked attention to her.

"Kiss me, thou beauteous one, the gems of whose crown are foot-lights," said the poet, when the custom ebbed for a moment.

"If thou comest near me," said the actress whirling the chopper, "I'll chop thy ugly little head off."

"Unless thou lendest me thy lips thou shalt not play in my comedy," said Pinchas angrily.

"*My* trouble!" said the leading lady, shrugging her shoulders.

Pinchas made several reappearances outside the open shop, with his insinuative finger on his nose and his insinuative smile on his face, but in the end went away with a flea in his ear and hunted up the actor-manager, the only person who made any money, to speak of, out of the performances. That gentleman had not yet consented to produce the play that Pinchas had ready in manuscript and which had been coveted by all the great theatres in the world, but which he, Pinchas, had reserved for the use of the only actor in Europe. The result of this inter-view was that the actor-manager yielded to Pinchas's solicitations, backed by frequent applications of poetic finger to poetic nose.

"But," said the actor-manager, with a sudden recollection, how about the besom?"

"The besom!" repeated Pinchas, nonplussed for once.

"Yes, thou sayest thou hast seen all the plays I have produced. Hast thou not noticed that I have a besom in all my plays?"

"Aha! Yes, I remember," said Pinchas.

"An old garden-besom it is," said the actor-manager. "And it is the cause of all my luck." He took up a house-broom that stood in the corner. "In comedy I sweep the floor with it – so – and the people grin; in comic-opera I beat time with it as I sing – so – and the people laugh; in farce I beat my mother-in-law with it – so – and the people roar; in tragedy I lean upon it – so – and the people thrill; in melodrama I sweep away the snow with it – so – and the people burst into tears. Usually I have my plays written beforehand and the authors are aware of the besom. Dost thou think," he concluded doubtfully, "that thou hast sufficient ingenuity to work in the besom now that the play is written?"

Pinchas put his finger to his nose and smiled reassuringly.

"It shall be all besom," he said.

"And when wilt thou read it to me?"

"Will tomorrow this time suit thee?"

"As honey a bear."

"Good, then!" said Pinchas; "I shall not fail."

The door closed upon him. In another moment it reopened a bit and he thrust his grinning face through the aperture.

"Ten percent of the receipts!" he said with his cajoling digito-nasal gesture.

"Certainly," rejoined the actor-manager briskly. "After paying the expenses – ten percent of the receipts."

"Thou wilt not forget?"

"I shall not forget."

Pinchas strode forth into the street and lit a new cigar in his exultation. How lucky the play was not yet written! Now he would be able to make it all turn round the axis of the besom. "It shall be all besom!" His own phrase rang in his ears like voluptuous marriage bells. Yes, it should, indeed, be all besom. With that besom he would sweep all his enemies – all the foul conspirators – in one clean sweep, down, down to Sheol. He would sweep them along the floor with it – so – and grin; he would beat time to their yells of agony – so – and laugh; he would beat them over the heads – so – and roar; he would lean upon it in statuesque greatness – so – and thrill; he would sweep away their remains with it – so – and weep for joy of countermining and quelling the long persecution.

All night he wrote the play at railway speed, like a night express – puffing out volumes of smoke as he panted along. "I dip my pen in their blood," he said from time to time, and threw back his head and laughed aloud in the silence of the small hours.

Pinchas had a good deal to do to explain the next day to the actor-manager where the fun came in. "Thou dost not grasp all the allusions, the back-handed slaps, the hidden poniards; perhaps not," the author acknowledged. "But the great heart of the people – it will understand."

The actor-manager was unconvinced, but he admitted there was a good deal of besom, and in consideration of the poet bating his terms to five percent of the receipts he agreed to give it a chance. The piece was billed widely in several streets under the title of "The Hornet of Judah," and the name of Melchitsedek Pinchas appeared in letters of the size stipulated by the finger on the nose.

But the leading actress threw up her part at the last moment, disgusted by the poet's amorous advances; Pinchas volunteered to play the part himself and, although his offer was rejected, he attired himself in skirts and streaked his complexion with red and white to replace the promoted second actress, and shaved off his beard.

But in spite of this heroic sacrifice, the gods were unpropitious. They chaffed the poet in polished Yiddish throughout the first two acts. There was only a sprinkling of audience (most of it paper) in the dimly-lit hall, for the fame of the great writer had not spread from Berlin, Mogadore, Constantinople and the rest of the universe.

No one could make head or tail of the piece with its incessant play of occult satire against clergymen with four mistresses, Rabbis who sold their daughters, stockbrokers ignorant of Hebrew and destitute of English, greengrocers blowing Messianic and their own trumpets, labour-leaders embezzling funds, and the like. In vain the actor-manager swept the floor with the besom, beat time with the besom, beat his mother-in-law with the besom, leaned on the besom, swept bits of white paper with the besom. The hall, empty of its usual crowd, was fuller of derisive laughter. At last the spectators tired of laughter and the rafters re-echoed with hoots. At the end of the second act, Melchitsedek Pinchas addressed the audience from the stage in his ample petticoats, his brow streaming with paint and perspiration. He spoke of the great English conspiracy and expressed his grief and astonishment at finding it had infected the entire Ghetto.

There was no third act. It was the poet's first – and last – appearance on any stage.

CHAPTER XXII

"For Auld Lang Syne, My Dear"

The learned say that Passover was a Spring festival even before it was associated with the Redemption from Egypt, but there is not much Nature to worship in the Ghetto and the historical elements of the Festival swamp all the others. Passover still remains the most picturesque of the "Three Festivals" with its entire transmogrification of things culinary, its thorough taboo of leaven. The audacious archæologist of the thirtieth century may trace back the origin of the festival to the Spring Cleaning, the annual revel of the English housewife, for it is now that the Ghetto whitewashes itself and scrubs itself and paints itself and pranks itself and purifies its pans in a baptism of fire. Now, too, the publican gets unto himself a white sheet and suspends it at his door and proclaims that he sells *Kosher rum* by permission of the Chief Rabbi. Now the confectioner exchanges his "stuffed monkeys," and his bolas and his jam-puffs, and his cheese-cakes for unleavened "palavas," and worsted balls and almond cakes. Time was when the Passover dietary was restricted to fruit and meat and vegetables, but year by year the circle is expanding, and it should not be beyond the reach of ingenuity to make bread itself Passoverian. It is now that the pious shopkeeper whose store is tainted with leaven sells his business to a friendly Christian, buying it back at the conclusion of the festival. Now the Shalotten *Shammos* is busy from morning to night filling up charity-forms artistically multiplying the poor man's children and dividing his rooms. Now is holocaust made of a people's bread-crumbs, and now is the national salutation changed to "How do the *Motsos* agree, with you?" half of the race growing facetious, and the other half finical over the spotted Passover cakes.

It was on the evening preceding the opening of Passover that Esther Ansell set forth to purchase a shilling's worth of fish in Petticoat Lane, involuntarily storing up in her mind vivid impressions of the bustling scene. It is one of the compensations of poverty that it allows no time for mourning. Daily duty is the poor man's nepenthe.

Esther and her father were the only two members of the family upon whom the death of Benjamin made a deep impression. He had been so long away from home that he was the merest shadow to the rest. But Moses bore the loss with resignation, his emotions discharging themselves in the daily *Kaddish.* Blent with his personal grief was a sorrow for the commentaries lost to Hebrew literature by his boy's premature transference to Paradise. Esther's grief was more bitter and defiant. All the children were delicate, but it was the first time death had taken one. The meaningless tragedy of Benjamin's end shook the child's soul to its depths. Poor lad! How horrible to be lying cold and ghastly beneath the winter snow! What had been the use of all his long preparations to write great novels? The name of Ansell would now become ingloriously extinct. She wondered whether *Our Own* would collapse and secretly felt it must. And then what of the hopes of worldly wealth she had built on Benjamin's genius? Alas! the emancipation of the Ansells from the yoke of poverty was clearly postponed. To her and her alone must the family now look for deliverance. Well, she would take up the mantle of the dead boy, and fill it as best she might. She clenched her little hands in iron determination. Moses Ansell knew nothing either of her doubts or her ambitions. Work was still plentiful three days a week, and he was unconscious he was not supporting his family in comparative affluence. But even with Esther the incessant grind of school-life and quasi-motherhood speedily rubbed away the sharper edges of sorrow, though the custom prohibiting obvious pleasures during the year of mourning went in no danger of transgression, for poor little Esther gadded neither to children's balls nor to theatres. Her thoughts were full of the prospects of piscine bargains, as she pushed her way through a crowd so closely wedged, and lit up by such a flare of gas from the shops and such streamers of flame from the barrows that the cold wind of early April lost its sting.

Two opposing currents of heavy-laden pedestrians were endeavouring in their progress to occupy the same strip of pavement at the same moment, and the laws of space kept them blocked till they yielded to its remorseless conditions. Rich and poor elbowed one another, ladies in satins and furs were jammed against wretched looking foreign women with their heads swathed in dirty handkerchiefs; rough, red-faced English betting men struggled good-humouredly with their greasy kindred from over the North Sea; and a sprinkling of Christian yokels surveyed the Jewish hucksters and chapmen with amused superiority.

For this was the night of nights, when the purchases were made for the festival, and great ladies of the West, leaving behind their daughters who played the piano and had a subscription at Mudie's, came down again to the beloved Lane to throw off the veneer of refinement, and plunge gloveless hands in barrels where pickled cucumbers weltered in their own "*russell*," and to pick fat juicy olives from the rich-heaped tubs. Ah, me! what tragic comedy lay behind the transient happiness of these sensuous faces, laughing and munching with the shamelessness of school-girls! For tonight they need not hanker in silence after the flesh-pots of Egypt. tonight they could laugh and talk over *Olov hasholom* times – "Peace be upon him" times – with their old cronies, and loosen the stays of social ambition, even while they dazzled the Ghetto with the splendours of their get-up and the halo of the West End whence they came. It was a scene without parallel in the history of the world – this phantasmagoria of grubs and butterflies, met together for auld lang syne in their beloved hatching-place. Such violent contrasts of wealth and poverty as might be looked for in romantic gold-fields, or in unsettled countries were evolved quite naturally amid a colourless civilization by a people with an incurable talent for the picturesque.

"Hullo! Can that be you, Betsy?" some grizzled shabby old man would observe in innocent delight to Mrs. Arthur Montmorenci; "Why so it is! I never would have believed my eyes! Lord, what a fine woman you've grown! And so you're little Betsy who used to bring her father's coffee in a brown jug when he and I stood side by side in the Lane! He used to sell slippers next to my cutlery stall for eleven years – Dear, dear, how time flies to be sure."

Then Betsy Montmorenci's creamy face would grow scarlet under the gas-jets, and she would glower and draw her sables around her, and look round involuntarily, to see if any of her Kensington friends were within earshot.

Another Betsy Montmorenci would feel Bohemian for this occasion only, and would receive old acquaintances' greeting elusively, and pass the old phrases and by-words with a strange sense of stolen sweets; while yet a third Betsy Montmorenci, a finer spirit this, and worthier of the name, would cry to a Betsy Jacobs:

"Is that you, Betsy, how *are* you? How *are* you? I'm so glad to see you. Won't you come and treat me to a cup of chocolate at Bonn's, just to show you haven't forgot *Olov hasholom* times?"

And then, having thus thrown the responsibility of stand-offishness on the poorer Betsy, the Montmorenci would launch into recollections of those good old "Peace be upon him" times till the grub forgot the splendours of the caterpillar in a joyous resurrection of ancient scandals. But few of the Montmorencis, whatever their species, left the Ghetto without pressing bits of gold into half-reluctant palms in shabby back-rooms where old friends or poor relatives mouldered.

Overhead, the stars burned silently, but no one looked up at them. Underfoot, lay the thick, black veil of mud, which the lane never lifted, but none looked down on it. It was impossible to think of aught but humanity in the bustle and confusion, in the cram and crush, in the wedge and the jam, in the squeezing and shouting, in the hubbub and medley. Such a jolly, rampant, screaming, fighting, maddening, jostling, polyglot, quarrelling, laughing broth of a Vanity Fair! Mendicants, vendors, buyers, gossips, showmen, all swelled the roar.

"Here's your cakes! All *yontovdik* (for the festival)! *Yontovdik* –"
"Braces, best braces, all –"
"*Yontovdik*! Only one shilling –"
"It's the Rav's orders, mum; all legs of mutton must be porged or my license –" "Cowcumbers! Cowcumbers!"
"Now's your chance –"
"The best trousers, gentlemen. Corst me as sure as I stand –"
"On your own head, you old –"
"*Arbah Kanfus* (four fringes)! *Arbah* –"
"My old man's been under an operation –"
"HokeyPokey! *Yontovdik*! Hokey –"
"Get out of the way, can't you –"
"By your life and mine, Betsy –"
"Gord blesh you, mishter, a toisand year shall ye live."
"Eat the best *Motsos*. Only fourpence –"
"The bones must go with, marm. I've cut it as lean as possible."
"*Charoises* (a sweet mixture). *Charoises! Moroire* (bitter herb)! *Chraine* (horseradish)! *Pesachdik* (for Passover)."
"Come and have a glass of Old Tom, along o'me, sonny."
"Fine plaice! Here y'are! Hi! where's yer pluck! S'elp me –"
"Bob! *Yontovdik*! *Yontovdik*! Only a bob!"
"Chuck steak and half a pound of fat."
"A slap in the eye, if you –"
"Gord bless you. Remember me to Jacob."
"*Shaink* (spare) *meer* a 'apenny, missis *lieben*, missis *croin* (dear) –"
"An unnatural death on you, you –"
"Lord! Sal, how you've altered!"
"Ladies, here you are –"
"I give you my word, sir, the fish will be home before you."
"Painted in the best style, for a tanner –"
"A spoonge, mister?"
"I'll cut a slice of this melon for you for –"
"She's dead, poor thing, peace be upon him."

"*Yontovdik!* Three bob for one purse containing –"

"The real live tattooed Hindian, born in the African Harchipellygo. Walk up."

"This way for the dwarf that will speak, dance, and sing."

"Tree lemons a penny. Tree lemons –"

"A *Shtibbur* (penny) for a poor blind man –"

"*Yontovdik! Yontovdik! Yontovdik! Yontovdik!*"

And in this last roar, common to so many of the mongers, the whole Babel would often blend for a moment and be swallowed up, re-emerging anon in its broken multiplicity.

Everybody Esther knew was in the crowd – she met them all sooner or later. In Wentworth Street, amid dead cabbage-leaves, and mud, and refuse, and orts, and offal, stood the woe-begone Meckish, offering his puny sponges, and wooing the charitable with grinning grimaces tempered by epileptic fits at judicious intervals. A few inches off, his wife in costly sealskin jacket, purchased salmon with a Maida Vale manner. Compressed in a corner was Shosshi Shmendrik, his coat-tails yellow with the yolks of dissolving eggs from a bag in his pocket. He asked her frantically, if she had seen a boy whom he had hired to carry home his codfish and his fowls, and explained that his missus was busy in the shop, and had delegated to him the domestic duties. It is probable, that if Mrs. Shmendrik, formerly the widow Finkelstein, ever received these dainties, she found her good man had purchased fish artificially inflated with air, and fowls fattened with brown paper. Hearty Sam Abrahams the bass chorister, whose genial countenance spread sunshine for yards around, stopped Esther and gave her a penny. Further, she met her teacher, Miss Miriam Hyams, and curtseyed to her, for Esther was not of those who jeeringly called "teacher" and "master" according to sex after her superiors, till the victims longed for Elisha's influence over bears. Later on, she was shocked to see her teacher's brother piloting bonny Bessie Sugarman through the thick of the ferment. Crushed between two barrows, she found Mrs. Belcovitch and Fanny, who were shopping together, attended by Pesach Weingott, all carrying piles of purchases.

"Esther, if you should see my Becky in the crowd, tell her where I am," said Mrs. Belcovitch. "She is with one of her chosen young men. I am so feeble, I can hardly crawl around, and my Becky ought to carry home the cabbages. She has well-matched legs, not one a thick one and one a thin one."

Around the fishmongers the press was great. The fish-trade was almost monopolized by English Jews – blonde, healthy-looking fellows, with brawny, bare arms, who were approached with dread by all but the bravest foreign Jewesses. Their scale of prices and politeness varied with the status of the buyer. Esther, who had an observant eye and ear for such things, often found amusement standing unobtrusively by. Tonight there was the usual comedy awaiting her enjoyment. A well-dressed dame came up to "Uncle Abe's" stall, where half a dozen lots of fishy miscellanæa were spread out.

"Good evening, madam. Cold night but fine. That lot? Well, you're an old customer and fish are cheap today, so I can let you have 'em for a sovereign. Eighteen? Well, it's hard, but – boy! take the lady's fish. Thank you. Good evening."

"How much that?" says a neatly dressed woman, pointing to a precisely similar lot.

"Can't take less than nine bob. Fish are dear today. You won't get anything cheaper in the Lane, by G– you won't. Five shillings! By my life and by my children's life, they cost me more than that. So sure as I stand here and – well, come, gie's seven and six and they're yours. You can't afford more? Well, 'old up your apron, old gal. I'll make it up out of the rich. By your life and mine, you've got a *Metsiah* (bargain) there!"

Here old Mrs. Shmendrik, Shosshils mother, came up, a rich Paisley shawl over her head in lieu of a bonnet. Lane women who went out without bonnets were on the same plane as Lane men who went out without collars.

One of the terrors of the English fishmongers was that they required the customer to speak English, thus fulfilling an important educative function in the community. They allowed a certain percentage of jargon-words, for they themselves took licenses in this direction, but they professed not to understand pure Yiddish.

"Abraham, 'ow mosh for dees lot," said old Mrs. Shmendrik, turning over a third similar heap and feeling the fish all over.

"Paws off!" said Abraham roughly. "Look here! I know the tricks of you Polakinties. I'll name you the lowest price and won't stand a farthing's bating. I'll lose by you, but you ain't going to worry me. Eight bob! There!"

"Avroomkely (dear little Abraham) take lebbenpence!"

"Elevenpence! By G–," cried Uncle Abe, desperately tearing his hair. "I knew it!" And seizing a huge plaice by the tail he whirled it round and struck Mrs. Shmendrik full in the face, shouting, "Take that, you old witch! Sling your hook or I'll murder you."

"Thou dog!" shrieked Mrs. Shmendrik, falling back on the more copious resources of her native idiom. "A black year on thee! Mayest thou swell and die! May the hand that struck me rot away! Mayest thou be burned alive! Thy father was a *Gonof* and thou art a *Gonof* and thy whole family are *Ganovim*. May Pharaoh's ten plagues –"

There was little malice at the back of it all – the mere imaginative exuberance of a race whose early poetry consisted in saying things twice over.

Uncle Abraham menacingly caught up the plaice, crying:

"May I be struck dead on the spot, if you ain't gone in one second I won't answer for the consequences. Now, then, clear off!"

"Come, Avroomkely," said Mrs. Shmendrik, dropping suddenly from invective to insinuativeness. "Take fourteenpence. *Shemah, beni!* Fourteen *Shtibbur's* a lot of *Gelt*."

" Are you a-going?" cried Abraham in a terrible rage. "Ten bob's my price now."

"Avroomkely, *noo, zoog* (say now)! Fourteenpence 'apenny. I am a poor voman. Here, fifteenpence."

Abraharn seized her by the shoulders and pushed her towards the wall, where she cursed picturesquely. Esther thought it was a bad time to attempt to get her own shilling's worth – she fought her way towards another fishmonger.

There was a kindly, weather-beaten old fellow with whom Esther had often chaffered job-lots when fortune smiled on the Ansells. Him, to her joy, Esther perceived – she saw a stack of gurnards on his improvised slab, and in imagination smelt herself frying them. Then a great shock as of a sudden icy douche traversed her frame, her heart seemed to stand still. For when she put her hand to her pocket to get her purse, she found but a thimble and a slate-pencil and a cotton handkerchief. It was some minutes before she could or would realise the truth that the four and sevenpence halfpenny on which so much depended was gone. Groceries and unleavened cakes Charity had given, raisin wine had been preparing for days, but fish and meat and all the minor accessories of a well-ordered Passover table – these were the prey of the pickpocket. A blank sense of desolation overcame the child, infinitely more horrible than that which she felt when she spilled the soup; the gurnards she could have touched with her finger seemed far off, inaccessible; in a moment more they and all things were blotted out by a hot rush of tears, and she was jostled as in a dream hither and thither by the double stream of crowd. Nothing since the death of Benjamin had given her so poignant a sense of the hollowness and uncertainty of existence. What would her father say, whose triumphant conviction that Providence had provided for his Passover was to be so rudely dispelled at the eleventh hour. Poor Moses! He had been so proud of having earned enough money to make a good *Yontov*, and was more convinced than ever that given a little capital to start with he could build up a colossal business! And now she would have to go home and spoil everybody's *Yontov*, and see the sour faces of her little ones round a barren *Seder* table. Oh, it was terrible! and the child wept piteously, unheeded in the block, unheard amid the Babel.

CHAPTER XXIII

The Dead Monkey

An old *Maaseh* the grandmother had told her came back to her fevered brain. In a town in Russia lived an old Jew who earned scarce enough to eat, and half of what he did earn was stolen from him in bribes to the officials to let him be. Persecuted and spat upon, he yet trusted in his God and praised His name. And it came on towards Passover and the winter was severe and the Jew was nigh starving and his wife had made no preparations for the Festival. And in the bitterness of her soul she derided her husband's faith and made mock of him, but he said, "Have patience, my wife! Our *Seder* board shall be spread as in the days of yore and as in former years." But the Festival drew nearer and nearer and there was nothing in the house. And the wife taunted her husband yet further, saying, "Dost thou think that Elijah the prophet will call upon thee or that the Messiah will come?" But he answered: "Elijah the prophet walketh the earth, never having died; who knows but that he will cast an eye my way?" Whereat his wife laughed outright. And the days wore on to within a few hours of Passover and the larder was still empty of provender and the old Jew still full of faith. Now it befell that the Governor of the City, a hard and cruel man, sat counting out piles of gold into packets for the payment of the salaries of the officials and at his side sat his pet monkey, and as he heaped up the pieces, so his monkey imitated him, making little packets of its own to the amusement of the Governor. And when the Governor could not pick up a piece easily, he moistened his forefinger, putting it to his mouth, whereupon the monkey followed suit each time; only deeming its master was devouring the gold, it swallowed a coin every time he put his finger to his lips. So that of a sudden it was taken ill and died. And one of his men said, "Lo, the creature is dead. What shall we do with it?" And the Governor was sorely vexed in spirit, because he could not make his accounts straight and he answered gruffly, "Trouble me not! Throw it into the house of the old Jew down the street." So the man took the carcass and threw it with thunderous violence into the passage of the Jew's house and ran off as hard as he could. And the good wife came bustling out in alarm and saw a carcass hanging over an iron bucket that stood in the passage. And she knew that it was the act of a Christian and she took up the carrion to bury it when Lo! a rain of gold-pieces came from the stomach ripped up by the sharp rim of the vessel. And she called to her husband. "Hasten! See what Elijah the prophet hath sent us." And she scurried into the market-place and bought wine and unleavened bread, and bitter herbs and all things necessary for the *Seder* table, and a little fish therewith which might be hastily cooked before the Festival came in, and the old couple were happy and gave the monkey honourable burial and sang blithely of the deliverance at the Red Sea and filled Elijah's goblet to the brim till the wine ran over upon the white cloth.

Esther gave a scornful little sniff as the thought of this happy dénouement flashed upon her. No miracle like that would happen to her or hers, nobody was likely to leave a dead monkey on the stairs of the garret – hardly even the "stuffed monkey" of contemporary confectionery. And then her queer little brain forgot its grief in sudden speculations as to what she would think if her four and sevenpence halfpenny came back. She had never yet doubted the existence of the Unseen Power; only its workings seemed so incomprehensibly indifferent to human joys and sorrows. Would she believe that her father was right in holding that a special Providence watched over him? The spirit of her brother Solomon came upon her and she felt that she would. Speculation had checked her sobs; she dried her tears in stony scepticism and, looking up, saw

Malka's gipsy-like face bending over her, breathing peppermint.

"What weepest thou, Esther?" she said not unkindly. "I did not know thou wast a gusher with the eyes."

"I've lost my purse," sobbed Esther, softened afresh by the sight of a friendly face.

"Ah, thou *Schlemihl!* Thou art like thy father. How much was in it?"

"Four and sevenpence halfpenny!" sobbed Esther.

"Tu, tu, tu, tu, tu!" ejaculated Malka in horror. "Thou art the ruin of thy father." Then turning to the fishmonger with whom she had just completed a purchase, she counted out thirty-five shillings into his hand. "Here, Esther," she said, "thou shalt carry my fish and I will give thee a shilling."

A small slimy boy who stood expectant by scowled at Esther as she painfully lifted the heavy basket and followed in the wake of her relative whose heart was swelling with self-approbation.

Fortunately Zachariah Square was near and Esther soon received her shilling with a proportionate sense of Providence. The fish was deposited at Milly's house, which was brightly illuminated and seemed to poor Esther a magnificent palace of light and luxury. Malka's own house, diagonally across the Square, was dark and gloomy. The two families being at peace, Milly's house was the headquarters of the clan and the clothes-brush. Everybody was home for *Yomtov.* Malka's husband, Michael, and Milly's husband, Ephraim, were sitting at the table smoking big cigars and playing Loo with Sam Levine and David Brandon, who had been seduced into making a fourth. The two young husbands had but that day returned from the country, for you cannot get unleavened bread at commercial hotels, and David in spite of a stormy crossing had arrived from Germany an hour earlier than he had expected, and not knowing what to do with himself had been surveying the humours of the Festival Fair till Sam met him and dragged him round to Zachariah Square. It was too late to call that night on Hannah to be introduced to her parents, especially as he had wired he would come the next day. There was no chance of Hannah being at the club, it was too busy a night for all angels of the hearth; even tomorrow, the even of the Festival, would be an awkward time for a young man to thrust his love-affairs upon a household given over to the more important matters of dietary preparation. Still David could not consent to live another whole day without seeing the light of his eyes.

Leah, inwardly projecting an orgie of comic operas and dances, was assisting Milly in the kitchen. Both young women were covered with flour and oil and grease, and their coarse handsome faces were flushed, for they had been busy all day drawing fowls, stewing prunes and pippins, gutting fish, melting fat, changing the crockery and doing the thousand and one things necessitated by gratitude for the discomfiture of Pharaoh at the Red Sea; Ezekiel slumbered upstairs in his crib.

"Mother," said Michael, pulling pensively at his whisker as he looked at his card. "This is Mr. Brandon, a friend of Sam's. Don't get up, Brandon, we don't make ceremonies here. Turn up yours – ah, the nine of trumps."

"Lucky men!" said Malka with festival flippancy. "While I must hurry off my supper so as to buy the fish, and Milly and Leah must sweat in the kitchen, you can squat yourselves down and play cards."

"Yes," laughed Sam, looking up and adding in Hebrew, "Blessed art thou, O Lord, who hath not made me a woman."

"Now, now," said David, putting his hand jocosely across the young man's mouth. "No more Hebrew. Remember what happened last time. Perhaps there's some mysterious significance even in that, and you'll find yourself let in for something before you know where you are."

"You're not going to prevent me talking the language of my Fathers," gurgled Sam, bursting into a merry operatic whistle when the pressure was removed.

"Milly! Leah!" cried Malka. "Come and look at my fish! Such a *Metsiah*! See, they're alive yet."

"They *are* beauties, mother," said Leah, entering with her sleeves half tucked up, showing the finely-moulded white arms in curious juxtaposition with the coarse red hands.

"Oy mother, they're alive!" said Milly, peering over her younger sister's shoulder.

Both knew by bitter experience that their mother considered herself a connoisseur in the purchase of fish.

"And how much do you think I gave for them?" went on Malka triumphantly.

"Two pounds ten," said Milly.

Malka's eyes twinkled and she shook her head.

"Two pounds fifteen," said Leah, with the air of hitting it now.

Still Malka shook her head.

"Here, Michael, what do you think I gave for all this lot?"

"Diamonds!" said Michael.

"Be not a fool, Michael," said Malka sternly. "Look here a minute."

"Eh? Oh!" said Michael looking up from his cards. "Don't bother, mother. My game!"

"Michael!" thundered Malka. "Will you look at this fish? How much do you think I gave for this splendid lot? Here, look at 'em, alive yet."

"Hm – Ha!" said Michael, taking his complex corkscrew combination out of his pocket and putting it back again. "Three guineas?"

"Three guineas!" laughed Malka, in good-humoured scorn. "Lucky I don't let *you* do my marketing."

"Yes, he'd be a nice fishy customer!" said Sam Levine with a guffaw.

"Ephraim, what think you I got this fish for? Cheap now, you know?"

"I don't know, mother," replied the twinkling-eyed Pole obediently. "Three pounds, perhaps, if you got it cheap."

Samuel and David duly appealed to, reduced the amount to two pounds five and two pounds respectively. Then, having got everybody's attention fixed upon her, she exclaimed:

"Thirty shillings!"

She could not resist nibbling off the five shillings. Everybody drew a long breath.

"Tu! Tu!" they ejaculated in chorus. "What a *Metsiah*!"

"Sam," said Ephraim immediately afterwards, "*You* turned up the ace."

Milly and Leah went back into the kitchen.

It was rather too quick a relapse into the common things of life and made Malka suspect the admiration was but superficial.

She turned, with a spice of ill-humour, and saw Esther still standing timidly behind her. Her face flushed for she knew the child had overheard her in a lie.

"What art thou waiting about for?" she said roughly in Yiddish. "Na! there's a peppermint."

"I thought you might want me for something else," said Esther, blushing but accepting the peppermint for Ikey. "And I – I –"

"Well, speak up! I won't bite thee." Malka continued to talk in Yiddish though the child answered her in English.

"I – I – nothing," said Esther, turning away.

"Here, turn thy face round, child," said Malka, putting her hand on the girl's forcibly averted head. "Be not so sullen, thy mother was like that, she'd want to bite my head off if I hinted thy father was not the man for her, and then she'd *schmull* and sulk for a week after. Thank God, we have no one like that in this house. I couldn't live for a day with people with such nasty tempers. Her temper worried her into the grave, though if thy father had not brought his mother over from Poland my poor cousin might have carried home my fish tonight instead of thee. Poor Gittel, peace be upon him! Come tell me what ails thee, or thy dead mother will be cross with thee."

Esther turned her head and murmured: "I thought you might lend me the three and sevenpence halfpenny!"

"Lend thee –?" exclaimed Malka. "Why, how can thou ever repay it?"

"Oh yes," affirmed Esther earnestly. "I have lots of money in the bank."

"Eh! what? In the bank!" gasped Malka.

"Yes, I won five pounds in the school and I'll pay you out of that."

"Thy father never told me that!" said Malka. "He kept that dark. Ah, he is a regular *Schnorrer*!"

"My father hasn't seen you since," retorted Esther hotly. "If you had come round when he was sitting *shiva* for Benjamin, peace be upon him, you would have known."

Malka got as red as fire. Moses had sent Solomon round to inform the *Mishpocha* of his affliction, but at a period when the most casual acquaintance thinks it his duty to call (armed with hard boiled eggs, a pound of sugar, or an ounce of tea) on the mourners condemned to sit on the floor for a week, no representative of the "family" had made an appearance. Moses took it meekly enough, but his mother insisted that such a slight from Zachariah Square would never have been received if he had married another woman, and Esther for once agreed with her grandmother's sentiments if not with her Hibernian expression of them.

But that the child should now dare to twit the head of the family with bad behaviour was intolerable to Malka, the more so as she had no defence.

"Thou impudent of face!" she cried sharply. "Dost thou forget whom thou talkest to?"

" No," retorted Esther. You are my father's cousin – that is why you ought to have come to see him."

"I am not thy father's cousin, God forbid!" cried Malka. "I was thy mother's cousin, God have mercy on her, and I wonder not you drove her into the grave between the lot of you. I am no relative of any of you, thank God, and from this day forwards I wash my hands of the lot of you, you ungrateful pack! Let thy father send you into the streets, with matches, not another thing will I do for thee."

"Ungrateful!" said Esther hotly. "Why, what have you ever done for us? When my poor mother was alive you made her scrub your floors and clean your windows, as if she was an Irishwoman."

"Impudent of face!" cried Malka, almost choking with rage. "What have I done for you? Why – why – I – I – shameless hussy! And this is what Judaism's coming to in England! This is the manners and religion they teach thee at thy school, eh? What have I–? Impudent of face! At this very moment thou holdest one of my shillings in thy hand."

"Take it!" said Esther. And threw the coin passionately to the floor, where it rolled about pleasantly for a terrible minute of human silence. The smoke-wreathed card-players looked up at last.

"Eh? Eh? What's this, my little girl," said Michael genially. "What makes you so naughty?"

A hysterical fit of sobbing was the only reply. In the bitterness of that moment Esther hated the whole world.

"Don't cry like that! Don't!" said David Brandon kindly.

Esther, her little shoulders heaving convulsively, put her hand on the latch.

"What's the matter with the girl, mother?" said Michael.

"She's *meshugga*!" said Malka. "Raving mad!" Her face was white and she spoke as if in self-defence. "She's such a *Schlemihl* that she lost her purse in the Lane, and I found her gushing with the eyes, and I let her carry home my fish and gave her a shilling and a peppermint, and thou seest how she turns on me, thou seest."

"Poor little thing!" said David impulsively. "Here, come here, my child."

Esther refused to budge.

"Come here," he repeated gently. "See, I will make up the loss to you. Take the pool. I've just won it, so I shan't miss it."

Esther sobbed louder, but she did not move.

David rose, emptied the heap of silver into his palm, walked over to Esther, and pushed it into her pocket. Michael got up and added half a crown to it, and the other two men followed suit. Then David opened the door, put her outside gently and said: "There! Run away, my little dear, and be more careful of pickpockets."

All this while Malka had stood frozen to the stony dignity of a dingy terra-cotta statue. But ere the door could close again on the child, she darted forward and seized her by the collar of her frock.

"Give me that money," she cried.

Half hypnotized by the irate swarthy face, Esther made no resistance while Malka rifled her pocket less dexterously than the first operator.

Malka counted it out.

"Seventeen and sixpence," she announced in terrible tones. How darest thou take all this money from strangers, and perfect strangers? Do my children think to shame me before my own relative?" And throwing the money violently into the plate she took out a gold coin and pressed it into the bewildered child's hand.

"There!" she shouted. "Hold that tight! It is a sovereign. And if ever I catch thee taking money from anyone in this house but thy mother's own cousin, I'll wash my hands of thee for ever. Go now! Go on! I can't afford any more, so it's useless waiting. Good night, and tell thy father I wish him a happy *Yontov*, and I hope he'll lose no more children."

She hustled the child into the Square and banged the door upon her, and Esther went about her mammoth marketing half-dazed, with an undercurrent of happiness, vaguely apologetic towards her father and his Providence.

Malka stooped down, picked up the clothes-brush from under the side-table, and strode silently and diagonally across the Square.

There was a moment's dread silence. The thunderbolt had fallen. The festival felicity of two households trembled in the balance. Michael muttered impatiently and went out on his wife's track.

"He's an awful fool," said Ephraim. "I should make her pay for her tantrums."

The card party broke up in confusion. David Brandon took his leave and strolled about aimlessly under the stars, his soul blissful with the sense of a good deed that had only superficially miscarried. His feet took him to Hannah's house. All the windows were lit up. His heart began to ache at the thought that his bright, radiant girl was beyond that doorstep he had never crossed.

He pictured the love-light in her eyes; for surely she was dreaming of him, as he of her. He took out his watch – the time was twenty to nine. After all, would it be so outrageous to call? He went away twice. The third time, defying the *convenances*, he knocked at the door, his heart beating almost as loudly.

CHAPTER XXIV

The Shadow of Religion

The little servant girl who opened the door for him looked relieved by the sight of him, for it might have been the Rebbitzin returning from the Lane with heaps of supplies and an accumulation of ill-humour. She showed him into the study, and in a few moments Hannah hurried in with a big apron and a general flavour of the kitchen.

"How dare you come tonight?" she began, but the sentence died on her lips.

"How hot your face is," he said, dinting the flesh fondly with his finger. "I see my little girl is glad to have me back."

"It's not that. It's the fire. I'm frying fish for *Yomtov*," she said, with a happy laugh.

"And yet you say you're not a good Jewess," he laughed back.

"You had no right to come and catch me like this," she pouted. "All greasy and dishevelled. I'm not made up to receive visitors."

"Call me a visitor?" he grumbled. "Judging by your appearance, I should say you were always made up. Why, you're perfectly radiant."

Then the talk became less intelligible. The first symptom of returning rationality was her inquiry –

"What sort of a journey did you have back?"

"The sea was rough, but I'm a good sailor."

"And the poor fellow's father and mother?"

"I wrote you about them."

"So you did; but only just a line."

"Oh, don't let us talk about the subject just now, dear, it's too painful. Come, let me kiss that little woe-begone look out of your eyes. There! Now, another – that was only for the right eye, this is for the left. But where's your mother?"

"Oh, you innocent!" she replied. "As if you hadn't watched her go out of the house!"

"'Pon my honour, not," he said smiling. "Why should I now? Am I not the accepted son-in-law of the house, you silly timid little thing? What a happy thought it was of yours to let the cat out of the bag. Come, let me give you another kiss for it – Oh, I really must. You deserve it, and whatever it costs me you shall be rewarded. There! Now, then! Where's the old man? I have to receive his blessing, I know, and I want to get it over."

"It's worth having, I can tell you, so speak more respectfully," said Hannah, more than half in earnest.

"*You* are the best blessing he can give me – and that's worth – well, I wouldn't venture to price it."

"It's not your line, eh?"

"I don't know, I have done a good deal in gems; but where is the Rabbi?"

"Up in the bedrooms, gathering the *Chomutz*. You know he won't trust anybody else. He creeps under all the beds, hunting with a candle for stray crumbs, and looks in all the wardrobes and the pockets of all my dresses. Luckily, I don't keep your letters there. I hope he won't set something alight – he did once. And one year – Oh, it was so funny! – after he had ransacked every hole and corner of the house, imagine his horror, in the middle of Passover to find a crumb of bread audaciously planted – where do you suppose? In his Passover prayer-book! But, oh!" – with a little scream – "you naughty boy! I quite forgot." She took him by the shoulders, and peered along his coat. "Have you brought any crumbs with you? This room's *pesachdik* already."

He looked dubious.

She pushed him towards the door. "Go out and give yourself a good shaking on the doorstep, or else we shall have to clean out the room all over again."

"Don't!" he protested. "I might shake out that."

"What?"

"The ring."

She uttered a little pleased sigh.

"Oh, have you brought that?"

"Yes, I got it while I was away. You know I believe the reason you sent me trooping to the continent in such haste, was you wanted to ensure your engagement ring being 'made in Germany.' It's had a stormy passage to England, has that ring. I suppose the advantage of buying rings in Germany is that you're certain not to get Paris diamonds in them, they are so intensely patriotic, the Germans. That was your idea, wasn't it, Hannah?"

"Oh, show it me! Don't talk so much," she said, smiling.

"No," he said, teasingly. "No more accidents for me! I'll wait to make sure – till your father and mother have taken me to their arms. Rabbinical law is so full of pitfalls – I might touch your finger this or that way, and then we should be married. And then, if your parents said 'no,' after all –"

"We should have to make the best of a bad job," she finished up laughingly.

"All very well," he went on in his fun, "but it would be a pretty kettle of fish."

"Heavens!" she cried, "so it will be. They will be charred to ashes." And turning tail, she fled to the kitchen, pursued by her lover. There, dead to the surprise of the servant, David Brandon fed his eyes on the fair incarnation of Jewish domesticity, type of the vestal virgins of Israel, Ministresses at the hearth. It was a very homely kitchen; the dressers glistening with speckless utensils, and the deep red glow of the coal over which the pieces of fish sputtered and crackled in their bath of oil, filling the room with a sense of deep peace and cosy comfort. David's imagination transferred the kitchen to his future home, and he was almost dazzled by the thought of actually inhabiting such a fairyland alone with Hannah. He had knocked about a great deal, not always innocently, but deep down at his heart was the instinct of well-ordered life. His past seemed joyless folly and chill emptiness. He felt his eyes growing humid as he looked at the frank-souled girl who had given herself to him. He was not humble, but for a moment he found himself wondering how he deserved the trust, and there was reverence in the touch with which he caressed her hair. In another moment the frying was complete, and the contents of the pan neatly added to the dish. Then the voice of Reb Shemuel crying for Hannah came down the kitchen stairs, and the lovers returned to the upper world. The Reb had a tiny harvest of crumbs in a brown paper, and wanted Hannah to stow it away safely till the morning, when, to make assurance doubly sure, a final expedition in search of leaven would be undertaken. Hannah received the packet and in return presented her betrothed.

Reb Shemuel had not of course expected him till the next morning, but he welcomed him as heartily as Hannah could desire.

"The Most High bless you!" he said in his charming foreign accents. "May you make my Hannah as good a husband as she will make you a wife."

"Trust me, Reb Shemuel," said David, grasping his great hand warmly.

"Hannah says you're a sinner in Israel," said the Reb, smiling playfully, though there was a touch of anxiety in the tones. "But I suppose you will keep a *kosher* house."

"Make your mind easy, sir," said David heartily. "We must, if it's only to have the pleasure of your dining with us sometimes."

The old man patted him gently on the shoulder.

"Ah, you will soon become a good Jew," he said. "My Hannah will teach you, God bless her." Reb Shemuel's voice was a bit husky. He bent down and kissed Hannah's forehead. "I was a bit *link* myself before I married my Simcha," he added encouragingly.

"No, no, not you," said David, smiling in response to the twinkle in the Reb's eye. "I warrant you never skipped a *Mitzvah* even as a bachelor."

"Oh yes, I did," replied the Reb, letting the twinkle develop to a broad smile, "for when I was a bachelor I hadn't fulfilled the precept to marry, don't you see?"

"Is marriage a *Mitzvah*, then?" inquired David, amused.

"Certainly. In our holy religion everything a man ought to do is a *Mitzvah*, even if it is pleasant."

"Oh, then, even I must have laid up some good deeds," laughed David, "for I have always enjoyed myself. Really, it isn't such a bad religion after all."

"Bad religion!" echoed Reb Shemuel genially. "Wait till you've tried it. You've never had a proper training, that's clear. Are your parents alive?"

"No, they both died when I was a child," said David, becoming serious.

"I thought so!" said Reb Shemuel. "Fortunately my Hannah's didn't." He smiled at the humour of the phrase and Hannah took his hand and pressed it tenderly. "Ah, it will be all right," said the Reb with a characteristic burst of optimism. "God is good. You have a sound Jewish heart at bottom, David, my son. Hannah, get the *Yomtovdik* wine. We will drink a glass for *Mazzoltov*, and I hope your mother will be back in time to join in."

Hannah ran into the kitchen feeling happier than she had over been in her life. She wept a little and laughed a little, and loitered a little to recover her composure and allow the two men to get to know each other a little.

"How is your Hannah's late husband?" inquired the Reb with almost a wink, for everything combined to make him jolly as a sandboy. "I understand he is a friend of yours."

"We used to be schoolboys together, that is all. Though strangely enough I just spent an hour with him. He is very well," answered David smiling. "He is about to marry again."

"His first love of course," said the Reb.

"Yes, people always come back to that," said David laughing.

"That's right, that's right," said the Reb. "I am glad there was no unpleasantness."

"Unpleasantness. No, how could there be? Leah knew it was only a joke. All's well that ends well, and we may perhaps all get married on the same day and risk another mix-up. Ha! Ha! Ha!"

"Is it your wish to marry soon, then?"

"Yes; there are too many long engagements among our people. They often go off."

"Then I suppose you have the means?"

"Oh yes, I can show you my –"

The old man waved his hand.

"I don't want to see anything. My girl must be supported decently – that is all I ask. What do you do for a living?"

"I have made a little money at the Cape and now I think of going into business."

"What business?"

"I haven't settled."

"You won't open on *Shabbos*," said the Reb anxiously.

David hesitated a second. In some business, Saturday is the best day. Still he felt that he was not quite radical enough to break the Sabbath deliberately, and since he had contemplated settling down, his religion had become rather more real to him. Besides he must sacrifice something for Hannah's sake.

"Have no fear, sir," he said cheerfully.

Reb Shemuel gripped his hand in grateful silence.

"You mustn't think me quite a lost soul," pursued David after a moment of emotion. "You don't remember me, but I had lots of bless-ings and halfpence from you when I was a lad. I dare say I valued the latter more in those days." He smiled to hide his emotion.

Reb Shemuel was beaming. "Did you, really?" he inquired. "I don't remember you. But then I have blessed so many little children. Of course you'll come to the *Seder* tomorrow evening and taste some of Hannah's cookery. You're one of the family now, you know."

"I shall be delighted to have the privilege of having *Seder* with you," replied David, his heart going out more and more to the fatherly old man.

"What *Shool* will you be going to for Passover? I can get you a seat in mine if you haven't arranged."

"Thank you, but I promised Mr. Birnbaum to come to the little synagogue of which he is President. It seems they have a scarcity of *Cohenim*, and they want me to bless the congregation, I suppose."

"What!" cried Reb Shemuel excitedly. "Are you a *Cohen*?"

"Of course I am. Why, they got me to bless them in the Transvaal last *Yom Kippur*. So you see I'm anything but a sinner in Israel." He laughed – but his laugh ended abruptly. Reb Shemuells face had grown white. His hands were trembling.

"What is the matter? You are ill," cried David.

The old man shook his head. Then he struck his brow with his fist. "*Ach, Gott!*" he cried. "Why did I not think of finding out before? But thank God I know it in time."

"Finding out what?" said David, fearing the old man's reason was giving way.

"My daughter cannot marry you," said Reb Shemuel in hushed, quavering tones.

"Eh? What?" said David blankly.

"It is impossible."

"What are you talking about, Reb Shemuel?"

"You are a *Cohen*. Hannah cannot marry a *Cohen*."

"Not marry a *Cohen*? Why, I thought they were Israel's aristocracy."

"That is why. A *Cohen* cannot marry a divorced woman."

The fit of trembling passed from the old Reb to the young man. His heart pulsed as with the stroke of a mighty piston. Without comprehending, Hannah's prior misadventure gave him a horrible foreboding of critical complications.

"Do you mean to say I can't marry Hannah?" he asked almost in a whisper.

"Such is the law. A woman who has had *Gett* may not marry a *Cohen*."

"But you surely wouldn't call Hannah a divorced woman?" he cried hoarsely.

"How shall I not? I gave her the divorce myself."

"Great God!" exclaimed David. "Then Sam has ruined our lives." He stood a moment in dazed horror, striving to grasp the terrible tangle. Then he burst forth. "This is some of your cursed Rabbinical laws, it is not Judaism, it is not true Judaism. God never made any such law."

"Hush!" said Reb Shemuel sternly. "It is the holy Torah. It is not even the Rabbis, of whom you speak like an Epicurean. It is in Leviticus, chapter 2 1, verse 7: '*Neither shall they take a woman put away from her husband; for he is holy unto his God. Thou shall sanctify him, therefore; for he offereth the bread of thy God; he shall be holy unto thee, for I the Lord which sanctify you am holy.*'"

For an instant David was overwhelmed by the quotation, for the Bible was still a sacred book to him. Then he cried indignantly:

"But God never meant it to apply to a case like this!"

"We must obey God's law," said Reb Shemuel.

"Then it is the devil's law!" shouted David, losing all control of himself.

The Reb's face grew dark as night. There was a moment of dread silence.

"Here you are, father," said Hannah, returning with the wine and some glasses which she had carefully dusted. Then she paused and gave a little cry, nearly losing her hold of the tray.

"What's the matter? What has happened?" she asked anxiously.

"Take away the wine – we shall drink nobody's health tonight," cried David brutally.

"My God!" said Hannah, all the hue of happiness dying out of her cheeks. She threw down the tray on the table and ran to her father's arms.

"What is it! Oh, what is it, father?" she cried. "You haven't had a quarrel?"

The old man was silent. The girl looked appealingly from one to the other.

"No, it's worse than that," said David in cold, harsh tones. "You remember your marriage in fun to Sam?"

"Yes. Merciful heavens! I guess it! There was something not valid in the *Gett* after all!"

Her anguish at the thought of losing him was so apparent that he softened a little.

"No, not that," he said more gently. "But this blessed religion of ours reckons you a divorced-woman, and so you can't marry me because I'm a *Cohen*."

"Can't marry you because you're a *Cohen*" repeated Hannah, dazed in her turn.

"We must obey the Torah," said Reb Shemuel again, in low, solemn tones. "It is your friend Levine who has erred, not the Torah."

"The Torah cannot visit a mere bit of fun so cruelly," protested David. "And on the innocent, too."

"Sacred things should not be jested with," said the old man in stern tones that yet quavered with sympathy and pity. "On his head is the sin; on his head is the responsibility."

"Father," cried Hannah in piercing tones, "can nothing be done?"

The old man shook his head sadly. The poor, pretty face was pallid with a pain too deep for tears. The shock was too sudden, too terrible. She sank helplessly into a chair.

"Something must be done, something shall be done," thundered David. "I will appeal to the Chief Rabbi."

"And what can he do? Can he go behind the Torah?" said Reb Shemuel pitifully.

"I won't ask him to. But if he has a grain of common sense he will see that our case is an exception, and cannot come under the Law."

"The Law knows no exceptions," said Reb Shemuel gently, quoting in Hebrew, 'The Law of God is perfect, enlightening the eyes.' Be patient, my dear children, in your affliction. It is the will of God. The Lord giveth and the Lord taketh away – bless ye the name of the Lord."

"Not I!" said David harshly. "But look to Hannah. She has fainted."

"No, I am all right," said Hannah wearily, opening the eyes she had closed. "Do not make so certain, father. Look at your books again.

Perhaps they do make an exception in such a case."

The Reb shook his head hopelessly.

"Do not expect that," he said. "Believe me, my Hannah, if there were a gleam of hope I would not hide it from you. Be a good girl, dear, and bear your trouble like a true Jewish maiden. Have faith in God, my child. He doeth all things for the best. Come now – rouse yourself. Tell David you will always be a friend, and that your father will love him as though he were indeed his son." He moved towards her and touched her tenderly. He felt a violent spasm traversing her bosom.

"I can't, father," she cried in a choking voice. "I can't. Don't ask me."

David leaned against the manuscript-littered table in stony silence. The stern granite faces of the old continental Rabbis seemed to frown down on him from the walls and he returned the frown with interest. His heart was full of bitterness, contempt, revolt. What a pack of knavish bigots they must all have been! Reb Shemuel bent down and took his daughter's head in his trembling palms. The eyes were closed again, the chest heaved painfully with silent sobs.

"Do you love him so much, Hannah?" whispered the old man.

Her sobs answered, growing loud at last.

"But you love your religion more, my child?" he murmured anxiously. "That will bring you peace."

Her sobs gave him no assurance. Presently the contagion of sobbing took him too.

"God! God!" he moaned. "What sin have I committed that thou shouldst punish my child thus?"

"Don't blame God!" burst forth David at last. "It's your own foolish bigotry. Is it not enough your daughter doesn't ask to marry a Christian? Be thankful, old man, for that and put away all this antiquated superstition. We're living in the nineteenth century."

"And what if we are!" said Reb Shemuel, blazing up in turn. "The Torah is eternal. Thank God for your youth, and your health and strength, and do not blaspheme Him because you cannot have all the desire of your heart or the inclination of your eyes."

"The desire of my heart," retorted David. "Do you imagine I am only thinking of my own suffering? Look at your daughter – think of what you are doing to her and beware before it is too late."

"Is it in my hand to do or to forbear?" asked the old man. "It is the Torah. Am I responsible for that?"

"Yes," said David, out of mere revolt. Then, seeking to justify himself, his face lit up with sudden inspiration. "Who need ever know? The *Maggid* is dead. Old Hyams has gone to America. So Hannah has told me. It's a thousand to one Leah's people never heard of the Law of Leviticus. If they had, it's another thousand to one against their putting two and two together. It requires a Talmudist like you to even dream of reckoning Hannah as an ordinary divorced woman. If they did, it's a third thousand to one against their telling anybody. There is no need for you to perform the ceremony yourself. Let her be married by some other minister – by the Chief Rabbi himself, and to make assurance doubly sure I'll not mention that I'm a *Cohen*." The words poured forth like a torrent, overwhelming the Reb for a moment. Hannah leaped up with a hysterical cry of joy.

"Yes, yes, father. It will be all right, after all. Nobody knows. Oh, thank God! thank God!"

There was a moment of tense silence. Then the old man's voice rose slowly and painfully.

"Thank God!" he repeated. "Do you dare mention the Name even when you propose to profane it? Do you ask me, your father, Reb Shemuel, to consent to such a profanation of the Name?"

"And why not?" said David angrily. "Whom else has a daughter the right to ask mercy from, if not her father?"

"God have mercy on me!" groaned the old Reb, covering his face with his hands.

"Come, come!" said David impatiently. "Be sensible. It's nothing unworthy of you at all. Hannah was never really married, so cannot be really divorced. We only ask you to obey the spirit of the Torah instead of the letter."

The old man shook his head, unwavering. His cheeks were white and wet, but his expression was stern and solemn.

"Just think!" went on David passionately. "What am I better than another Jew – than yourself for instance – that I shouldn't marry a divorced woman?"

"It's the Law. You area *Cohen* – a priest."

"A priest, Ha! Ha! Ha!" laughed David bitterly. "A priest – in the nineteenth century! When the Temple has been destroyed these two thousand years."

"It will be rebuilt, please God," said Reb Shemuel. "We must be ready for it."

"Oh yes, I'll be ready – Ha! Ha! Ha! A priest! Holy unto the Lord – I a priest! Ha! Ha! Ha! Do you know what my holiness consists in? In eating *tripha* meat, and going to *Shool* a few times a year! And I, I am too holy to marry *your* daughter. Oh, it is rich!" He ended in uncontrollable mirth, slapping his knee in ghastly enjoyment.

His laughter rang terrible. Reb Shemuel trembled from head to foot. Hannah's cheek was drawn and white. She seemed overwrought beyond endurance. There followed a silence only less terrible than David's laughter.

"A *Cohen*," burst forth David again. "A holy *Cohen* up to date. Do you know what the boys say about us priests when we're blessing you common people? They say that if you look on us once during that sacred function, you'll get blind, and if you look on us a second time you'll die. A nice reverent joke that, eh! Ha! Ha! Ha! You're blind already, Reb Shemuel. Beware you don't look at me again or I'll commence to bless you. Ha! Ha! Ha!"

Again the terrible silence.

"Ah well," David resumed, his bitterness welling forth in irony. "And so the first sacrifice the priest is called upon to make is that of your daughter. But I won't, Reb Shemuel, mark my words; I won't, not till she offers her own throat to the knife. If she and I are parted, on you and you alone the guilt must rest. *You* will have to perform the sacrifice."

"What God wishes me to do I will do," said the old man in a broken voice. "What is it to that which our ancestors suffered for the glory of the Name?"

"Yes, but it seems you suffer by proxy," retorted David, savagely.

"My God! Do you think I would not die to make Hannah happy?" faltered the old man. "But God has laid the burden on her – and I can only help her to bear it. And now, sir, I must beg you to go. You do but distress my child."

"What say you, Hannah? Do you wish me to go?"

"Yes – What is the use – now?" breathed Hannah through white quivering lips.

"My child!" said the old man pitifully, while he strained her to his breast.

"All right!" said David in strange harsh tones, scarcely recognizable as his. "I see you are your father's daughter."

He took his hat and turned his back upon the tragic embrace.

"David!" She called his name in an agonized hoarse voice. She held her arms towards him. He did not turn round.

"David!" Her voice rose to a shriek. "You will not leave me?"

He faced her exultant.

"Ah, you will come with me. You will be my wife."

No – no – not now, not now. I cannot answer you now. Let me think – goodbye, dearest, goodbye." She burst out weeping. David took her in his arms and kissed her passionately. Then he went out hurriedly.

Hannah wept on – her father holding her hand in piteous silence.

"Oh, it is cruel, your religion," she sobbed. "Cruel, cruel!"

"Hannah! Shemuel! Where are you?" suddenly came the excited voice of Simcha from the passage. "Come and look at the, lovely fowls I've bought – and such *Metsiahs*. They're worth double. Oh, what a beautiful *Yomtov* we shall have!"

CHAPTER XXV

Seder Night

"Prosaic miles of street stretch all around,
Astir with restless, hurried life, and spanned
By arches that with thund'rous trains resound,
And throbbing wires that galvanize the land;
Gin palaces in tawdry splendour stand;
The newsboys shriek of mangled bodies found;
The last burlesque is playing in the Strand –
In modern prose, all poetry seems drowned.
Yet in ten thousand homes this April night
An ancient people celebrates its birth
To Freedom, with a reverential mirth,
With customs quaint and many a hoary rite,
Waiting until, its tarnished glories bright,
Its God shall be the God of all the Earth."

To an imaginative child like Esther, *Seder* night was a charmed time. The strange symbolic dishes – the bitter herbs and the sweet mixture of apples, almonds, spices and wine, the roasted bone and the lamb, the salt water and the four cups of raisin wine, the great round unleavened cakes, with their mottled surfaces, some specially thick and sacred, the special Hebrew melodies and verses with their jingle of rhymes and assonances, the quaint ceremonial with its striking moments, as when the finger was dipped in the wine and the drops sprinkled over the shoulder in repudiation of the ten plagues of Egypt cabalistically magnified to two hundred and fifty; all this penetrated deep into her consciousness and made the recurrence of every Passover coincide with a rush of pleasant anticipations and a sense of the special privilege of being born a happy Jewish child. Vaguely, indeed, did she co-ordinate the celebration with the history enshrined in it or with the prospective history of her race. It was like a tale out of the fairy-books, this miraculous deliverance of her forefathers in the dim haze of antiquity; true enough but not more definitely realized on that account. And yet not easily dissoluble links were being forged with her race, which has anticipated Positivism in vitalizing history by making it religion.

The *Matzoth* that Esther ate were not dainty – they were coarse, of the quality called "seconds," for even the unleavened bread of charity is not necessarily delicate eating – but few things melted sweeter on the palate than a segment of a *Matso* dipped in cheap raisin wine; the unconventionality of the food made life less common, more picturesque. Simple Ghetto children into whose existence the ceaseless round of fast and feast, of prohibited and enjoyed pleasures, of varying species of food, brought change and relief! Imprisoned in the area of a few narrow streets, unlovely and sombre, muddy and ill-smelling, immured in dreary houses and surrounded with mean and depressing sights and sounds, the spirit of childhood took radiance and colour from its own inner light and the alchemy of youth could still transmute its lead to gold. No little princess in the courts of fairyland could feel a fresher interest and pleasure in life than Esther sitting at the *Seder* table, where her father – no longer a slave in Egypt – leaned royally upon two chairs supplied with pillows as the *Din* prescribes. Not even the monarch's prime minister could have had a meaner opinion of Pharaoh than Moses Ansell in this symbolically sybaritic attitude. A live dog is better than a dead lion, as a great teacher in Israel had said. How much better then a live lion than a dead dog? Pharaoh, for all his purple and fine linen and his treasure cities, was at the bottom of the Red Sea, smitten with two hundred and fifty plagues, and even if, as tradition asserted, he had been made to live on and on to be King of Nineveh, and to give ear to the warnings of Jonah, prophet and whale-explorer, even so he was but dust and ashes for other sinners to cover themselves withal; but he, Moses Ansell, was the honoured master of his household, enjoying a foretaste of the lollings of the righteous in Paradise; nay, more, dispensing hospitality to the poor and the hungry. Little fleas have lesser fleas, and Moses Ansell had never fallen so low but that, on this night of nights when the slave sits with the master on equal terms, he could manage to entertain a Passover guest, usually some newly-arrived Greener, or some nondescript waif and stray returned to Judaism for the occasion and accepting a seat at the board in that spirit of *camaraderie* which is one of the most delightful features of the Jewish pauper. *Seder* was a ceremonial to be taken in none too solemn and sober a spirit, and there was an abundance of unreproved giggling throughout from the little ones, especially in those happy days when mother was alive and tried to steal the *Afikuman* or *Matso* specially laid aside for the final morsel, only to be surrendered to father when he promised to grant her whatever she wished. Alas! it is to be feared Mrs. Ansell's wishes did not soar high. There was more giggling when the youngest talking son – it was poor Benjamin in Esther's earliest recollections – opened the ball by inquiring in a peculiarly pitched incantation and with an air of blank ignorance why this night differed from all other nights – in view of the various astonishing peculiarities of food and behaviour (enumerated in detail) visible to his vision. To which Moses and the *Bube* and the rest of the company (including the questioner) invariably replied in corresponding sing-song: "Slaves have we been in Egypt," proceeding to recount at great length, stopping for refreshment in the middle, the never-cloying tale of the great deliverance, with irrelevant digressions concerning Haman and Daniel and the wise men of Bona Berak, the whole of this most ancient of the world's extant domestic rituals terminating with an allegorical ballad like the "house that jack built," concerning a kid that was eaten by a cat, which was bitten by a dog, which was beaten by a stick, which was burned by a fire, which was quenched by some water, which was drunk by an ox, which was slaughtered by a slaughterer, who was slain by the Angel of Death, who was slain by the Holy One, blessed be He.

In wealthy houses this *Hagadah* was read from manuscripts with rich illuminations – the one development of pictorial art among the Jews – but the Ansells had wretchedly-printed little books containing quaint but unintentionally comic woodcuts, pre-Raphaelite in perspective and ludicrous in draughtsmanship, depicting the Miracles of the Redemption, Moses burying the Egyptian, and sundry other passages of the text. In one a king was praying in the Temple to an exploding bomb intended to represent the Shechinah or divine glory. In another, Sarah attired in a matronly cap and a fashionable jacket and skirt, was standing behind the door of the tent, a solid detached villa on the brink of a lake, whereon ships and gondolas floated, what time Abraham welcomed the three celestial messengers, unobtrusively disguised with heavy pinions. What delight as the quaffing of each of the four cups of wine loomed in sight, what disappointment and mutual bantering when the cup had merely to be raised in the hand, what chaff of the greedy Solomon who was careful not to throw away a drop during the digital manœuvres when the wine must be jerked from the cup at the mention of each plague. And what a solemn moment was that when the tallest goblet was filled to the brim for the delectation of the prophet Elijah and the door thrown open for his entry. Could one almost hear the rustling of the prophet's spirit through the room? And what though the level of the wine subsided not a barley-corn? Elijah, though there was no difficulty in his being in all parts of the world simultaneously, could hardly compass the greater miracle of emptying so many million goblets. Historians have traced this custom of opening the door to the necessity of asking the world to look in and see for itself that no blood of Christian child figured in the ceremonial – and for once science has illumined naive superstition with a tragic glow more poetic still. For the London Ghetto persecution had dwindled to an occasional bellowing through the keyhole, as the local rowdies heard the unaccustomed melodies trolled forth from jocund lungs and then the singers would stop for a moment, startled, and some one would say: "Oh, it's only a Christian rough," and take up the thread of song.

And then, when the *Afikuman* had been eaten and the last cup of wine drunk, and it was time to go to bed, what a sweet sense of sanctity and security still reigned. No need to say your prayers tonight, beseeching the guardian of Israel, who neither slumbereth nor sleepeth, to watch over you and chase away the evil spirits; the angels are with you – Gabriel on your right and Raphael on your left, and Michael behind you. All about the Ghetto the light of the Passover rested, transfiguring the dreary rooms and illumining the grey lives.

Dutch Debby sat beside Mrs. Simons at the table of that good soul's married daughter; the same who had suckled little Sarah. Esther's frequent eulogiums had secured the poor lonely narrow-chested seamstress this enormous concession and privilege. Bobby squatted on the mat in the passage ready to challenge Elijah. At this table there were two pieces of fried fish sent to Mrs. Simons by Esther Ansell. They represented the greatest revenge of Esther's life, and she felt remorseful towards Malka, remembering to whose gold she owed this proud moment. She made up her mind to write her a letter of apology in her best hand.

At the Belcovitches' the ceremonial was long, for the master of it insisted on translating the Hebrew into jargon, phrase by phrase; but no one found it tedious, especially after supper. Pesach was there, hand in hand with Fanny, their wedding very near now; and Becky lolled royally in all her glory, aggressive of ringlet, insolently unattached, a conscious beacon of bedazzlement to the pauper *Pollack* we last met at Reb Shemuel's Sabbath table, and there, too, was Chayah, she of the ill-matched legs. Be sure that Malka had returned the clothes-brush, and was throned in complacent majesty at Milly's table; and that Sugarman the *Shadchan* forgave his monocular consort her lack of a fourth uncle; while Joseph Strelitski, dreamer of dreams, rich with commissions from "Passover" cigars, brooded on the Great Exodus. Nor could the Shalotten *Shammos* be other than beaming, ordering the complex ceremonial with none to contradict; nor Karlkammer be otherwise than in the seven hundred and seventy-seventh heaven, which, calculated by

Gematriyah, can easily be reduced to the seventh.

Shosshi Shmendrik did not fail to explain the deliverance to the ex-widow Finkelstein, nor Guedalyah, the greengrocer, omit to hold his annual revel at the head of half a hundred merry "pauper-aliens." Christian roughs bawled derisively in the street, especially when doors were opened for Elijah; but hard words break no bones, and the Ghetto was uplifted above insult.

Melchitsedek Pinchas was the Passover guest at Reb Shemuel's table, for the reek of his Sabbath cigar had not penetrated to the old man's nostrils. It was a great night for Pinchas; wrought up to fervid national-istic aspirations by the memory of the Egyptian deliverance, which he yet regarded as mythical in its details. It was a terrible night for Hannah, sitting opposite to him under the fire of his poetic regard. She was pale and rigid, moving and speaking mechanically. Her father glanced towards her every now and again, compassionately, but with trust that the worst was over. Her mother realised the crisis much less keenly than he, not having been in the heart of the storm. She had never even seen her intended son-in-law except through the lens of a camera. She was sorry – that was all. Now that Hannah had broken the ice, and encour-aged one young man, there was hope for the others.

Hannah's state of mind was divined by neither parent. Love itself is blind in those tragic silences which divide souls.

All night, after that agonizing scene, she did not sleep; the feverish activity of her mind rendered that impossible, and unerring instinct told her that David was awake also – that they two, amid the silence of a sleeping city, wrestled in the darkness with the same terrible problem, and were never so much at one as in this their separation. A letter came for her in the morning. It was unstamped, and had evidently been dropped into the letter-box by David's hand. It appointed an interview at ten o'clock at a corner of the Ruins; of course, he could not come to the house. Hannah was out with a little basket to make some purchases. There was a cheery hum of life about the Ghetto; a pleasant festival bustle; the air resounded with the, raucous clucking of innumerable fowls on their way to the feather-littered, blood-stained shambles, where professional cut-throats wielded sacred knives; boys armed with little braziers of glowing coal ran about the Ruins, offering halfpenny pyres for the immolation of the last crumbs of leaven. Nobody paid the slightest attention to the two tragic figures whose lives turned on the brief moments of conversation snatched in the thick of the hurrying crowd.

David's clouded face lightened a little as he saw Hannah advancing towards him.

"I knew you would come," he said, taking her hand for a moment. His palm burned, hers was cold and limp. The stress of a great tempest of emotion had driven the blood from her face and limbs, but inwardly she was on fire. As they looked each read revolt in the other's eyes.

"Let us walk on," he said.

They moved slowly forwards. The ground was slippery and muddy under foot. The sky was grey. But the gayety of the crowds neutralized the dull squalor of the scene.

"Well," he said, in a low tone.

"I thought you had something to propose," she murmured.

"Let me carry your basket."

"No, no; go on. What have you determined?"

"Not to give you up, Hannah, while I live."

"Ah!" she said quietly. "I have thought it all over, too, and I shall not leave you. But our marriage by Jewish law is impossible; we could not marry at any synagogue without my father's knowledge; and he would at once inform the authorities of the bar to our union."

"I know, dear. But let us go to America, where no one will know. There we shall find plenty of Rabbis to marry us. There is nothing to tie me to this country. I can start my business in America just as well as here. Your parents, too, will think more kindly of you when you are across the seas. Forgiveness is easier at a distance. What do you say, dear?"

She shook her head.

"Why should we be married in a synagogue?" she asked.

"Why?" repeated he, puzzled.

"Yes, why?"

"Because we are Jews."

"You would use Jewish forms to outwit Jewish laws?" she asked quietly.

"No, no. Why should you put it that way? I don't doubt the Bible is all right in making the laws it does. After the first heat of my anger was over, I saw the whole thing in its proper bearings. Those laws about priests were only intended for the days when we had a Temple, and in any case they cannot apply to a merely farcical divorce like yours. It is these old fools, – I beg your pardon, – it is these fanatical Rabbis who insist on giving them a rigidity God never meant them to have, just as they still make a fuss about *kosher* meat. In America they are less strict; besides, they will not know I am a *Cohen*."

"No, David," said Hannah firmly. "There must be no more deceit. What need have we to seek the sanction of any Rabbi? If Jewish law cannot marry us without our hiding something, then I will have nothing to do with Jewish law. You know my opinions; I haven't gone so deeply into religious questions as you have –"

"Don't be sarcastic," he interrupted.

"I have always been sick to death of this eternal ceremony, this endless coil of laws winding round us and cramping our lives at every turn; and now it has become too oppressive to be borne any longer. Why should we let it ruin our lives? And why, if we determine to break from it, shall we pretend to keep to it? What do you care for Judaism? You eat *triphas*, you smoke on *Shabbos* when you want to –"

"Yes, I know, perhaps I'm wrong. But everybody does it now-a-days. When I was a boy nobody dared be seen riding in a bus on *Shabbos* – now you meet lots. But all that is only old-fashioned Judaism. There must be a God, else we shouldn't be here, and it's impossible to believe that Jesus was He. A man must have some religion, and there isn't anything better. But that's neither here nor there. If you don't care for my plan," he concluded anxiously, "what's yours?"

"Let us be married honestly by a Registrar."

"Any way you like, dear," he said readily, "so long as we are married —and quickly."

"As quickly as you like."

He seized her disengaged hand and pressed it passionately.

"That's my own darling Hannah. Oh, if you could realise what I felt last night when you seemed to be drifting away from me." ·

There was an interval of silence, each thinking excitedly. Then David said:

"But have you the courage to do this and remain in London?"

"I have courage for anything. But, as you say, it might be better to travel. It will be less of a break if we break away altogether – change everything at once. It sounds contradictory, but you understand what I mean."

"Perfectly. It is difficult to live a new life with all the old things round you. Besides, why should we give our friends the chance to cold-shoulder us? They will find all sorts of malicious reasons why we were not married in a *Shool*, and if they hit on the true one they may even regard our marriage as illegal. Let us go to America, as I proposed."

"Very well. Do we go direct from London?"

"No, from Liverpool."

"Then we can be married at Liverpool before sailing?"

"A good idea. But when do we start?"

"At once. Tonight. The sooner the better."

He looked at her quickly. "Do you mean it?" he said. His heart beat violently as if it would burst. Waves of dazzling colour swam before his eyes.

"I mean it," she said gravely and quietly. "Do you think I could face my father and mother, knowing I was about to wound them to the heart? Each day of delay would be torture to me. Oh, why is religion such a curse?" She paused, overwhelmed for a moment by the emotion she had been suppressing. She resumed in the same quiet manner. "Yes, we must break away at once. We have kept our last Passover. We shall have to eat leavened food – it will be a decisive break. Take me to Liverpool, David, this very day. You are my chosen husband; I trust in you."

She looked at him frankly with her dark eyes that stood out in lustrous relief against the pale skin. He gazed into those eyes, and a flash as from the inner heaven of purity pierced his soul.

"Thank you, dearest," he said in a voice with tears in it.

They walked on silently. Speech was as superfluous as it was inadequate. When they spoke again their voices were calm. The peace that comes of resolute decision was theirs at last, and each was full of the joy of daring greatly for the sake of their mutual love. Petty as their departure from convention might seem to the stranger, to them it loomed as a violent breach with all the traditions of the Ghetto and their past lives; they were venturing forth into untrodden paths, holding each other's hand.

Jostling the loquacious crowd, in the unsavory by-ways of the Ghetto, in the grey chillness of a cloudy morning, Hannah seemed to herself to walk in enchanted gardens, breathing the scent of love's own roses mingled with the keen salt air that blew in from the sea of liberty. A fresh, new blessed life was opening before her. The clogging vapours of the past were rolling away at last. The unreasoning instinctive rebellion, bred of ennui and brooding dissatisfaction with the conditions of her existence and the people about her, had by a curious series of accidents been hastened to its acutest development; thought had at last fermented into active resolution, and the anticipation of action flooded her soul with peace and joy, in which all recollection of outside humanity was submerged.

"What time can you be ready by?" he said before they parted.

"Any time," she answered. "I can take nothing with me. I dare not pack anything. I suppose I can get necessaries in Liverpool. I have merely my hat and cloak to put on."

"But that will be enough," he said ardently. "I want but you."

"I know it, dear," she answered gently. "If you were as other Jewish young men I could not give up all else for you."

"You shall never regret it, Hannah," he said, moved to his depths, as the full extent of her sacrifice for love dawned upon him. He was a vagabond on the face of the earth, but she was tearing herself away from deep roots in the soil of home, as well as from the conventions of her circle and her sex. Once again he trembled with a sense of unworthiness, a sudden anxious doubt if he were noble enough to repay her trust. Mastering his emotion, he went on: "I reckon my packing and arrangements for leaving the country will take me all day at least. I must see my bankers if nobody else. I shan't take leave of anybody, that would arouse suspicion. I will be at the corner of your street with a cab at nine, and we'll catch the ten o'clock express from Euston. If we missed that, we should have to wait till midnight. It will be dark; no one is likely to notice me. I will get a dressing-case for you and anything else I can think of and add it to my luggage."

"Very well," she said simply.

They did not kiss; she gave him her hand, and, with a sudden inspiration, he slipped the ring he had brought the day before on her finger. The tears came into her eyes as she saw what he had done. They looked at each other through a mist, feeling bound beyond human intervention.

"Goodbye," she faltered.

"Goodbye," he said. "At nine."

"At nine," she breathed. And hurried off without looking behind.

It was a hard day, the minutes crawling reluctantly into the hours, the hours dragging themselves wearily on towards the night. It was typical April weather – squalls and sunshine in capricious succession. When it drew towards dusk she put on her best clothes for the Festival, stuffing a few precious mementoes into her pockets and wearing her father's portrait next to her lover's at her breast. She hung a travelling cloak and a hat on a peg near the hall door ready to hand as she left the house. Of little use was she in the kitchen that day, but her mother was tender to her as knowing her sorrow. Time after time Hannah ascended to her bedroom to take a last look at the things she had grown so tired of – the little iron bed, the wardrobe, the framed lithographs, the jug and basin with their floral designs. All things seemed strangely dear now she was seeing them for the last time. Hannah turned over everything – even the little curling iron, and the cardboard box full of tags and rags of ribbon and chiffon and lace and crushed artificial flowers, and the fans with broken sticks and the stays with broken ribs, and the petticoats with dingy frills and the twelve-button ball gloves with dirty fingers, and the soiled pink wraps. Some of her books, especially her school prizes, she would have liked to take with her – but that could not be. She went over the rest of the house, too, from top to bottom. It weakened her but she could not conquer the impulse of farewell. Finally she wrote a letter to her parents and hid it under her looking-glass, knowing they would search her room for traces of her. She looked curiously at herself as she did so; the colour had not returned to her cheeks. She knew she was pretty and always strove to look nice for the mere pleasure of the thing. All her instincts were æsthetic. Now she had the air of a saint wrought up to spiritual exaltation. She was almost frightened by the vision. She had seen her face frowning, weeping, overcast with gloom, never with an expression so fateful. It seemed as if her resolution was writ large upon every feature for all to read.

In the evening she accompanied her father to *Shool*. She did not often go in the evening, and the thought of going only suddenly occurred to her. Heaven alone knew if she would ever enter a synagogue again – the visit would be part of her systematic farewell. Reb Shemuel took it as a symptom of resignation to the will of God, and he laid his hand lightly on her head in silent blessing, his eyes uplifted gratefully to Heaven. Too late Hannah felt the misconception and was remorseful. For the festival occasion Reb Shemuel elected to worship at the Great Synagogue; Hannah, seated among the sparse occupants of the Ladies' Gallery and mechanically fingering a *Machzor*, looked down for the last time on the crowded auditorium where the men sat in high hats and holiday garments. Tall wax-candles twinkled everywhere, in great gilt chandeliers depending from the ceiling, in sconces stuck about the window ledges, in candelabra branching from the walls. There was an air of holy joy about the solemn old structure with its massive pillars, its small side-windows, high ornate roof, and skylights, and its gilt-lettered tablets to the memory of pious donors.

The congregation gave the responses with joyous unction.

Some of the worshippers tempered their devotion by petty gossip and the beadle marshalled the men in low hats within the iron railings, sonorously sounding his automatic amens. But tonight Hannah had no eye for the humours that were wont to awaken her scornful amusement – a real emotion possessed her, the same emotion of farewell which she had experienced in her own bedroom. Her eyes wandered towards the Ark, surmounted by the stone tablets of the Decalogue, and the sad dark orbs filled with the brooding light of childish reminiscence. Once when she was a little girl her father told her that on Passover night an angel sometimes came out of the doors of the Ark from among the scrolls of the Law. For years she looked out for that angel, keeping her eyes patiently fixed on the curtain. At last she gave him up, concluding her vision was insufficiently purified or that he was exhibiting at other synagogues. Tonight her childish fancy recurred to her – she found herself involuntarily looking towards the Ark and half-expectant of the angel.

She had not thought of the *Seder* service she would have to partially sit through, when she made her appointment with David in the morning, but when during the day it occurred to her, a cynical smile traversed her lips. How apposite it was! Tonight would mark *her* exodus from slavery. Like her ancestors leaving Egypt, she, too, would partake of a meal in haste, staff in hand ready for the journey. With what stout heart would she set forth, she, too, towards the promised land! Thus had she thought some hours since, but her mood was changed now. The nearer the *Seder* approached, the more she shrank from the family ceremonial. A panic terror almost seized her now, in the synagogue, when the picture of the domestic interior flashed again before her mental vision – she felt like flying into the street, on towards her lover without ever looking behind. Oh, why could David not have fixed the hour earlier, so as to spare her an ordeal so trying to the nerves? The black-stoled choir was singing sweetly, Hannah banished her foolish flutter of alarm by joining in quietly, for congregational singing was regarded rather as an intrusion on the privileges of the choir and calculated to put them out in their elaborate four-part fugues unaided by an organ.

"With everlasting love hast Thou loved the house of Israel, Thy people," she sang: "a Law and commandments, statutes and judgments hast thou taught us. Therefore, O Lord our God, when we lie down and when we rise up we will meditate on Thy statutes: yea, we will rejoice in the words of Thy Law and in Thy commandments for ever, for they are our life and the length of our days, and will meditate on them day and night. And mayest Thou never take away Thy love from us. Blessed art Thou, O Lord, who lovest Thy people Israel."

Hannah scanned the English version of the Hebrew in her *Machzor* as she sang. Though she could translate every word, the meaning of what she sang was never completely conceived by her consciousness. The power of song over the soul depends but little on the words. Now the words seem fateful, pregnant with special message. Her eyes were misty when the fugues were over. Again she looked towards the Ark with its beautifully embroidered curtain, behind which were the precious scrolls with their silken swathes and their golden bells and shields and pomegranates. Ah, if the angel would come out now! If only the dazzling vision gleamed for a moment on the white steps. Oh, why did he not come and save her?

Save her? From what? She asked herself the question fiercely, in defiance of the still, small voice. What wrong had she ever done that she so young and gentle should be forced to make so cruel a choice between the old and the new? This was the synagogue she should have been married in; stepping gloriously and honourably under the canopy, amid the pleasant excitement of a congratulatory company. And now she was being driven to exile and the chillness of secret nuptials. No, no; she did not want to be saved in the sense of being kept in the fold; it was the creed that was culpable, not she.

The service drew to an end. The choir sang the final hymn, the *Chazan* giving the last verse at great length and with many musical flourishes.

"The dead will God quicken in the abundance of His loving kindness. Blessed for evermore be His glorious name."

There was a clattering of reading-flaps and seat-lids and the congregation poured out, amid the buzz of mutual "Good *Yomtovs*." Hannah rejoined her father, the sense of injury and revolt still surging in her breast. In the fresh starlit air, stepping along the wet gleaming pavements, she shook off the last influences of the synagogue; all her thoughts converged on the meeting with David, on the wild flight northwards while good Jews were sleeping off the supper in celebration of their Redemption: her blood coursed quickly through her veins, she was in a fever of impatience for the hour to come.

And thus it was that she sat at the *Seder* table, as in a dream, with images of desperate adventure flitting in her brain. The face of her lover floated before her eyes, close, close to her own as it should have been tonight had there been justice in Heaven. Now and again the scene about her flashed in upon her consciousness, piercing her to the heart. When Levi asked the introductory question, it set her wondering what would become of him? Would manhood bring enfranchisement to him as womanhood was doing to her? What sort of life would he lead the poor Reb and his wife? The omens were scarcely auspicious; but a man's charter is so much wider than a woman's; and Levi might do much without paining them as she would pain them. Poor father! The white hairs were predominating in his beard, she had never noticed before how old he was getting. And mother – her face was quite wrinkled. Ah, well; we must all grow old. What a curious man Melchitsedek Pinchas was, singing so heartily the wonderful story. Judaism certainly produced some curious types. A smile crossed her face as she thought of herself as his bride.

At supper she strove to eat a little, knowing she would need it. In bringing some plates from the kitchen she looked at her hat and cloak, carefully hung up on the peg in the hall nearest the street door. It would take but a second to slip them on. She nodded her head towards them, as who should say "Yes, we shall meet again very soon." During the meal she found herself listening to the poet's monologues delivered in his high-pitched creaking voice.

Melchitsedek Pinchas had much to say about a certain actor-manager who had spoiled the greatest jargon-play of the century and a certain labour-leader who, out of the funds of his gulls, had subsidized the audience to stay away, and (though here the Reb cut him short for Hannah's sake) a certain leading lady, one of the quartette of mistresses of a certain clergyman, who had been beguiled by her paramour into joining the great English conspiracy to hound down Melchitsedek Pinchas, – all of whom he would shoot presently and had in the meantime enshrined like dead flies in the amber of immortal acrostics. The wind began to shake the shutters as they finished supper and presently the rain began to patter afresh against the panes. Reb Shemuel distributed the pieces of *Afikuman* with a happy sigh, and, lolling on his pillows and almost forgetting his family troubles in the sense of Israel's blessedness, began to chant the Grace like the saints in the Psalm who sing aloud on their couches. The little Dutch clock on the mantelpiece began to strike. Hannah did not move. Pale and trembling she sat riveted to her chair. One – two – three – four – five – six – seven – eight. She counted the strokes, as if to count them was the only means of telling the hour, as if her eyes had not been following the hands creeping, creeping. She had a mad hope the striking would cease with the eight and there would he still time to think. Nine! She waited, her ear longing for the tenth stroke. If it were only ten o'clock, it would be too late. The danger would be over. She sat, mechanically watching the hands. They crept on. It was five minutes past the hour. She felt sure that David was already at the corner of the street, getting wet and a little impatient. She half rose from her chair. It was not a nice night for an elopement. She sank back into her seat. Perhaps they had best wait till tomorrow night. She would go and tell David so. But then he would not mind the weather; once they had met he would bundle her into the cab and they would roll off, leaving the old world irrevocably behind. She sat in a paralysis of volition; rigid on her chair, magnetized by the warm comfortable room, the old familiar furniture, the Passover table – with its white table-cloth and its decanter and wine-glasses, the faces of her father and mother eloquent with the appeal of a thousand memories. The clock ticked on loudly, fiercely, like a summoning drum; the rain beat an impatient tattoo on the window-panes, the wind rattled the doors and casements. "Go forth, go forth," they caned, "go forth where your lover waits you, to bear you off into the new and the unknown." And the louder they called the louder Reb Shemuel trolled his hilarious Grace: *May He who maketh Peace in the High Heavens, bestow Peace upon us and upon all Israel and say ye, Amen.*

The hands of the clock crept on. It was half-past nine. Hannah sat lethargic, numb, unable to think, her strung-up nerves grown flaccid, her eyes full of bitter-sweet tears, her soul floating along as in a trance on the waves of a familiar melody. Suddenly she became aware that the others had risen and that her father was motioning to her. Instinctively she understood; rose automatically and went to the door; then a great shock of returning recollection whelmed her soul. She stood rooted to the floor. Her father had filled Elijah's goblet with wine and it was her annual privilege to open the door for the prophet's entry. Intuitively she knew that David was pacing madly in front of the house, not daring to make known his presence, and perhaps cursing her cowardice. A chill terror seized her. She was afraid to face him – his will was strong and mighty; her fevered imagination figured it as the wash of a great ocean breaking on the doorstep threatening to sweep her off into the roaring whirlpool of doom. She threw the door of the room wide and paused as if her duty were done.

"*Nu, nu,*" muttered Reb Shemuel, indicating the outer door. It was so near that he always had that opened, too.

Hannah tottered forwards through the few feet of hall. The cloak and hat on the peg nodded to her sardonically. A wild thrill of answering defiance shot through her: she stretched out her hands towards them. "Fly, fly; it is your last chance," said the blood throbbing in her ears. But her hand dropped to her side and in that brief instant of terrible illumination, Hannah saw down the whole long vista of her future life, stretching straight and unlovely between great blank walls, on, on to a solitary grave; knew that the strength had been denied her to diverge to the right or left, that for her there would be neither Exodus nor Redemption. Strong in the conviction of her weakness she noisily threw open the street door. The face of David, sallow and ghastly, loomed upon her in the darkness. Great drops of rain fell from his hat and ran down his cheeks like tears. His clothes seemed soaked with rain.

"At last!" he exclaimed in a hoarse, glad whisper. "What has kept you?"

"*Boruch Habo*! (Welcome art thou who arrivest)" came the voice of Reb Shemuel from within, greeting the prophet.

"Hush!" said Hannah. "Listen a moment."

The sing-song undulations of the old Rabbis voice mingled harshly with the wail of the wind: "*Pour out Thy wrath on the heathen who acknowledge Thee not and upon the Kingdoms which invoke not Thy name, for they have devoured Jacob and laid waste his Temple. Pour out Thy indignation upon them and cause Thy fierce anger to overtake them. Pursue them in wrath and destroy them from under the heavens of the Lord.*"

"Quick, Hannah!" whispered David. "We can't wait a moment more. Put on your things. We shall miss the train."

A sudden inspiration came to her. For answer she drew his ring out of her pocket and slipped it into his hand.

"Goodbye!" she murmured in a strange hollow voice, and slammed the street door in his face.

"Hannah!"

His startled cry of agony and despair penetrated the woodwork, muffled to an inarticulate shriek. He rattled the door violently in unreasoning frenzy.

"Who's that? What's that noise?" asked the Rebbitzin.

"Only some Christian rough shouting in the street," answered Hannah.

It was truer than she knew.

* * * * *

The rain fell faster, the wind grew shriller, but the Children of the Ghetto basked by their firesides in faith and hope and contentment. Hunted from shore to shore through the ages, they had found the national aspiration – Peace – in a country where Passover came without menace of blood. In the garret of Number 1 Royal Street little Esther Ansell sat brooding, her heart full of a vague tender poetry and penetrated by the beauties of Judaism, which, please God, she would always cling to; her childish vision looking forward hopefully to the larger life that the years would bring.

Also available in the Victorian Series

In Darkest London
Margaret Harkness

ISBN 1 900 355 28 0

Margaret Harkness was born at Upton-upon-Severn in 1854, the daughter of an Anglican priest. In 1877 she went to London to train as a nurse but in 1881 decided to become a writer and soon began earning a meagre living as a journalist. She became interested in the social problems of London's East End and in 1888 joined a group based around the Social Democratic Federation's journal 'Justice', in which she published several of her articles.

The novels which she came to write, based on her experience living with the unemployed in the slums of London, are excellent examples of the social realist genre which had become popular in the late 1800s and was read by many in the reform movements of the day, including Fredrich Engels who complimented her books as being both political and artistic.

In Darkest London is set in Whitechapel, in the epicentre of the East End ghetto, and has long been considered one of the best sources of social description and commentary for its time. It gives a penetrating insight into the lives and labours of the people who lived in one of the most impoverished areas of England during the late Victorian period.

To purchase this book or to find out details of other
Black Apollo Press publications, visit our website at
www.blackapollo.com